Dynamite Enterta...

The Complete ALICE in Wonderland

story by
LEWIS CARROLL

adapted by
LEAH MOORE & JOHN REPPION

illustrated by
ÉRICA AWANO

colored by
ÉRICA AWANO issues 1-3, issue 4 pages 1-26
ALE STARLING issue 4 pages 27-34
JAZREEL ROJALES issue 4 pages 35-40

lettered by
SIMON BOWLAND

collection and logo design by
JASON ULLMEYER

This volume collects issues 1-4 of the Dynamite series, *The Complete Alice in Wonderland*.

"For Edward," - Moore & Reppion

DYNAMITE®

Nick Barrucci, CEO / Publisher
Juan Collado, President / COO

Joe Rybandt, Senior Editor
Rachel Pinnelas, Associate Editor

Jason Ullmeyer, Design Director
Geoff Harkins, Graphic Designer
Chris Caniano, Digital Associate
Rachel Kilbury, Digital Assistant

Brandon Dante Primavera, Director of IT/Operations
Rich Young, Director of Business Development

Keith Davidsen, Marketing Manager
Pat O'Connell, Sales Manager

www.DYNAMITE.com   Facebook /Dynamitecomics   Instagram /Dynamitecomics
Tumblr dynamitecomics.tumblr.com   Twitter @Dynamitecomics   YouTube /Dynamitecomics

THE COMPLETE ALICE IN WONDERLAND™. First printing. Contains materials originally published in The Complete Alice In Wonderland #1-4. Published by Dynamite Entertainment. 113 Gaither Dr., STE 205, Mt. Laurel, NJ 08054. The Complet Alice in Wonderland is ™ & © 2016 Dynamite Characters, llc. All Rights Reserved. Dynamite, Dynamite Entertainment & its logo are ® 2016 Dynamite. All Rights Reserved. All names, characters, events, and locales in this publication are entirely fictional. Any resemblance to actual persons (living or dead), events or places, without satiric intent, is coincidental. No portion of this book may be reproduced by any means (digital or print) without the written permission of Dynamite Entertainment except for review purposes. The scanning, uploading and distribution of this book via the Internet or via any other means without the permission of the publisher is illegal and punishable by law. Please purchase only authorized electronic editions, and do not participate in or encourage electronic piracy of copyrighted materials. **Printed in China.**

For media rights, foreign rights, promotions, licensing, and advertising: marketing@dynamite.com

ISBN-10: 1-60690-973-8   ISBN-13: 978-1-60690-973-7   First Printing   10 9 8 7 6 5 4 3 2 1

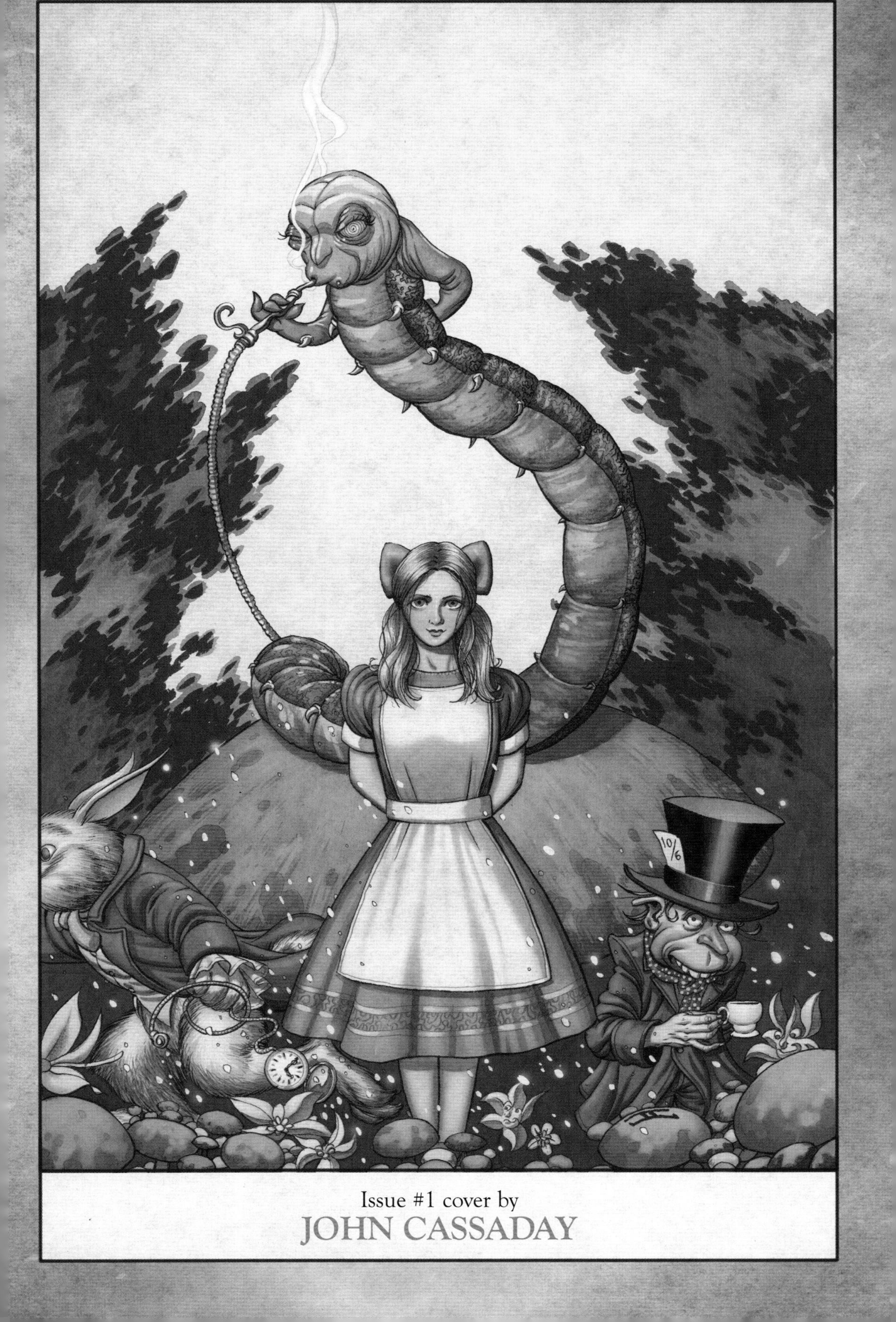
10/6

Issue #1 cover by
JOHN CASSADAY

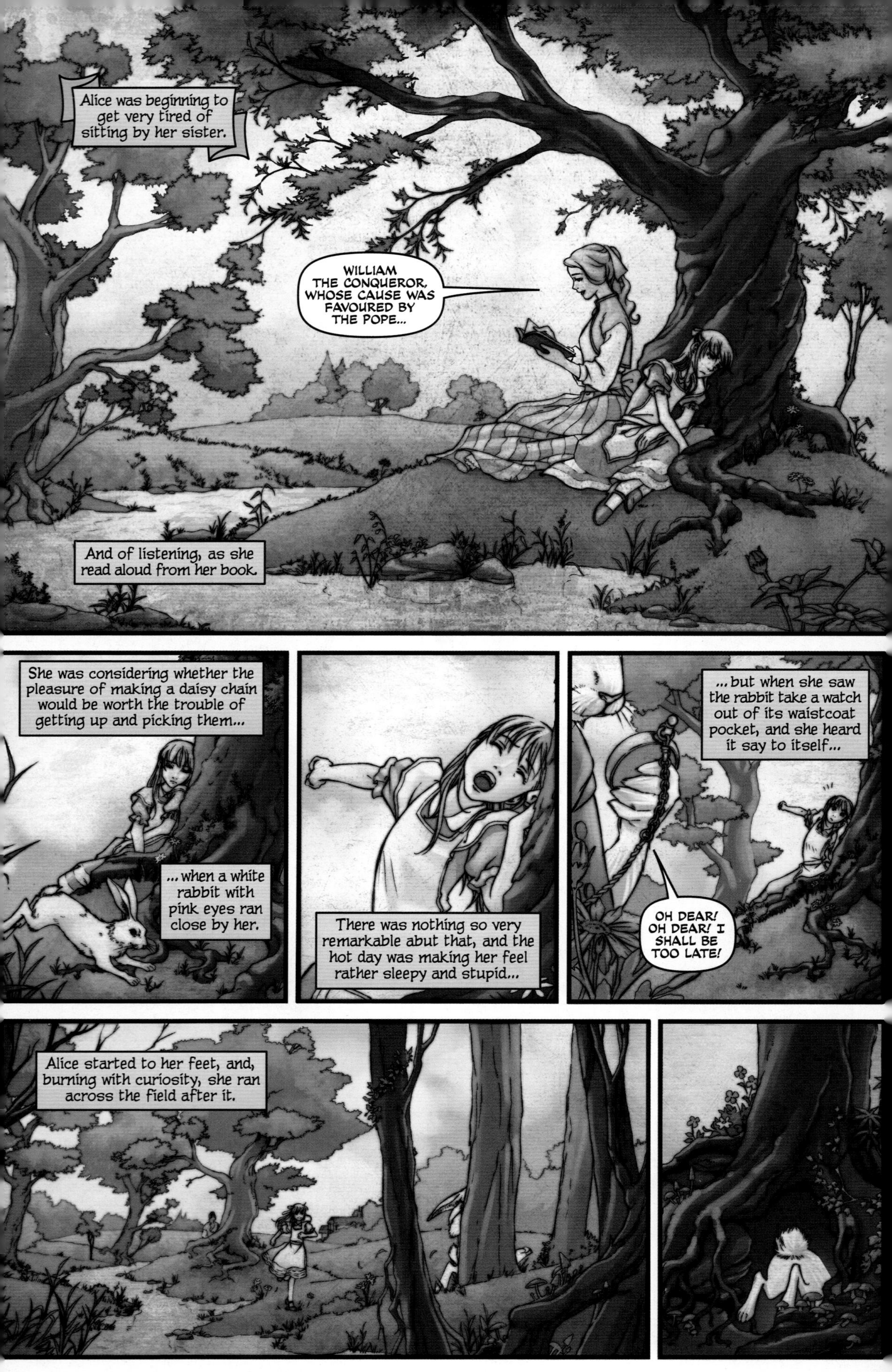
Alice was beginning to get very tired of sitting by her sister.
WILLIAM THE CONQUEROR, WHOSE CAUSE WAS FAVOURED BY THE POPE...
And of listening, as she read aloud from her book.
She was considering whether the pleasure of making a daisy chain would be worth the trouble of getting up and picking them...
...when a white rabbit with pink eyes ran close by her.
There was nothing so very remarkable abut that, and the hot day was making her feel rather sleepy and stupid...
...but when she saw the rabbit take a watch out of its waistcoat pocket, and she heard it say to itself...
OH DEAR! OH DEAR! I SHALL BE TOO LATE!
Alice started to her feet, and, burning with curiosity, she ran across the field after it.

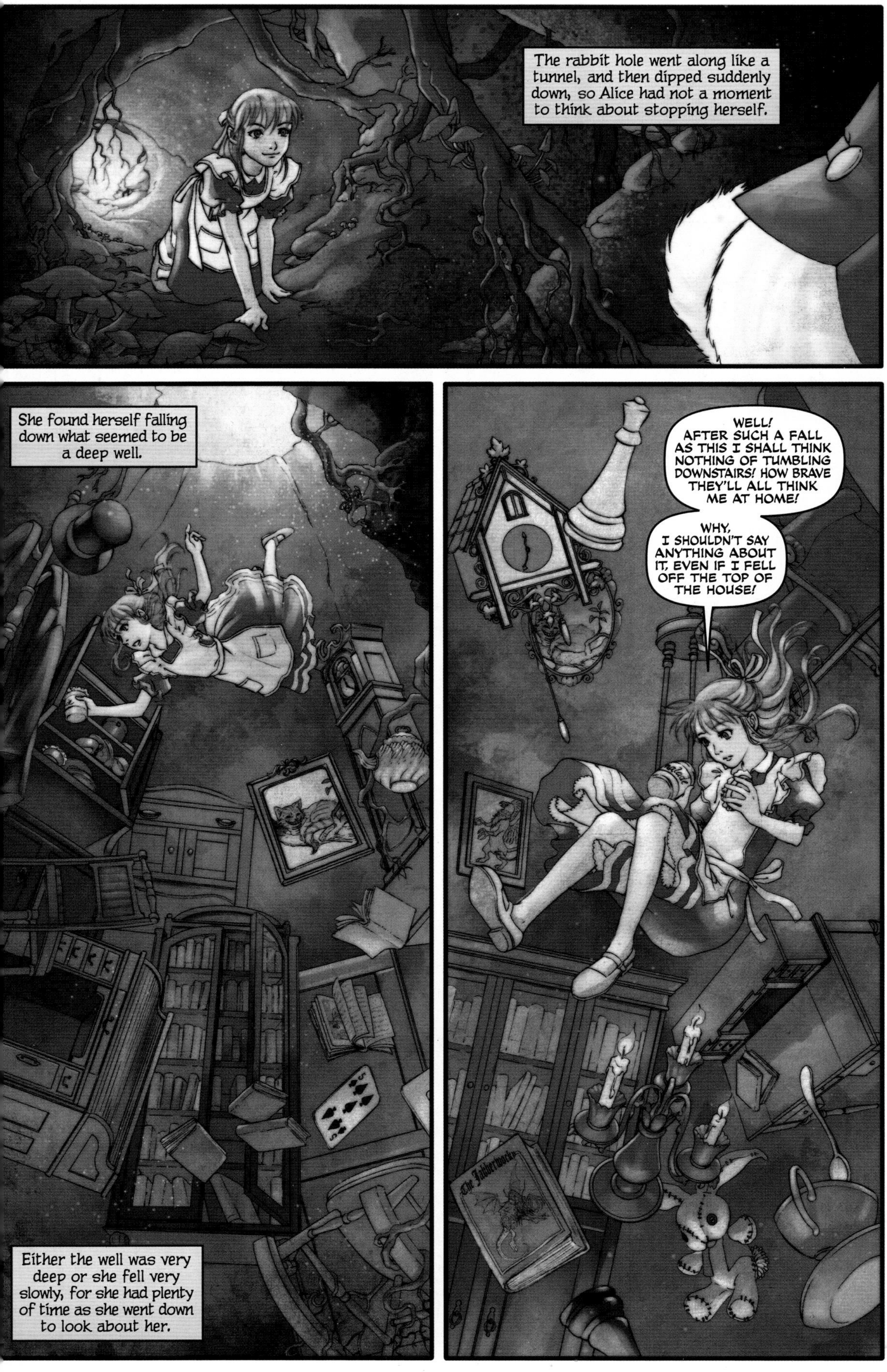
The rabbit hole went along like a tunnel, and then dipped suddenly down, so Alice had not a moment to think about stopping herself.
She found herself falling down what seemed to be a deep well.
Either the well was very deep or she fell very slowly, for she had plenty of time as she went down to look about her.
WELL! AFTER SUCH A FALL AS THIS I SHALL THINK NOTHING OF TUMBLING DOWNSTAIRS! HOW BRAVE THEY'LL ALL THINK ME AT HOME!
WHY, I SHOULDN'T SAY ANYTHING ABOUT IT, EVEN IF I FELL OFF THE TOP OF THE HOUSE!

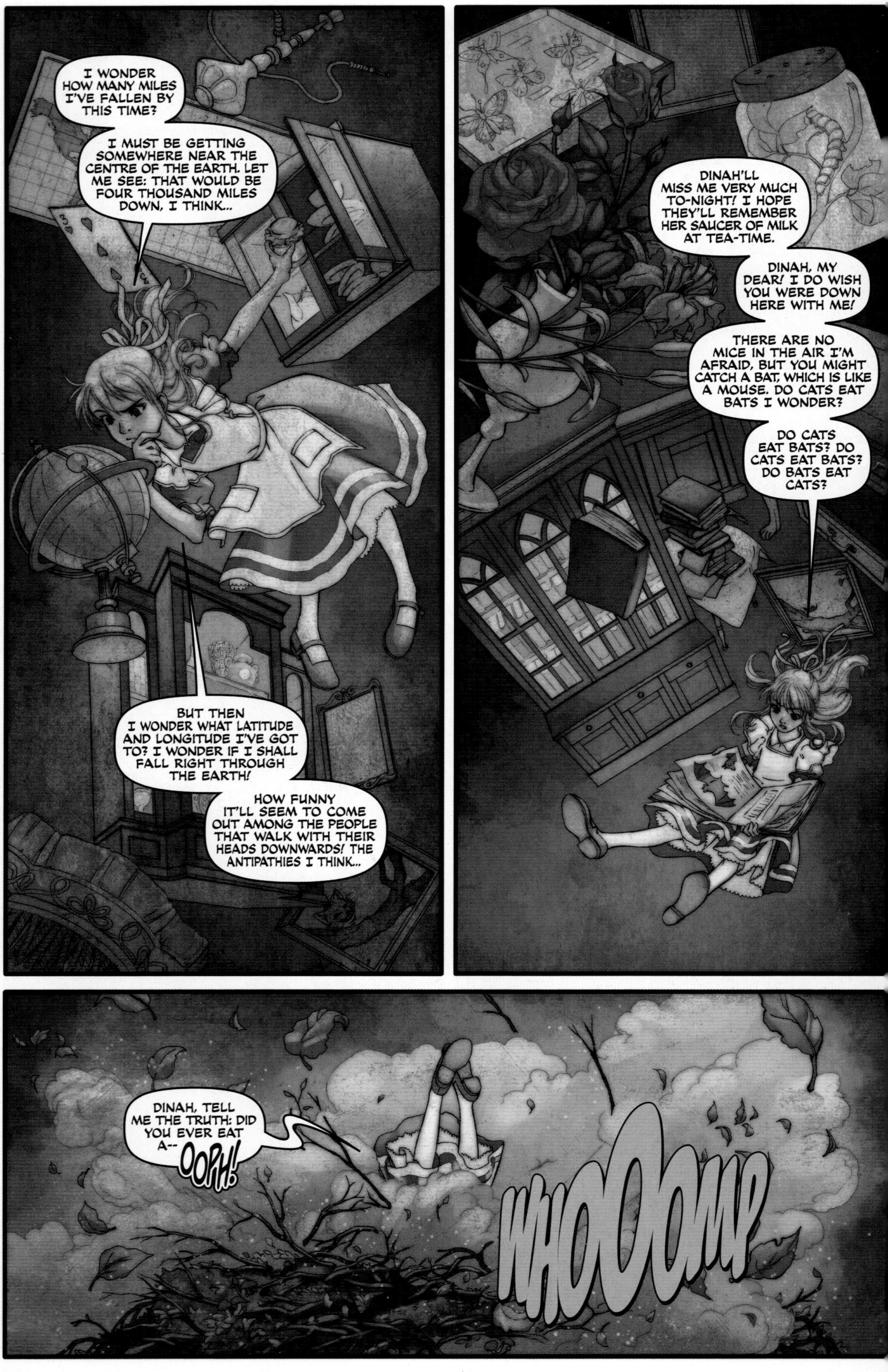
I WONDER HOW MANY MILES I'VE FALLEN BY THIS TIME?
I MUST BE GETTING SOMEWHERE NEAR THE CENTRE OF THE EARTH. LET ME SEE: THAT WOULD BE FOUR THOUSAND MILES DOWN, I THINK...
BUT THEN I WONDER WHAT LATITUDE AND LONGITUDE I'VE GOT TO? I WONDER IF I SHALL FALL RIGHT THROUGH THE EARTH!
HOW FUNNY IT'LL SEEM TO COME OUT AMONG THE PEOPLE THAT WALK WITH THEIR HEADS DOWNWARDS! THE ANTIPATHIES I THINK...
DINAH'LL MISS ME VERY MUCH TO-NIGHT! I HOPE THEY'LL REMEMBER HER SAUCER OF MILK AT TEA-TIME.
DINAH, MY DEAR! I DO WISH YOU WERE DOWN HERE WITH ME!
THERE ARE NO MICE IN THE AIR I'M AFRAID, BUT YOU MIGHT CATCH A BAT, WHICH IS LIKE A MOUSE. DO CATS EAT BATS I WONDER?
DO CATS EAT BATS? DO CATS EAT BATS? DO BATS EAT CATS?
DINAH, TELL ME THE TRUTH: DID YOU EVER EAT A--
OOPH!
WHOOOMP

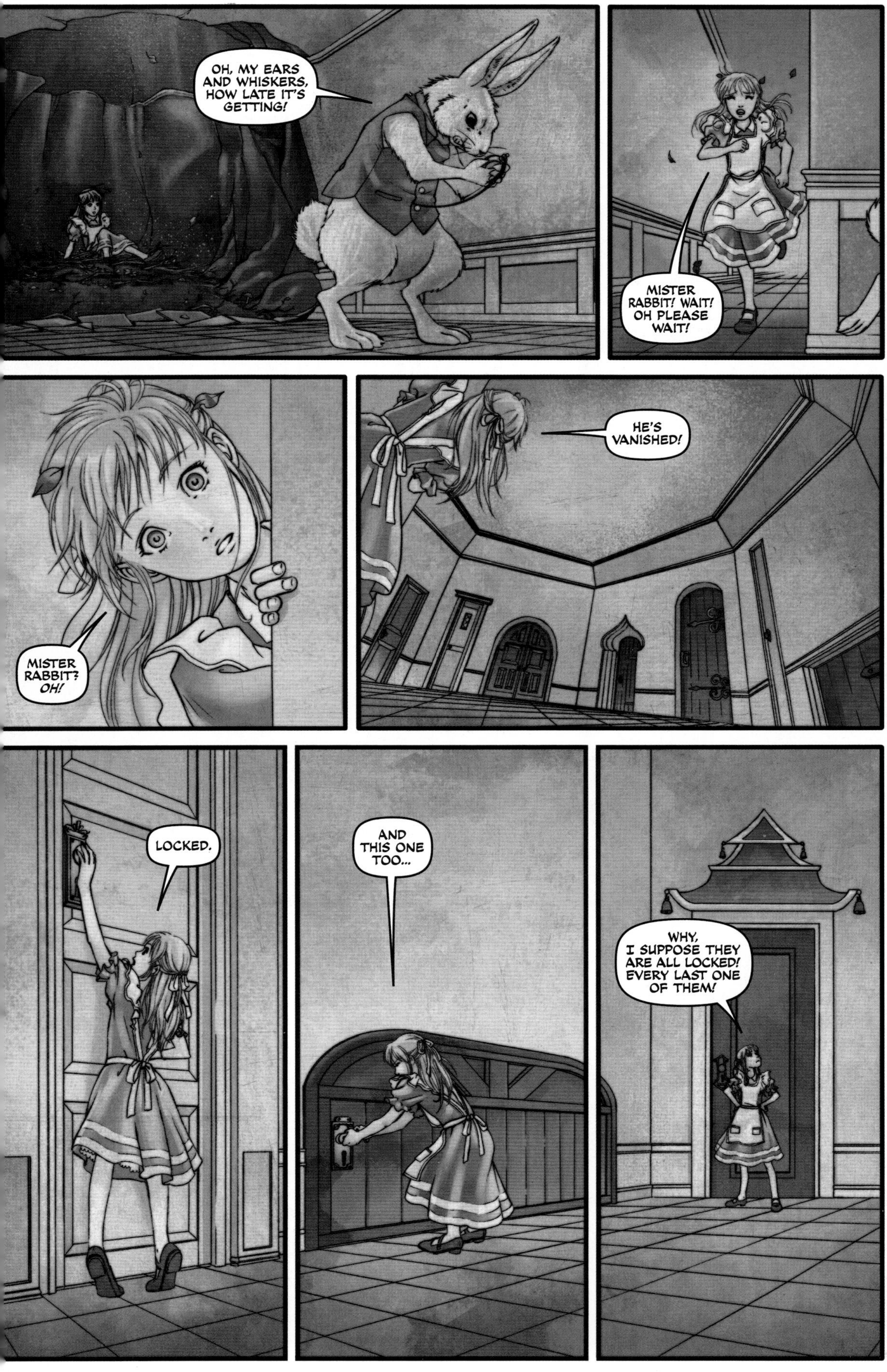
OH, MY EARS AND WHISKERS, HOW LATE IT'S GETTING!
MISTER RABBIT! WAIT! OH PLEASE WAIT!
MISTER RABBIT? OH!
HE'S VANISHED!
LOCKED.
AND THIS ONE TOO...
WHY, I SUPPOSE THEY ARE ALL LOCKED! EVERY LAST ONE OF THEM!

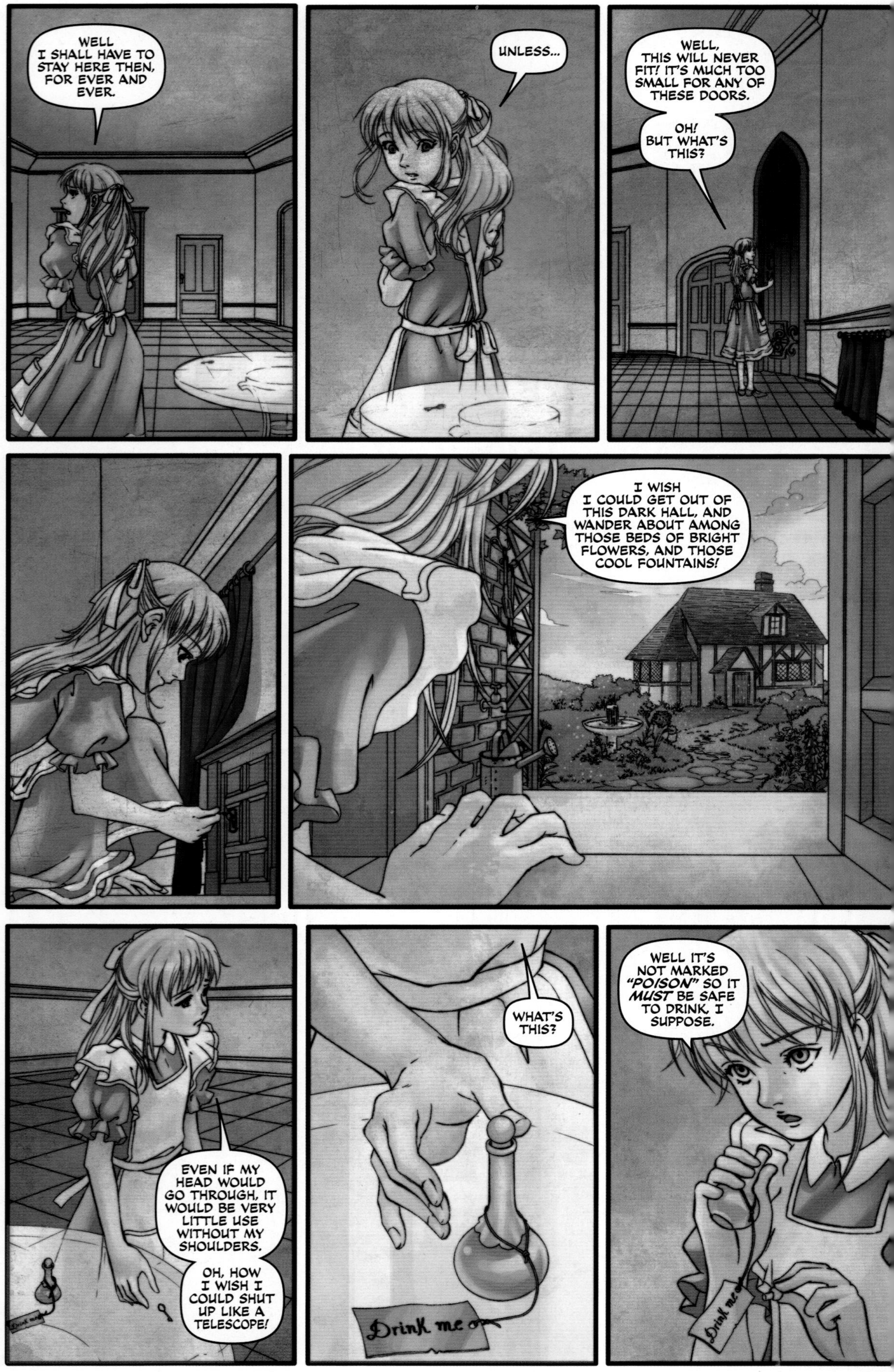
WELL I SHALL HAVE TO STAY HERE THEN, FOR EVER AND EVER.
UNLESS...
WELL, THIS WILL NEVER FIT! IT'S MUCH TOO SMALL FOR ANY OF THESE DOORS.
OH! BUT WHAT'S THIS?
I WISH I COULD GET OUT OF THIS DARK HALL, AND WANDER ABOUT AMONG THOSE BEDS OF BRIGHT FLOWERS, AND THOSE COOL FOUNTAINS!
EVEN IF MY HEAD WOULD GO THROUGH, IT WOULD BE VERY LITTLE USE WITHOUT MY SHOULDERS.
OH, HOW I WISH I COULD SHUT UP LIKE A TELESCOPE!
WHAT'S THIS?
Drink me
WELL IT'S NOT MARKED *"POISON"* SO IT *MUST* BE SAFE TO DRINK, I SUPPOSE.
Drink me

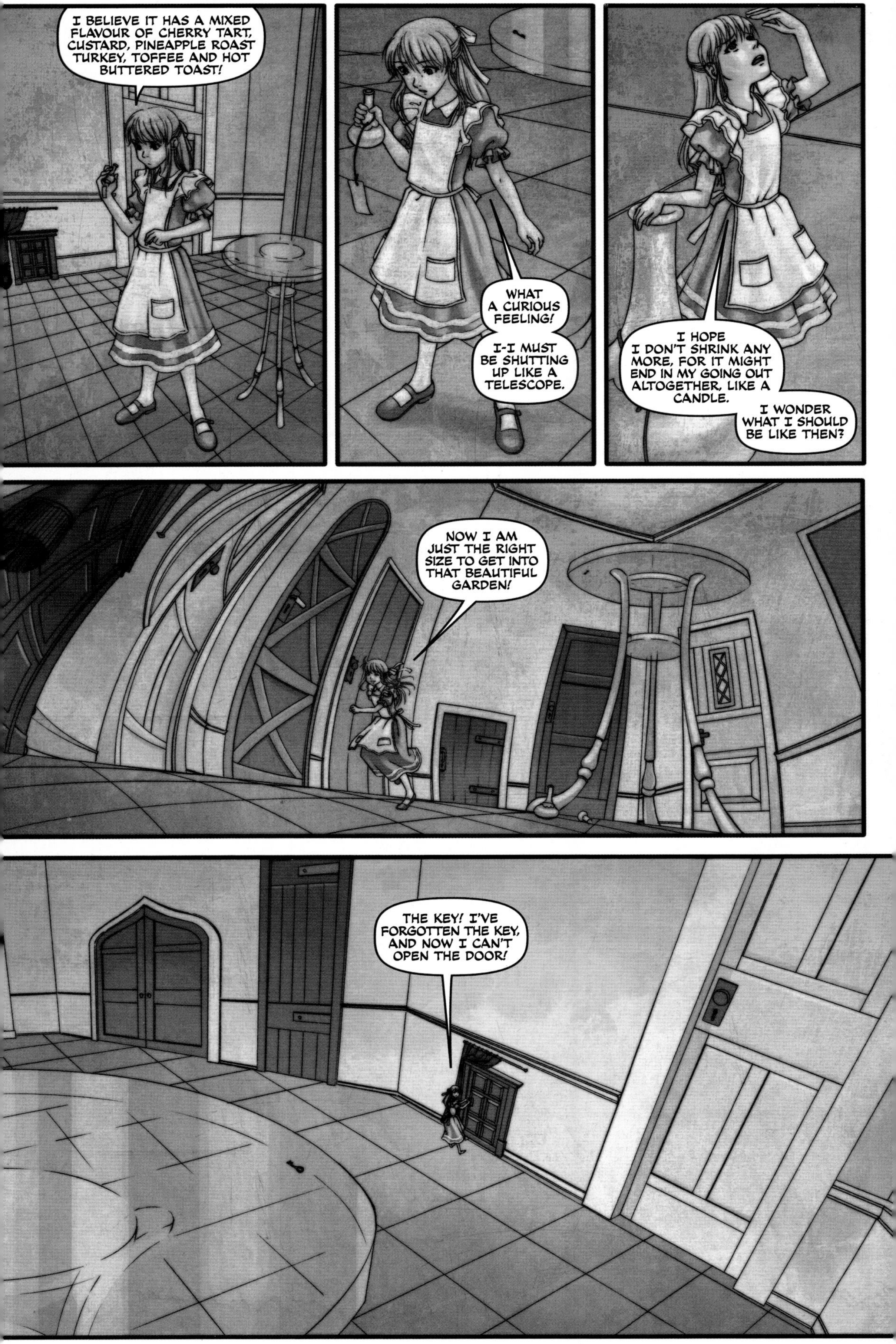
I BELIEVE IT HAS A MIXED FLAVOUR OF CHERRY TART, CUSTARD, PINEAPPLE ROAST TURKEY, TOFFEE AND HOT BUTTERED TOAST!
WHAT A CURIOUS FEELING!
I-I MUST BE SHUTTING UP LIKE A TELESCOPE.
I HOPE I DON'T SHRINK ANY MORE, FOR IT MIGHT END IN MY GOING OUT ALTOGETHER, LIKE A CANDLE.
I WONDER WHAT I SHOULD BE LIKE THEN?
NOW I AM JUST THE RIGHT SIZE TO GET INTO THAT BEAUTIFUL GARDEN!
THE KEY! I'VE FORGOTTEN THE KEY, AND NOW I CAN'T OPEN THE DOOR!

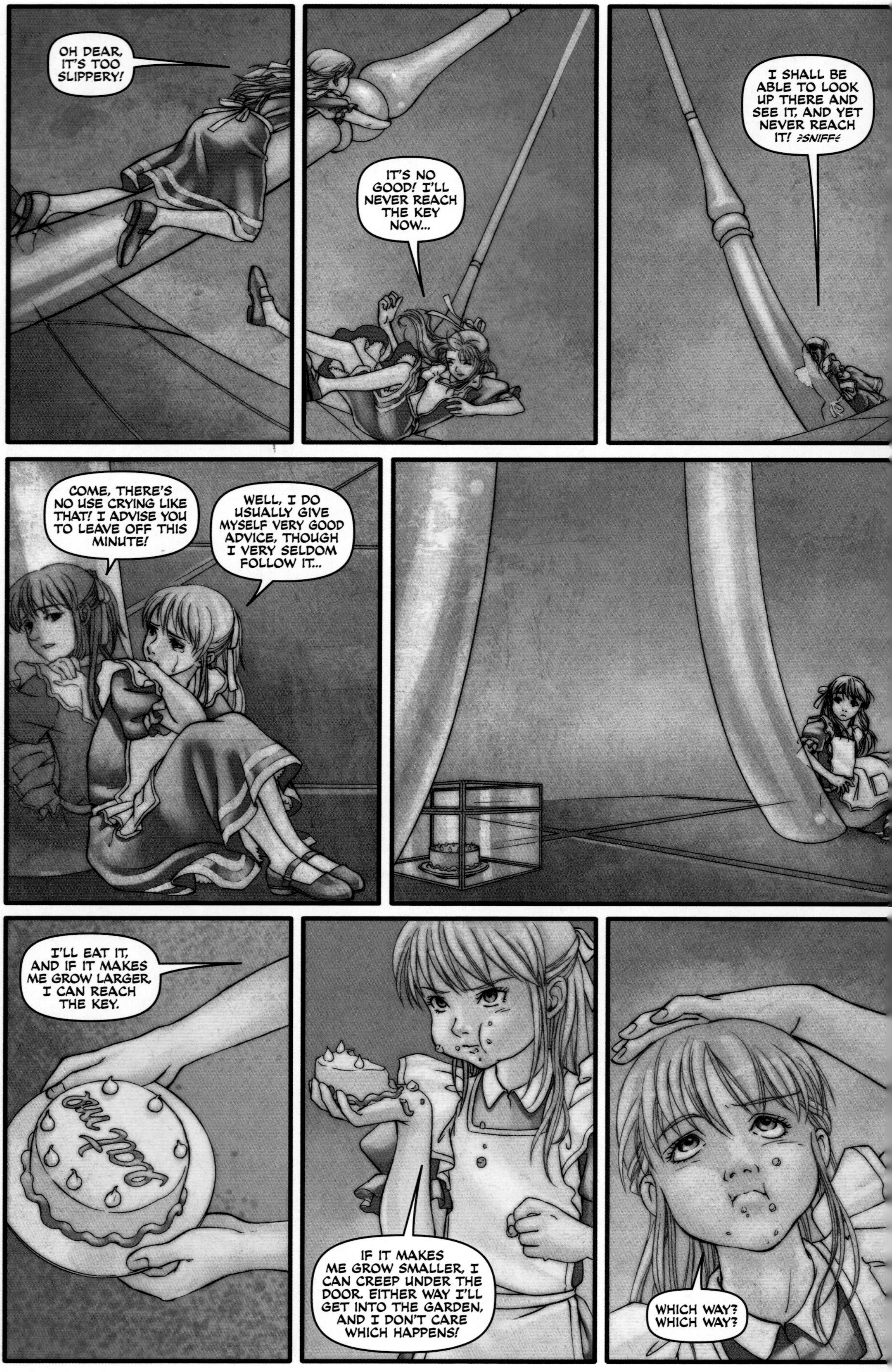
OH DEAR, IT'S TOO SLIPPERY!
IT'S NO GOOD! I'LL NEVER REACH THE KEY NOW...
I SHALL BE ABLE TO LOOK UP THERE AND SEE IT, AND YET NEVER REACH IT! SNIFF
COME, THERE'S NO USE CRYING LIKE THAT! I ADVISE YOU TO LEAVE OFF THIS MINUTE!
WELL, I DO USUALLY GIVE MYSELF VERY GOOD ADVICE, THOUGH I VERY SELDOM FOLLOW IT...
I'LL EAT IT, AND IF IT MAKES ME GROW LARGER, I CAN REACH THE KEY.
EAT ME
IF IT MAKES ME GROW SMALLER, I CAN CREEP UNDER THE DOOR. EITHER WAY I'LL GET INTO THE GARDEN, AND I DON'T CARE WHICH HAPPENS!
WHICH WAY? WHICH WAY?

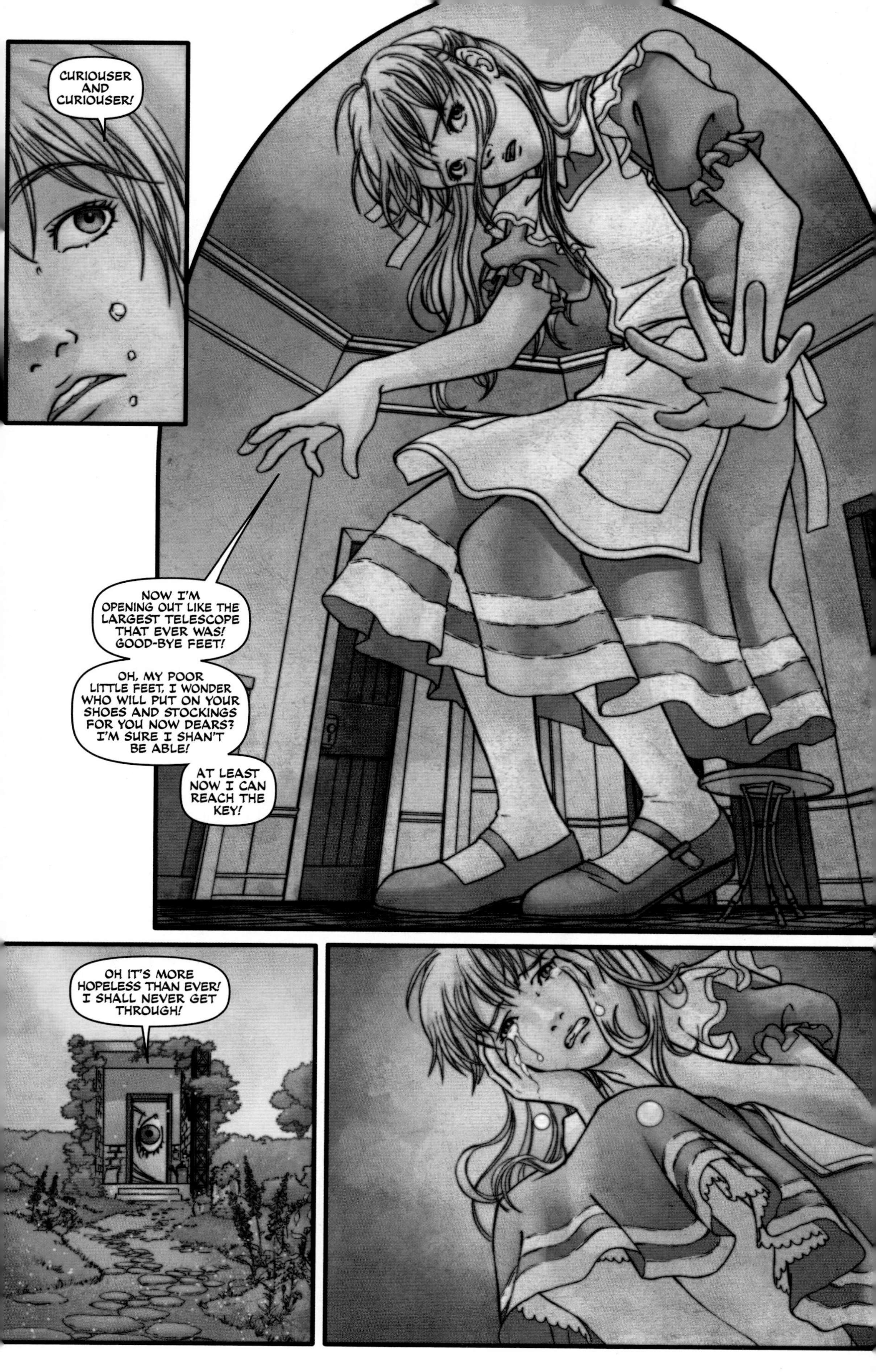
CURIOUSER AND CURIOUSER!
NOW I'M OPENING OUT LIKE THE LARGEST TELESCOPE THAT EVER WAS! GOOD-BYE FEET!
OH, MY POOR LITTLE FEET, I WONDER WHO WILL PUT ON YOUR SHOES AND STOCKINGS FOR YOU NOW DEARS? I'M SURE I SHAN'T BE ABLE!
AT LEAST NOW I CAN REACH THE KEY!
OH IT'S MORE HOPELESS THAN EVER! I SHALL NEVER GET THROUGH!

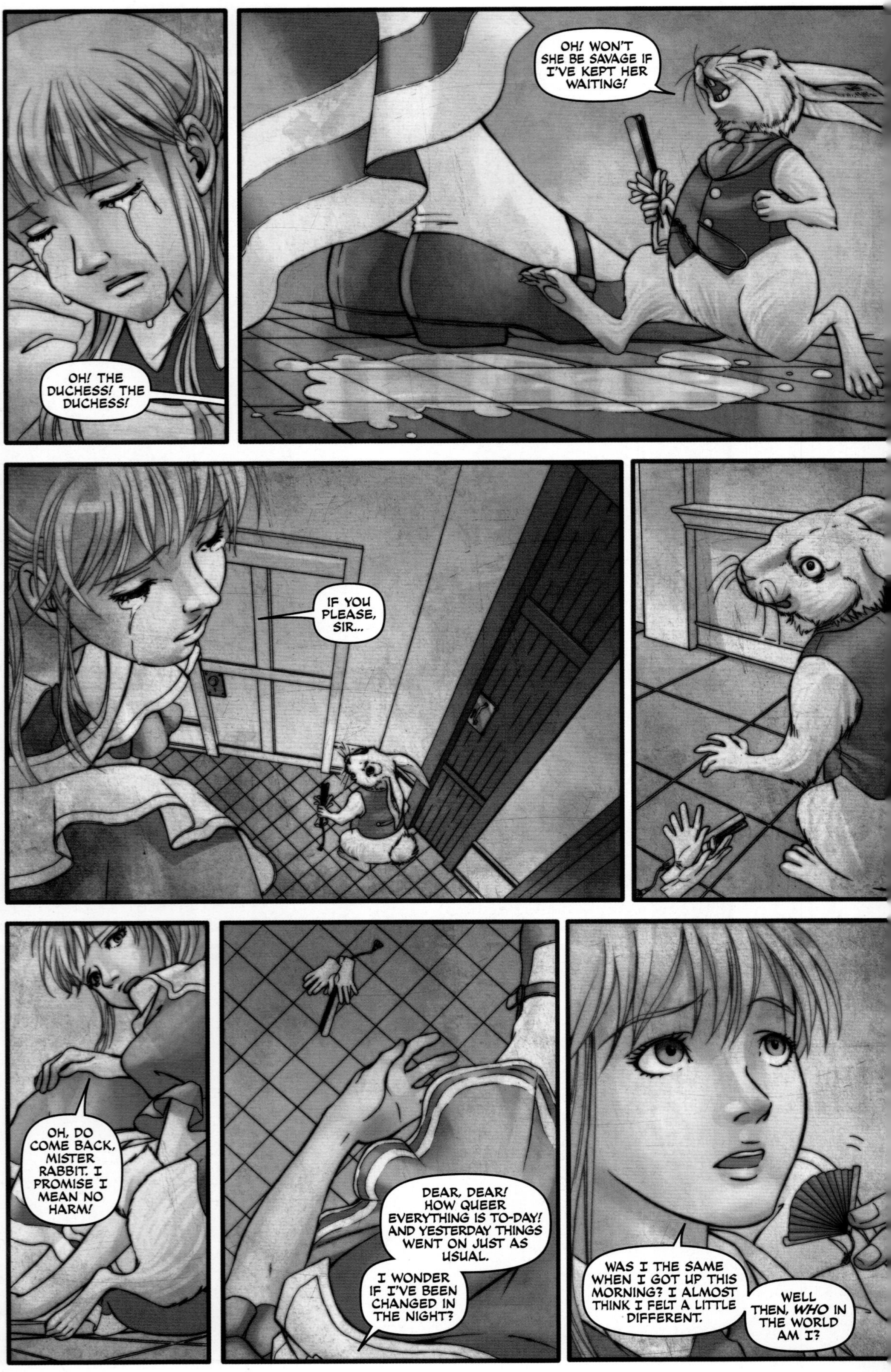
OH! THE DUCHESS! THE DUCHESS!
OH! WON'T SHE BE SAVAGE IF I'VE KEPT HER WAITING!
IF YOU PLEASE, SIR...
OH, DO COME BACK, MISTER RABBIT. I PROMISE I MEAN NO HARM!
DEAR, DEAR! HOW QUEER EVERYTHING IS TO-DAY! AND YESTERDAY THINGS WENT ON JUST AS USUAL.
I WONDER IF I'VE BEEN CHANGED IN THE NIGHT?
WAS I THE SAME WHEN I GOT UP THIS MORNING? I ALMOST THINK I FELT A LITTLE DIFFERENT.
WELL THEN, WHO IN THE WORLD AM I?

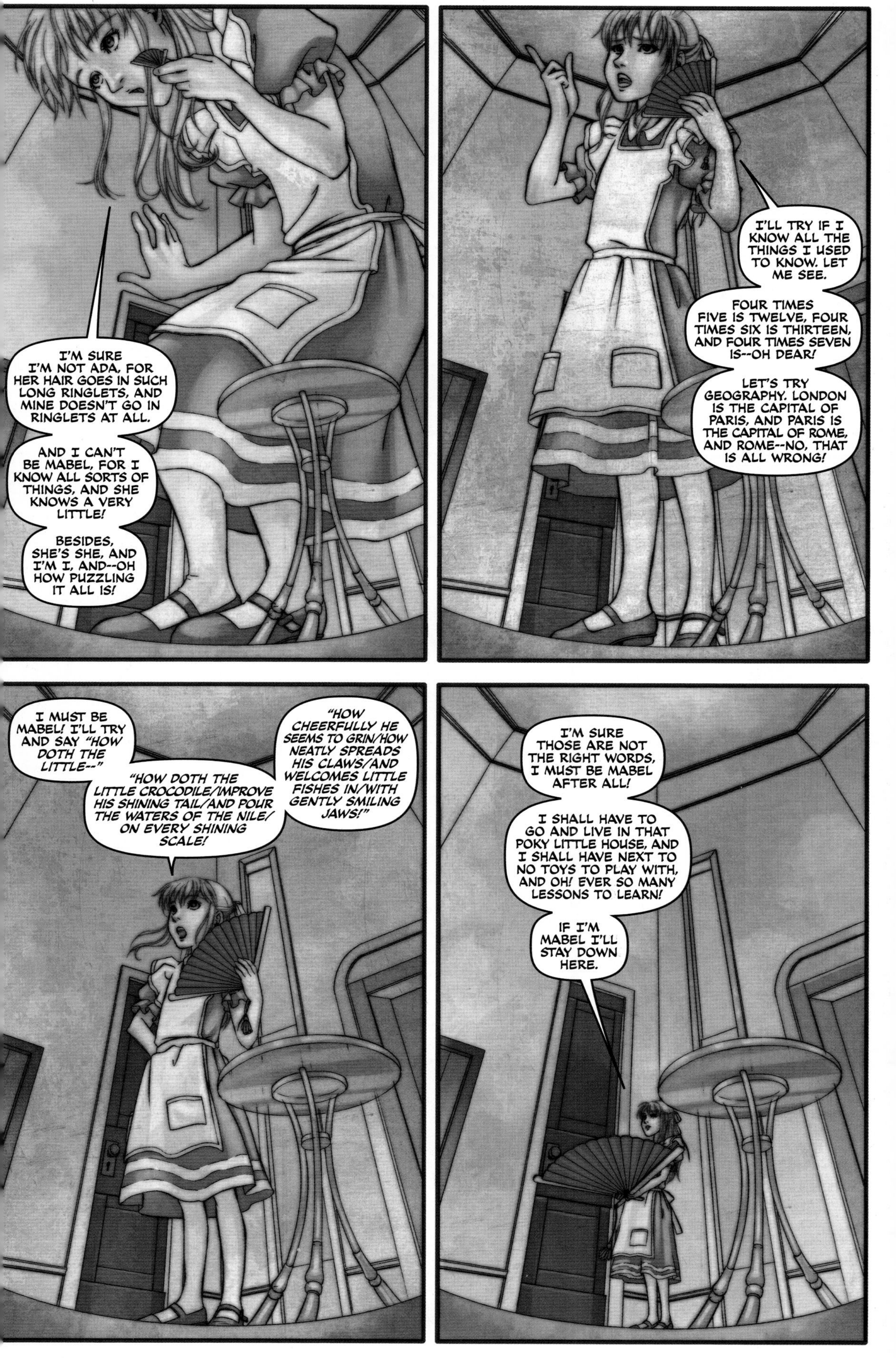
I'M SURE I'M NOT ADA, FOR HER HAIR GOES IN SUCH LONG RINGLETS, AND MINE DOESN'T GO IN RINGLETS AT ALL.
AND I CAN'T BE MABEL, FOR I KNOW ALL SORTS OF THINGS, AND SHE KNOWS A VERY LITTLE!
BESIDES, SHE'S SHE, AND I'M I, AND--OH HOW PUZZLING IT ALL IS!
I'LL TRY IF I KNOW ALL THE THINGS I USED TO KNOW. LET ME SEE.
FOUR TIMES FIVE IS TWELVE, FOUR TIMES SIX IS THIRTEEN, AND FOUR TIMES SEVEN IS--OH DEAR!
LET'S TRY GEOGRAPHY. LONDON IS THE CAPITAL OF PARIS, AND PARIS IS THE CAPITAL OF ROME, AND ROME--NO, THAT IS ALL WRONG!
I MUST BE MABEL! I'LL TRY AND SAY "HOW DOTH THE LITTLE--"
"HOW DOTH THE LITTLE CROCODILE/IMPROVE HIS SHINING TAIL/AND POUR THE WATERS OF THE NILE/ ON EVERY SHINING SCALE!
"HOW CHEERFULLY HE SEEMS TO GRIN/HOW NEATLY SPREADS HIS CLAWS/AND WELCOMES LITTLE FISHES IN/WITH GENTLY SMILING JAWS!"
I'M SURE THOSE ARE NOT THE RIGHT WORDS, I MUST BE MABEL AFTER ALL!
I SHALL HAVE TO GO AND LIVE IN THAT POKY LITTLE HOUSE, AND I SHALL HAVE NEXT TO NO TOYS TO PLAY WITH, AND OH! EVER SO MANY LESSONS TO LEARN!
IF I'M MABEL I'LL STAY DOWN HERE.

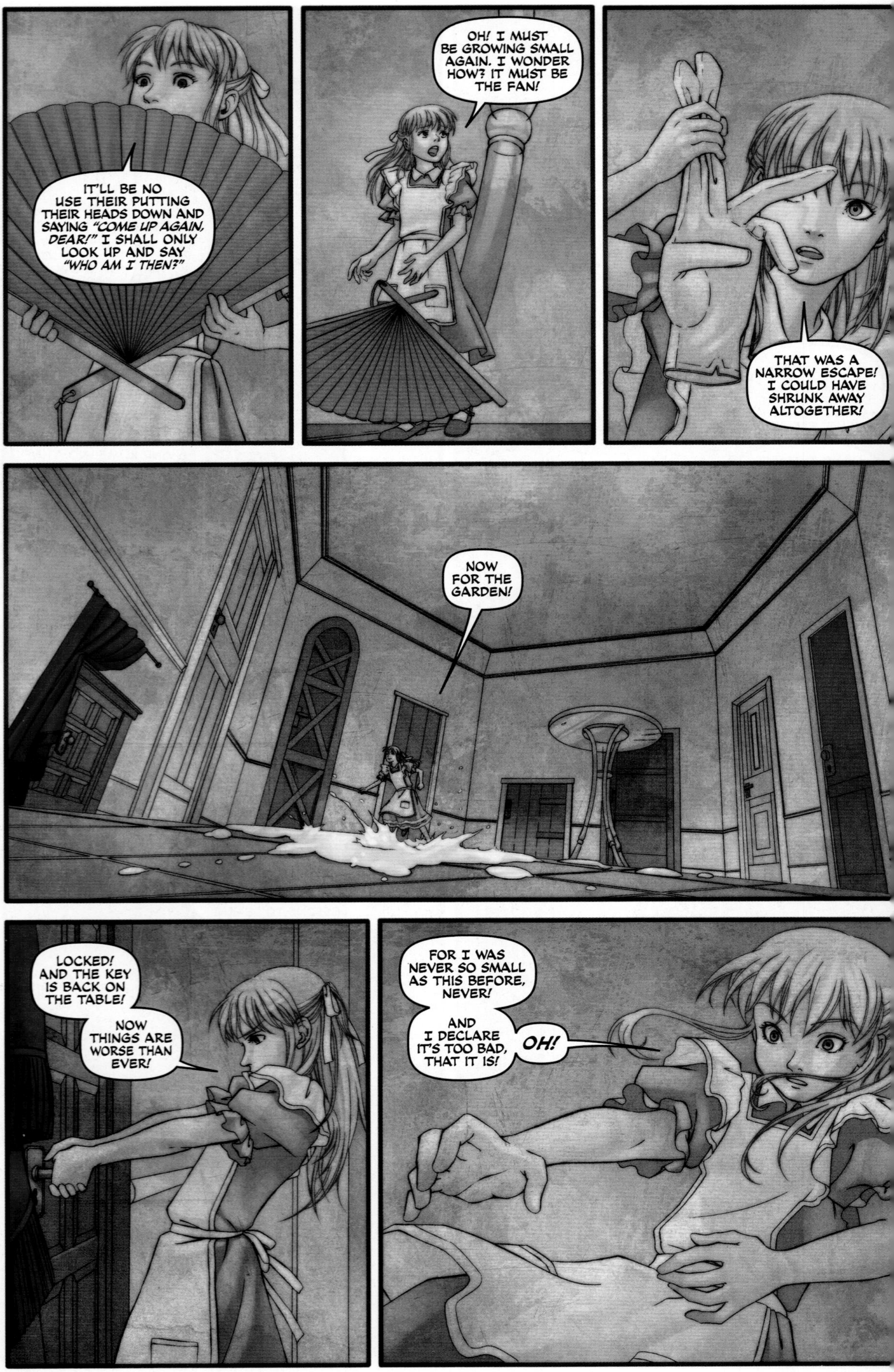
IT'LL BE NO USE THEIR PUTTING THEIR HEADS DOWN AND SAYING "COME UP AGAIN, DEAR!" I SHALL ONLY LOOK UP AND SAY "WHO AM I THEN?"
OH! I MUST BE GROWING SMALL AGAIN. I WONDER HOW? IT MUST BE THE FAN!
THAT WAS A NARROW ESCAPE! I COULD HAVE SHRUNK AWAY ALTOGETHER!
NOW FOR THE GARDEN!
LOCKED! AND THE KEY IS BACK ON THE TABLE!
NOW THINGS ARE WORSE THAN EVER!
FOR I WAS NEVER SO SMALL AS THIS BEFORE, NEVER!
AND I DECLARE IT'S TOO BAD, THAT IT IS!
OH!

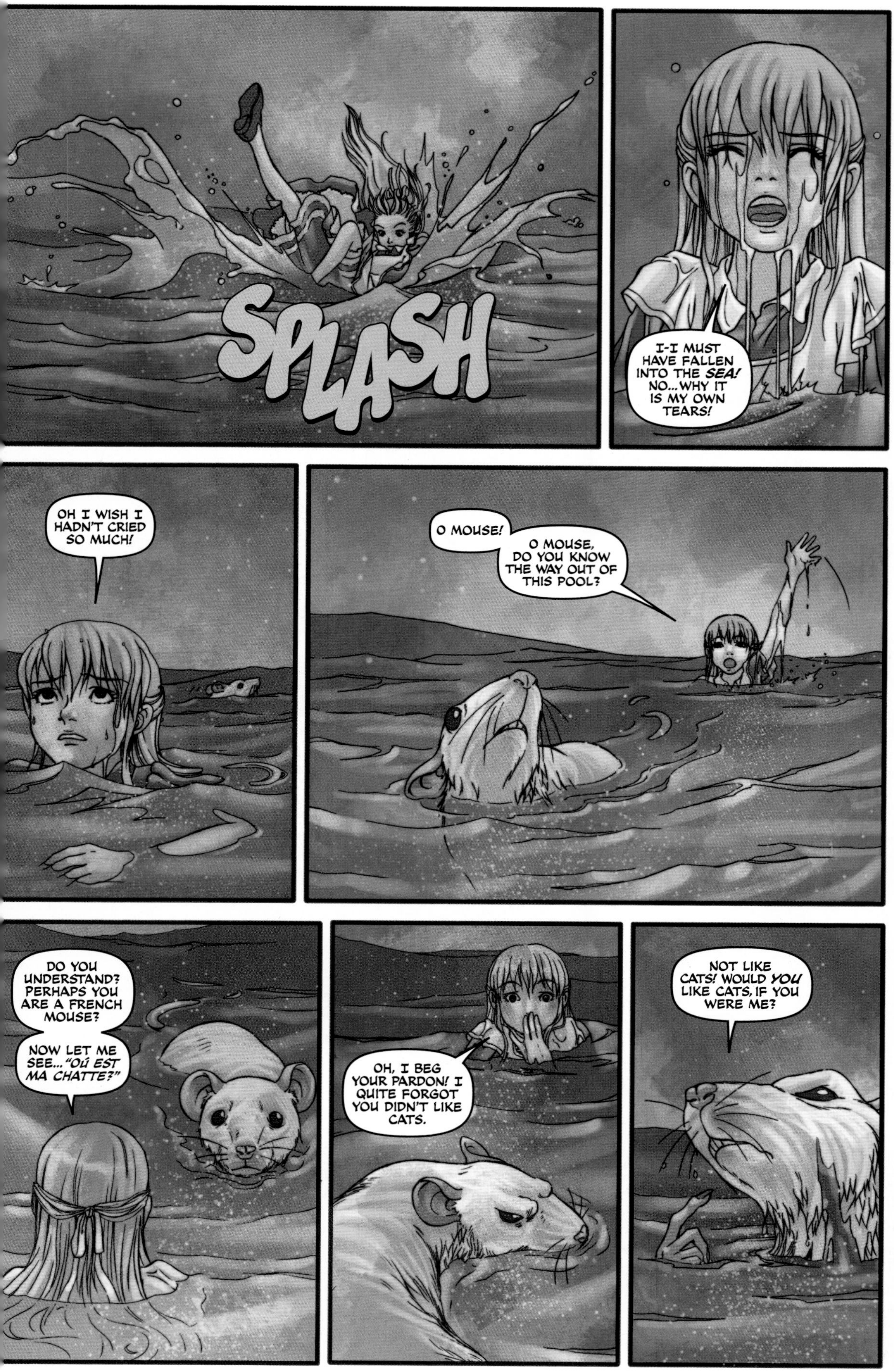
SPLASH
I-I MUST HAVE FALLEN INTO THE SEA! NO...WHY IT IS MY OWN TEARS!
OH I WISH I HADN'T CRIED SO MUCH!
O MOUSE!
O MOUSE, DO YOU KNOW THE WAY OUT OF THIS POOL?
DO YOU UNDERSTAND? PERHAPS YOU ARE A FRENCH MOUSE?
NOW LET ME SEE... "OÙ EST MA CHATTE?"
OH, I BEG YOUR PARDON! I QUITE FORGOT YOU DIDN'T LIKE CATS.
NOT LIKE CATS! WOULD YOU LIKE CATS, IF YOU WERE ME?

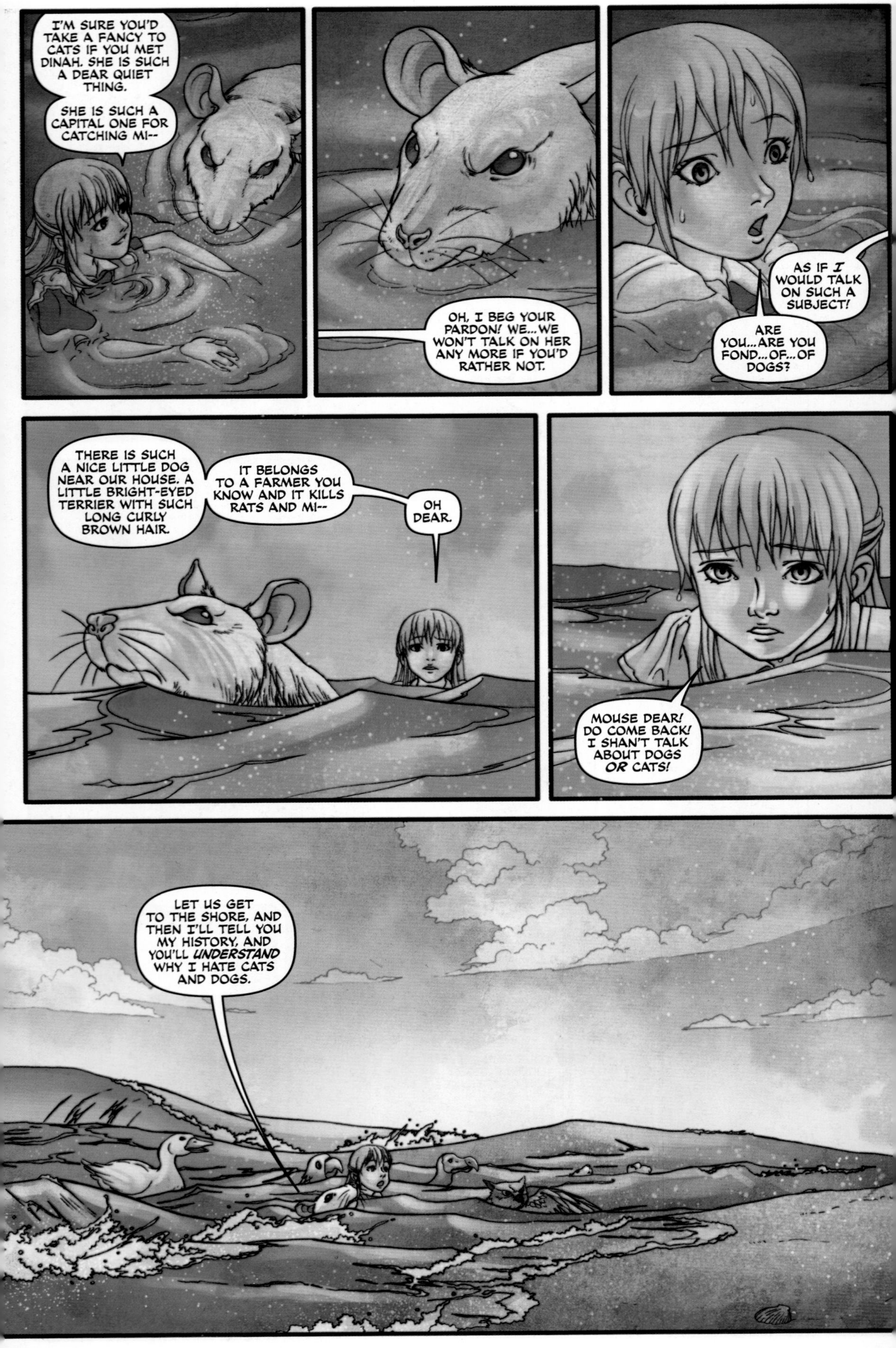
I'M SURE YOU'D TAKE A FANCY TO CATS IF YOU MET DINAH. SHE IS SUCH A DEAR QUIET THING.
SHE IS SUCH A CAPITAL ONE FOR CATCHING MI--
OH, I BEG YOUR PARDON! WE...WE WON'T TALK ON HER ANY MORE IF YOU'D RATHER NOT.
AS IF I WOULD TALK ON SUCH A SUBJECT!
ARE YOU...ARE YOU FOND...OF...OF DOGS?
THERE IS SUCH A NICE LITTLE DOG NEAR OUR HOUSE. A LITTLE BRIGHT-EYED TERRIER WITH SUCH LONG CURLY BROWN HAIR.
IT BELONGS TO A FARMER YOU KNOW AND IT KILLS RATS AND MI--
OH DEAR.
MOUSE DEAR! DO COME BACK! I SHAN'T TALK ABOUT DOGS OR CATS!
LET US GET TO THE SHORE, AND THEN I'LL TELL YOU MY HISTORY, AND YOU'LL UNDERSTAND WHY I HATE CATS AND DOGS.

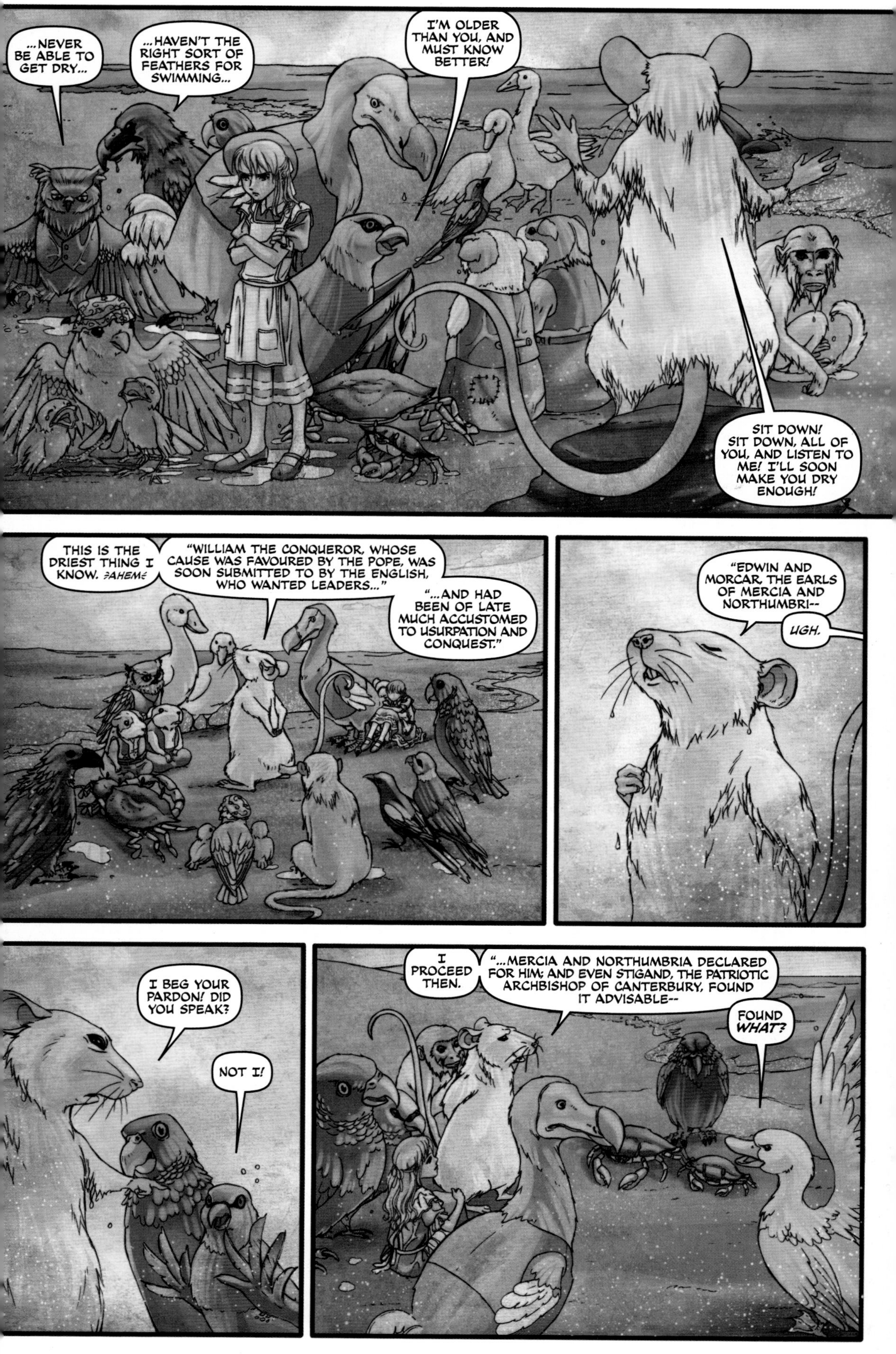
...NEVER BE ABLE TO GET DRY...
...HAVEN'T THE RIGHT SORT OF FEATHERS FOR SWIMMING...
I'M OLDER THAN YOU, AND MUST KNOW BETTER!
SIT DOWN! SIT DOWN, ALL OF YOU, AND LISTEN TO ME! I'LL SOON MAKE YOU DRY ENOUGH!
THIS IS THE DRIEST THING I KNOW. ƎAHEMƐ
"WILLIAM THE CONQUEROR, WHOSE CAUSE WAS FAVOURED BY THE POPE, WAS SOON SUBMITTED TO BY THE ENGLISH, WHO WANTED LEADERS..."
"...AND HAD BEEN OF LATE MUCH ACCUSTOMED TO USURPATION AND CONQUEST."
"EDWIN AND MORCAR, THE EARLS OF MERCIA AND NORTHUMBRI--
UGH.
I BEG YOUR PARDON! DID YOU SPEAK?
NOT I!
I PROCEED THEN.
"...MERCIA AND NORTHUMBRIA DECLARED FOR HIM; AND EVEN STIGAND, THE PATRIOTIC ARCHBISHOP OF CANTERBURY, FOUND IT ADVISABLE--
FOUND WHAT?

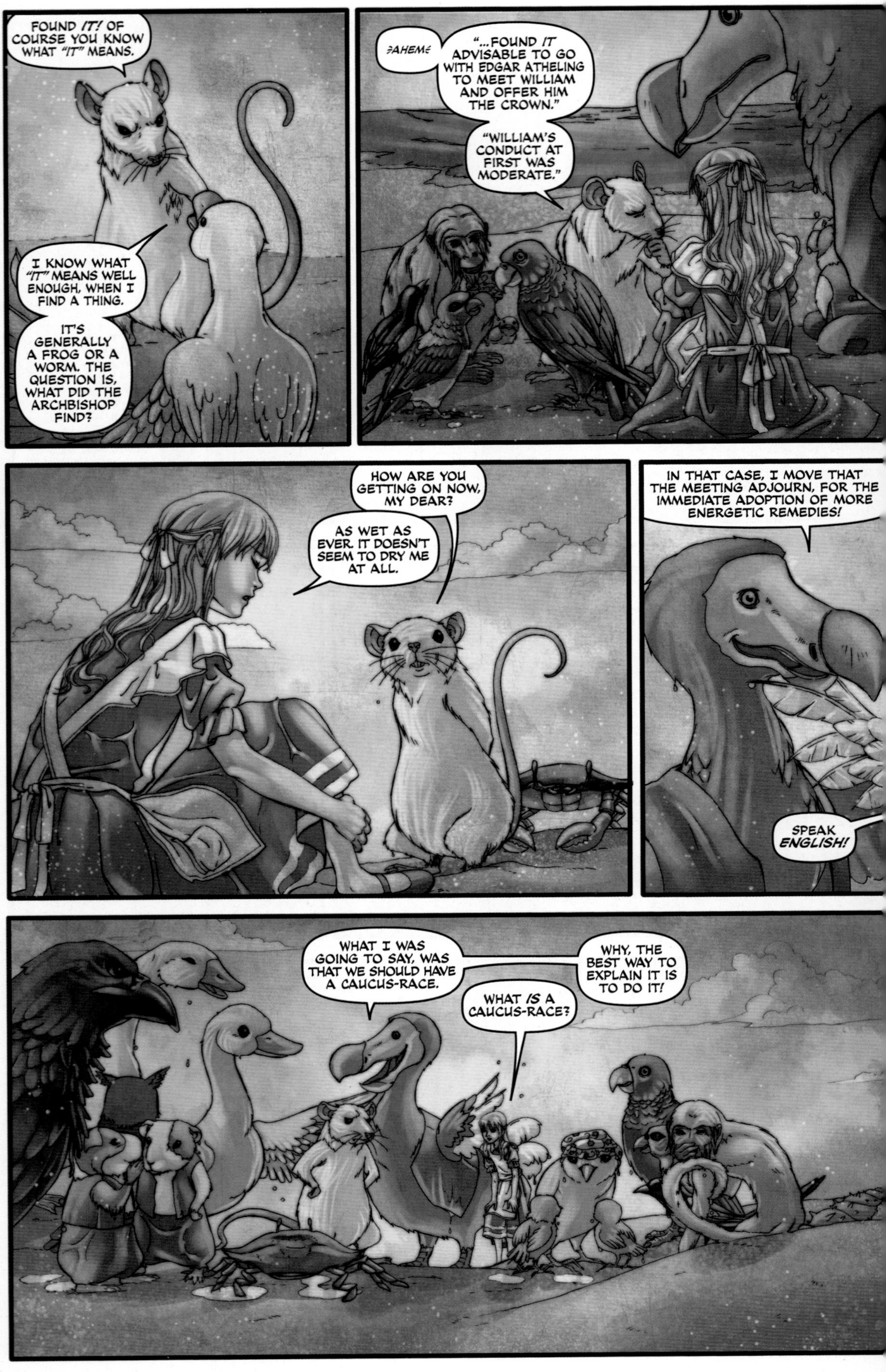
FOUND IT! OF COURSE YOU KNOW WHAT "IT" MEANS.
I KNOW WHAT "IT" MEANS WELL ENOUGH, WHEN I FIND A THING.
IT'S GENERALLY A FROG OR A WORM. THE QUESTION IS, WHAT DID THE ARCHBISHOP FIND?
AHEM
"...FOUND IT ADVISABLE TO GO WITH EDGAR ATHELING TO MEET WILLIAM AND OFFER HIM THE CROWN."
"WILLIAM'S CONDUCT AT FIRST WAS MODERATE."
HOW ARE YOU GETTING ON NOW, MY DEAR?
AS WET AS EVER. IT DOESN'T SEEM TO DRY ME AT ALL.
IN THAT CASE, I MOVE THAT THE MEETING ADJOURN, FOR THE IMMEDIATE ADOPTION OF MORE ENERGETIC REMEDIES!
SPEAK ENGLISH!
WHAT I WAS GOING TO SAY, WAS THAT WE SHOULD HAVE A CAUCUS-RACE.
WHAT IS A CAUCUS-RACE?
WHY, THE BEST WAY TO EXPLAIN IT IS TO DO IT!

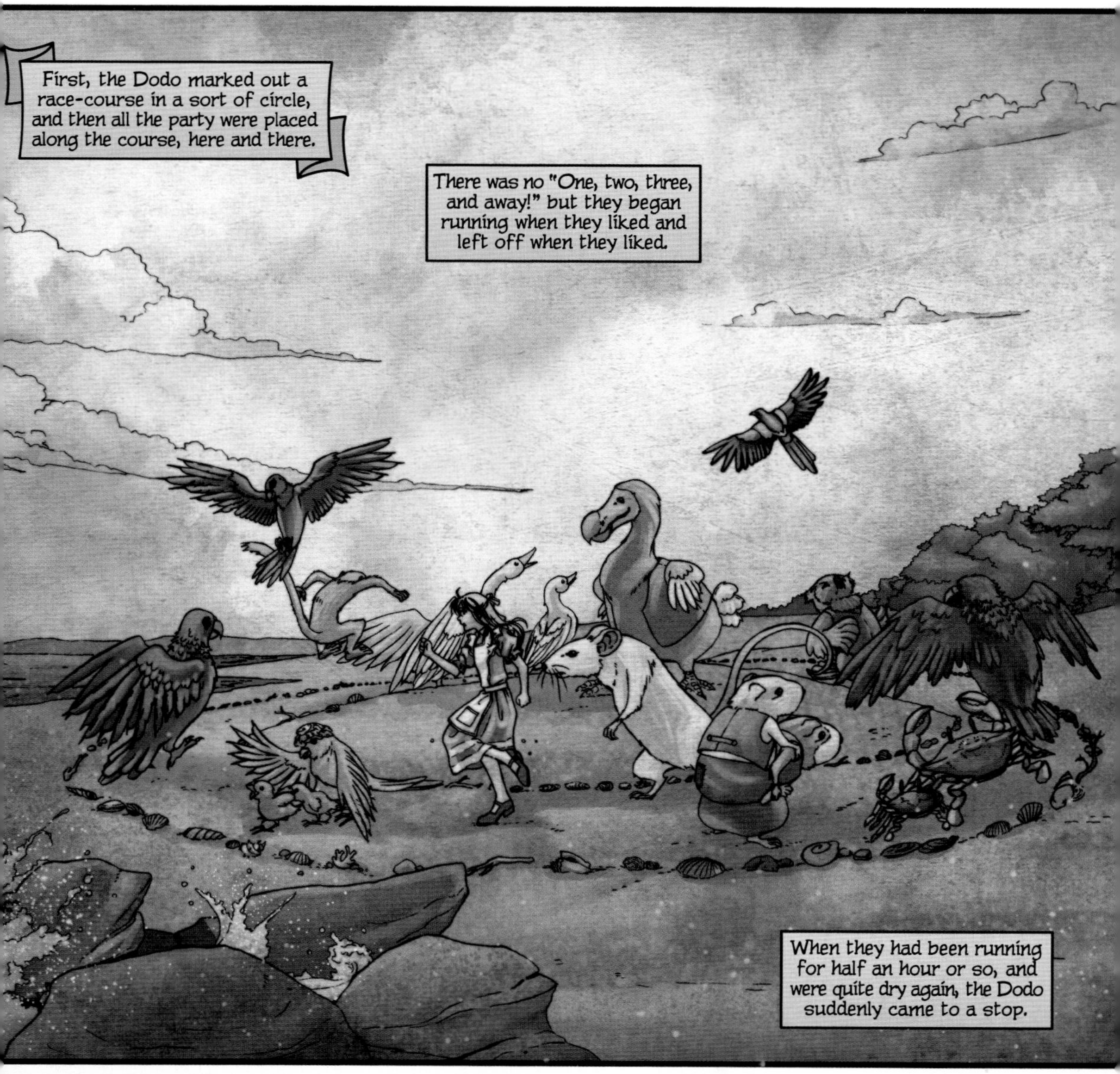
First, the Dodo marked out a race-course in a sort of circle, and then all the party were placed along the course, here and there.
There was no "One, two, three, and away!" but they began running when they liked and left off when they liked.
When they had been running for half an hour or so, and were quite dry again, the Dodo suddenly came to a stop.

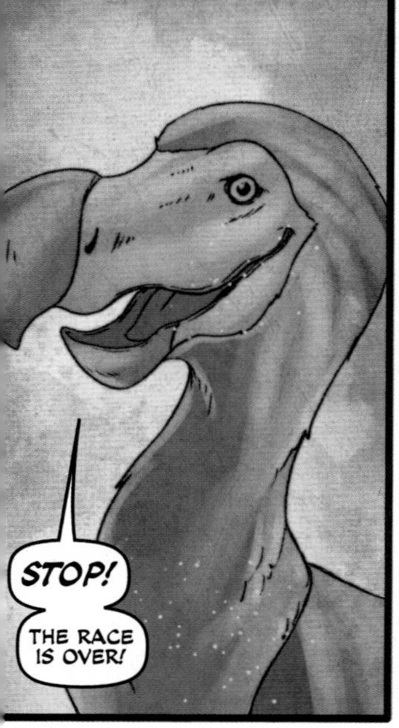
STOP!
THE RACE IS OVER!

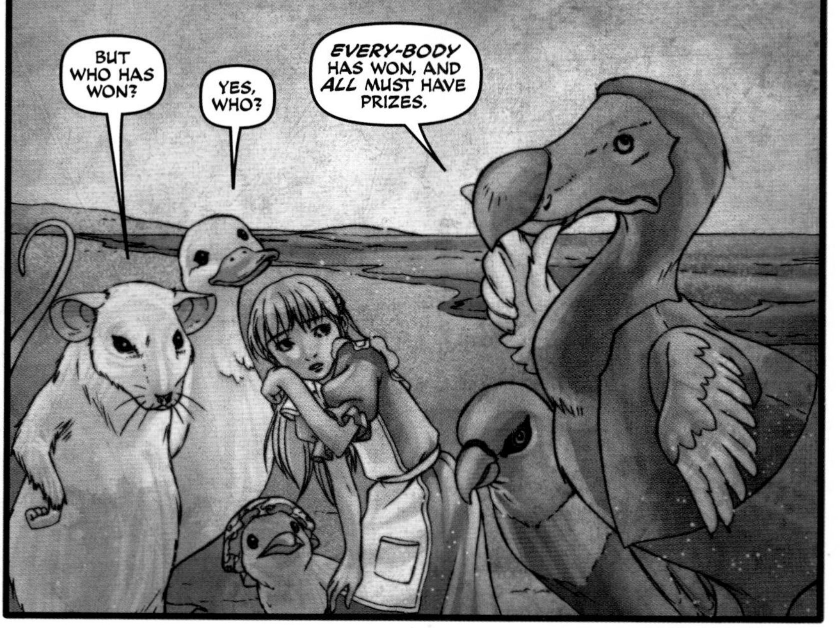
BUT WHO HAS WON?
YES, WHO?
EVERY-BODY HAS WON, AND ALL MUST HAVE PRIZES.

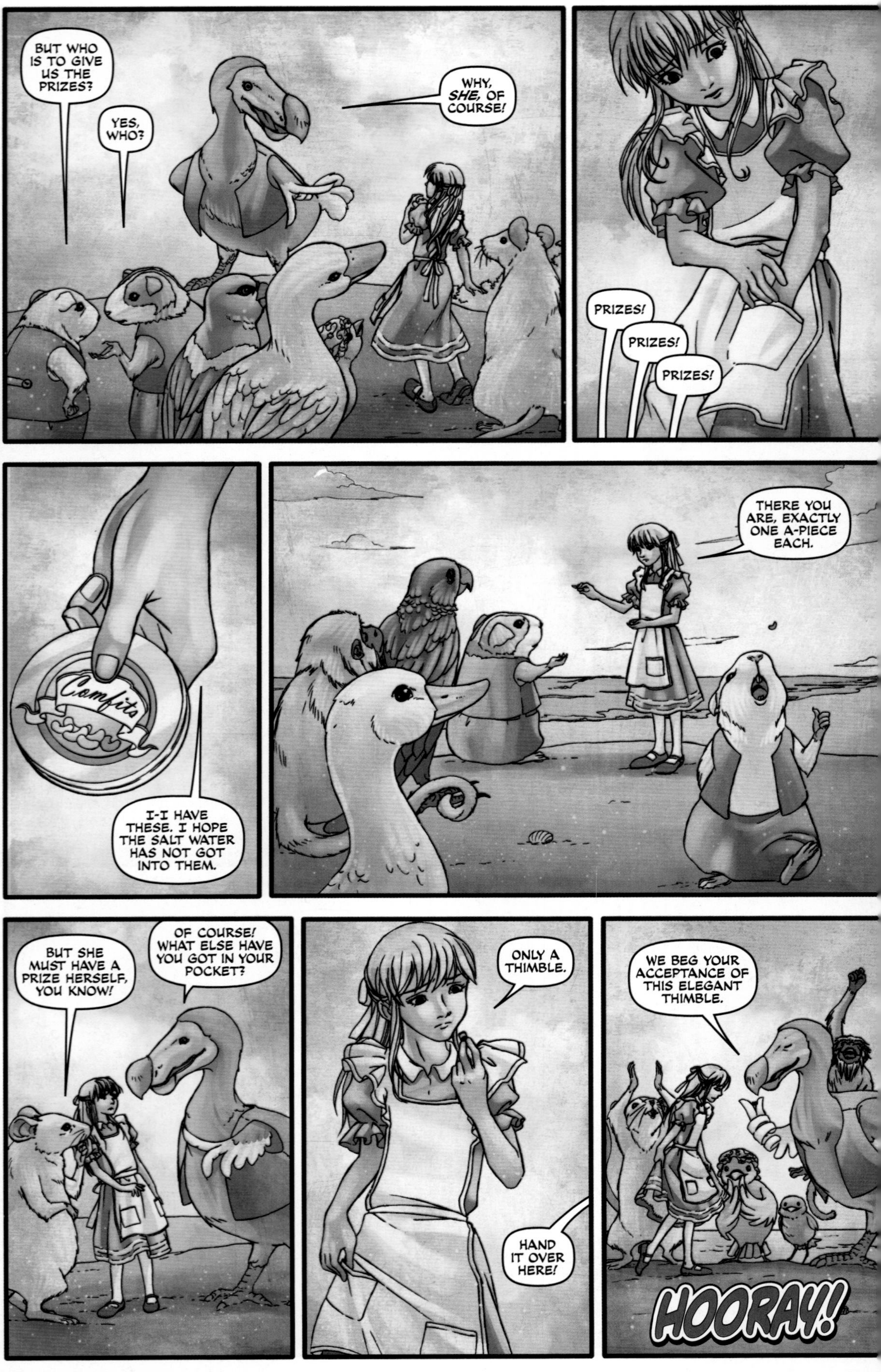
BUT WHO IS TO GIVE US THE PRIZES?
YES, WHO?
WHY, *SHE,* OF COURSE!
PRIZES!
PRIZES!
PRIZES!
Comfits
I-I HAVE THESE. I HOPE THE SALT WATER HAS NOT GOT INTO THEM.
THERE YOU ARE, EXACTLY ONE A-PIECE EACH.
BUT SHE MUST HAVE A PRIZE HERSELF, YOU KNOW!
OF COURSE! WHAT ELSE HAVE YOU GOT IN YOUR POCKET?
ONLY A THIMBLE.
HAND IT OVER HERE!
WE BEG YOUR ACCEPTANCE OF THIS ELEGANT THIMBLE.
HOORAY!

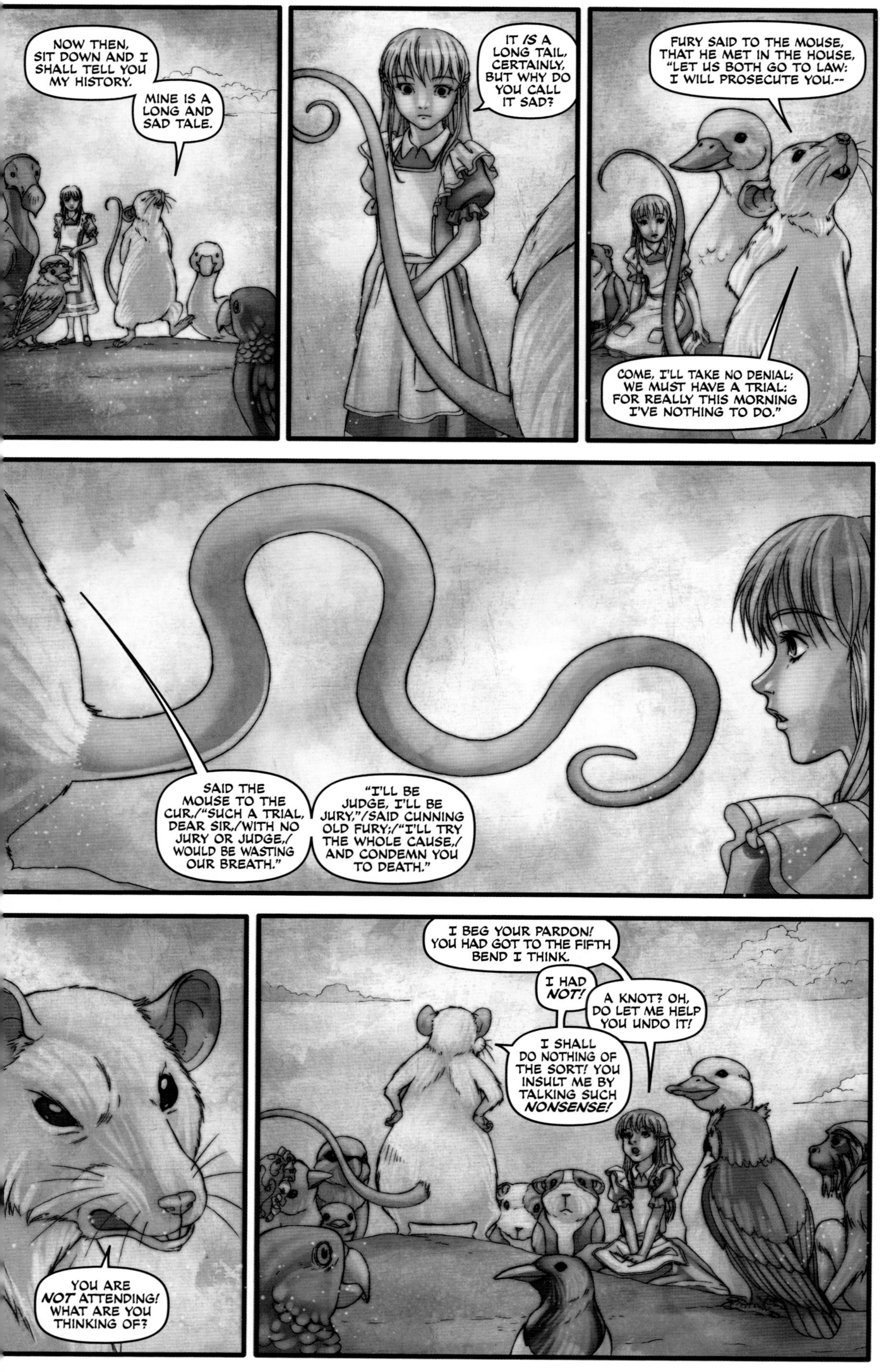

NOW THEN, SIT DOWN AND I SHALL TELL YOU MY HISTORY.
MINE IS A LONG AND SAD TALE.
IT *IS* A LONG TAIL, CERTAINLY, BUT WHY DO YOU CALL IT SAD?
FURY SAID TO THE MOUSE, THAT HE MET IN THE HOUSE, "LET US BOTH GO TO LAW: I WILL PROSECUTE YOU.--
COME, I'LL TAKE NO DENIAL; WE MUST HAVE A TRIAL: FOR REALLY THIS MORNING I'VE NOTHING TO DO."
SAID THE MOUSE TO THE CUR,/"SUCH A TRIAL, DEAR SIR,/WITH NO JURY OR JUDGE,/ WOULD BE WASTING OUR BREATH."
"I'LL BE JUDGE, I'LL BE JURY,"/SAID CUNNING OLD FURY;/"I'LL TRY THE WHOLE CAUSE,/ AND CONDEMN YOU TO DEATH."
YOU ARE *NOT* ATTENDING! WHAT ARE YOU THINKING OF?
I BEG YOUR PARDON! YOU HAD GOT TO THE FIFTH BEND I THINK.
I HAD *NOT!*
A KNOT? OH, DO LET ME HELP YOU UNDO IT!
I SHALL DO NOTHING OF THE SORT! YOU INSULT ME BY TALKING SUCH *NONSENSE!*

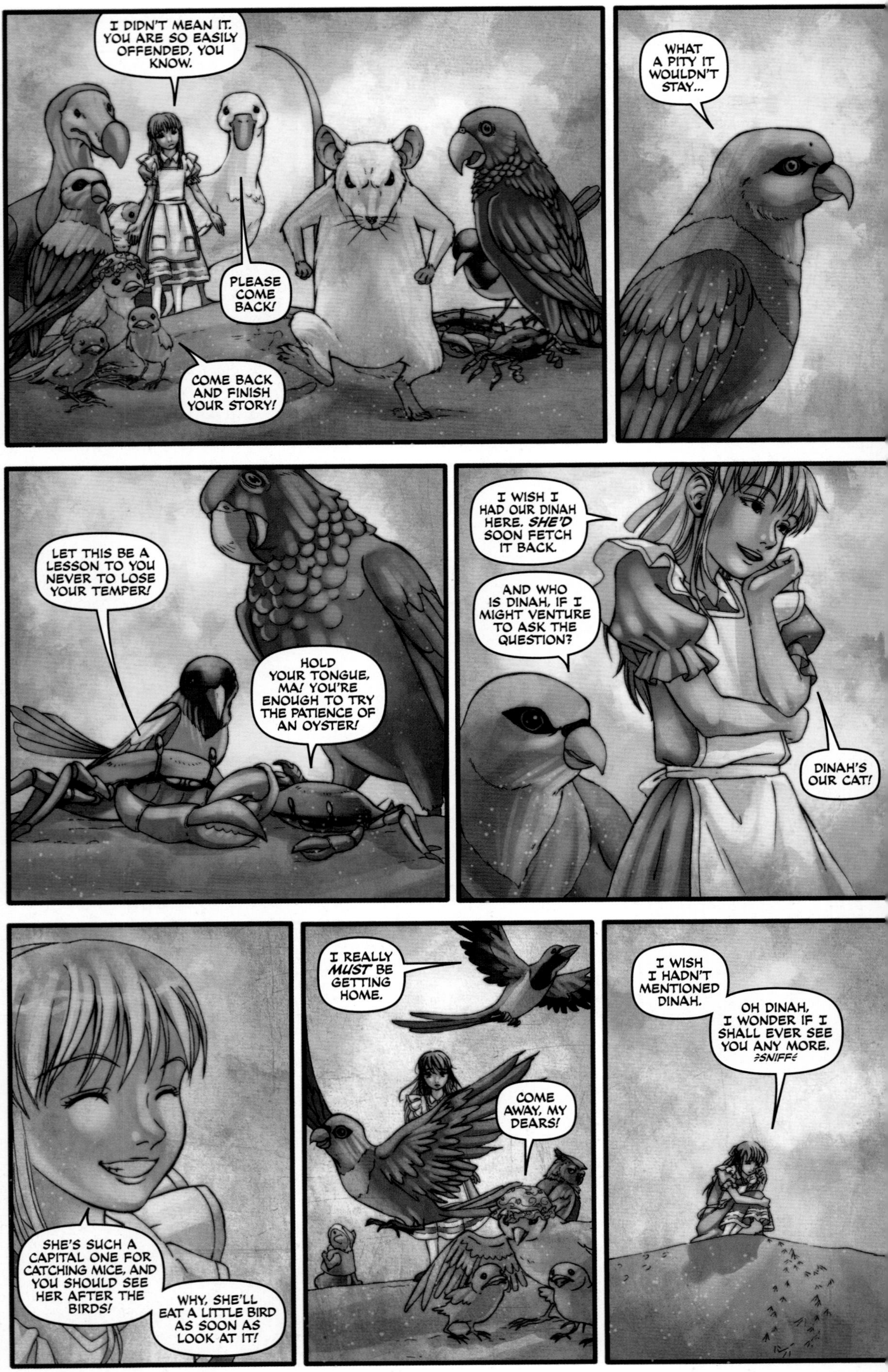

I DIDN'T MEAN IT. YOU ARE SO EASILY OFFENDED, YOU KNOW.
PLEASE COME BACK!
COME BACK AND FINISH YOUR STORY!
WHAT A PITY IT WOULDN'T STAY...
LET THIS BE A LESSON TO YOU NEVER TO LOSE YOUR TEMPER!
HOLD YOUR TONGUE, MA! YOU'RE ENOUGH TO TRY THE PATIENCE OF AN OYSTER!
I WISH I HAD OUR DINAH HERE. SHE'D SOON FETCH IT BACK.
AND WHO IS DINAH, IF I MIGHT VENTURE TO ASK THE QUESTION?
DINAH'S OUR CAT!
SHE'S SUCH A CAPITAL ONE FOR CATCHING MICE, AND YOU SHOULD SEE HER AFTER THE BIRDS!
WHY, SHE'LL EAT A LITTLE BIRD AS SOON AS LOOK AT IT!
I REALLY MUST BE GETTING HOME.
COME AWAY, MY DEARS!
I WISH I HADN'T MENTIONED DINAH.
OH DINAH, I WONDER IF I SHALL EVER SEE YOU ANY MORE.
SNIFF

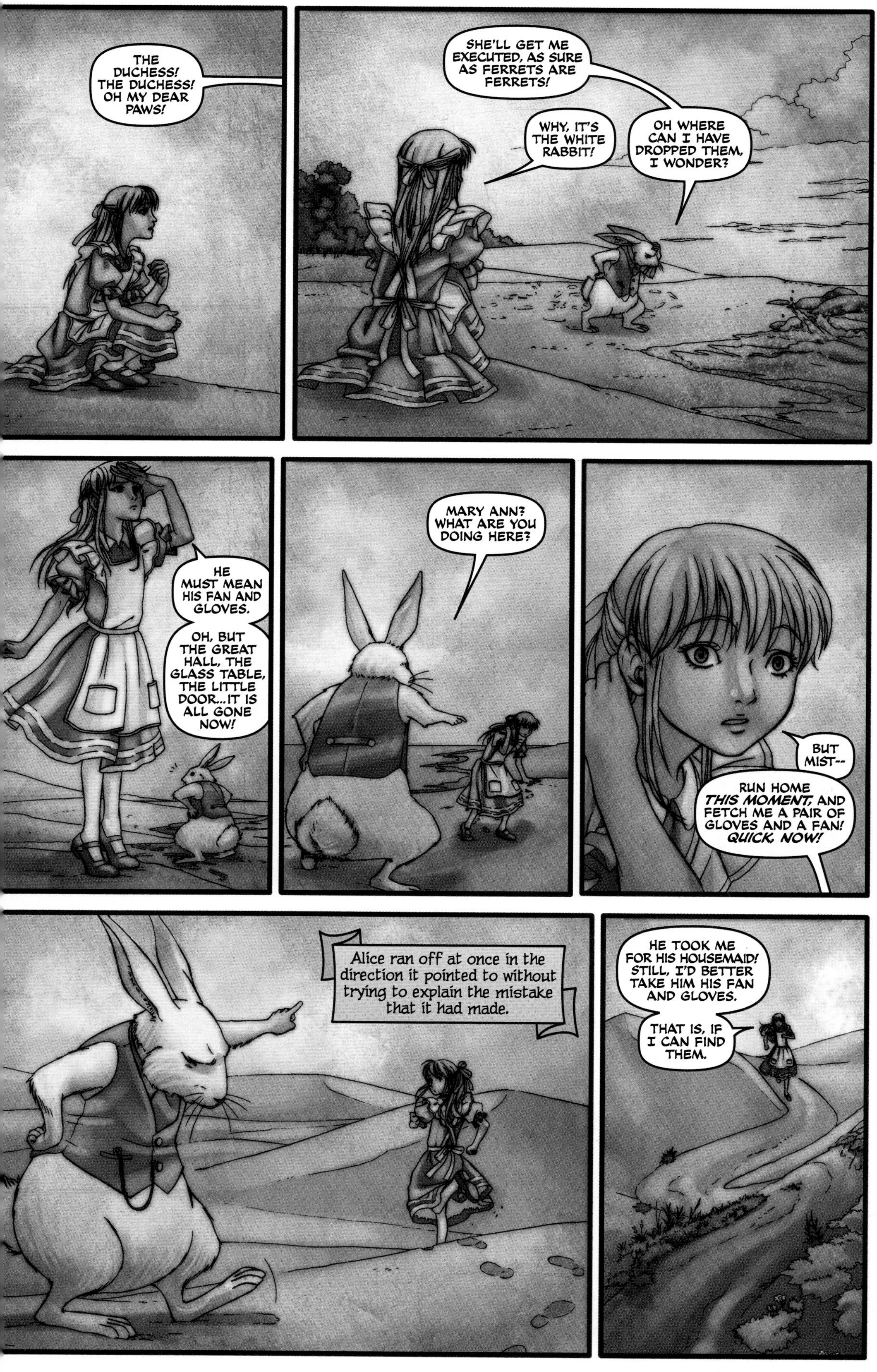
THE DUCHESS! THE DUCHESS! OH MY DEAR PAWS!
SHE'LL GET ME EXECUTED, AS SURE AS FERRETS ARE FERRETS!
OH WHERE CAN I HAVE DROPPED THEM, I WONDER?
WHY, IT'S THE WHITE RABBIT!
HE MUST MEAN HIS FAN AND GLOVES.
OH, BUT THE GREAT HALL, THE GLASS TABLE, THE LITTLE DOOR...IT IS ALL GONE NOW!
MARY ANN? WHAT ARE YOU DOING HERE?
BUT MIST--
RUN HOME THIS MOMENT, AND FETCH ME A PAIR OF GLOVES AND A FAN! QUICK, NOW!
Alice ran off at once in the direction it pointed to without trying to explain the mistake that it had made.
HE TOOK ME FOR HIS HOUSEMAID! STILL, I'D BETTER TAKE HIM HIS FAN AND GLOVES.
THAT IS, IF I CAN FIND THEM.

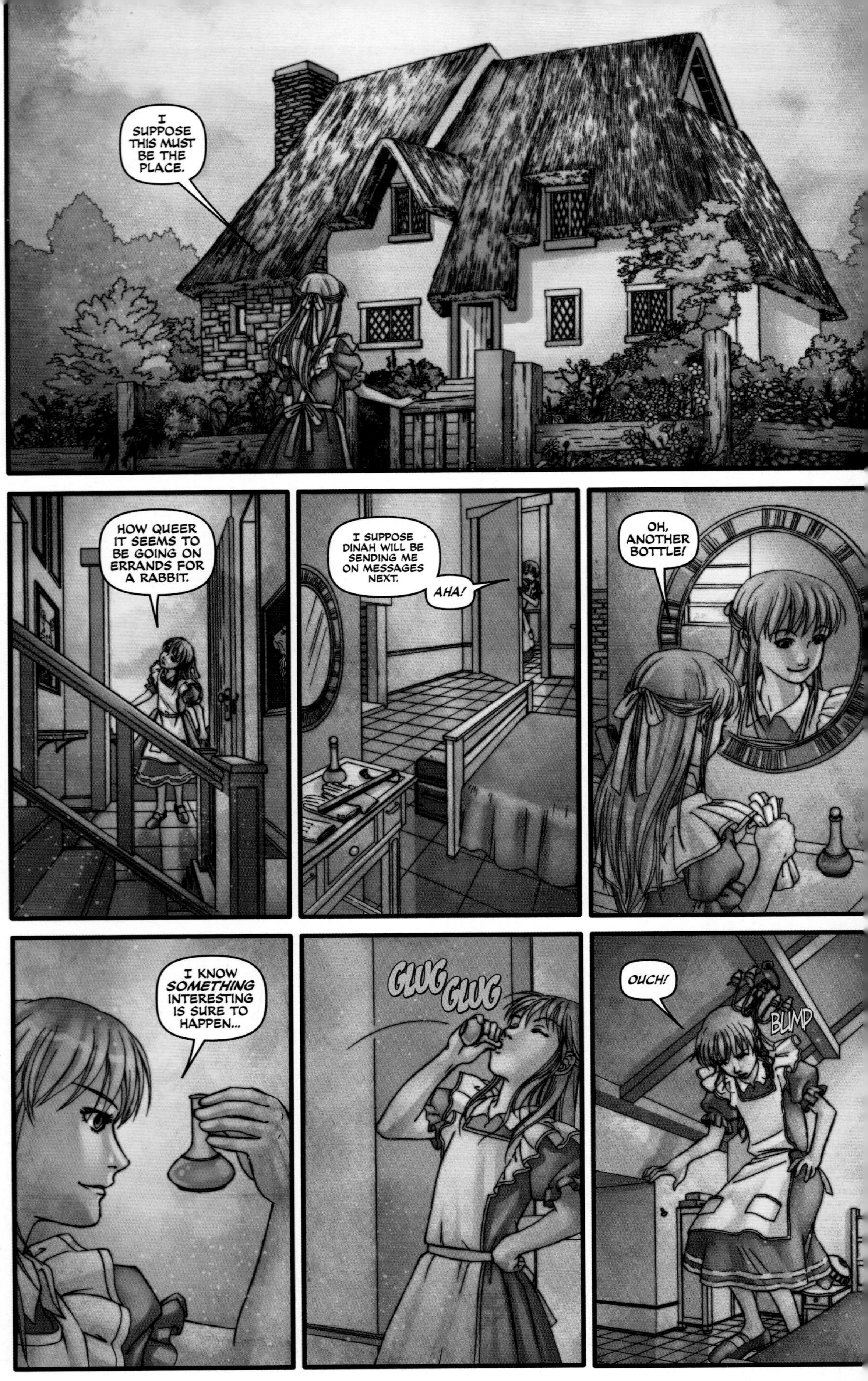
I SUPPOSE THIS MUST BE THE PLACE.
HOW QUEER IT SEEMS TO BE GOING ON ERRANDS FOR A RABBIT.
I SUPPOSE DINAH WILL BE SENDING ME ON MESSAGES NEXT.
AHA!
OH, ANOTHER BOTTLE!
I KNOW SOMETHING INTERESTING IS SURE TO HAPPEN...
GLUG GLUG
OUCH!
BUMP

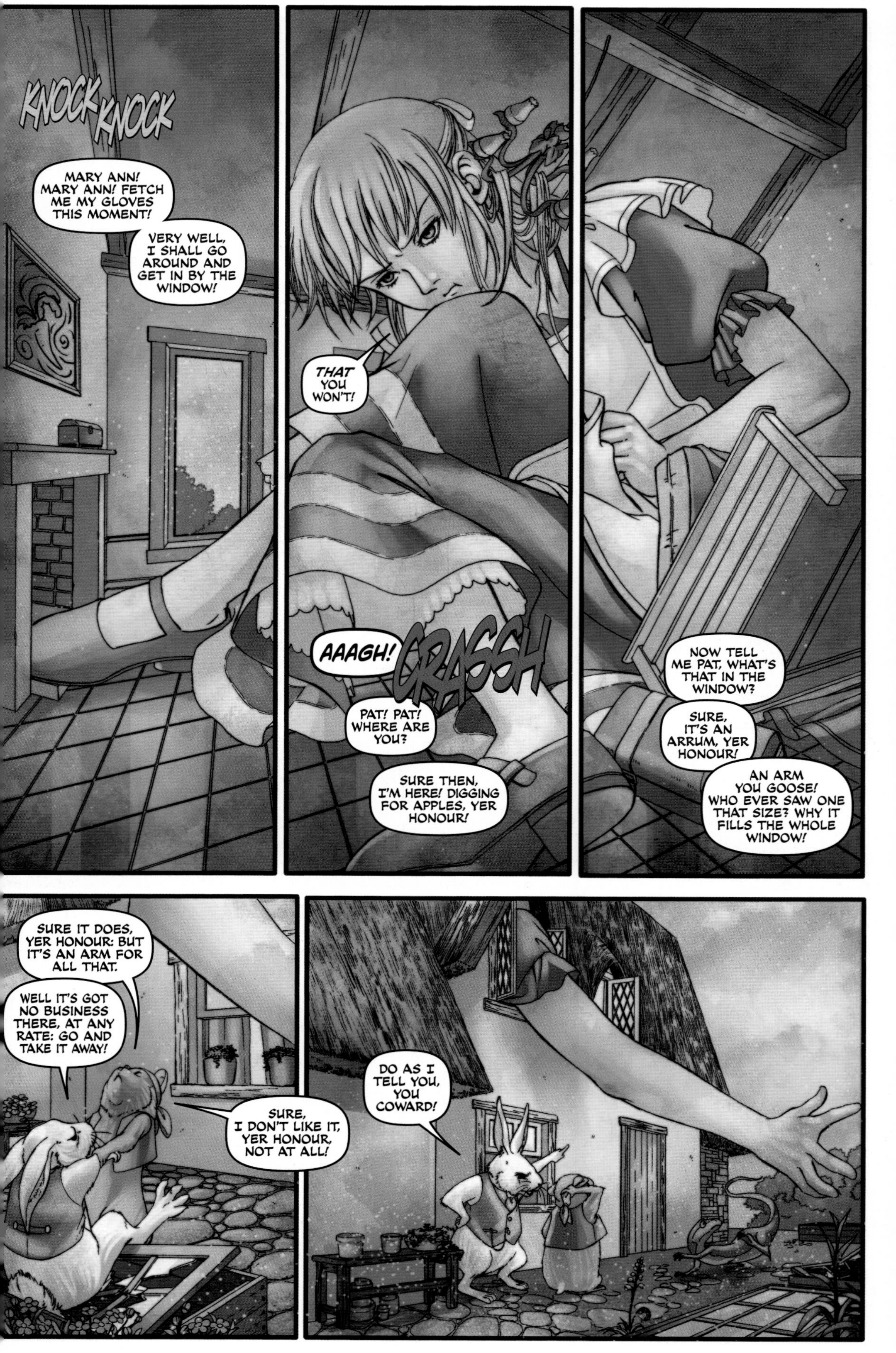
KNOCK KNOCK
MARY ANN! MARY ANN! FETCH ME MY GLOVES THIS MOMENT!
VERY WELL, I SHALL GO AROUND AND GET IN BY THE WINDOW!
THAT YOU WON'T!
AAAGH!
CRASSH
PAT! PAT! WHERE ARE YOU?
SURE THEN, I'M HERE! DIGGING FOR APPLES, YER HONOUR!
NOW TELL ME PAT, WHAT'S THAT IN THE WINDOW?
SURE, IT'S AN ARRUM, YER HONOUR!
AN ARM YOU GOOSE! WHO EVER SAW ONE THAT SIZE? WHY IT FILLS THE WHOLE WINDOW!
SURE IT DOES, YER HONOUR: BUT IT'S AN ARM FOR ALL THAT.
WELL IT'S GOT NO BUSINESS THERE, AT ANY RATE: GO AND TAKE IT AWAY!
SURE, I DON'T LIKE IT, YER HONOUR, NOT AT ALL!
DO AS I TELL YOU, YOU COWARD!

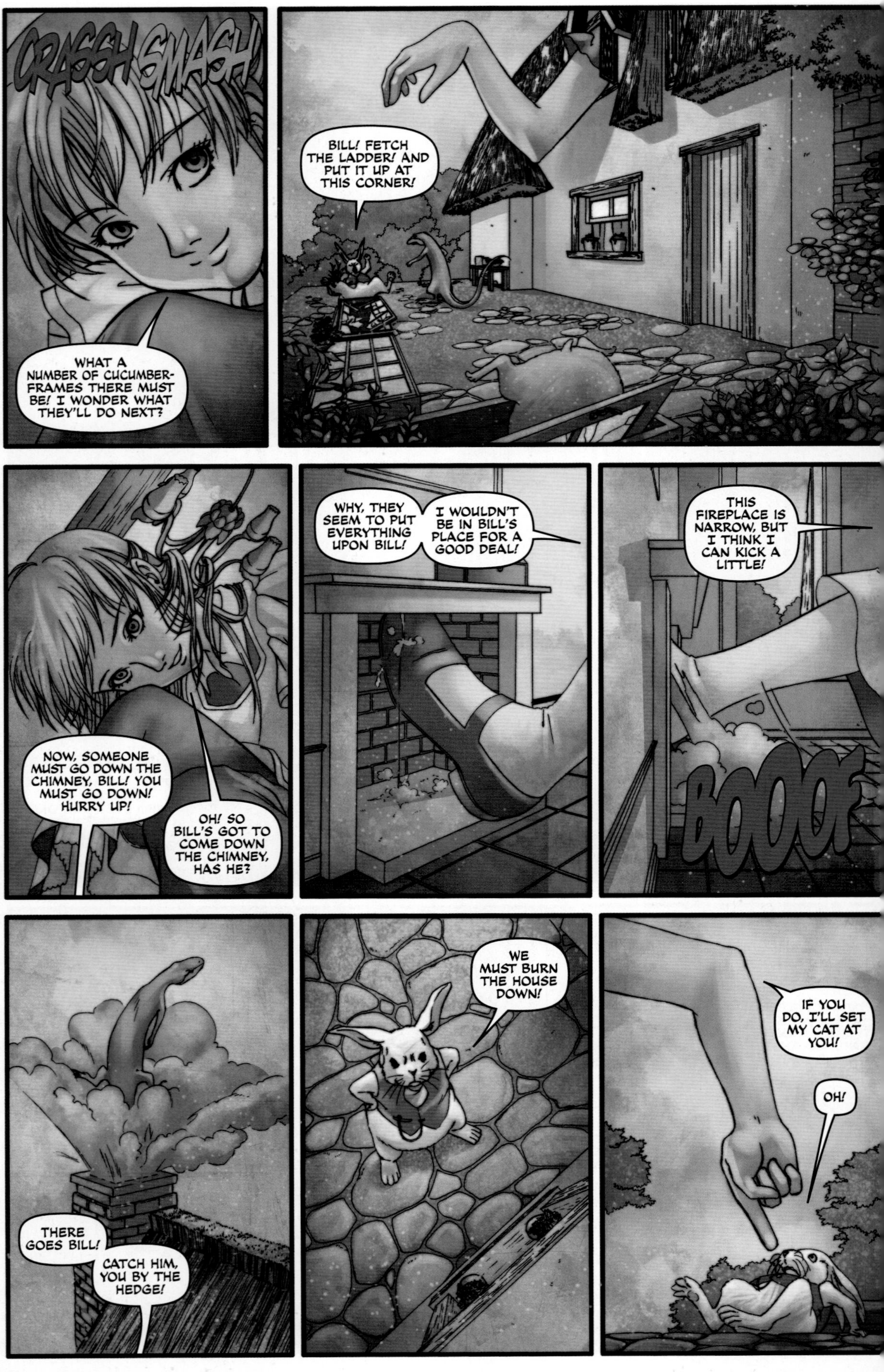
CRASSH SMASH!
WHAT A NUMBER OF CUCUMBER-FRAMES THERE MUST BE! I WONDER WHAT THEY'LL DO NEXT?
BILL! FETCH THE LADDER! AND PUT IT UP AT THIS CORNER!
NOW, SOMEONE MUST GO DOWN THE CHIMNEY, BILL! YOU MUST GO DOWN! HURRY UP!
OH! SO BILL'S GOT TO COME DOWN THE CHIMNEY, HAS HE?
WHY, THEY SEEM TO PUT EVERYTHING UPON BILL!
I WOULDN'T BE IN BILL'S PLACE FOR A GOOD DEAL!
THIS FIREPLACE IS NARROW, BUT I THINK I CAN KICK A LITTLE!
BOOOF
THERE GOES BILL!
CATCH HIM, YOU BY THE HEDGE!
WE MUST BURN THE HOUSE DOWN!
IF YOU DO, I'LL SET MY CAT AT YOU!
OH!

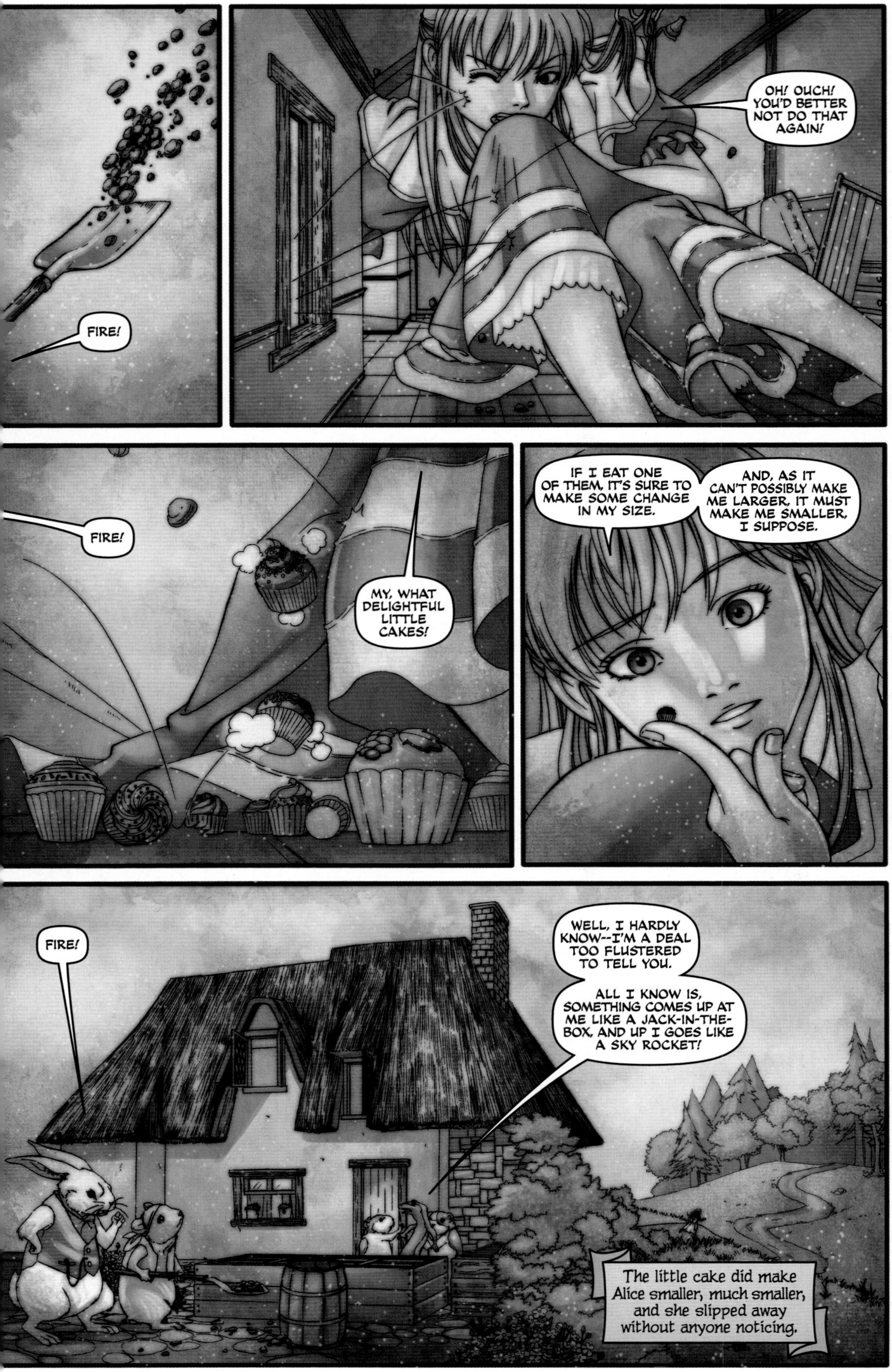
FIRE!
OH! OUCH! YOU'D BETTER NOT DO THAT AGAIN!
FIRE!
MY, WHAT DELIGHTFUL LITTLE CAKES!
IF I EAT ONE OF THEM, IT'S SURE TO MAKE SOME CHANGE IN MY SIZE.
AND, AS IT CAN'T POSSIBLY MAKE ME LARGER, IT MUST MAKE ME SMALLER, I SUPPOSE.
FIRE!
WELL, I HARDLY KNOW--I'M A DEAL TOO FLUSTERED TO TELL YOU.
ALL I KNOW IS, SOMETHING COMES UP AT ME LIKE A JACK-IN-THE-BOX, AND UP I GOES LIKE A SKY ROCKET!
The little cake did make Alice smaller, much smaller, and she slipped away without anyone noticing.

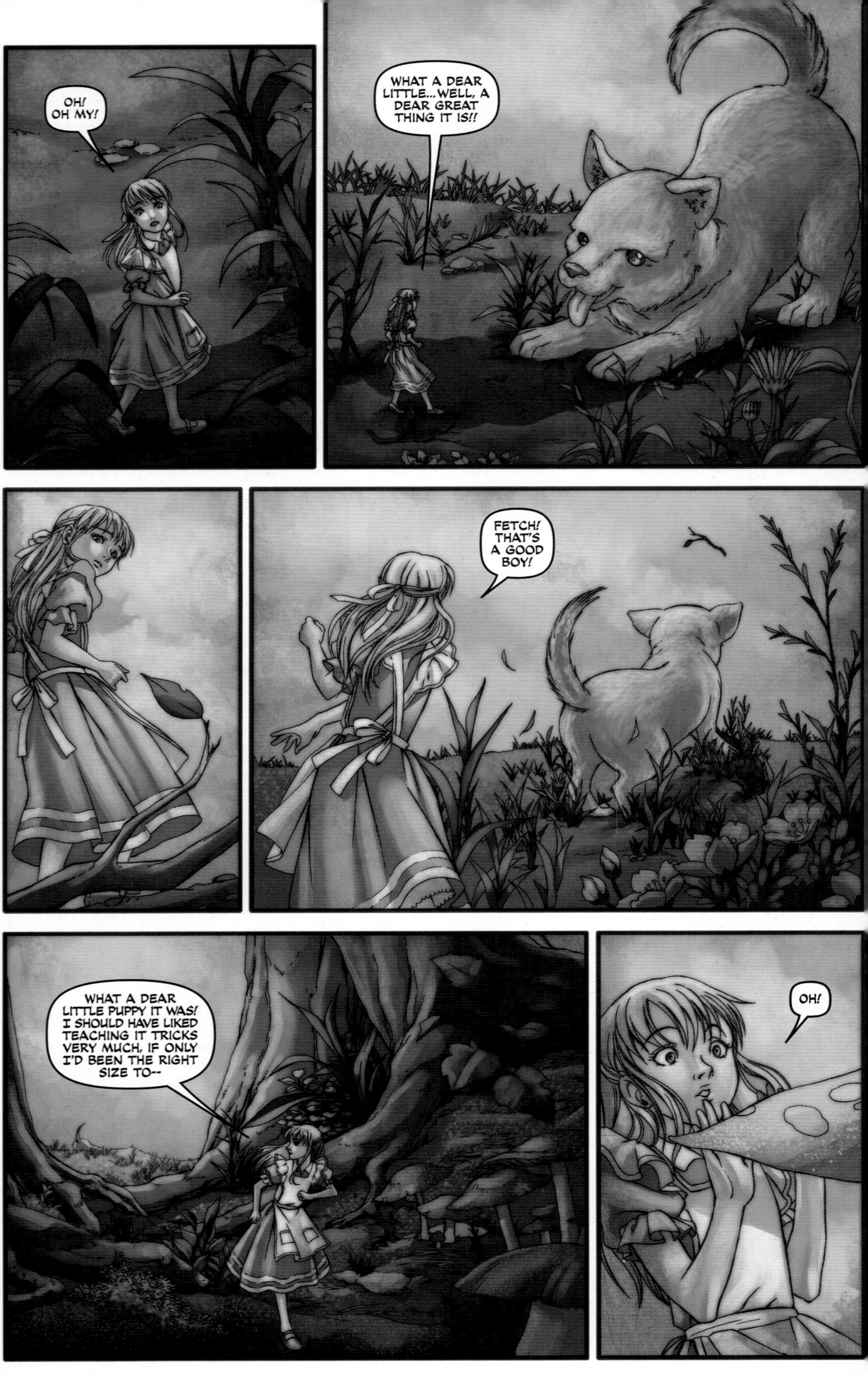
OH! OH MY!
WHAT A DEAR LITTLE...WELL, A DEAR GREAT THING IT IS!!
FETCH! THAT'S A GOOD BOY!
WHAT A DEAR LITTLE PUPPY IT WAS! I SHOULD HAVE LIKED TEACHING IT TRICKS VERY MUCH, IF ONLY I'D BEEN THE RIGHT SIZE TO--
OH!

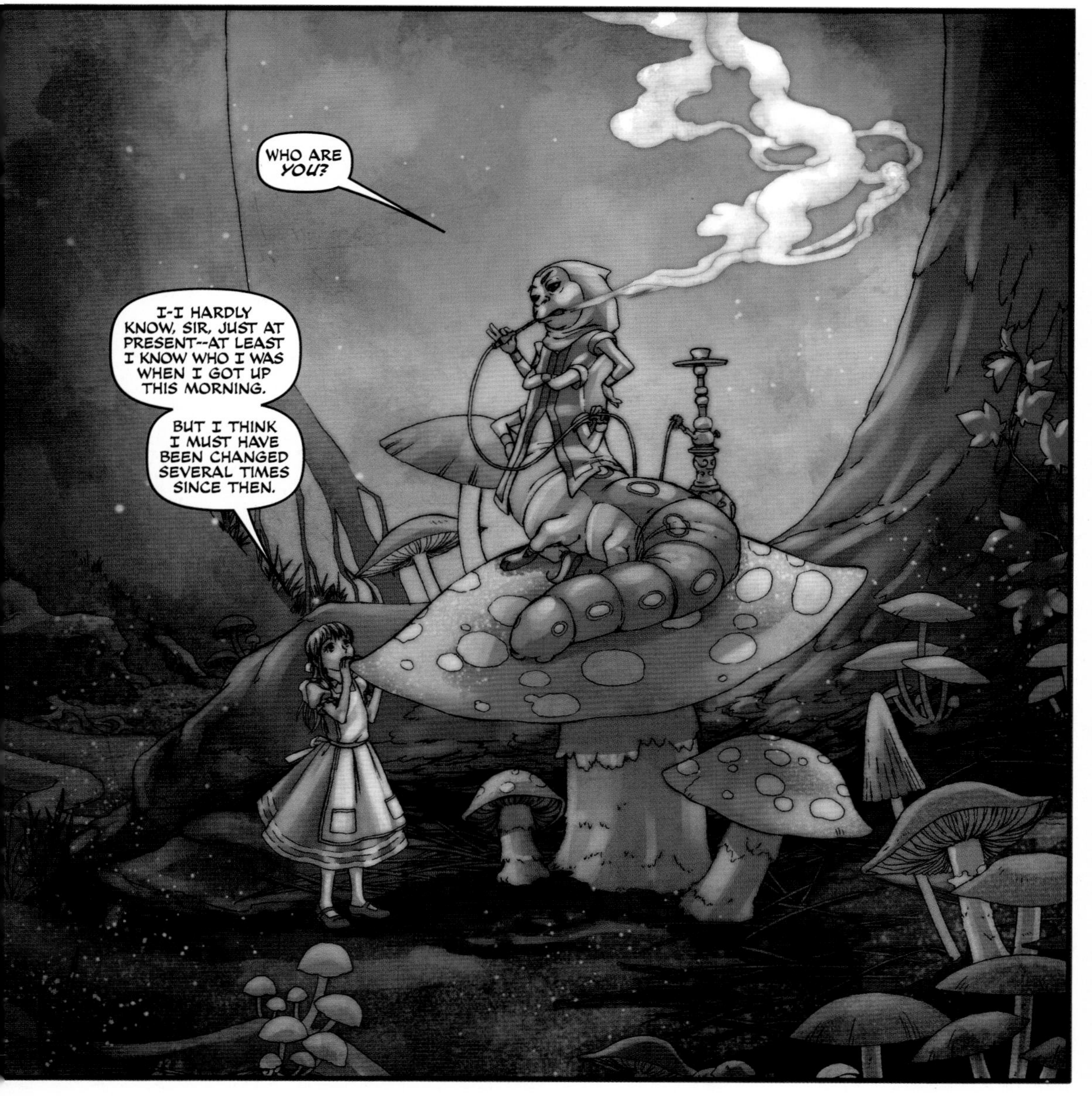
WHO ARE YOU?
I-I HARDLY KNOW, SIR, JUST AT PRESENT--AT LEAST I KNOW WHO I WAS WHEN I GOT UP THIS MORNING.
BUT I THINK I MUST HAVE BEEN CHANGED SEVERAL TIMES SINCE THEN.

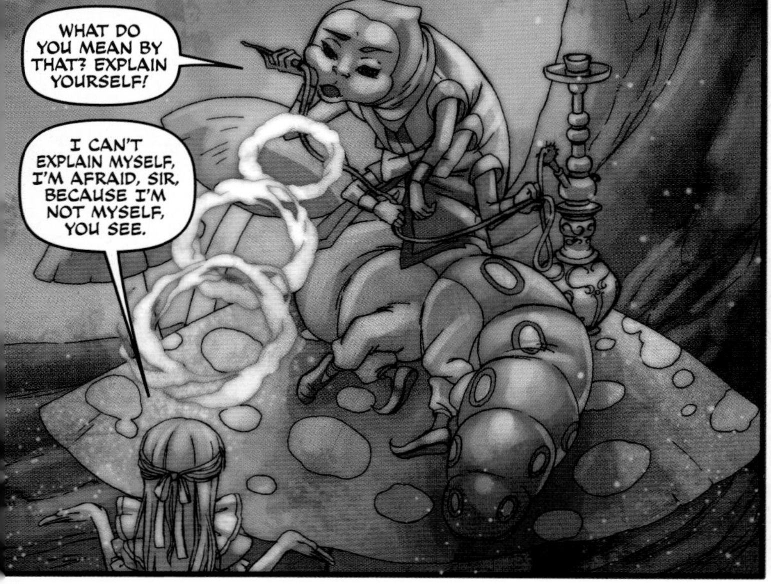
WHAT DO YOU MEAN BY THAT? EXPLAIN YOURSELF!
I CAN'T EXPLAIN MYSELF, I'M AFRAID, SIR, BECAUSE I'M NOT MYSELF, YOU SEE.

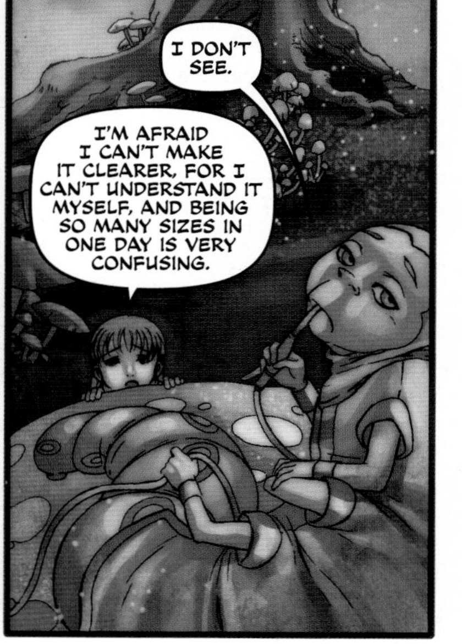
I DON'T SEE.
I'M AFRAID I CAN'T MAKE IT CLEARER, FOR I CAN'T UNDERSTAND IT MYSELF, AND BEING SO MANY SIZES IN ONE DAY IS VERY CONFUSING.

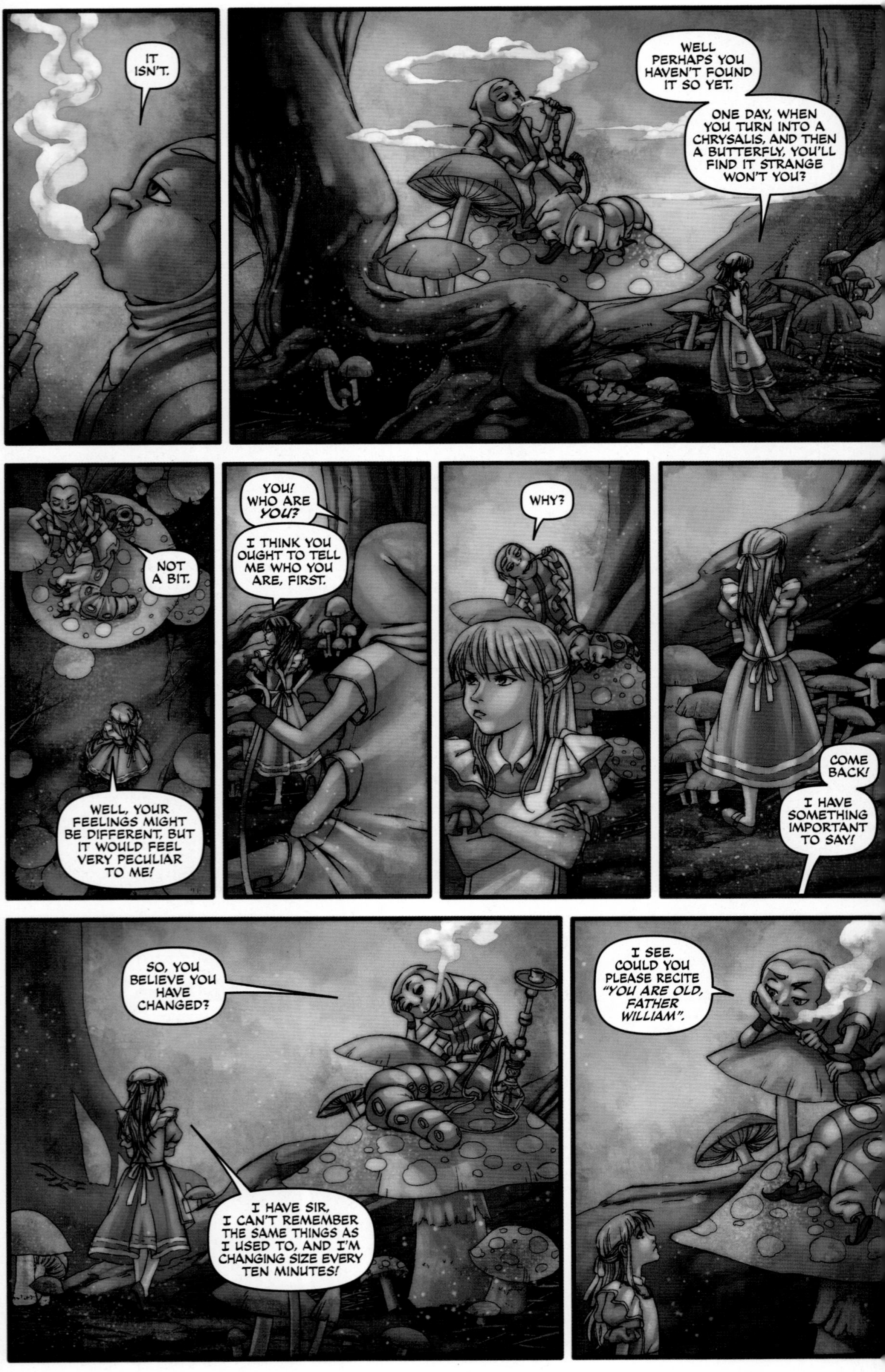
IT ISN'T.
WELL PERHAPS YOU HAVEN'T FOUND IT SO YET.
ONE DAY, WHEN YOU TURN INTO A CHRYSALIS, AND THEN A BUTTERFLY, YOU'LL FIND IT STRANGE WON'T YOU?
NOT A BIT.
WELL, YOUR FEELINGS MIGHT BE DIFFERENT, BUT IT WOULD FEEL VERY PECULIAR TO ME!
YOU! WHO ARE YOU?
I THINK YOU OUGHT TO TELL ME WHO YOU ARE, FIRST.
WHY?
COME BACK!
I HAVE SOMETHING IMPORTANT TO SAY!
SO, YOU BELIEVE YOU HAVE CHANGED?
I HAVE SIR, I CAN'T REMEMBER THE SAME THINGS AS I USED TO, AND I'M CHANGING SIZE EVERY TEN MINUTES!
I SEE. COULD YOU PLEASE RECITE "YOU ARE OLD, FATHER WILLIAM".

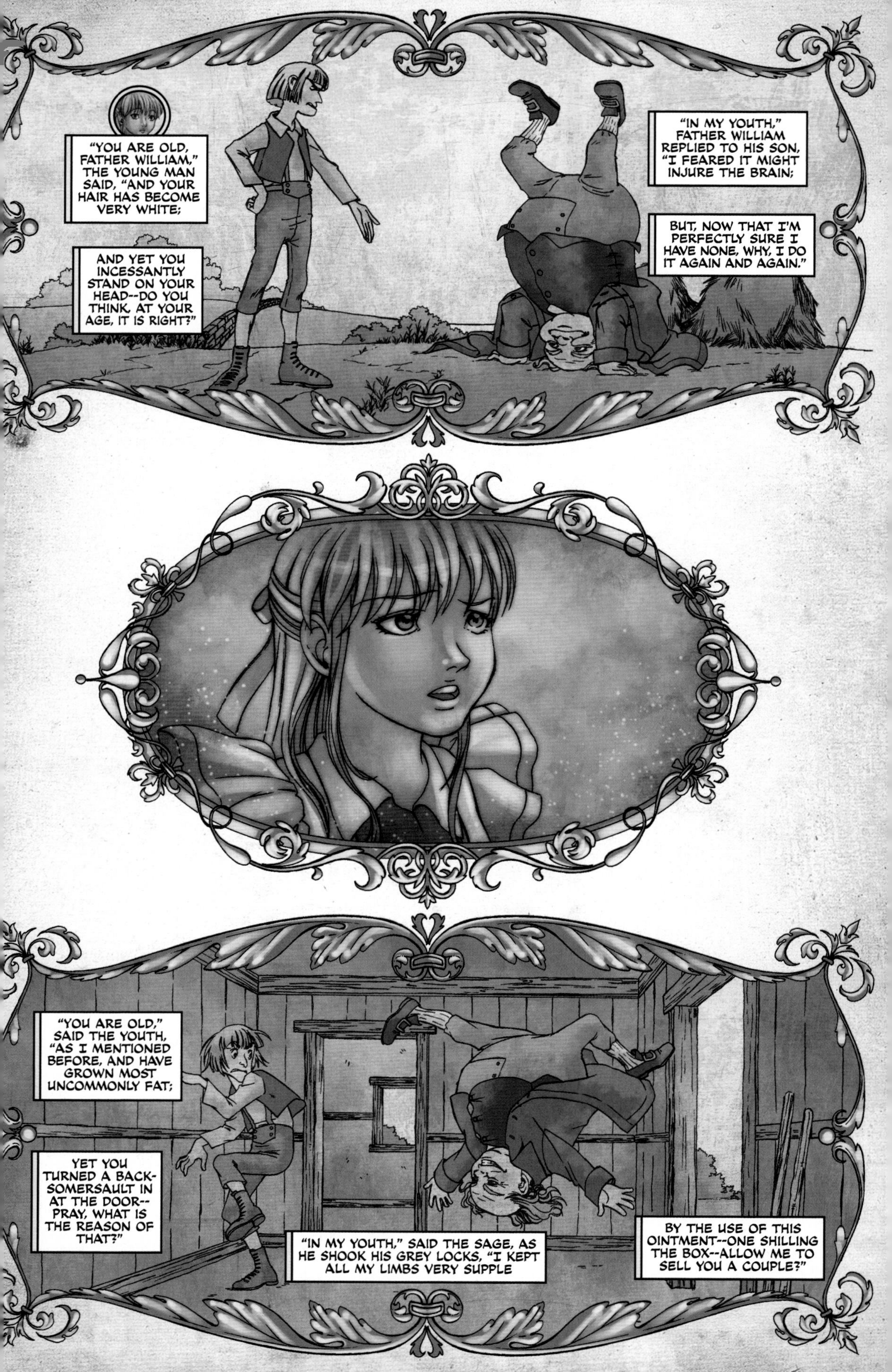
"YOU ARE OLD, FATHER WILLIAM," THE YOUNG MAN SAID, "AND YOUR HAIR HAS BECOME VERY WHITE;
AND YET YOU INCESSANTLY STAND ON YOUR HEAD--DO YOU THINK, AT YOUR AGE, IT IS RIGHT?"
"IN MY YOUTH," FATHER WILLIAM REPLIED TO HIS SON, "I FEARED IT MIGHT INJURE THE BRAIN;
BUT, NOW THAT I'M PERFECTLY SURE I HAVE NONE, WHY, I DO IT AGAIN AND AGAIN."
"YOU ARE OLD," SAID THE YOUTH, "AS I MENTIONED BEFORE, AND HAVE GROWN MOST UNCOMMONLY FAT;
YET YOU TURNED A BACK-SOMERSAULT IN AT THE DOOR--PRAY, WHAT IS THE REASON OF THAT?"
"IN MY YOUTH," SAID THE SAGE, AS HE SHOOK HIS GREY LOCKS, "I KEPT ALL MY LIMBS VERY SUPPLE
BY THE USE OF THIS OINTMENT--ONE SHILLING THE BOX--ALLOW ME TO SELL YOU A COUPLE?"

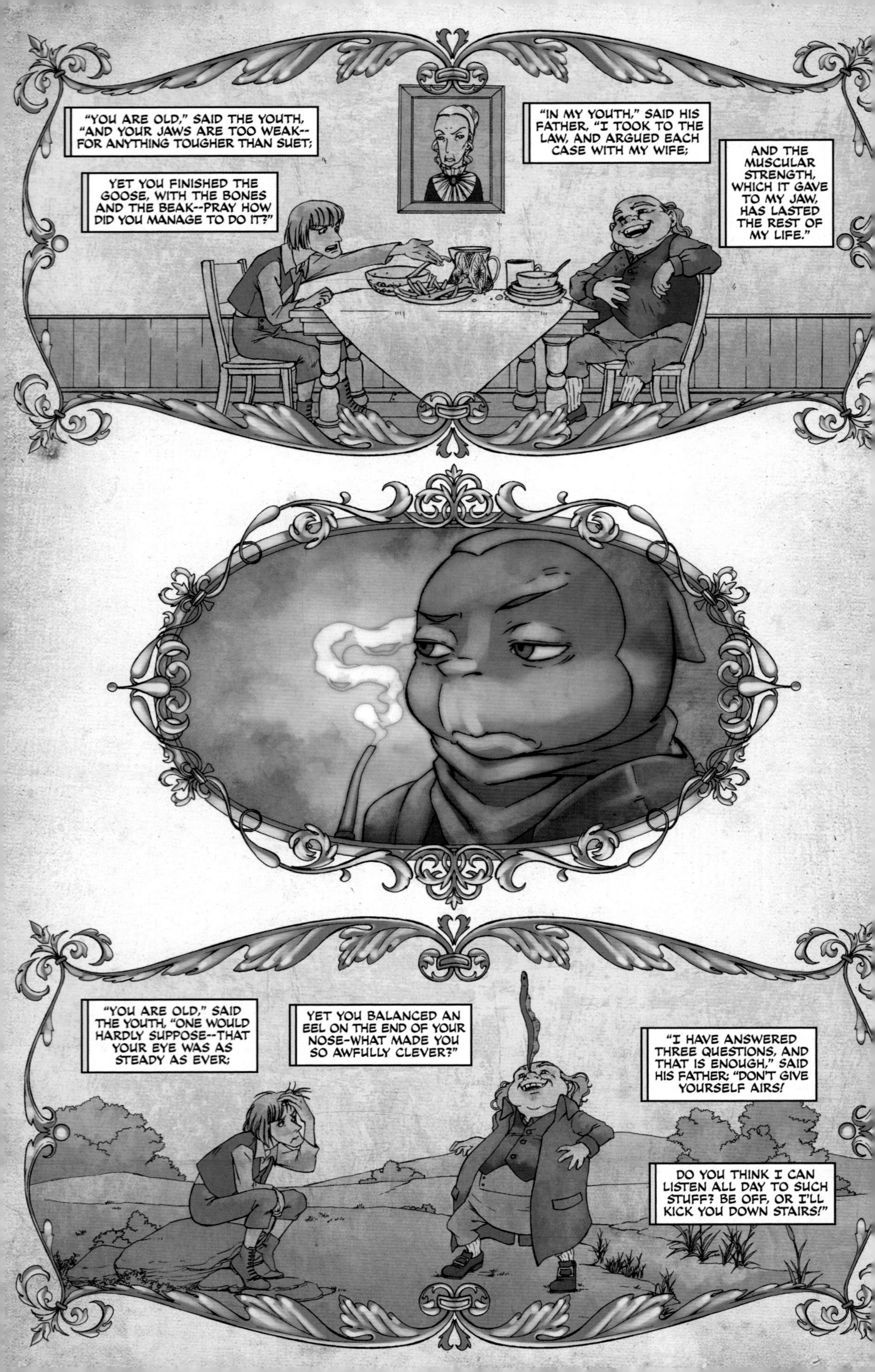
"YOU ARE OLD," SAID THE YOUTH, "AND YOUR JAWS ARE TOO WEAK--FOR ANYTHING TOUGHER THAN SUET;
YET YOU FINISHED THE GOOSE, WITH THE BONES AND THE BEAK--PRAY HOW DID YOU MANAGE TO DO IT?"
"IN MY YOUTH," SAID HIS FATHER, "I TOOK TO THE LAW, AND ARGUED EACH CASE WITH MY WIFE;
AND THE MUSCULAR STRENGTH, WHICH IT GAVE TO MY JAW, HAS LASTED THE REST OF MY LIFE."
"YOU ARE OLD," SAID THE YOUTH, "ONE WOULD HARDLY SUPPOSE--THAT YOUR EYE WAS AS STEADY AS EVER;
YET YOU BALANCED AN EEL ON THE END OF YOUR NOSE-WHAT MADE YOU SO AWFULLY CLEVER?"
"I HAVE ANSWERED THREE QUESTIONS, AND THAT IS ENOUGH," SAID HIS FATHER; "DON'T GIVE YOURSELF AIRS!
DO YOU THINK I CAN LISTEN ALL DAY TO SUCH STUFF? BE OFF, OR I'LL KICK YOU DOWN STAIRS!"

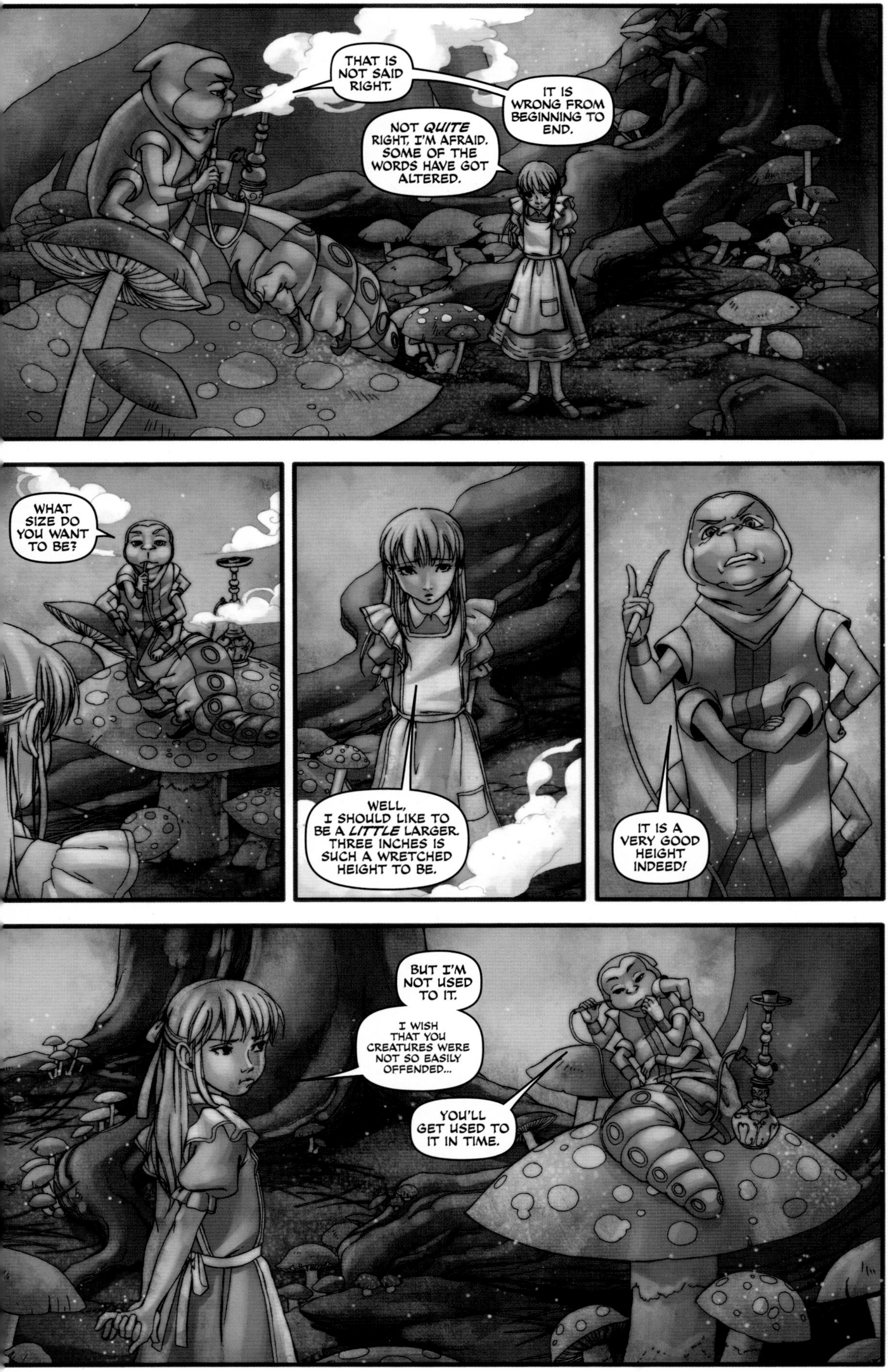
THAT IS NOT SAID RIGHT.
IT IS WRONG FROM BEGINNING TO END.
NOT QUITE RIGHT, I'M AFRAID. SOME OF THE WORDS HAVE GOT ALTERED.
WHAT SIZE DO YOU WANT TO BE?
WELL, I SHOULD LIKE TO BE A LITTLE LARGER. THREE INCHES IS SUCH A WRETCHED HEIGHT TO BE.
IT IS A VERY GOOD HEIGHT INDEED!
BUT I'M NOT USED TO IT.
I WISH THAT YOU CREATURES WERE NOT SO EASILY OFFENDED...
YOU'LL GET USED TO IT IN TIME.

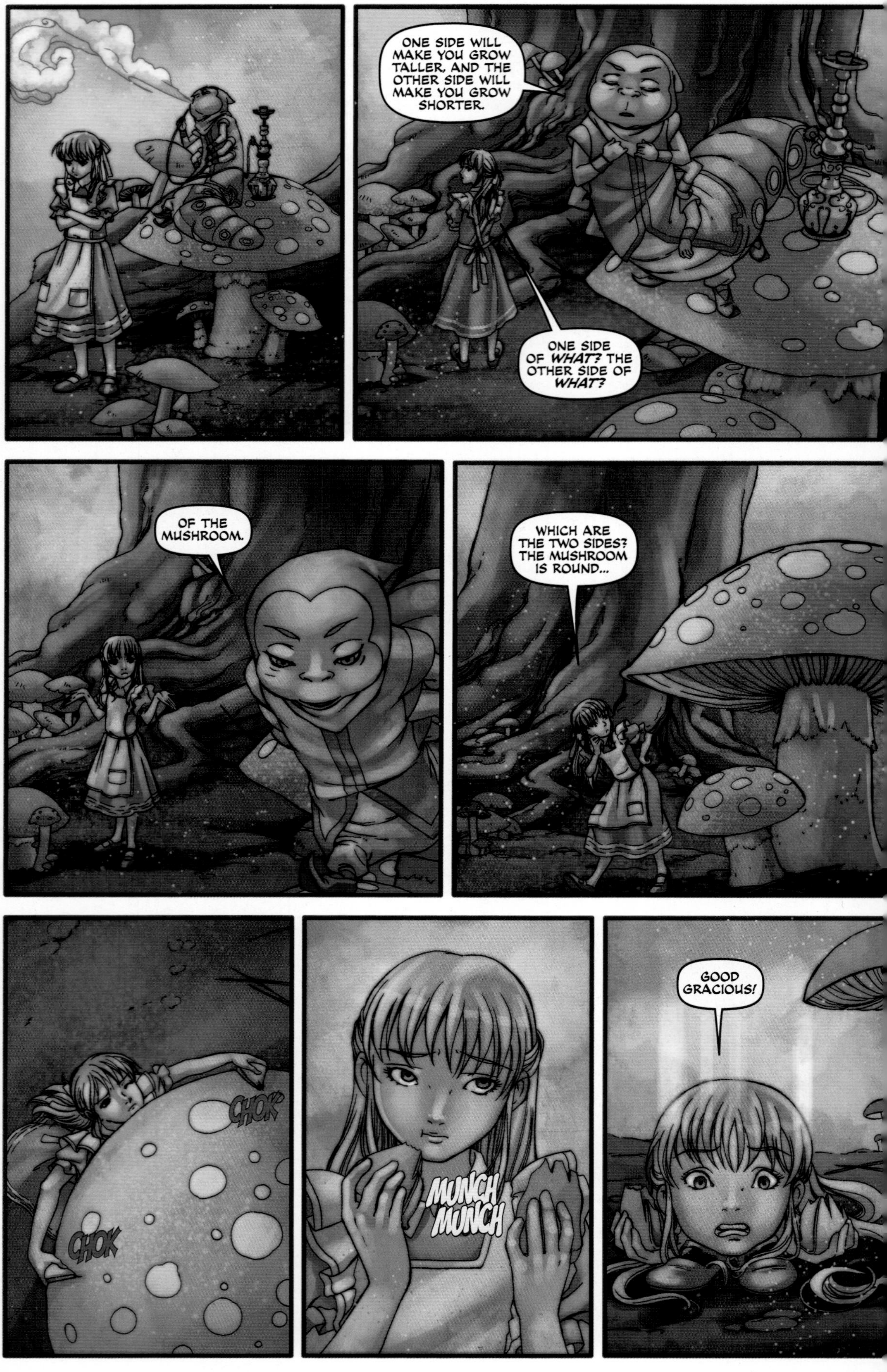
ONE SIDE WILL MAKE YOU GROW TALLER, AND THE OTHER SIDE WILL MAKE YOU GROW SHORTER.
ONE SIDE OF *WHAT?* THE OTHER SIDE OF *WHAT?*
OF THE MUSHROOM.
WHICH ARE THE TWO SIDES? THE MUSHROOM IS ROUND...
CHOK
CHOK
MUNCH MUNCH
GOOD GRACIOUS!

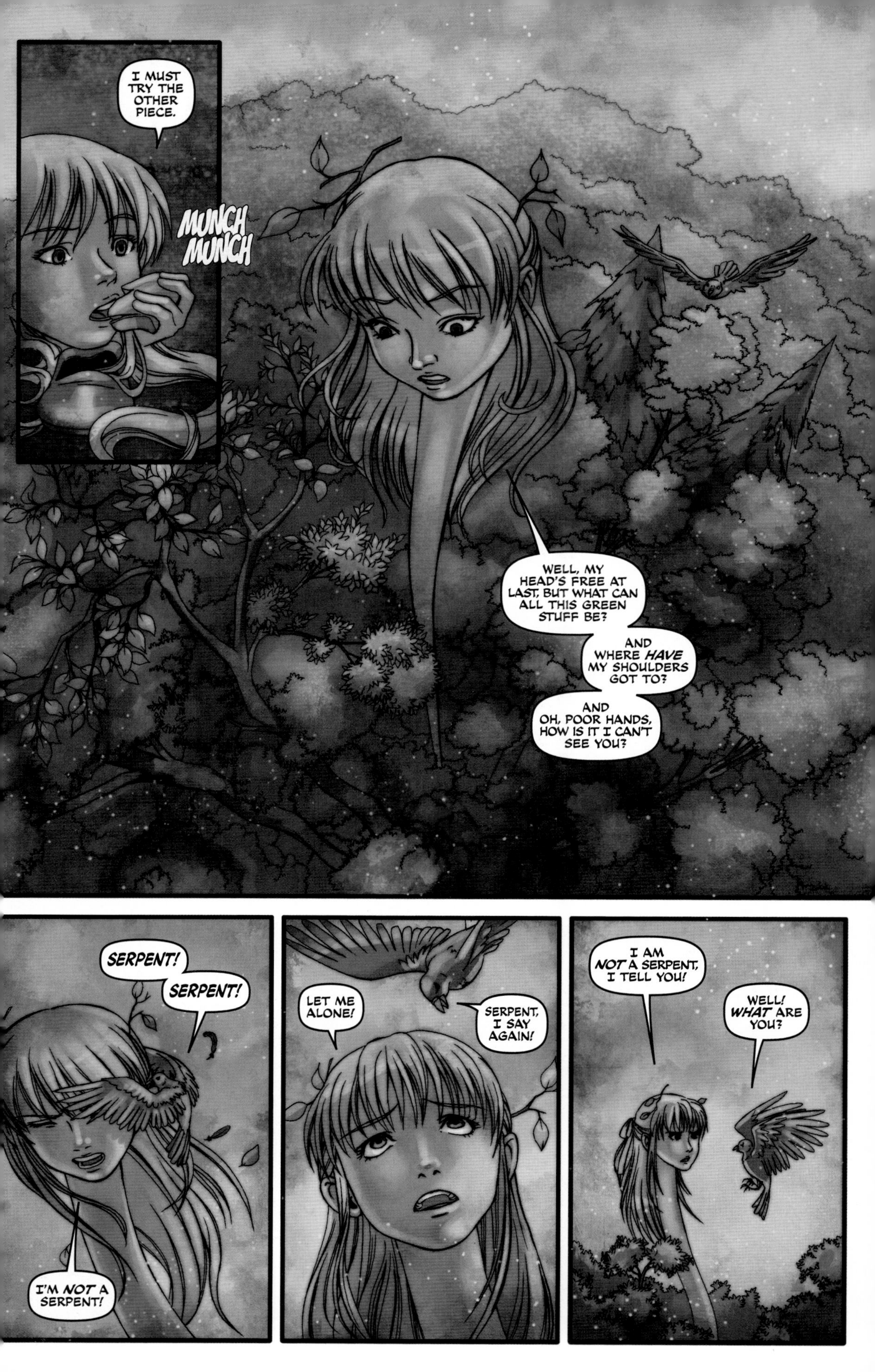
I MUST TRY THE OTHER PIECE.
MUNCH MUNCH
WELL, MY HEAD'S FREE AT LAST, BUT WHAT CAN ALL THIS GREEN STUFF BE?
AND WHERE *HAVE* MY SHOULDERS GOT TO?
AND OH, POOR HANDS, HOW IS IT I CAN'T SEE YOU?
SERPENT!
SERPENT!
I'M *NOT* A SERPENT!
LET ME ALONE!
SERPENT, I SAY AGAIN!
I AM *NOT* A SERPENT, I TELL YOU!
WELL! *WHAT* ARE YOU?

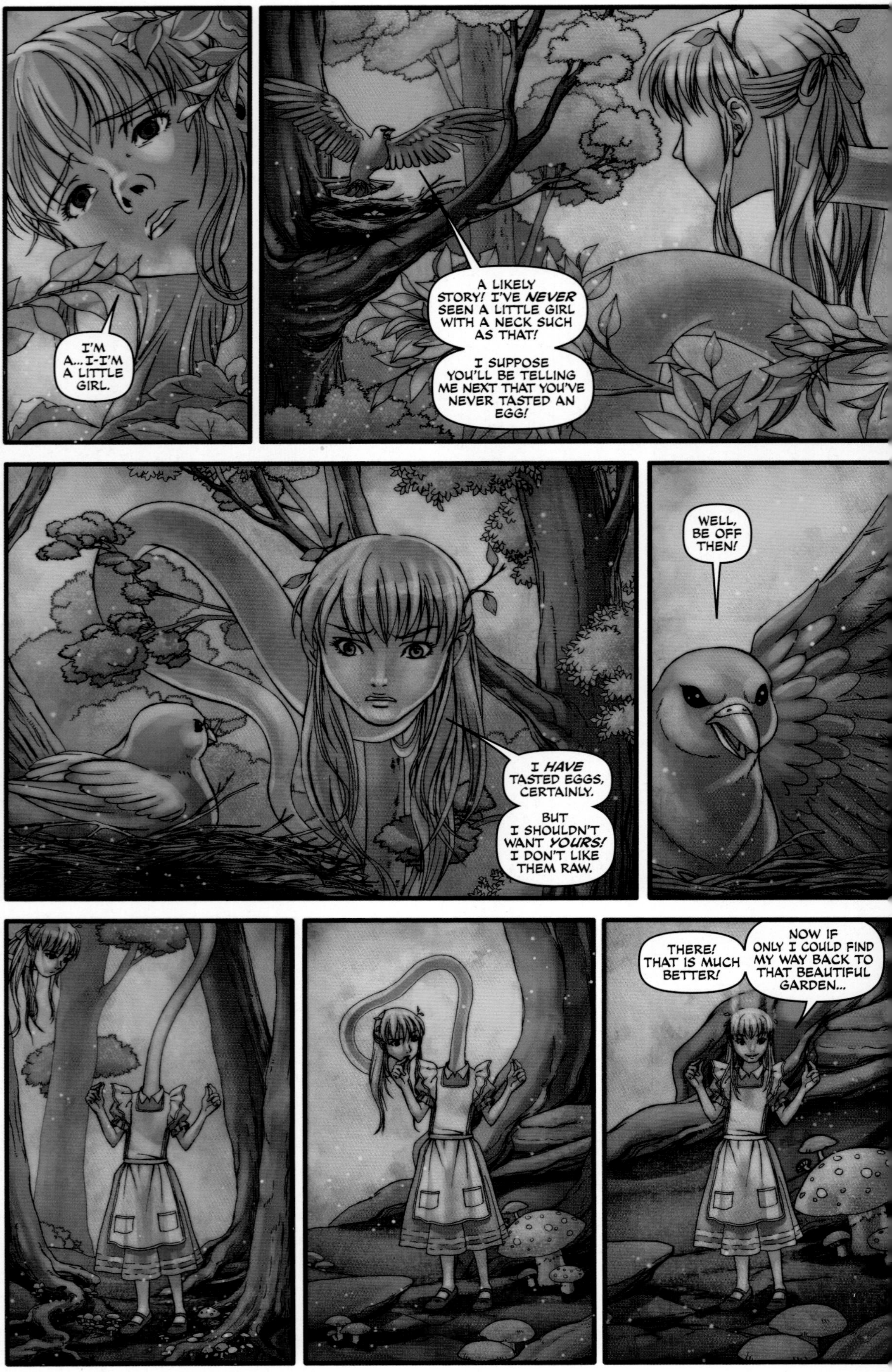
I'M A... I-I'M A LITTLE GIRL.
A LIKELY STORY! I'VE NEVER SEEN A LITTLE GIRL WITH A NECK SUCH AS THAT!
I SUPPOSE YOU'LL BE TELLING ME NEXT THAT YOU'VE NEVER TASTED AN EGG!
I HAVE TASTED EGGS, CERTAINLY.
BUT I SHOULDN'T WANT YOURS! I DON'T LIKE THEM RAW.
WELL, BE OFF THEN!
THERE! THAT IS MUCH BETTER!
NOW IF ONLY I COULD FIND MY WAY BACK TO THAT BEAUTIFUL GARDEN...

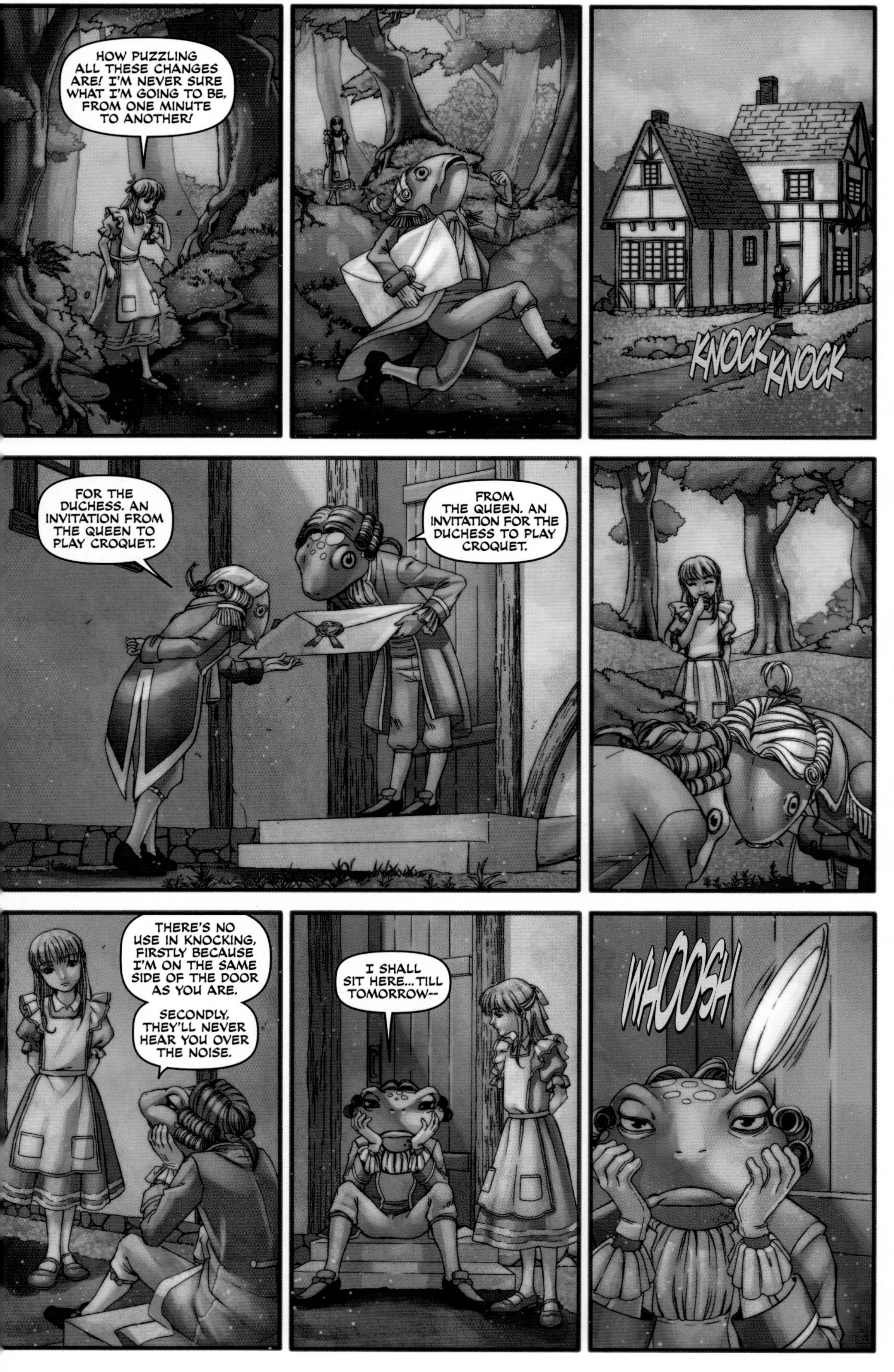
HOW PUZZLING ALL THESE CHANGES ARE! I'M NEVER SURE WHAT I'M GOING TO BE, FROM ONE MINUTE TO ANOTHER!
KNOCK KNOCK
FOR THE DUCHESS. AN INVITATION FROM THE QUEEN TO PLAY CROQUET.
FROM THE QUEEN. AN INVITATION FOR THE DUCHESS TO PLAY CROQUET.
THERE'S NO USE IN KNOCKING, FIRSTLY BECAUSE I'M ON THE SAME SIDE OF THE DOOR AS YOU ARE.
SECONDLY, THEY'LL NEVER HEAR YOU OVER THE NOISE.
I SHALL SIT HERE... TILL TOMORROW--
WHOOSH

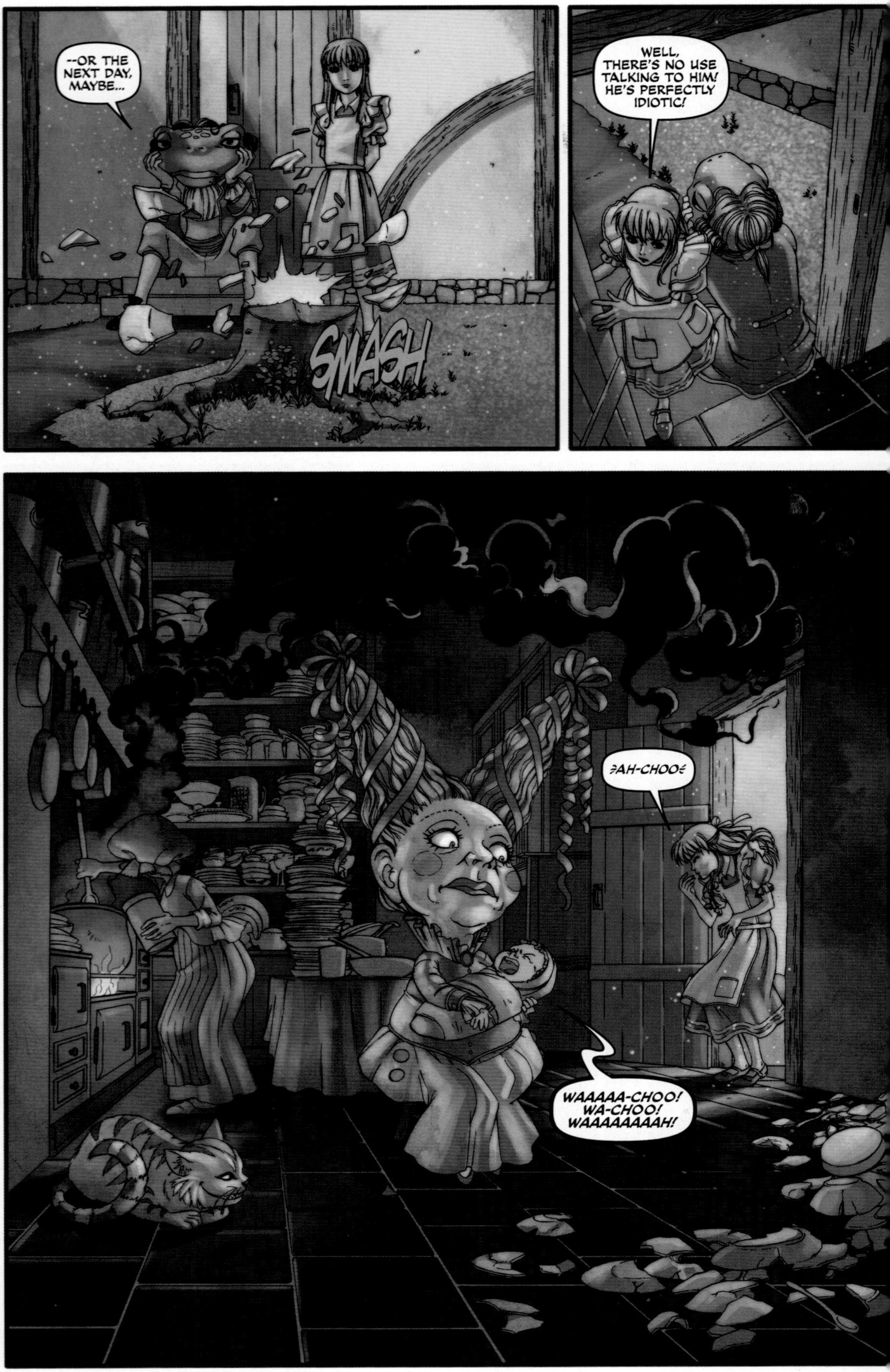
--OR THE NEXT DAY, MAYBE...
SMASH
WELL, THERE'S NO USE TALKING TO HIM! HE'S PERFECTLY IDIOTIC!
AH-CHOO
WAAAAA-CHOO! WA-CHOO! WAAAAAAAAH!

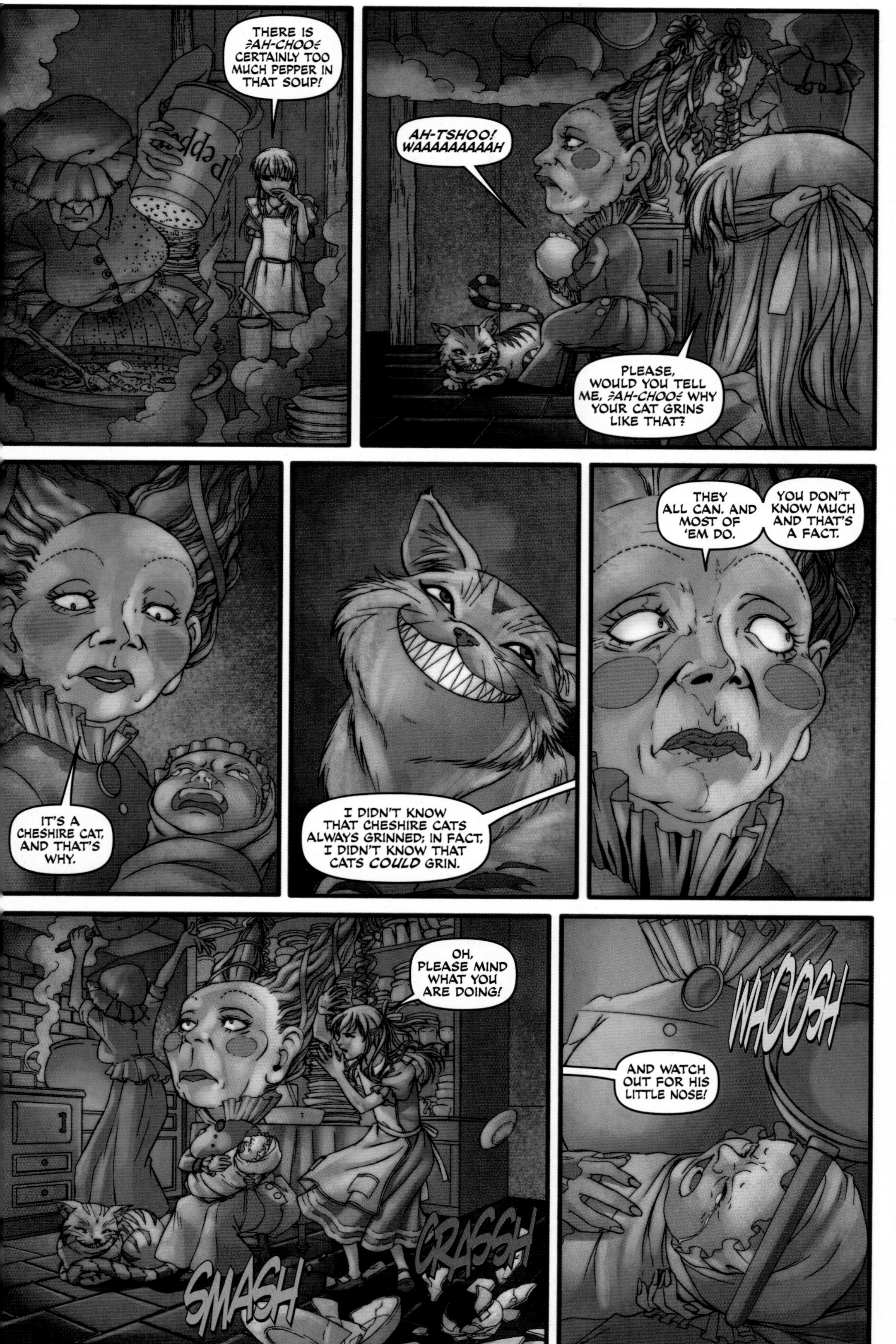
THERE IS ƎAH-CHOOƐ CERTAINLY TOO MUCH PEPPER IN THAT SOUP!
AH-TSHOO! WAAAAAAAAAH
PLEASE, WOULD YOU TELL ME, ƎAH-CHOOƐ WHY YOUR CAT GRINS LIKE THAT?
IT'S A CHESHIRE CAT, AND THAT'S WHY.
I DIDN'T KNOW THAT CHESHIRE CATS ALWAYS GRINNED; IN FACT, I DIDN'T KNOW THAT CATS COULD GRIN.
THEY ALL CAN. AND MOST OF 'EM DO.
YOU DON'T KNOW MUCH AND THAT'S A FACT.
OH, PLEASE MIND WHAT YOU ARE DOING!
CRASSH
SMASH
WHOOSH
AND WATCH OUT FOR HIS LITTLE NOSE!

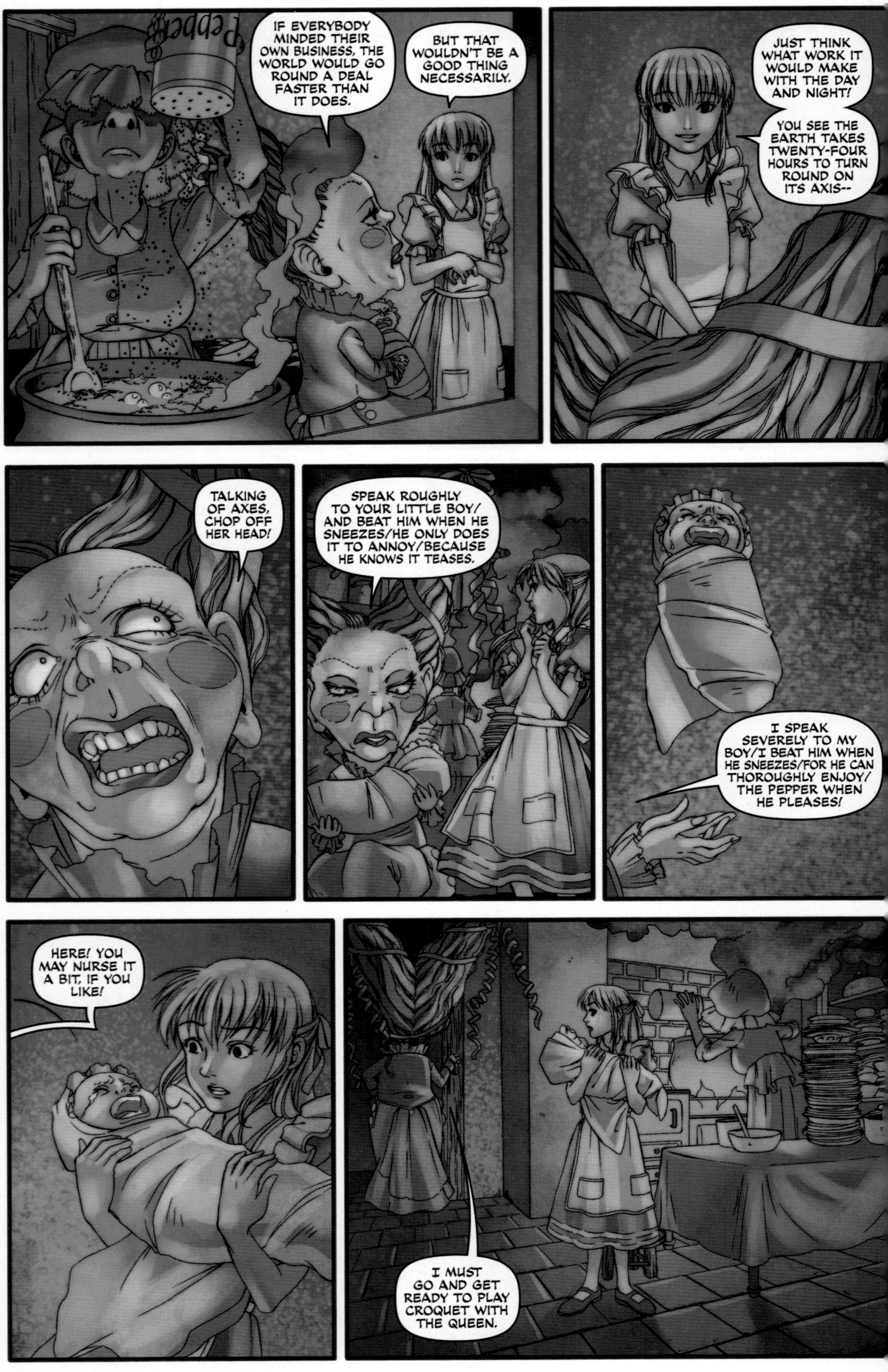

Pepper
IF EVERYBODY MINDED THEIR OWN BUSINESS, THE WORLD WOULD GO ROUND A DEAL FASTER THAN IT DOES.
BUT THAT WOULDN'T BE A GOOD THING NECESSARILY.
JUST THINK WHAT WORK IT WOULD MAKE WITH THE DAY AND NIGHT!
YOU SEE THE EARTH TAKES TWENTY-FOUR HOURS TO TURN ROUND ON ITS AXIS--
TALKING OF AXES, CHOP OFF HER HEAD!
SPEAK ROUGHLY TO YOUR LITTLE BOY/ AND BEAT HIM WHEN HE SNEEZES/HE ONLY DOES IT TO ANNOY/BECAUSE HE KNOWS IT TEASES.
I SPEAK SEVERELY TO MY BOY/I BEAT HIM WHEN HE SNEEZES/FOR HE CAN THOROUGHLY ENJOY/ THE PEPPER WHEN HE PLEASES!
HERE! YOU MAY NURSE IT A BIT, IF YOU LIKE!
I MUST GO AND GET READY TO PLAY CROQUET WITH THE QUEEN.

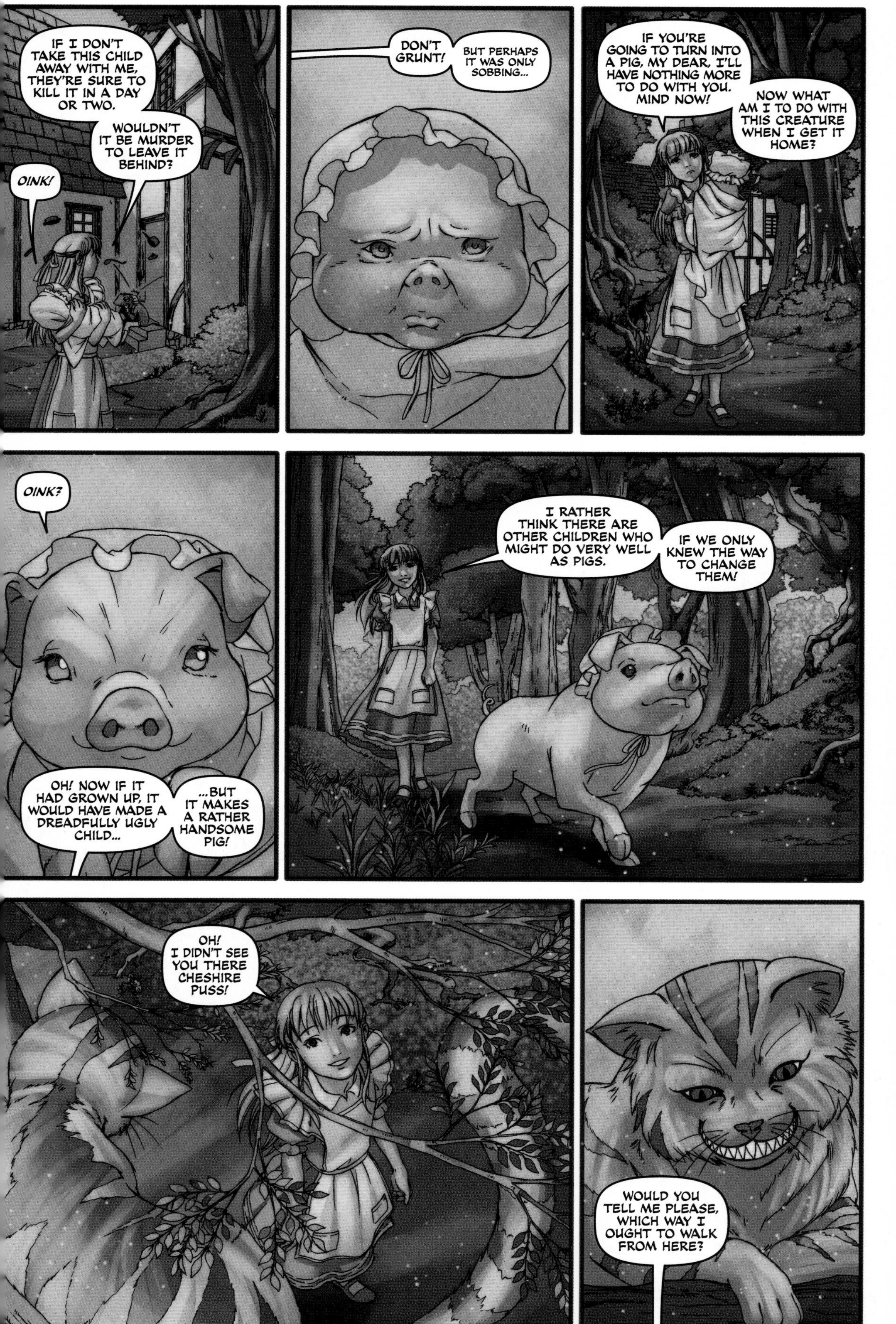
IF I DON'T TAKE THIS CHILD AWAY WITH ME, THEY'RE SURE TO KILL IT IN A DAY OR TWO.
WOULDN'T IT BE MURDER TO LEAVE IT BEHIND?
OINK!
DON'T GRUNT!
BUT PERHAPS IT WAS ONLY SOBBING...
IF YOU'RE GOING TO TURN INTO A PIG, MY DEAR, I'LL HAVE NOTHING MORE TO DO WITH YOU. MIND NOW!
NOW WHAT AM I TO DO WITH THIS CREATURE WHEN I GET IT HOME?
OINK?
OH! NOW IF IT HAD GROWN UP, IT WOULD HAVE MADE A DREADFULLY UGLY CHILD...
...BUT IT MAKES A RATHER HANDSOME PIG!
I RATHER THINK THERE ARE OTHER CHILDREN WHO MIGHT DO VERY WELL AS PIGS.
IF WE ONLY KNEW THE WAY TO CHANGE THEM!
OH! I DIDN'T SEE YOU THERE CHESHIRE PUSS!
WOULD YOU TELL ME PLEASE, WHICH WAY I OUGHT TO WALK FROM HERE?

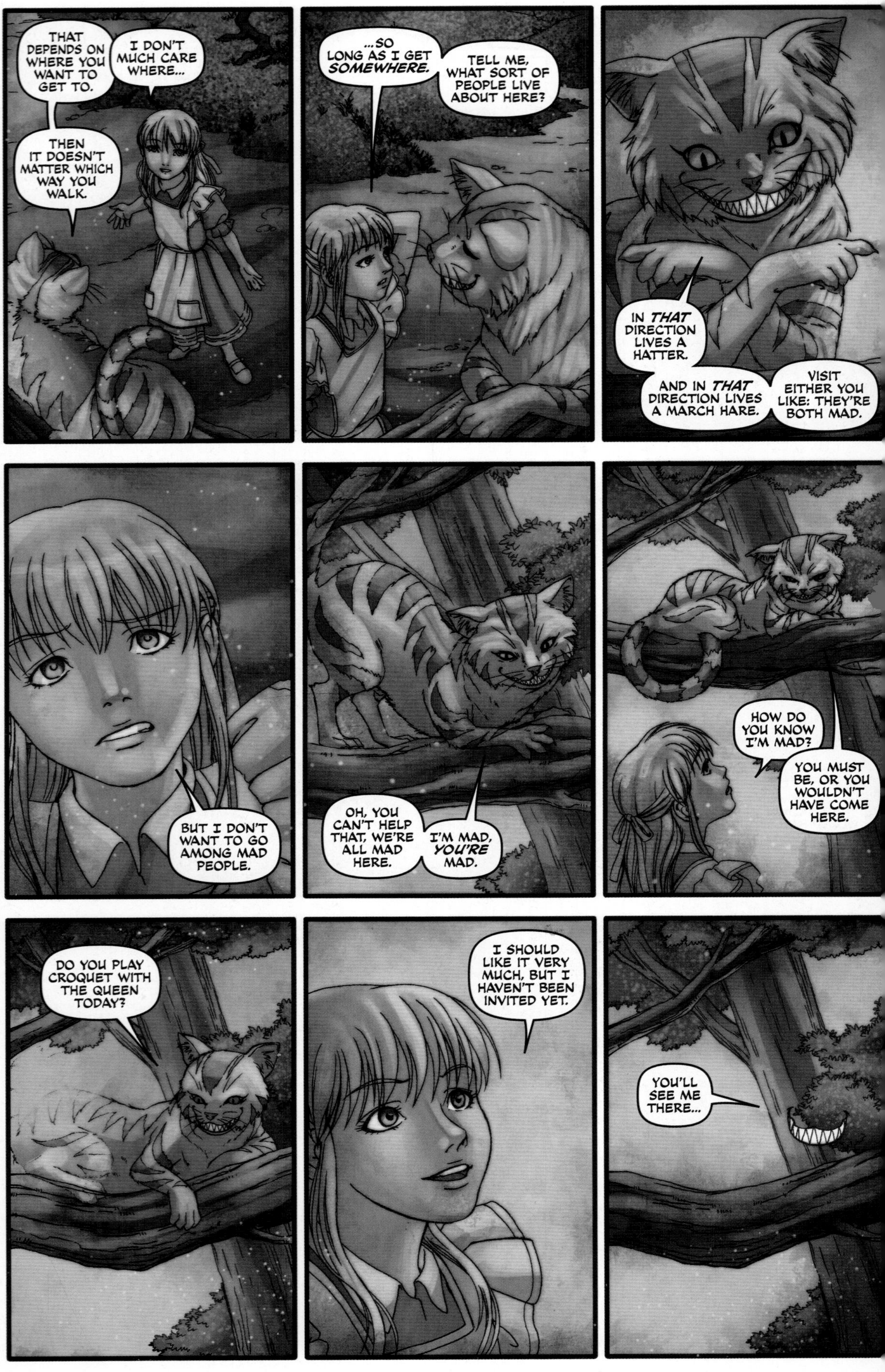
THAT DEPENDS ON WHERE YOU WANT TO GET TO.
I DON'T MUCH CARE WHERE...
THEN IT DOESN'T MATTER WHICH WAY YOU WALK.
...SO LONG AS I GET *SOMEWHERE.*
TELL ME, WHAT SORT OF PEOPLE LIVE ABOUT HERE?
IN *THAT* DIRECTION LIVES A HATTER.
AND IN *THAT* DIRECTION LIVES A MARCH HARE.
VISIT EITHER YOU LIKE: THEY'RE BOTH MAD.
BUT I DON'T WANT TO GO AMONG MAD PEOPLE.
OH, YOU CAN'T HELP THAT, WE'RE ALL MAD HERE.
I'M MAD, *YOU'RE* MAD.
HOW DO YOU KNOW I'M MAD?
YOU MUST BE, OR YOU WOULDN'T HAVE COME HERE.
DO YOU PLAY CROQUET WITH THE QUEEN TODAY?
I SHOULD LIKE IT VERY MUCH, BUT I HAVEN'T BEEN INVITED YET.
YOU'LL SEE ME THERE...

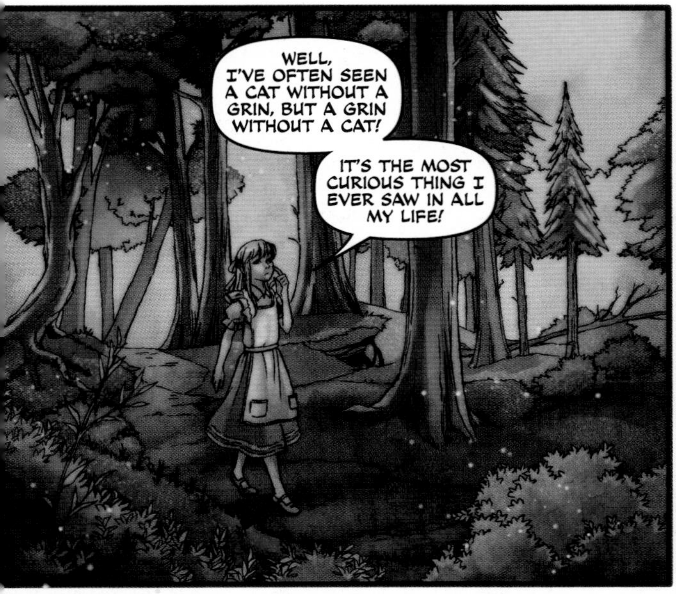
WELL, I'VE OFTEN SEEN A CAT WITHOUT A GRIN, BUT A GRIN WITHOUT A CAT!
IT'S THE MOST CURIOUS THING I EVER SAW IN ALL MY LIFE!

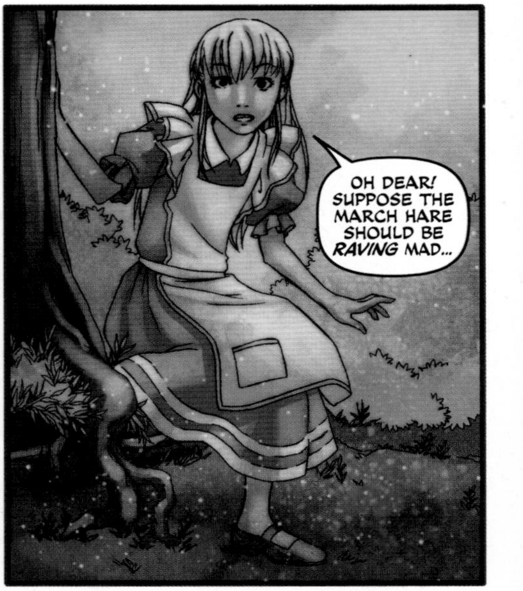
OH DEAR! SUPPOSE THE MARCH HARE SHOULD BE *RAVING* MAD...

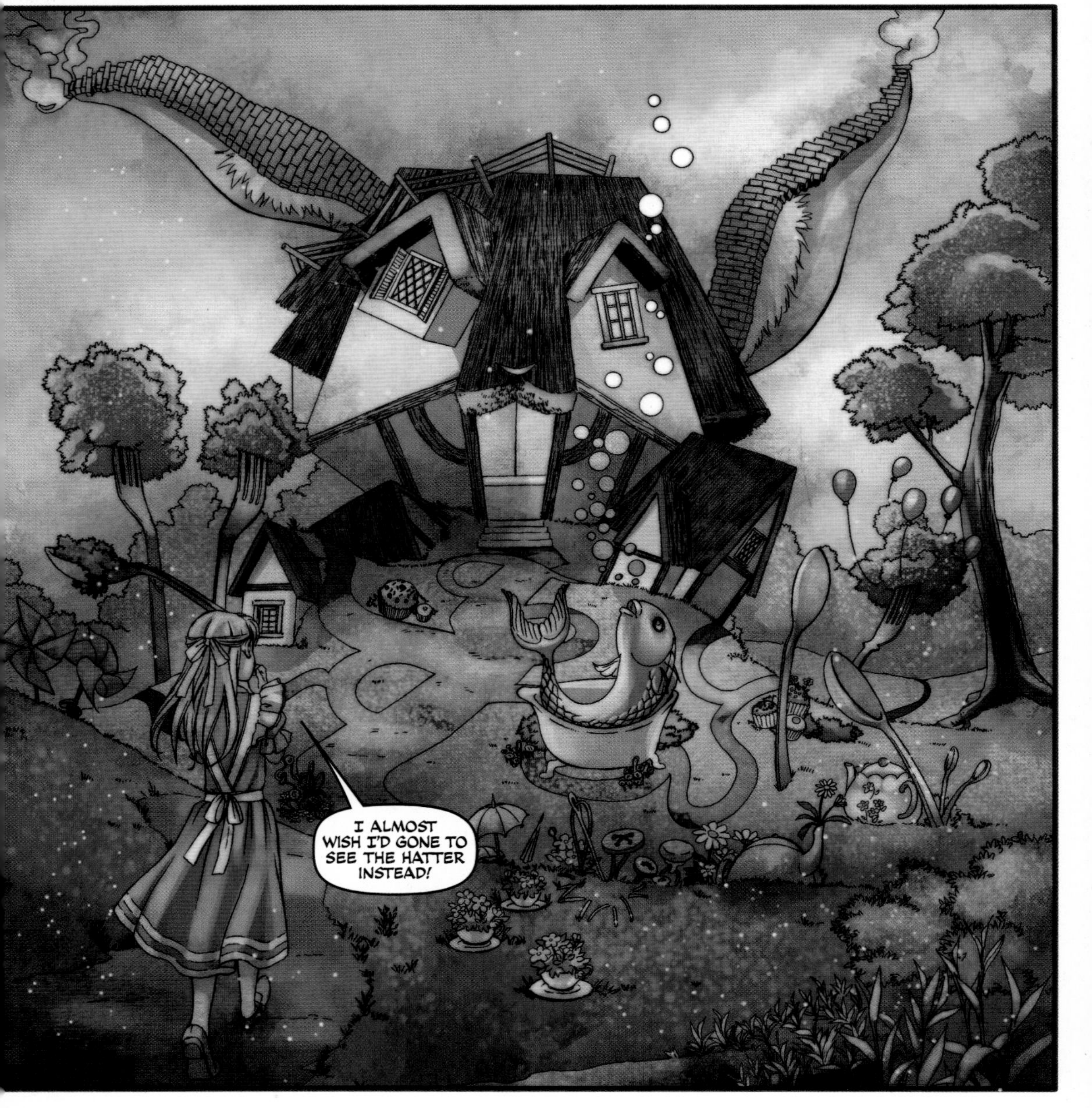
I ALMOST WISH I'D GONE TO SEE THE HATTER INSTEAD!

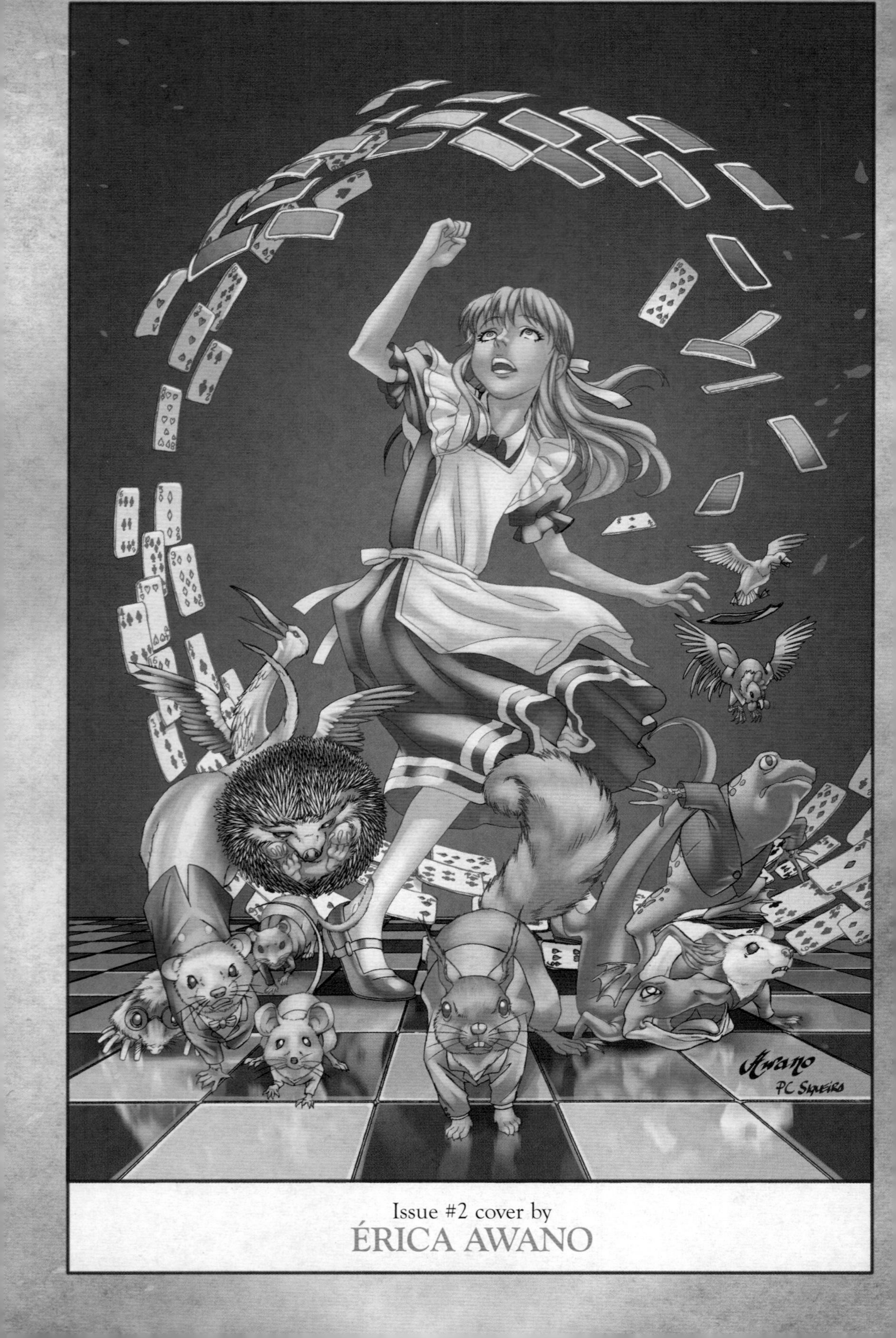
Awano
PC Siqueira

Issue #2 cover by
ÉRICA AWANO

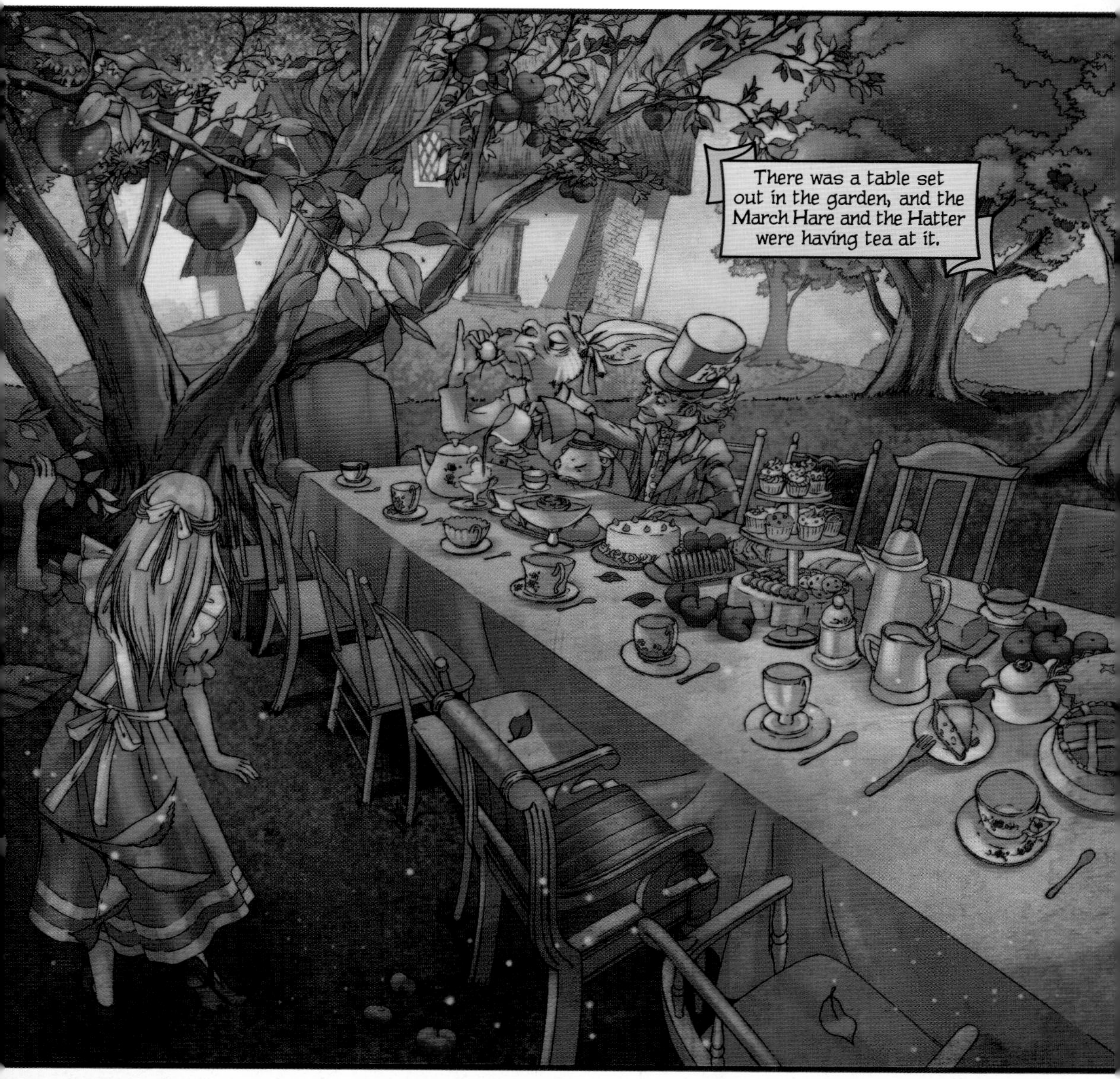
There was a table set out in the garden, and the March Hare and the Hatter were having tea at it.

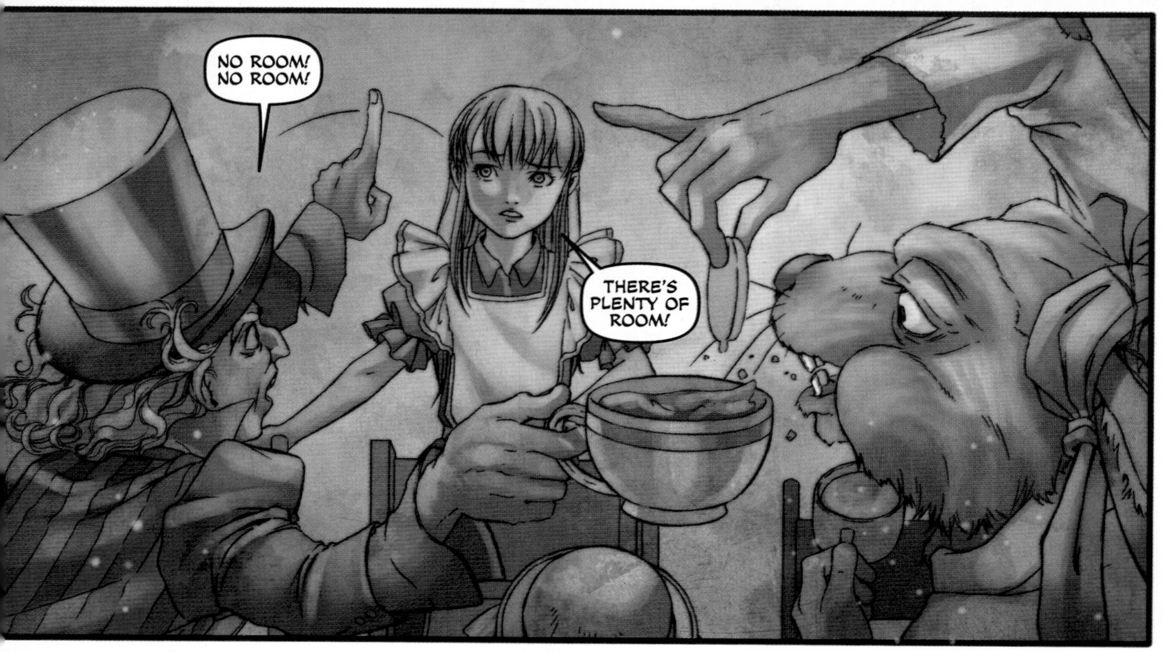
NO ROOM! NO ROOM!
THERE'S PLENTY OF ROOM!

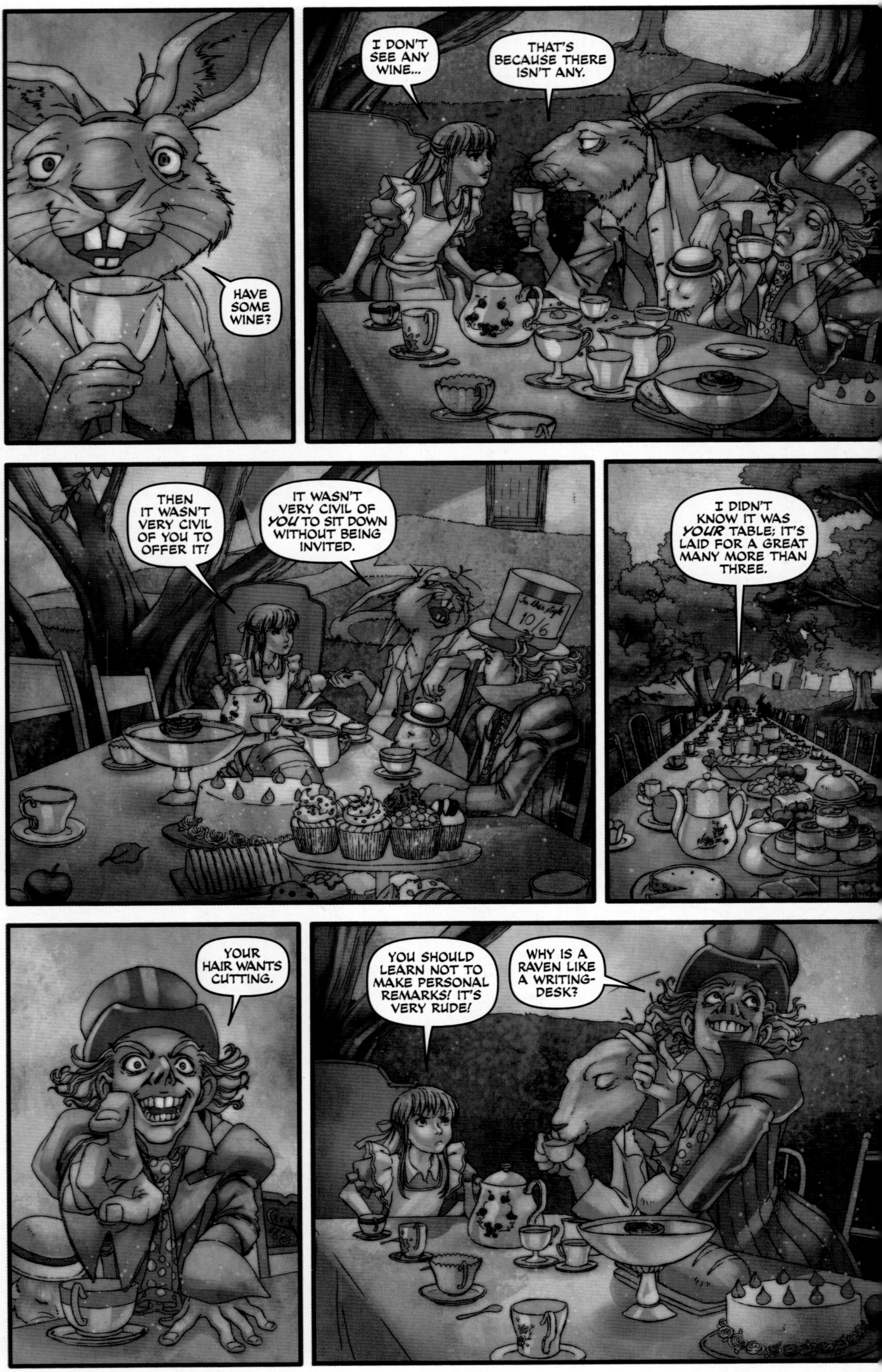
HAVE SOME WINE?
I DON'T SEE ANY WINE...
THAT'S BECAUSE THERE ISN'T ANY.
THEN IT WASN'T VERY CIVIL OF YOU TO OFFER IT!
IT WASN'T VERY CIVIL OF YOU TO SIT DOWN WITHOUT BEING INVITED.
I DIDN'T KNOW IT WAS YOUR TABLE; IT'S LAID FOR A GREAT MANY MORE THAN THREE.
YOUR HAIR WANTS CUTTING.
YOU SHOULD LEARN NOT TO MAKE PERSONAL REMARKS! IT'S VERY RUDE!
WHY IS A RAVEN LIKE A WRITING-DESK?

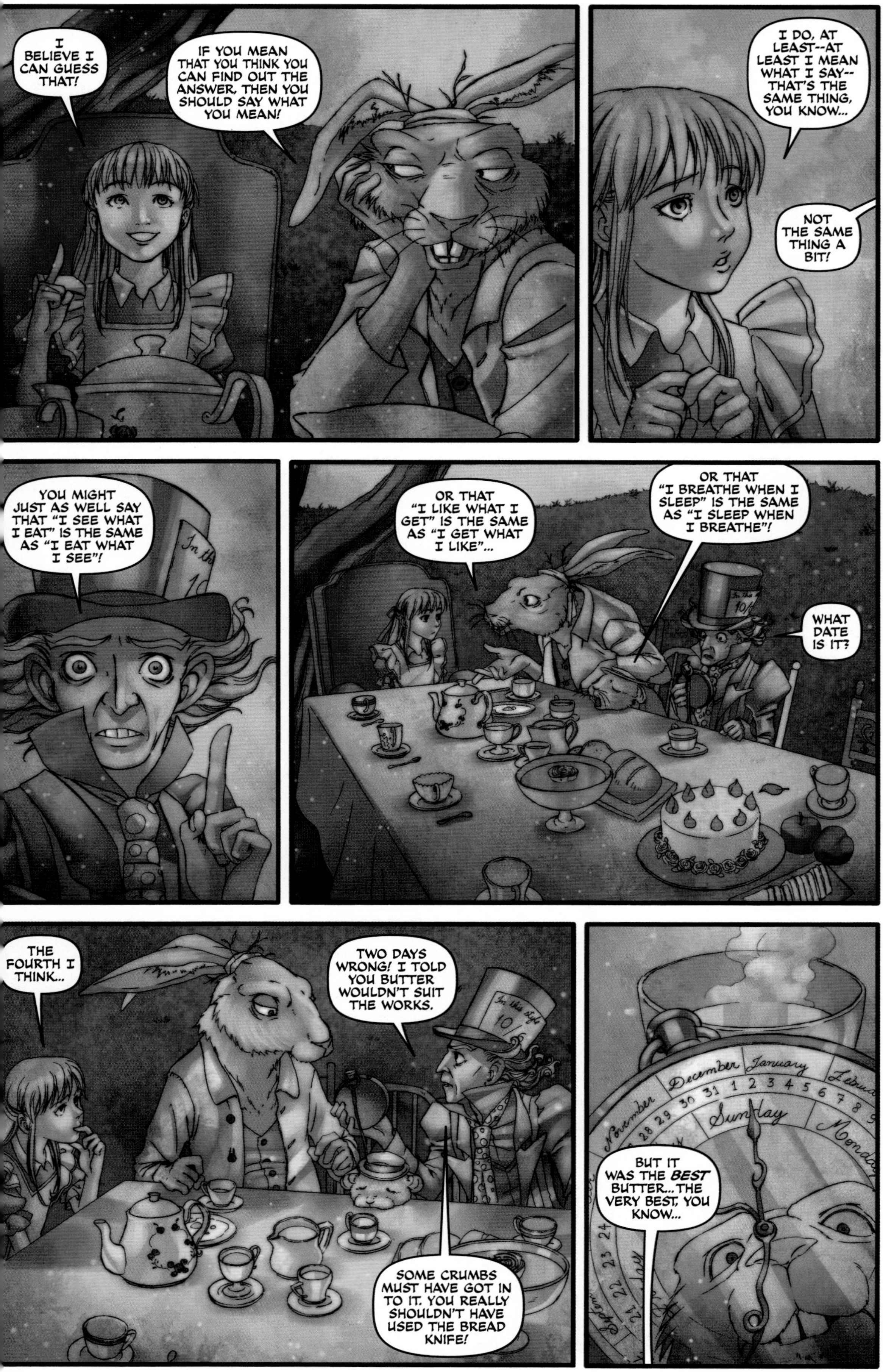

I BELIEVE I CAN GUESS THAT!
IF YOU MEAN THAT YOU THINK YOU CAN FIND OUT THE ANSWER, THEN YOU SHOULD SAY WHAT YOU MEAN!
I DO, AT LEAST--AT LEAST I MEAN WHAT I SAY--THAT'S THE SAME THING, YOU KNOW...
NOT THE SAME THING A BIT!
YOU MIGHT JUST AS WELL SAY THAT "I SEE WHAT I EAT" IS THE SAME AS "I EAT WHAT I SEE"!
OR THAT "I LIKE WHAT I GET" IS THE SAME AS "I GET WHAT I LIKE"...
OR THAT "I BREATHE WHEN I SLEEP" IS THE SAME AS "I SLEEP WHEN I BREATHE"!
WHAT DATE IS IT?
THE FOURTH I THINK...
TWO DAYS WRONG! I TOLD YOU BUTTER WOULDN'T SUIT THE WORKS.
SOME CRUMBS MUST HAVE GOT IN TO IT. YOU REALLY SHOULDN'T HAVE USED THE BREAD KNIFE!
December January
November
Sunday
BUT IT WAS THE *BEST* BUTTER...THE VERY BEST, YOU KNOW...

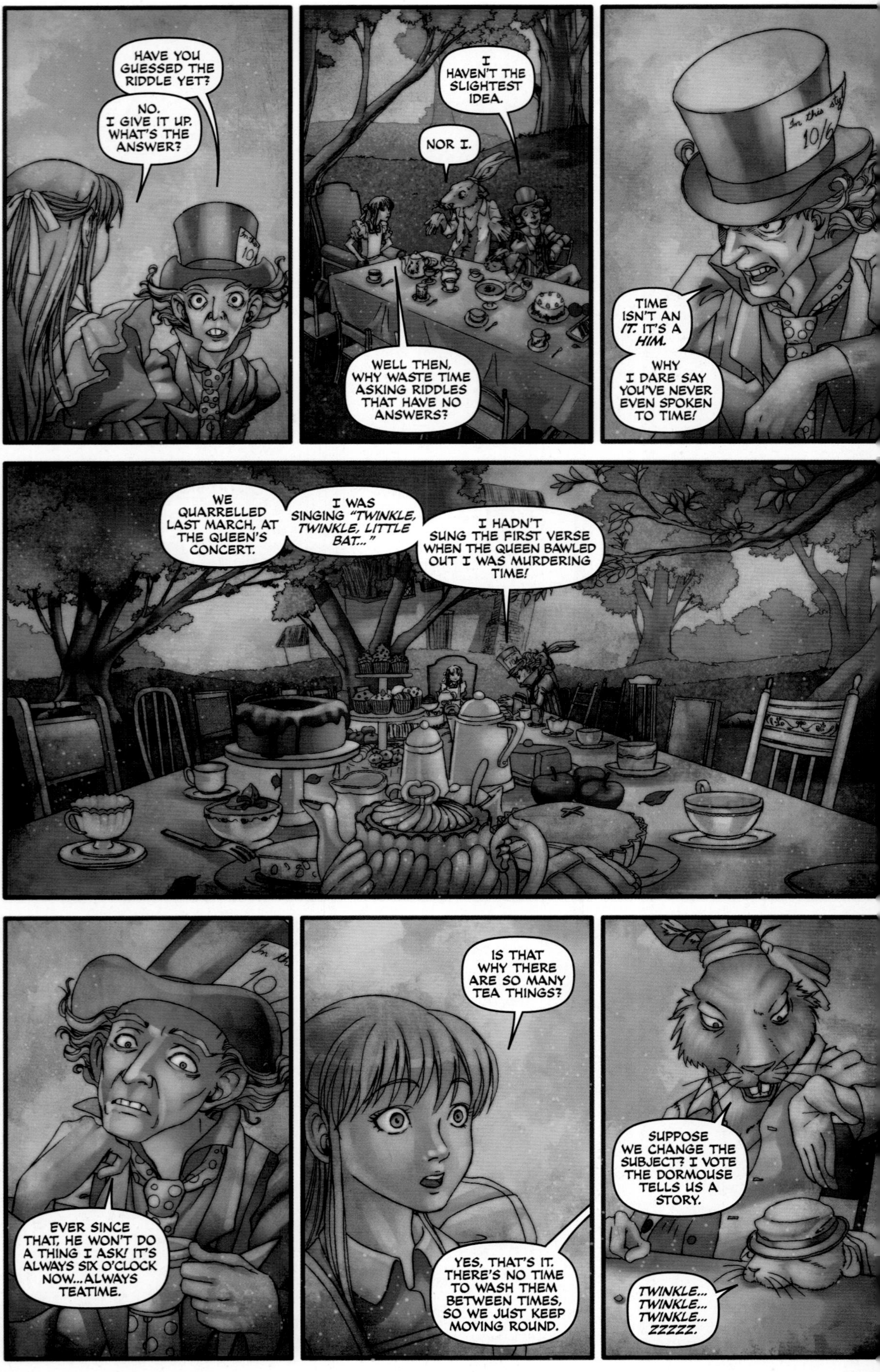
HAVE YOU GUESSED THE RIDDLE YET?
NO. I GIVE IT UP. WHAT'S THE ANSWER?
I HAVEN'T THE SLIGHTEST IDEA.
NOR I.
WELL THEN, WHY WASTE TIME ASKING RIDDLES THAT HAVE NO ANSWERS?
TIME ISN'T AN *IT.* IT'S A *HIM.*
WHY I DARE SAY YOU'VE NEVER EVEN SPOKEN TO TIME!
WE QUARRELLED LAST MARCH, AT THE QUEEN'S CONCERT.
I WAS SINGING *"TWINKLE, TWINKLE, LITTLE BAT..."*
I HADN'T SUNG THE FIRST VERSE WHEN THE QUEEN BAWLED OUT I WAS MURDERING TIME!
EVER SINCE THAT, HE WON'T DO A THING I ASK! IT'S ALWAYS SIX O'CLOCK NOW...ALWAYS TEATIME.
IS THAT WHY THERE ARE SO MANY TEA THINGS?
YES, THAT'S IT. THERE'S NO TIME TO WASH THEM BETWEEN TIMES, SO WE JUST KEEP MOVING ROUND.
SUPPOSE WE CHANGE THE SUBJECT? I VOTE THE DORMOUSE TELLS US A STORY.
TWINKLE... TWINKLE... TWINKLE... ZZZZZ.

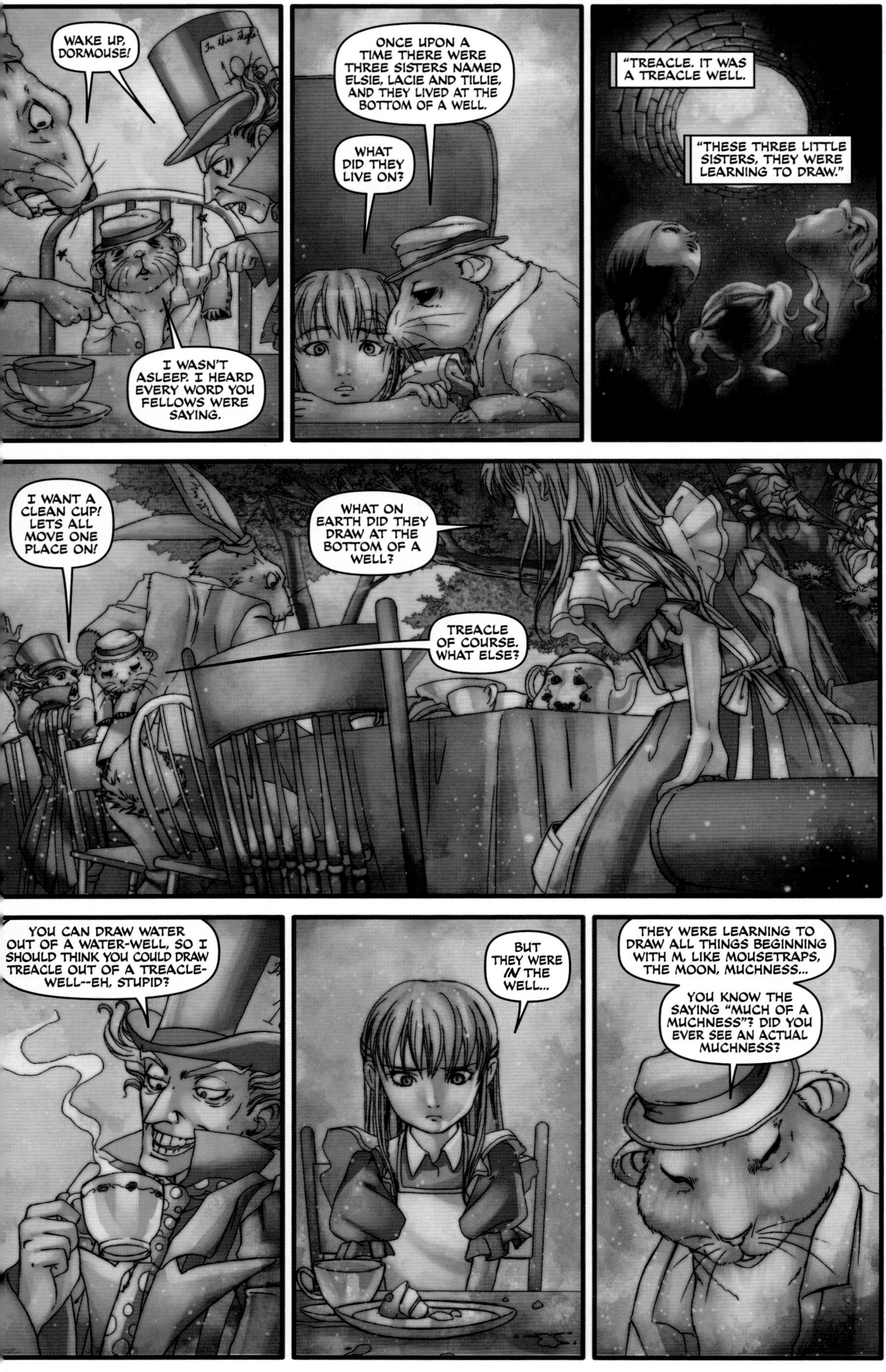
WAKE UP, DORMOUSE!
In this Style 10/6
I WASN'T ASLEEP. I HEARD EVERY WORD YOU FELLOWS WERE SAYING.
ONCE UPON A TIME THERE WERE THREE SISTERS NAMED ELSIE, LACIE AND TILLIE, AND THEY LIVED AT THE BOTTOM OF A WELL.
WHAT DID THEY LIVE ON?
"TREACLE. IT WAS A TREACLE WELL.
"THESE THREE LITTLE SISTERS, THEY WERE LEARNING TO DRAW."
I WANT A CLEAN CUP! LETS ALL MOVE ONE PLACE ON!
WHAT ON EARTH DID THEY DRAW AT THE BOTTOM OF A WELL?
TREACLE OF COURSE. WHAT ELSE?
YOU CAN DRAW WATER OUT OF A WATER-WELL, SO I SHOULD THINK YOU COULD DRAW TREACLE OUT OF A TREACLE-WELL--EH, STUPID?
BUT THEY WERE *IN* THE WELL...
THEY WERE LEARNING TO DRAW ALL THINGS BEGINNING WITH M, LIKE MOUSETRAPS, THE MOON, MUCHNESS...
YOU KNOW THE SAYING "MUCH OF A MUCHNESS"? DID YOU EVER SEE AN ACTUAL MUCHNESS?

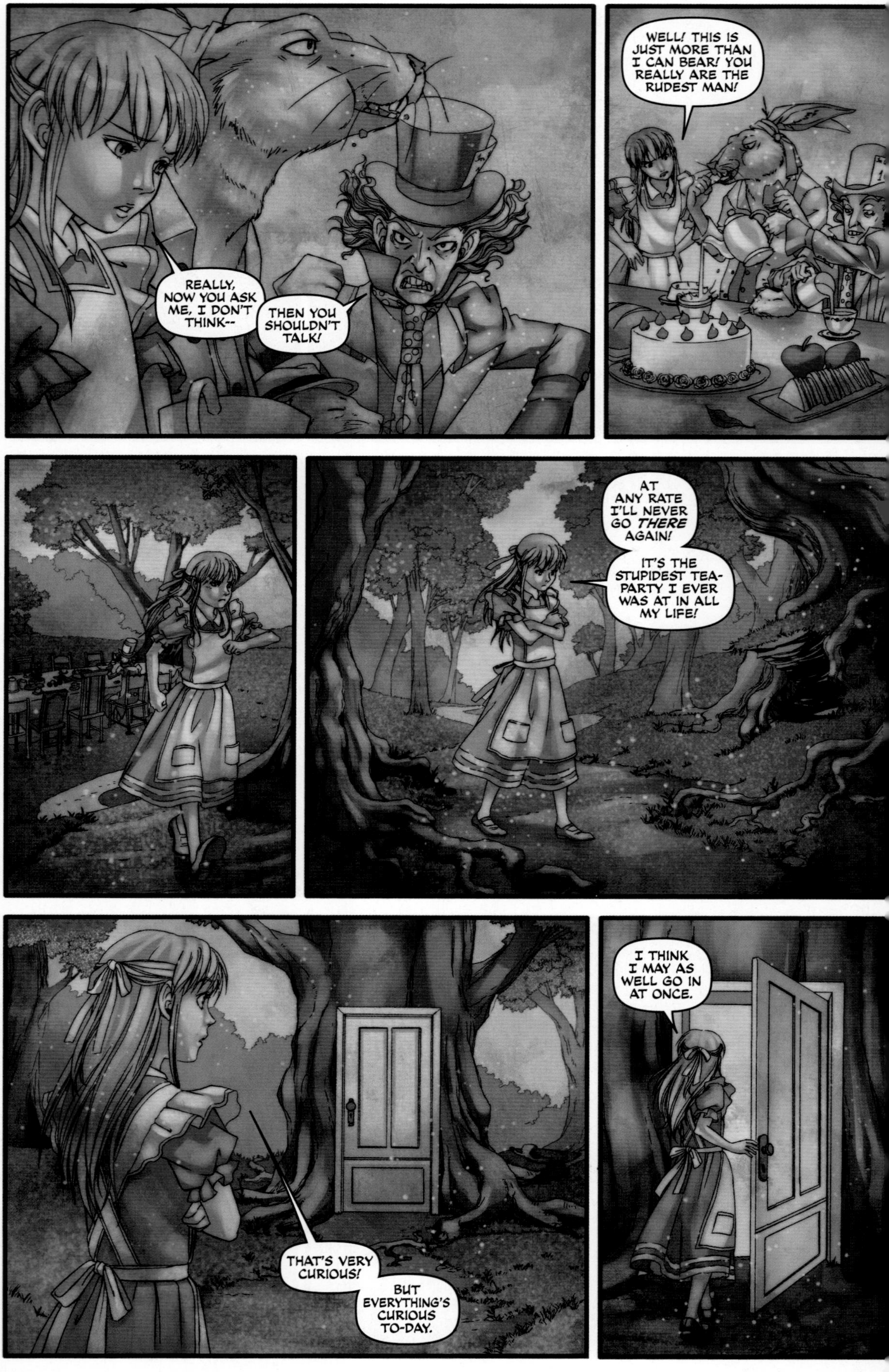
REALLY, NOW YOU ASK ME, I DON'T THINK--
THEN YOU SHOULDN'T TALK!
WELL! THIS IS JUST MORE THAN I CAN BEAR! YOU REALLY ARE THE RUDEST MAN!
AT ANY RATE I'LL NEVER GO *THERE* AGAIN!
IT'S THE STUPIDEST TEA-PARTY I EVER WAS AT IN ALL MY LIFE!
THAT'S VERY CURIOUS!
BUT EVERYTHING'S CURIOUS TO-DAY.
I THINK I MAY AS WELL GO IN AT ONCE.

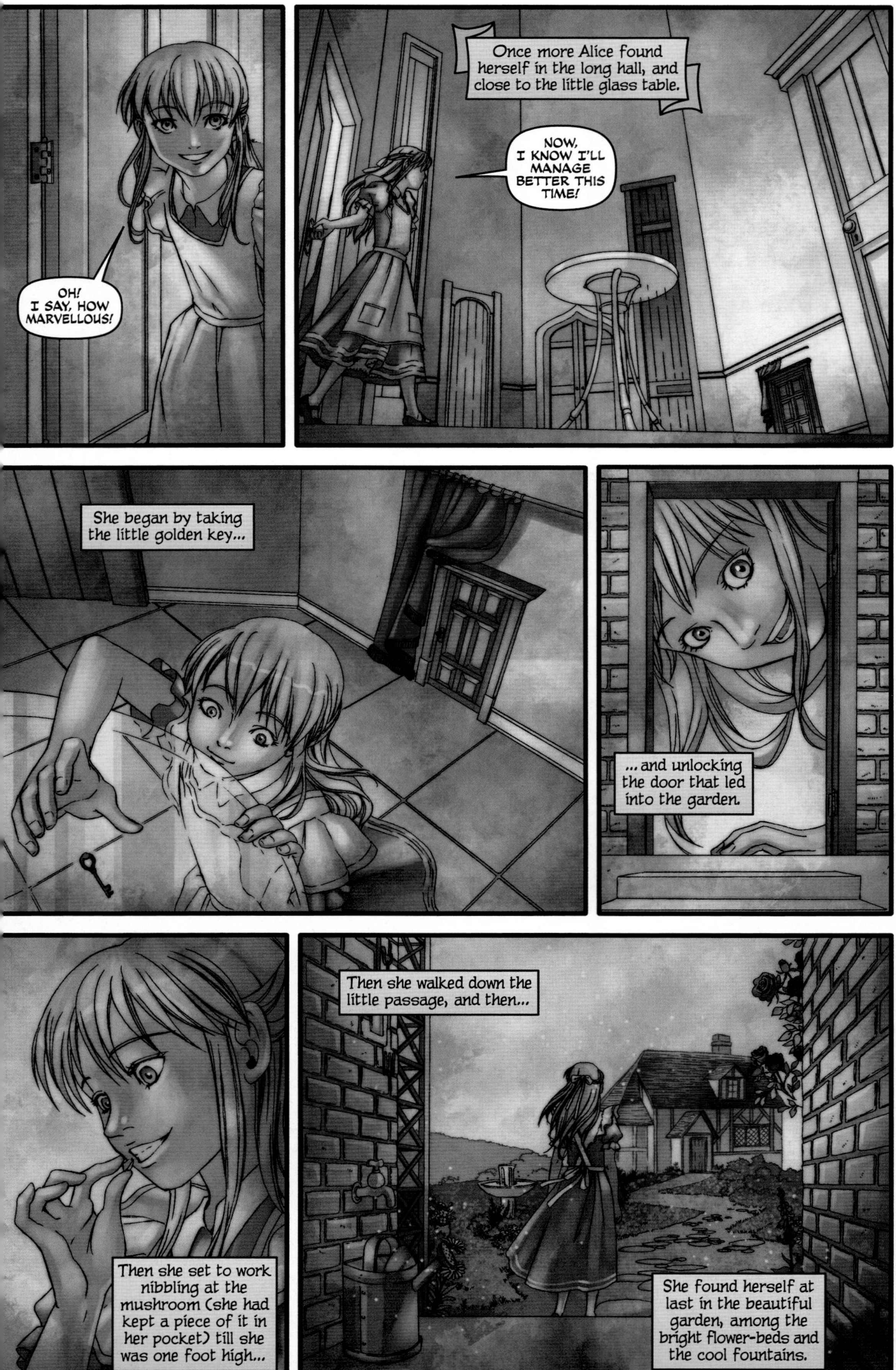
OH! I SAY, HOW MARVELLOUS!
Once more Alice found herself in the long hall, and close to the little glass table.
NOW, I KNOW I'LL MANAGE BETTER THIS TIME!
She began by taking the little golden key...
... and unlocking the door that led into the garden.
Then she set to work nibbling at the mushroom (she had kept a piece of it in her pocket) till she was one foot high...
Then she walked down the little passage, and then...
She found herself at last in the beautiful garden, among the bright flower-beds and the cool fountains.

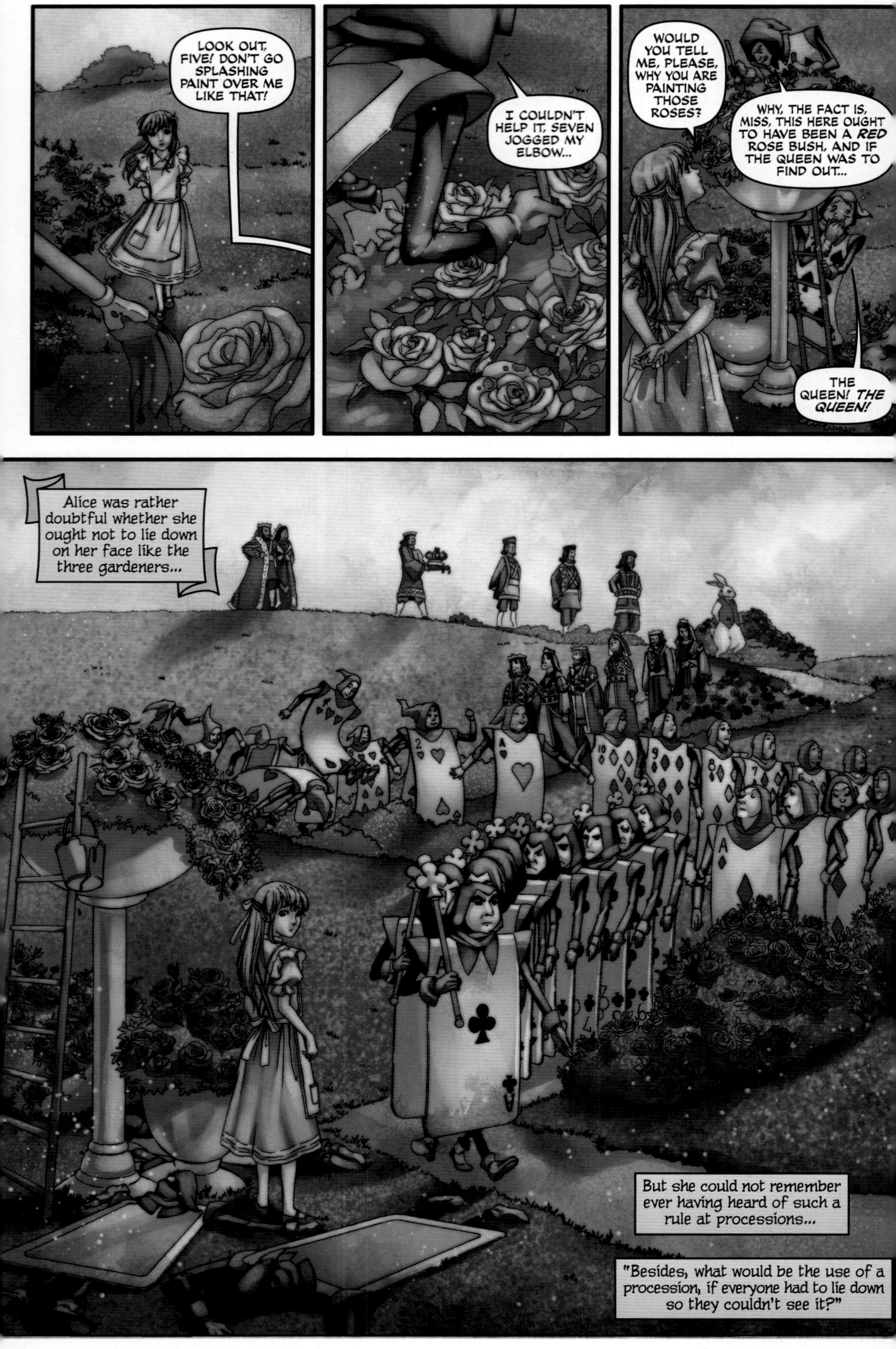
LOOK OUT, FIVE! DON'T GO SPLASHING PAINT OVER ME LIKE THAT!
I COULDN'T HELP IT, SEVEN JOGGED MY ELBOW...
WOULD YOU TELL ME, PLEASE, WHY YOU ARE PAINTING THOSE ROSES?
WHY, THE FACT IS, MISS, THIS HERE OUGHT TO HAVE BEEN A RED ROSE BUSH, AND IF THE QUEEN WAS TO FIND OUT...
THE QUEEN! THE QUEEN!
Alice was rather doubtful whether she ought not to lie down on her face like the three gardeners...
But she could not remember ever having heard of such a rule at processions...
"Besides, what would be the use of a procession, if everyone had to lie down so they couldn't see it?"

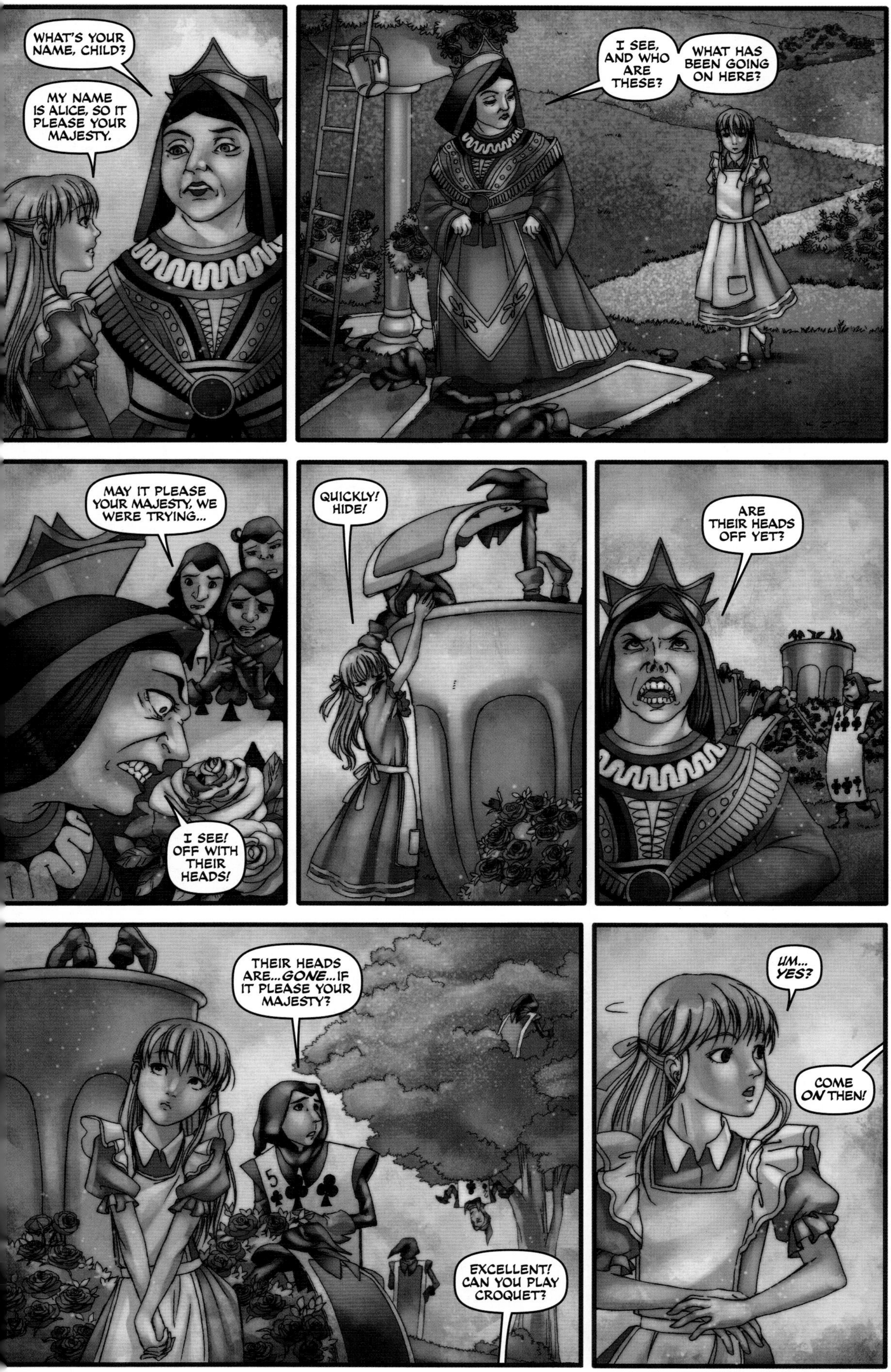
WHAT'S YOUR NAME, CHILD?
MY NAME IS ALICE, SO IT PLEASE YOUR MAJESTY.
I SEE, AND WHO ARE THESE?
WHAT HAS BEEN GOING ON HERE?
MAY IT PLEASE YOUR MAJESTY, WE WERE TRYING...
I SEE! OFF WITH THEIR HEADS!
QUICKLY! HIDE!
ARE THEIR HEADS OFF YET?
THEIR HEADS ARE...*GONE*...IF IT PLEASE YOUR MAJESTY?
EXCELLENT! CAN YOU PLAY CROQUET?
UM... YES?
COME *ON* THEN!

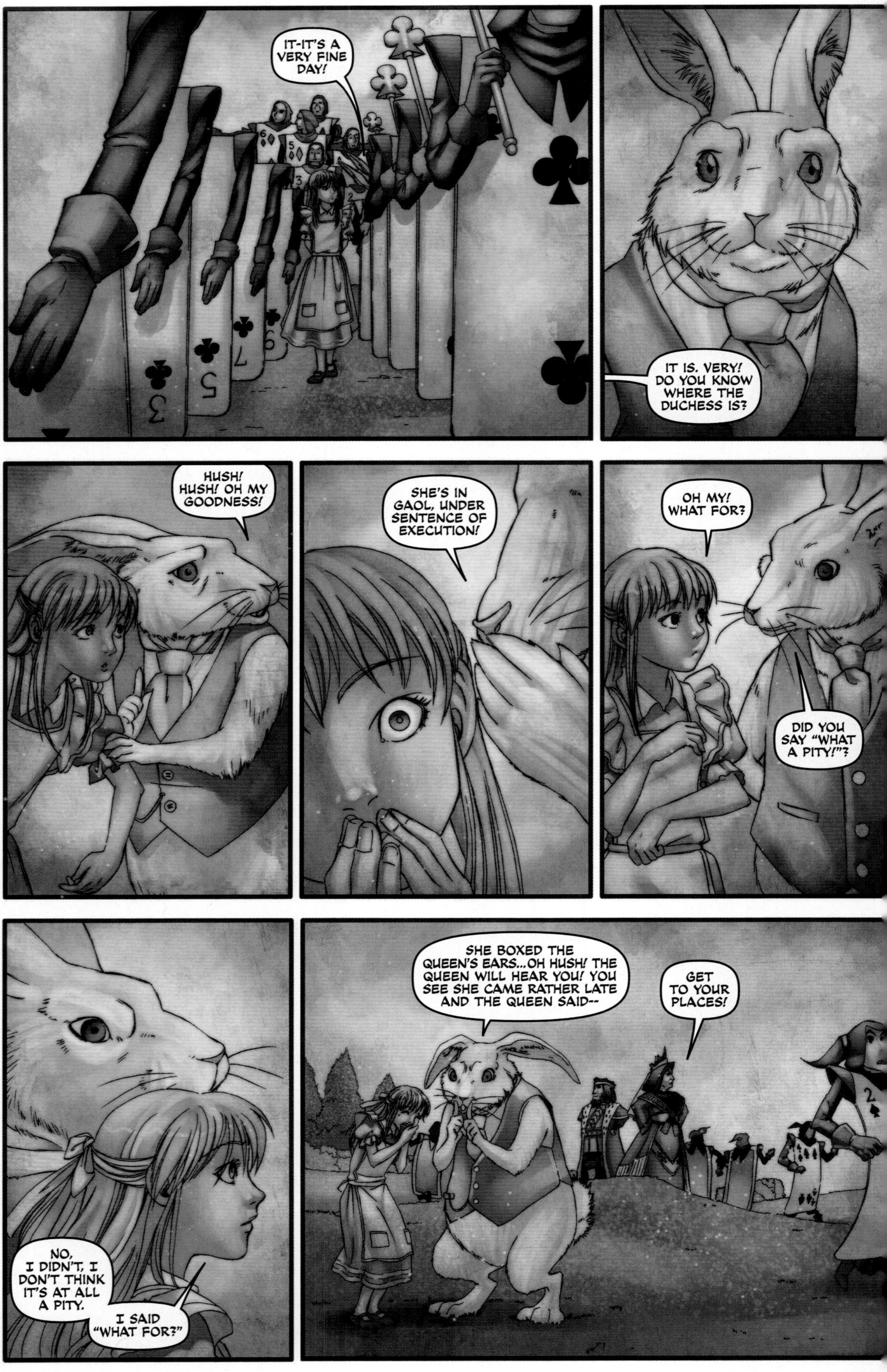
IT-IT'S A VERY FINE DAY!
IT IS. VERY! DO YOU KNOW WHERE THE DUCHESS IS?
HUSH! HUSH! OH MY GOODNESS!
SHE'S IN GAOL, UNDER SENTENCE OF EXECUTION!
OH MY! WHAT FOR?
DID YOU SAY "WHAT A PITY!"?
NO, I DIDN'T, I DON'T THINK IT'S AT ALL A PITY.
I SAID "WHAT FOR?"
SHE BOXED THE QUEEN'S EARS...OH HUSH! THE QUEEN WILL HEAR YOU! YOU SEE SHE CAME RATHER LATE AND THE QUEEN SAID--
GET TO YOUR PLACES!

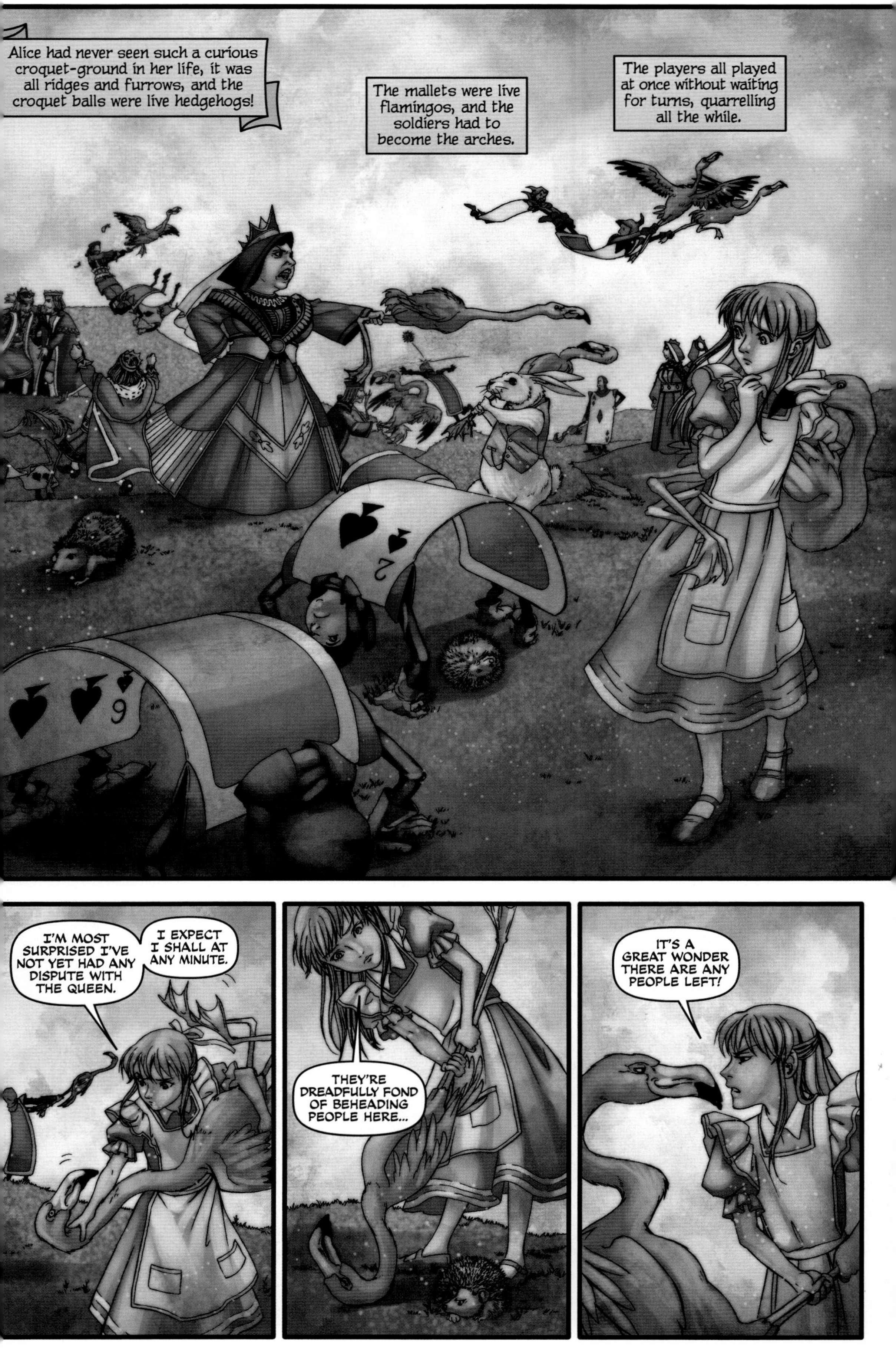
Alice had never seen such a curious croquet-ground in her life, it was all ridges and furrows, and the croquet balls were live hedgehogs!
The mallets were live flamingos, and the soldiers had to become the arches.
The players all played at once without waiting for turns, quarrelling all the while.
I'M MOST SURPRISED I'VE NOT YET HAD ANY DISPUTE WITH THE QUEEN.
I EXPECT I SHALL AT ANY MINUTE.
THEY'RE DREADFULLY FOND OF BEHEADING PEOPLE HERE...
IT'S A GREAT WONDER THERE ARE ANY PEOPLE LEFT!

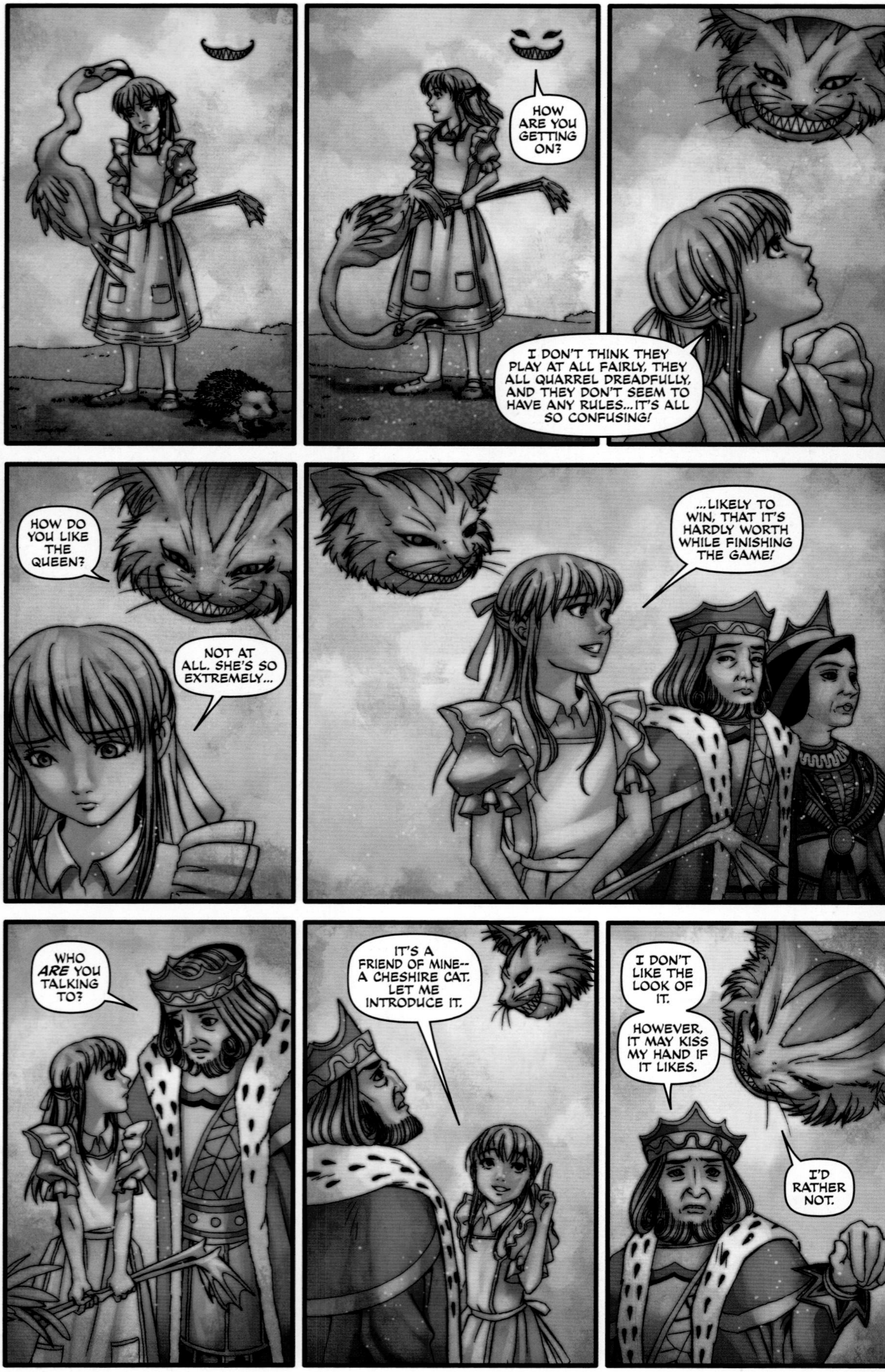
HOW ARE YOU GETTING ON?
I DON'T THINK THEY PLAY AT ALL FAIRLY, THEY ALL QUARREL DREADFULLY, AND THEY DON'T SEEM TO HAVE ANY RULES...IT'S ALL SO CONFUSING!
HOW DO YOU LIKE THE QUEEN?
NOT AT ALL. SHE'S SO EXTREMELY...
...LIKELY TO WIN, THAT IT'S HARDLY WORTH WHILE FINISHING THE GAME!
WHO *ARE* YOU TALKING TO?
IT'S A FRIEND OF MINE--A CHESHIRE CAT. LET ME INTRODUCE IT.
I DON'T LIKE THE LOOK OF IT.
HOWEVER, IT MAY KISS MY HAND IF IT LIKES.
I'D RATHER NOT.

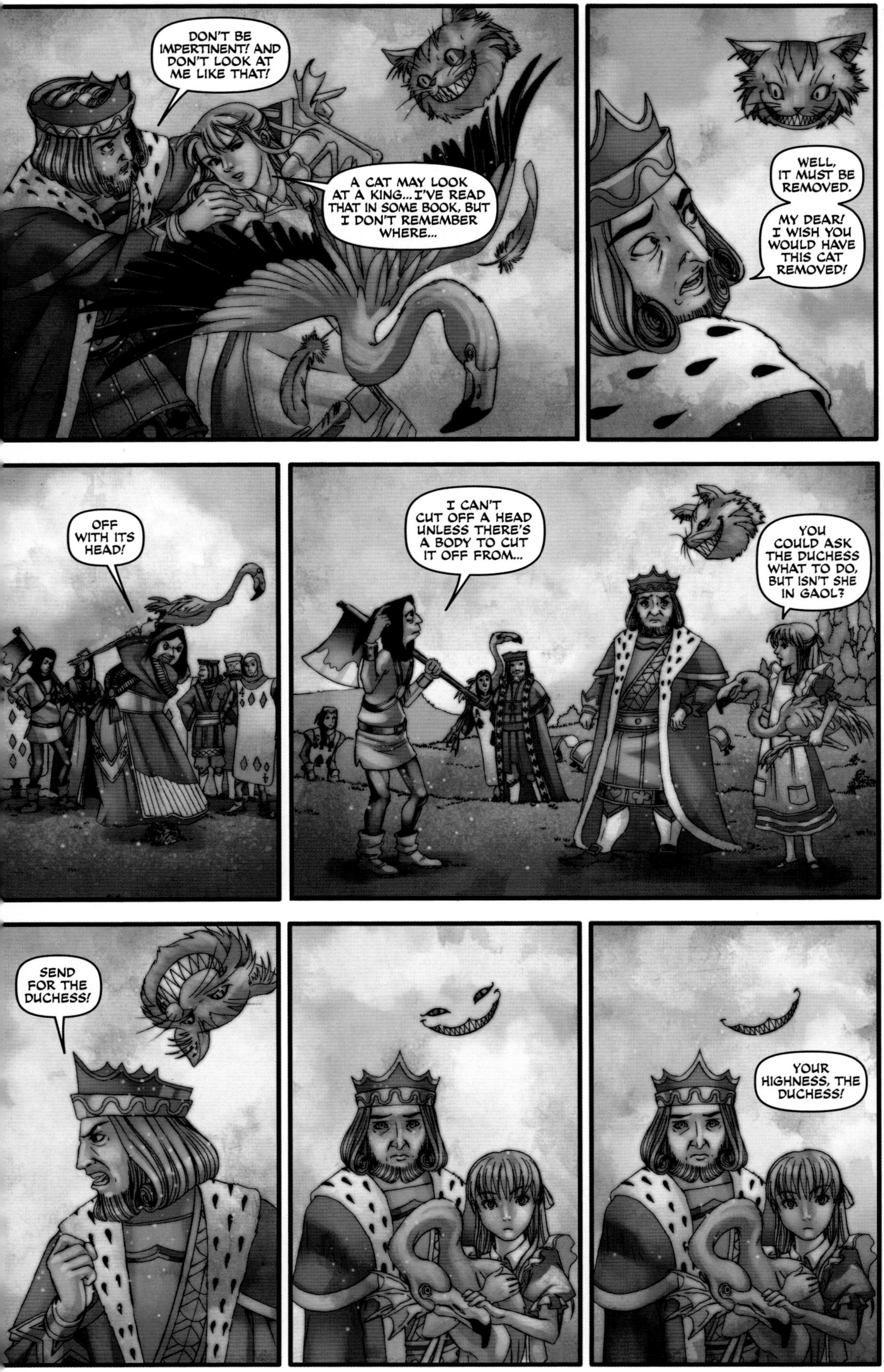
DON'T BE IMPERTINENT! AND DON'T LOOK AT ME LIKE THAT!
A CAT MAY LOOK AT A KING... I'VE READ THAT IN SOME BOOK, BUT I DON'T REMEMBER WHERE...
WELL, IT MUST BE REMOVED.
MY DEAR! I WISH YOU WOULD HAVE THIS CAT REMOVED!
OFF WITH ITS HEAD!
I CAN'T CUT OFF A HEAD UNLESS THERE'S A BODY TO CUT IT OFF FROM...
YOU COULD ASK THE DUCHESS WHAT TO DO, BUT ISN'T SHE IN GAOL?
SEND FOR THE DUCHESS!
YOUR HIGHNESS, THE DUCHESS!

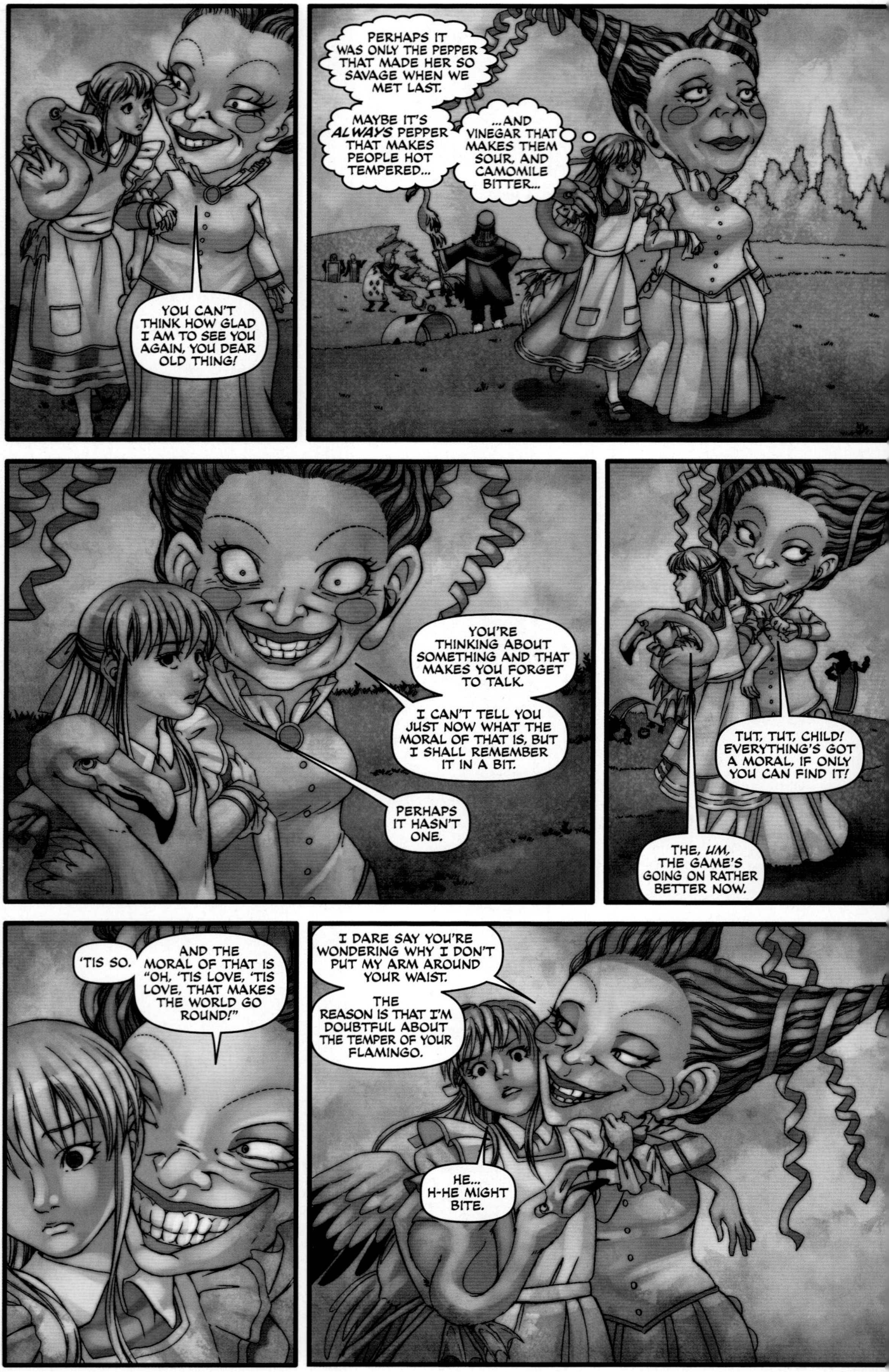

YOU CAN'T THINK HOW GLAD I AM TO SEE YOU AGAIN, YOU DEAR OLD THING!
PERHAPS IT WAS ONLY THE PEPPER THAT MADE HER SO SAVAGE WHEN WE MET LAST.
MAYBE IT'S *ALWAYS* PEPPER THAT MAKES PEOPLE HOT TEMPERED...
...AND VINEGAR THAT MAKES THEM SOUR, AND CAMOMILE BITTER...
YOU'RE THINKING ABOUT SOMETHING AND THAT MAKES YOU FORGET TO TALK.
I CAN'T TELL YOU JUST NOW WHAT THE MORAL OF THAT IS, BUT I SHALL REMEMBER IT IN A BIT.
PERHAPS IT HASN'T ONE.
TUT, TUT, CHILD! EVERYTHING'S GOT A MORAL, IF ONLY YOU CAN FIND IT!
THE, *UM*, THE GAME'S GOING ON RATHER BETTER NOW.
'TIS SO.
AND THE MORAL OF THAT IS "OH, 'TIS LOVE, 'TIS LOVE, THAT MAKES THE WORLD GO ROUND!"
I DARE SAY YOU'RE WONDERING WHY I DON'T PUT MY ARM AROUND YOUR WAIST.
THE REASON IS THAT I'M DOUBTFUL ABOUT THE TEMPER OF YOUR FLAMINGO.
HE... H-HE MIGHT BITE.

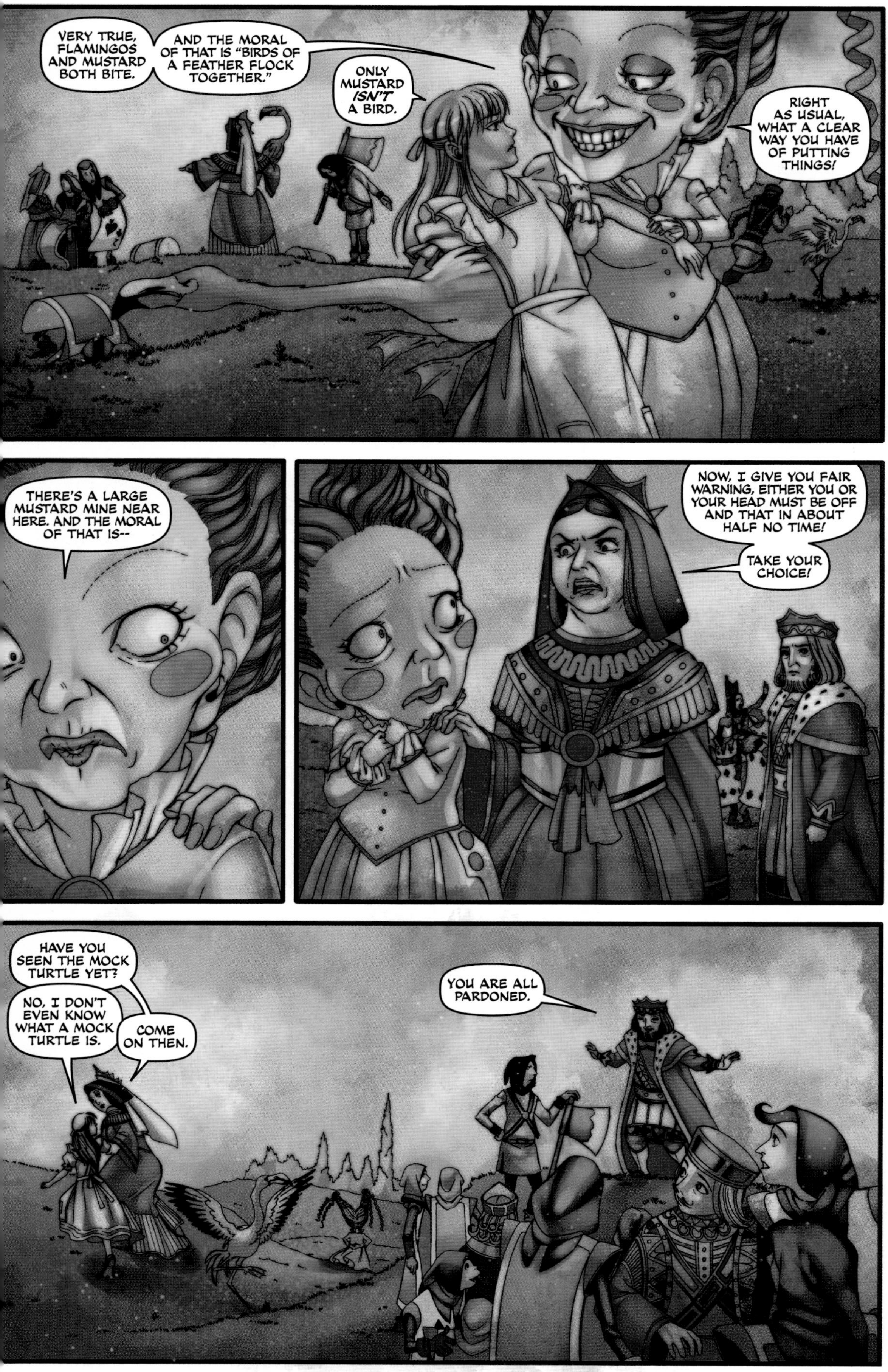

VERY TRUE, FLAMINGOS AND MUSTARD BOTH BITE.
AND THE MORAL OF THAT IS "BIRDS OF A FEATHER FLOCK TOGETHER."
ONLY MUSTARD ISN'T A BIRD.
RIGHT AS USUAL, WHAT A CLEAR WAY YOU HAVE OF PUTTING THINGS!
THERE'S A LARGE MUSTARD MINE NEAR HERE. AND THE MORAL OF THAT IS--
NOW, I GIVE YOU FAIR WARNING, EITHER YOU OR YOUR HEAD MUST BE OFF AND THAT IN ABOUT HALF NO TIME!
TAKE YOUR CHOICE!
HAVE YOU SEEN THE MOCK TURTLE YET?
NO, I DON'T EVEN KNOW WHAT A MOCK TURTLE IS.
COME ON THEN.
YOU ARE ALL PARDONED.

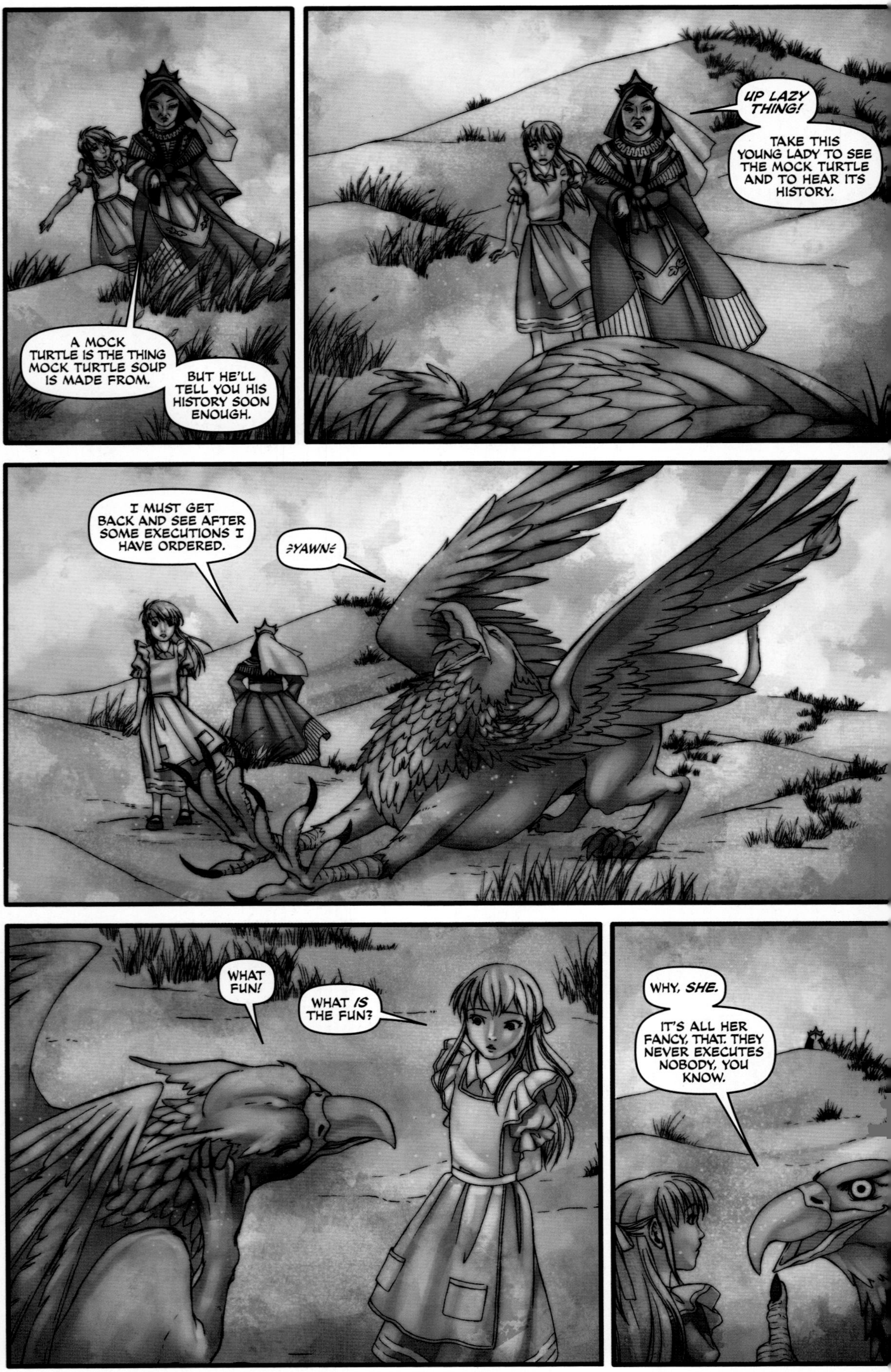
A MOCK TURTLE IS THE THING MOCK TURTLE SOUP IS MADE FROM.
BUT HE'LL TELL YOU HIS HISTORY SOON ENOUGH.
UP LAZY THING!
TAKE THIS YOUNG LADY TO SEE THE MOCK TURTLE AND TO HEAR ITS HISTORY.
I MUST GET BACK AND SEE AFTER SOME EXECUTIONS I HAVE ORDERED.
YAWN
WHAT FUN!
WHAT *IS* THE FUN?
WHY, *SHE.*
IT'S ALL HER FANCY, THAT. THEY NEVER EXECUTES NOBODY, YOU KNOW.

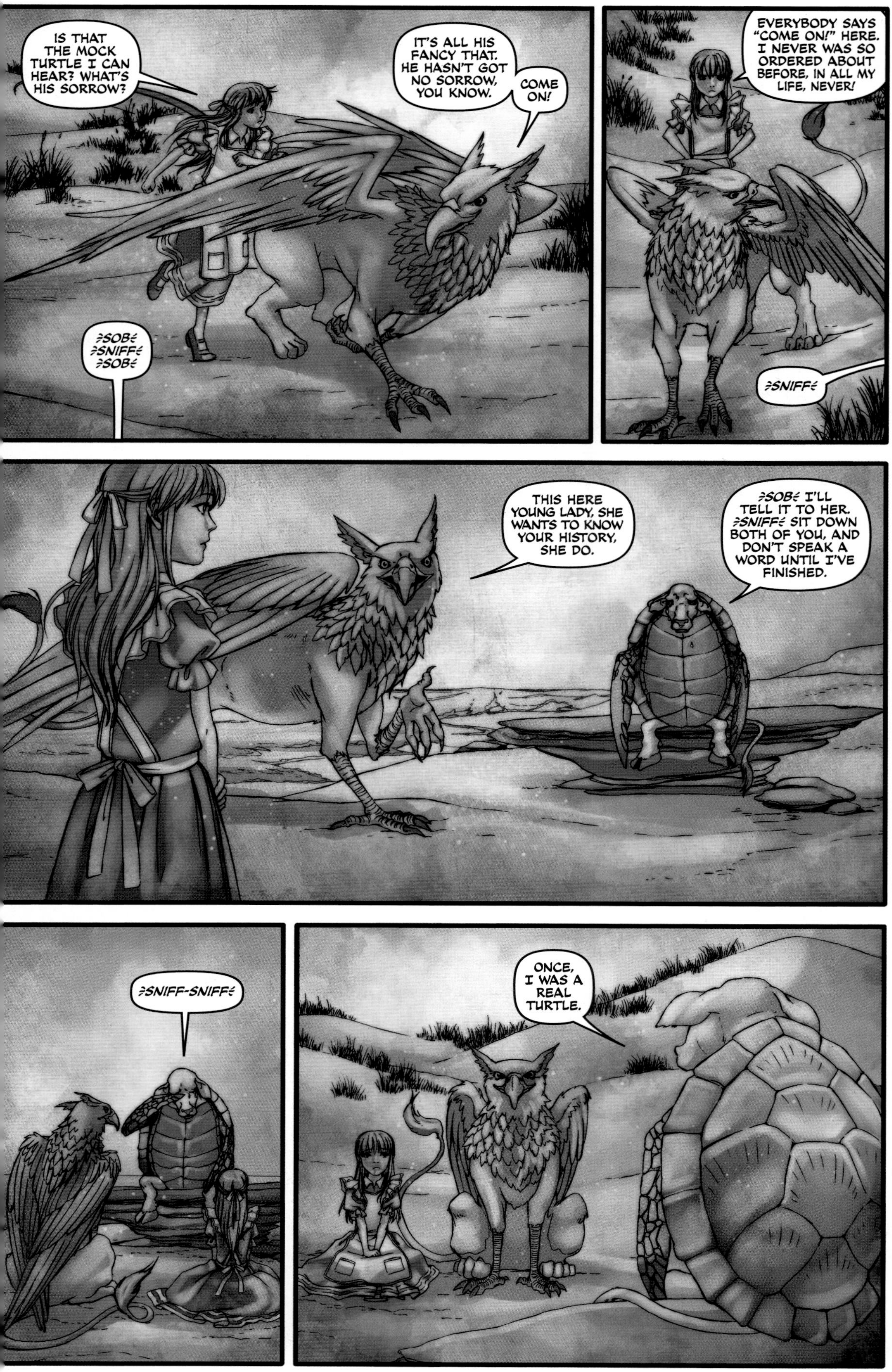
IS THAT THE MOCK TURTLE I CAN HEAR? WHAT'S HIS SORROW?
IT'S ALL HIS FANCY THAT. HE HASN'T GOT NO SORROW, YOU KNOW.
COME ON!
SOB SNIFF SOB
EVERYBODY SAYS "COME ON!" HERE. I NEVER WAS SO ORDERED ABOUT BEFORE, IN ALL MY LIFE, NEVER!
SNIFF
THIS HERE YOUNG LADY, SHE WANTS TO KNOW YOUR HISTORY, SHE DO.
SOB I'LL TELL IT TO HER. SNIFF SIT DOWN BOTH OF YOU, AND DON'T SPEAK A WORD UNTIL I'VE FINISHED.
SNIFF-SNIFF
ONCE, I WAS A REAL TURTLE.

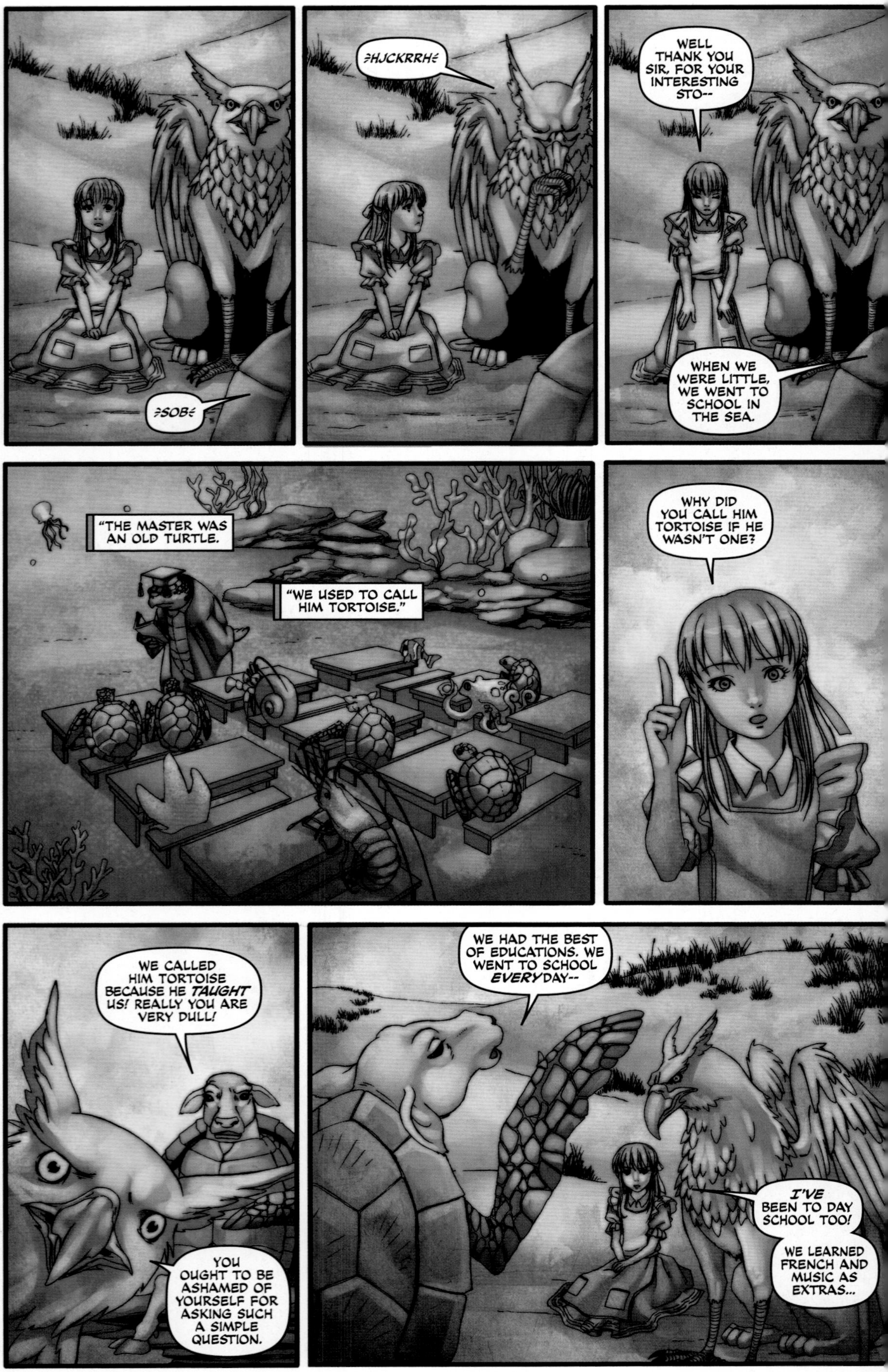

⁇SOB⁇
⁇HJCKRRH⁇
WELL THANK YOU SIR, FOR YOUR INTERESTING STO--
WHEN WE WERE LITTLE, WE WENT TO SCHOOL IN THE SEA.
"THE MASTER WAS AN OLD TURTLE.
"WE USED TO CALL HIM TORTOISE."
WHY DID YOU CALL HIM TORTOISE IF HE WASN'T ONE?
WE CALLED HIM TORTOISE BECAUSE HE *TAUGHT* US! REALLY YOU ARE VERY DULL!
YOU OUGHT TO BE ASHAMED OF YOURSELF FOR ASKING SUCH A SIMPLE QUESTION.
WE HAD THE BEST OF EDUCATIONS. WE WENT TO SCHOOL *EVERY*DAY--
I'VE BEEN TO DAY SCHOOL TOO!
WE LEARNED FRENCH AND MUSIC AS EXTRAS...

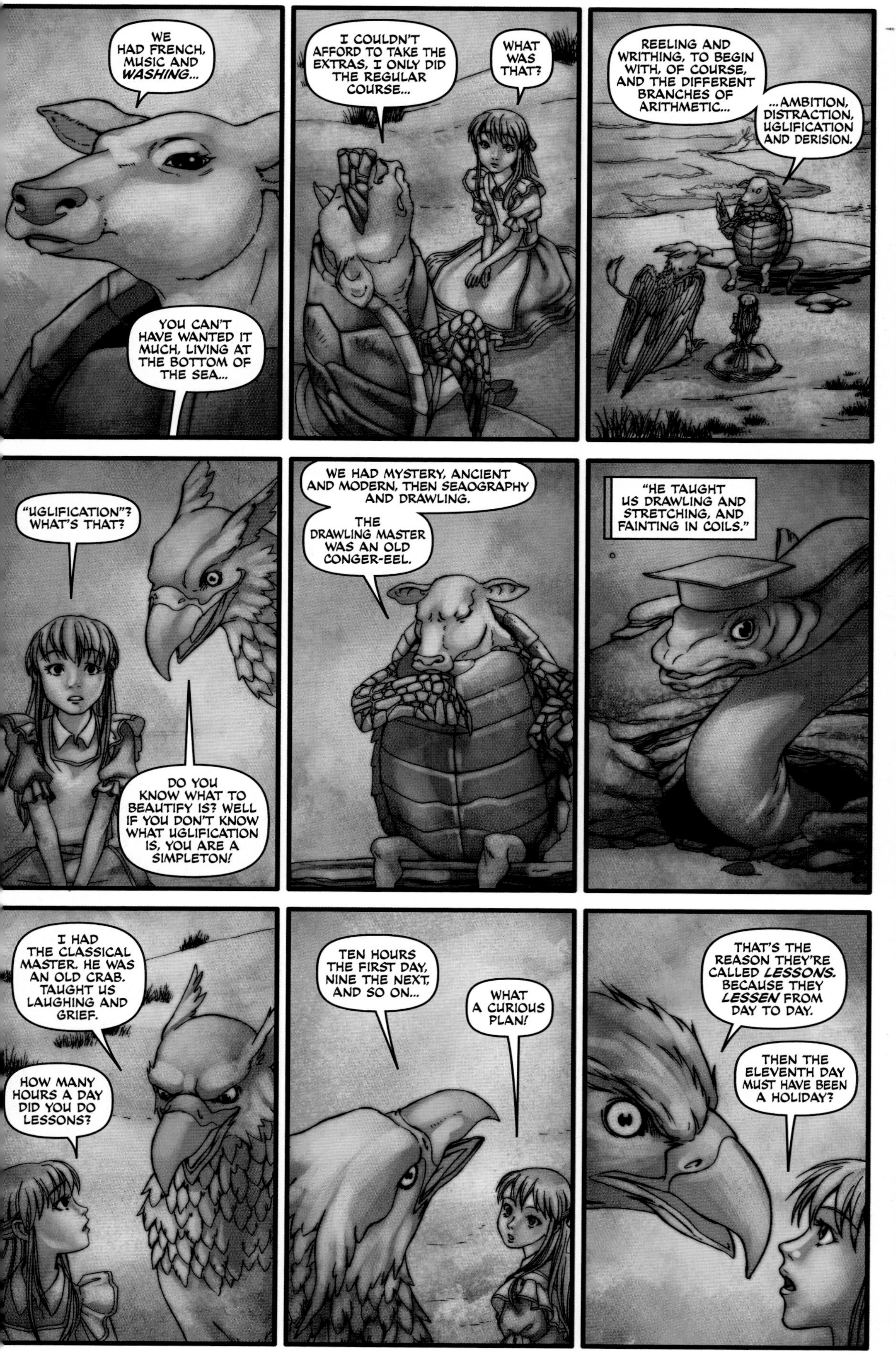
WE HAD FRENCH, MUSIC AND WASHING...
YOU CAN'T HAVE WANTED IT MUCH, LIVING AT THE BOTTOM OF THE SEA...
I COULDN'T AFFORD TO TAKE THE EXTRAS, I ONLY DID THE REGULAR COURSE...
WHAT WAS THAT?
REELING AND WRITHING, TO BEGIN WITH, OF COURSE, AND THE DIFFERENT BRANCHES OF ARITHMETIC...
...AMBITION, DISTRACTION, UGLIFICATION AND DERISION.
"UGLIFICATION"? WHAT'S THAT?
DO YOU KNOW WHAT TO BEAUTIFY IS? WELL IF YOU DON'T KNOW WHAT UGLIFICATION IS, YOU ARE A SIMPLETON!
WE HAD MYSTERY, ANCIENT AND MODERN, THEN SEAOGRAPHY AND DRAWLING.
THE DRAWLING MASTER WAS AN OLD CONGER-EEL.
"HE TAUGHT US DRAWLING AND STRETCHING, AND FAINTING IN COILS."
I HAD THE CLASSICAL MASTER. HE WAS AN OLD CRAB. TAUGHT US LAUGHING AND GRIEF.
HOW MANY HOURS A DAY DID YOU DO LESSONS?
TEN HOURS THE FIRST DAY, NINE THE NEXT, AND SO ON...
WHAT A CURIOUS PLAN!
THAT'S THE REASON THEY'RE CALLED LESSONS. BECAUSE THEY LESSEN FROM DAY TO DAY.
THEN THE ELEVENTH DAY MUST HAVE BEEN A HOLIDAY?

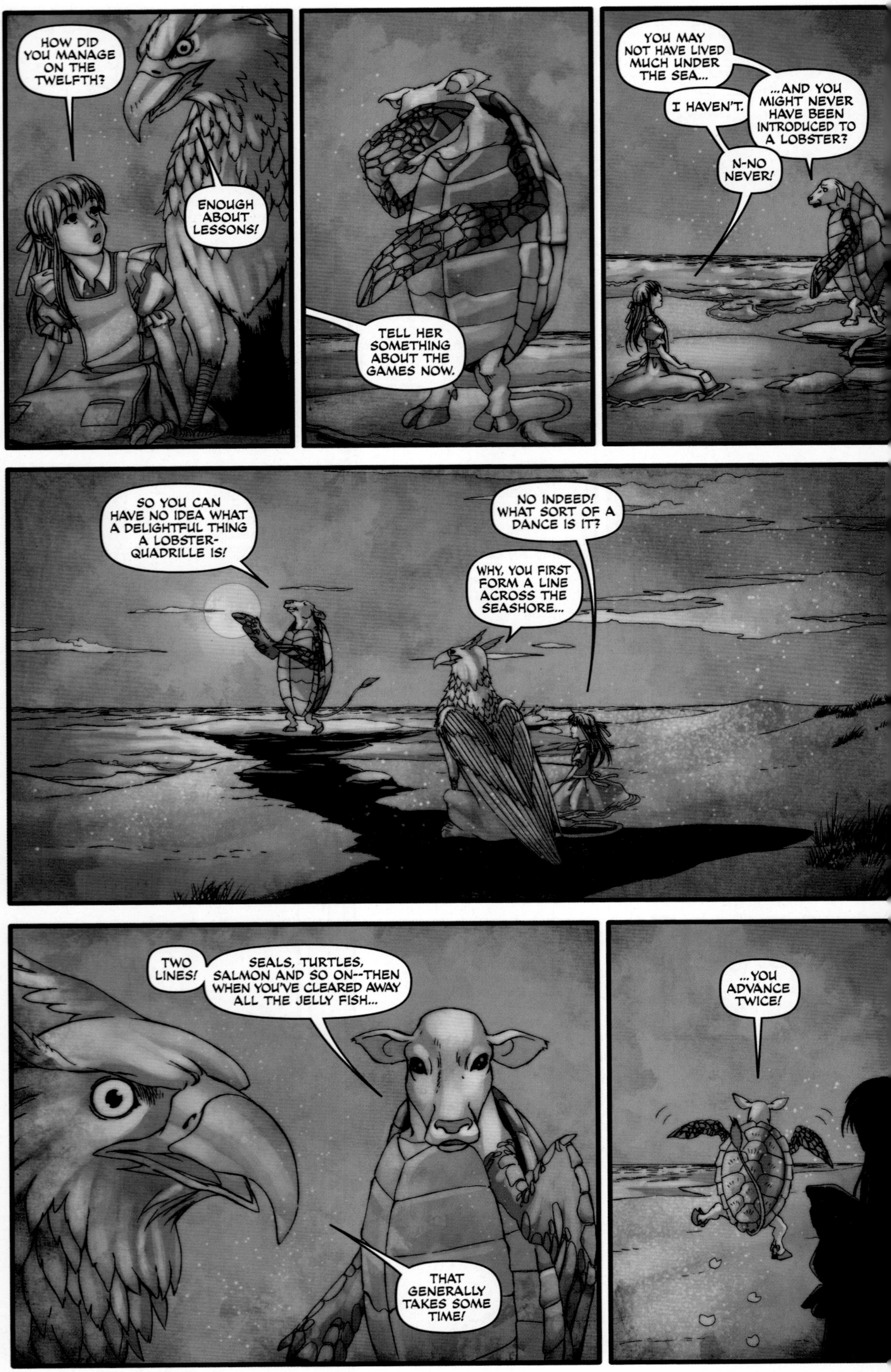
HOW DID YOU MANAGE ON THE TWELFTH?
ENOUGH ABOUT LESSONS!
TELL HER SOMETHING ABOUT THE GAMES NOW.
YOU MAY NOT HAVE LIVED MUCH UNDER THE SEA...
I HAVEN'T.
...AND YOU MIGHT NEVER HAVE BEEN INTRODUCED TO A LOBSTER?
N-NO NEVER!
SO YOU CAN HAVE NO IDEA WHAT A DELIGHTFUL THING A LOBSTER-QUADRILLE IS!
NO INDEED! WHAT SORT OF A DANCE IS IT?
WHY, YOU FIRST FORM A LINE ACROSS THE SEASHORE...
TWO LINES!
SEALS, TURTLES, SALMON AND SO ON--THEN WHEN YOU'VE CLEARED AWAY ALL THE JELLY FISH...
THAT GENERALLY TAKES SOME TIME!
...YOU ADVANCE TWICE!

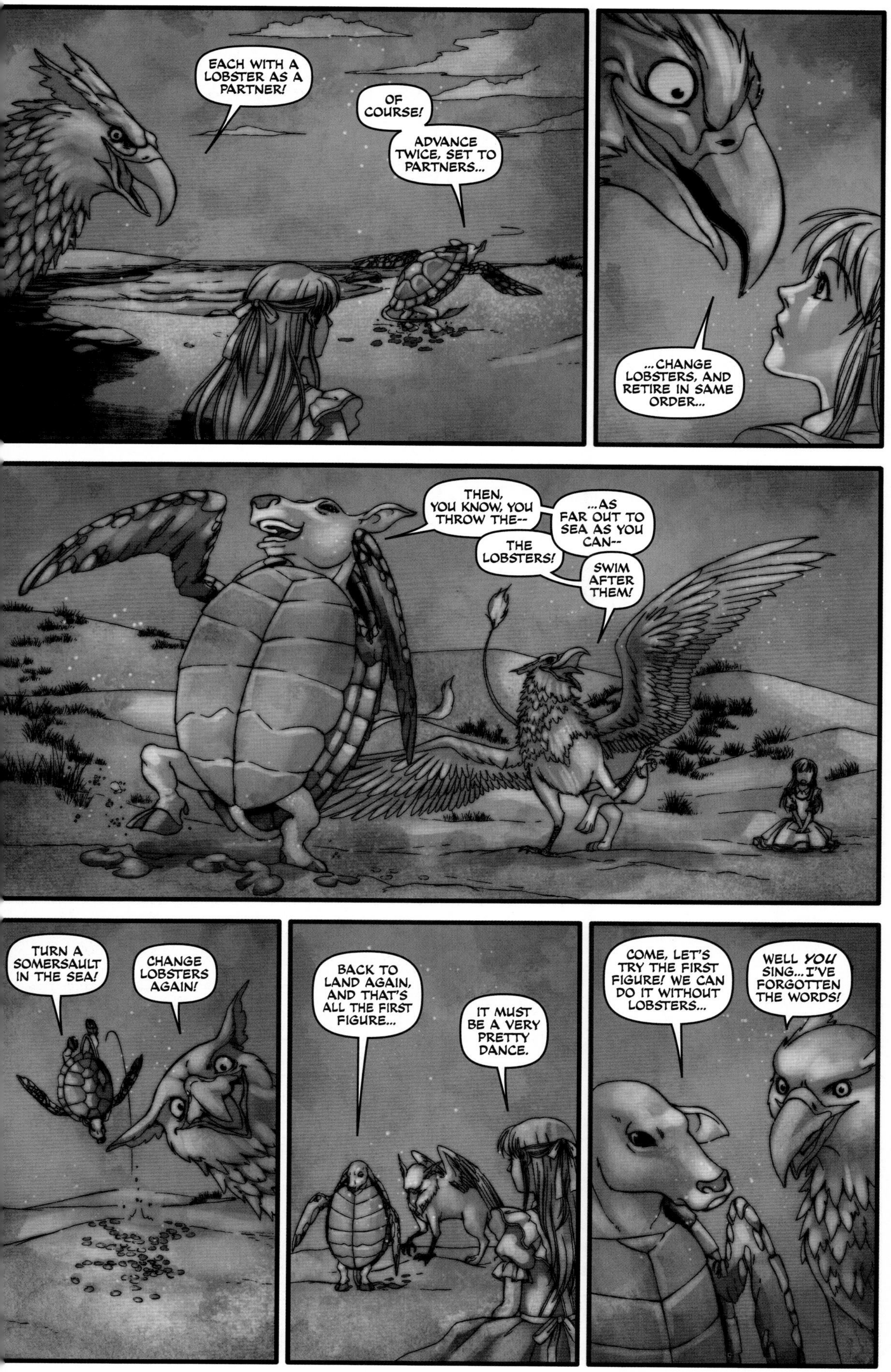
EACH WITH A LOBSTER AS A PARTNER!
OF COURSE!
ADVANCE TWICE, SET TO PARTNERS...
...CHANGE LOBSTERS, AND RETIRE IN SAME ORDER...
THEN, YOU KNOW, YOU THROW THE--
...AS FAR OUT TO SEA AS YOU CAN--
THE LOBSTERS!
SWIM AFTER THEM!
TURN A SOMERSAULT IN THE SEA!
CHANGE LOBSTERS AGAIN!
BACK TO LAND AGAIN, AND THAT'S ALL THE FIRST FIGURE...
IT MUST BE A VERY PRETTY DANCE.
COME, LET'S TRY THE FIRST FIGURE! WE CAN DO IT WITHOUT LOBSTERS...
WELL *YOU* SING...I'VE FORGOTTEN THE WORDS!

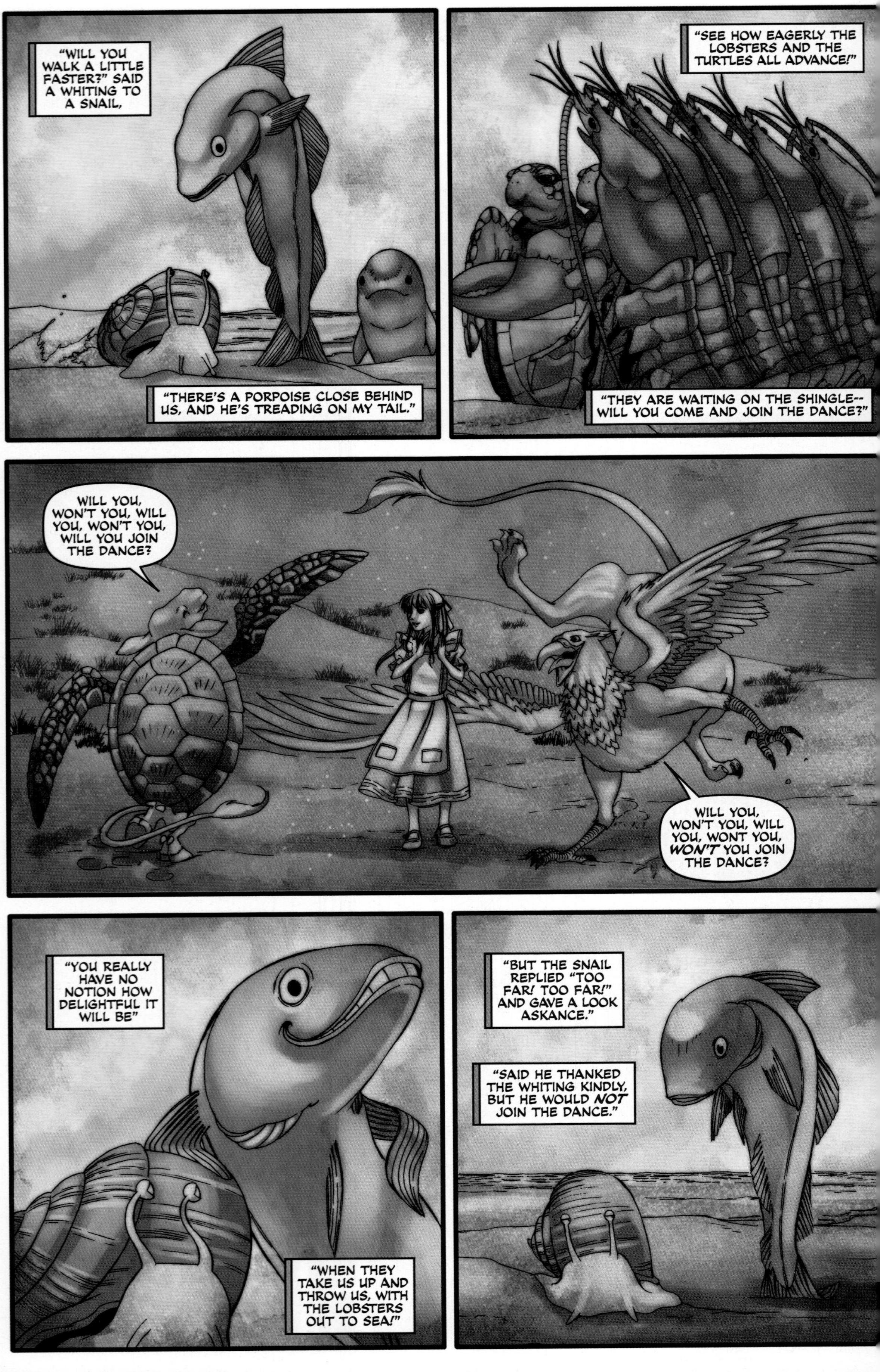
"WILL YOU WALK A LITTLE FASTER?" SAID A WHITING TO A SNAIL,
"THERE'S A PORPOISE CLOSE BEHIND US, AND HE'S TREADING ON MY TAIL."
"SEE HOW EAGERLY THE LOBSTERS AND THE TURTLES ALL ADVANCE!"
"THEY ARE WAITING ON THE SHINGLE-- WILL YOU COME AND JOIN THE DANCE?"
WILL YOU, WON'T YOU, WILL YOU, WON'T YOU, WILL YOU JOIN THE DANCE?
WILL YOU, WON'T YOU, WILL YOU, WONT YOU, *WON'T* YOU JOIN THE DANCE?
"YOU REALLY HAVE NO NOTION HOW DELIGHTFUL IT WILL BE"
"WHEN THEY TAKE US UP AND THROW US, WITH THE LOBSTERS OUT TO SEA!"
"BUT THE SNAIL REPLIED "TOO FAR! TOO FAR!" AND GAVE A LOOK ASKANCE."
"SAID HE THANKED THE WHITING KINDLY, BUT HE WOULD *NOT* JOIN THE DANCE."

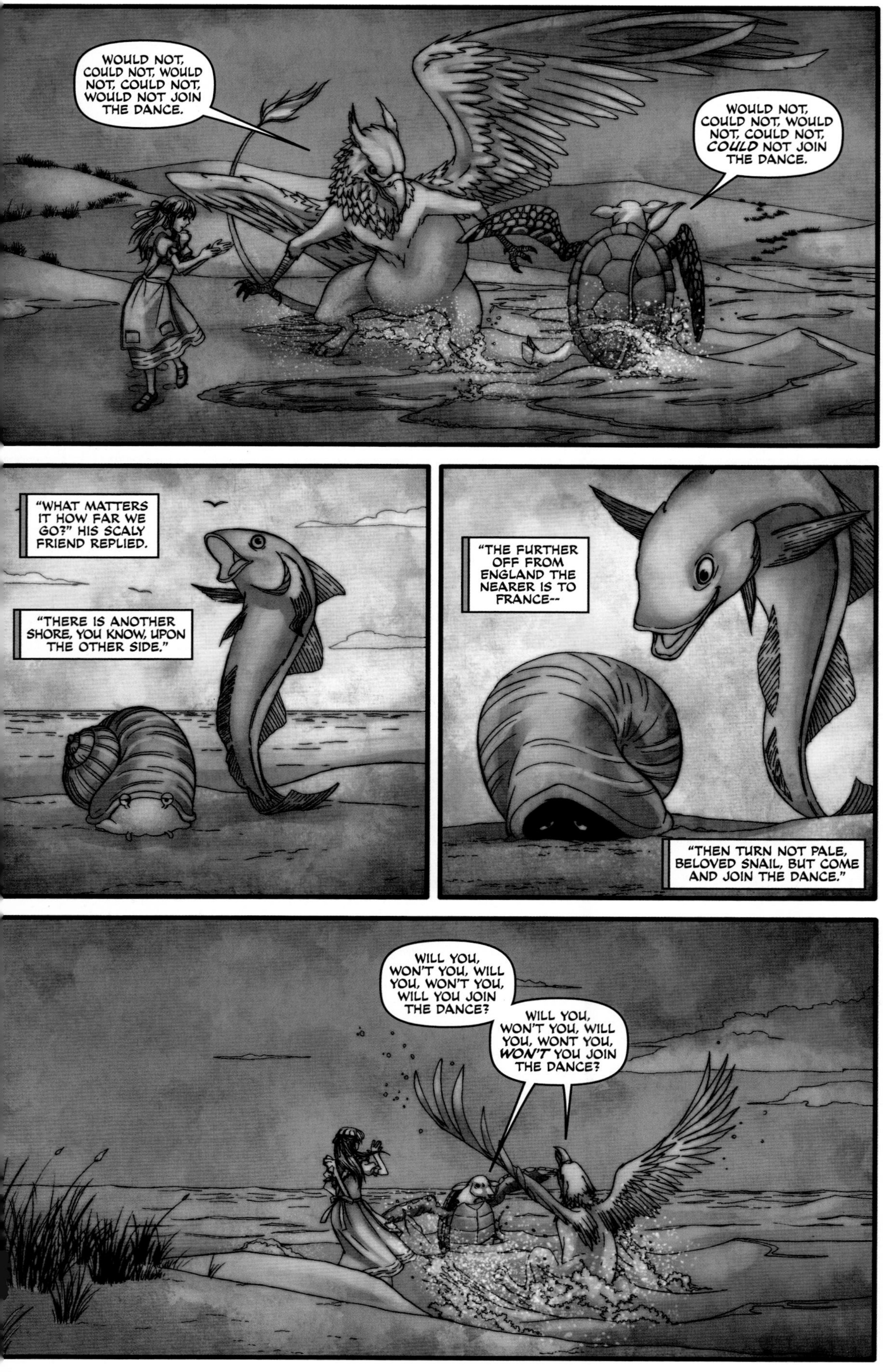
WOULD NOT, COULD NOT, WOULD NOT, COULD NOT, WOULD NOT JOIN THE DANCE.
WOULD NOT, COULD NOT, WOULD NOT, COULD NOT, *COULD* NOT JOIN THE DANCE.
"WHAT MATTERS IT HOW FAR WE GO?" HIS SCALY FRIEND REPLIED.
"THERE IS ANOTHER SHORE, YOU KNOW, UPON THE OTHER SIDE."
"THE FURTHER OFF FROM ENGLAND THE NEARER IS TO FRANCE--
"THEN TURN NOT PALE, BELOVED SNAIL, BUT COME AND JOIN THE DANCE."
WILL YOU, WON'T YOU, WILL YOU, WON'T YOU, WILL YOU JOIN THE DANCE?
WILL YOU, WON'T YOU, WILL YOU, WONT YOU, *WON'T* YOU JOIN THE DANCE?

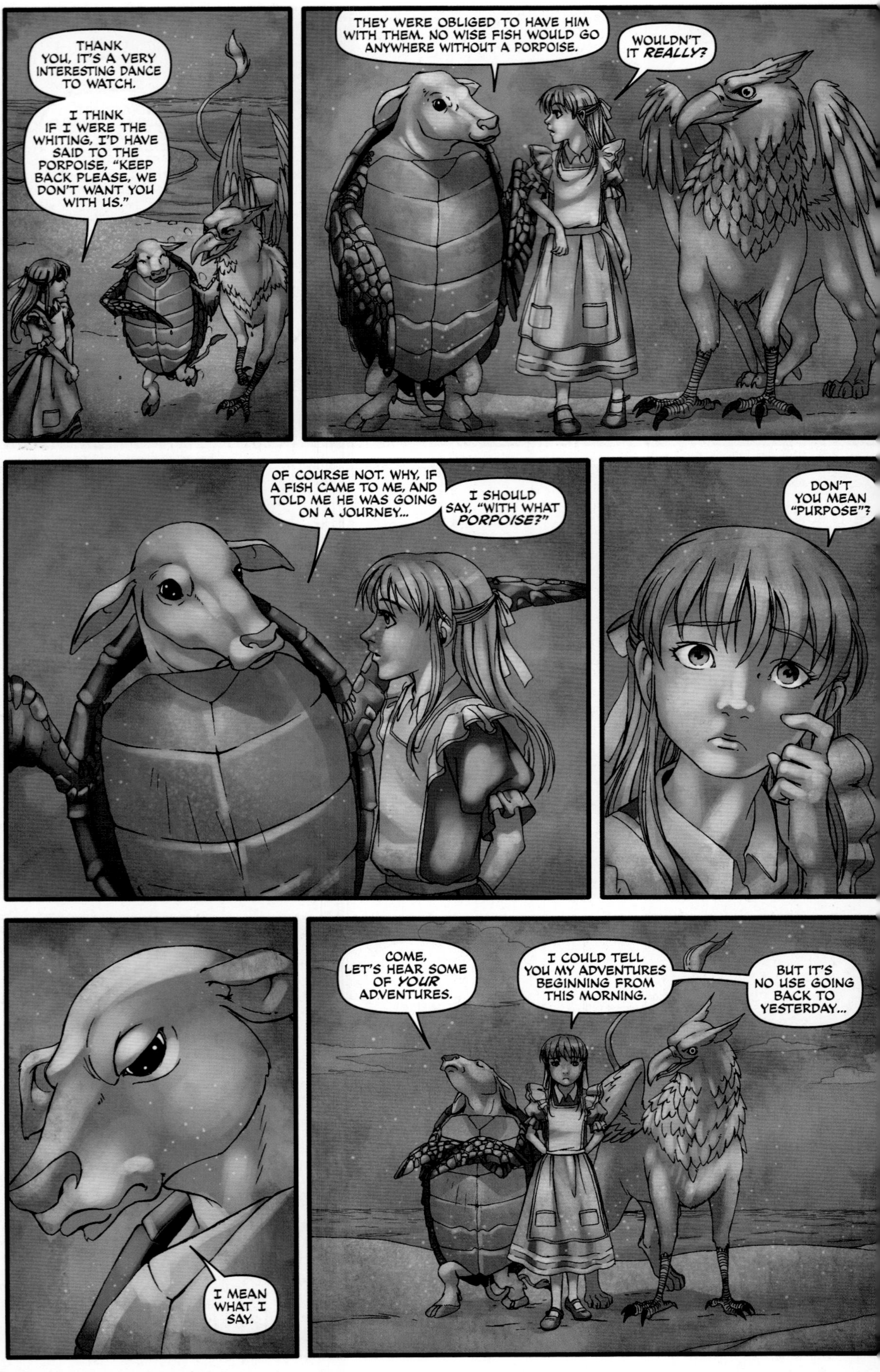
THANK YOU, IT'S A VERY INTERESTING DANCE TO WATCH.
I THINK IF I WERE THE WHITING, I'D HAVE SAID TO THE PORPOISE, "KEEP BACK PLEASE, WE DON'T WANT YOU WITH US."
THEY WERE OBLIGED TO HAVE HIM WITH THEM. NO WISE FISH WOULD GO ANYWHERE WITHOUT A PORPOISE.
WOULDN'T IT *REALLY*?
OF COURSE NOT. WHY, IF A FISH CAME TO ME, AND TOLD ME HE WAS GOING ON A JOURNEY...
I SHOULD SAY, "WITH WHAT *PORPOISE?*"
DON'T YOU MEAN "PURPOSE"?
I MEAN WHAT I SAY.
COME, LET'S HEAR SOME OF *YOUR* ADVENTURES.
I COULD TELL YOU MY ADVENTURES BEGINNING FROM THIS MORNING.
BUT IT'S NO USE GOING BACK TO YESTERDAY...

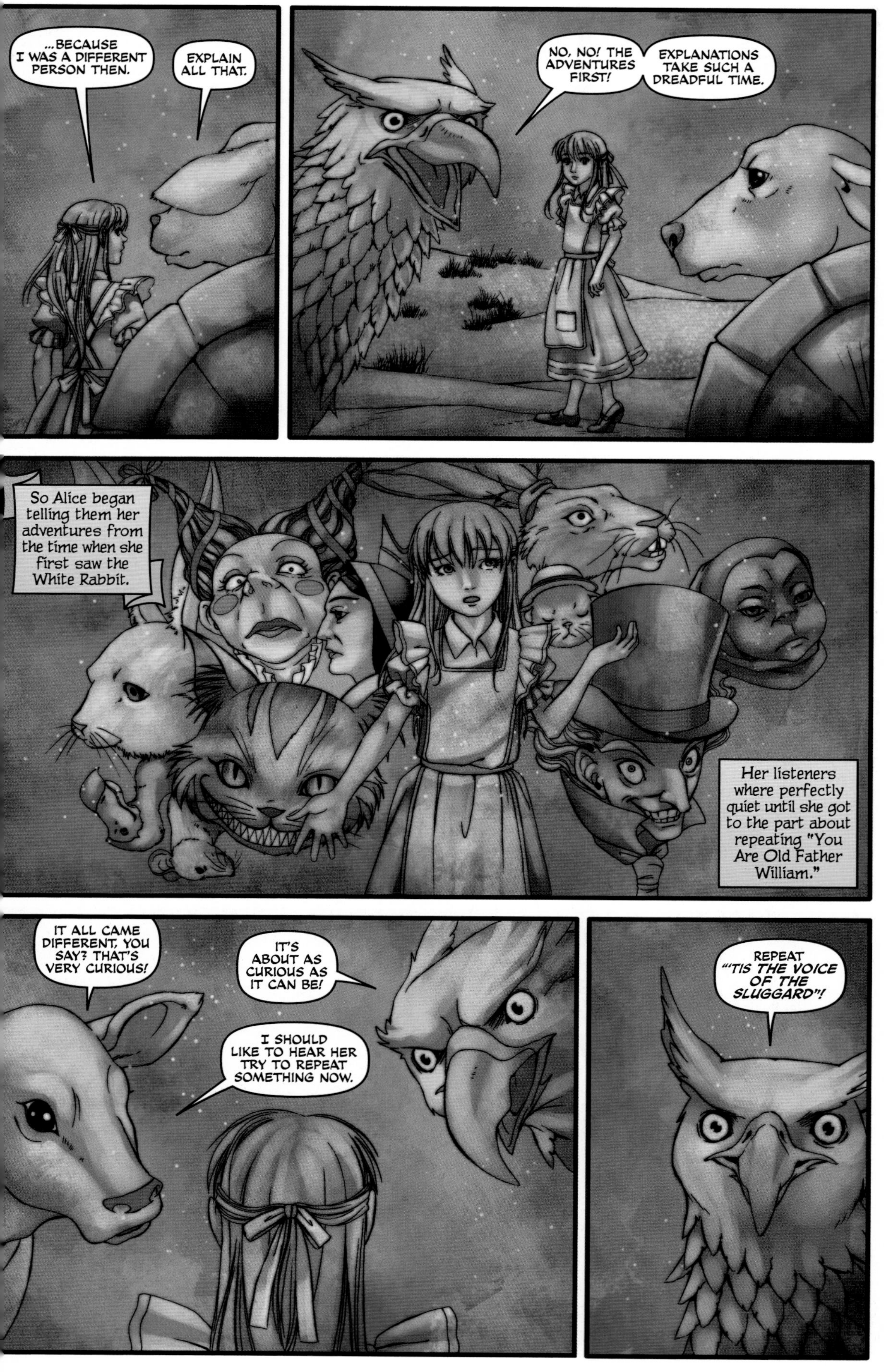
...BECAUSE I WAS A DIFFERENT PERSON THEN.
EXPLAIN ALL THAT.
NO, NO! THE ADVENTURES FIRST!
EXPLANATIONS TAKE SUCH A DREADFUL TIME.
So Alice began telling them her adventures from the time when she first saw the White Rabbit.
Her listeners where perfectly quiet until she got to the part about repeating "You Are Old Father William."
IT ALL CAME DIFFERENT, YOU SAY? THAT'S VERY CURIOUS!
IT'S ABOUT AS CURIOUS AS IT CAN BE!
I SHOULD LIKE TO HEAR HER TRY TO REPEAT SOMETHING NOW.
REPEAT "'TIS THE VOICE OF THE SLUGGARD"!

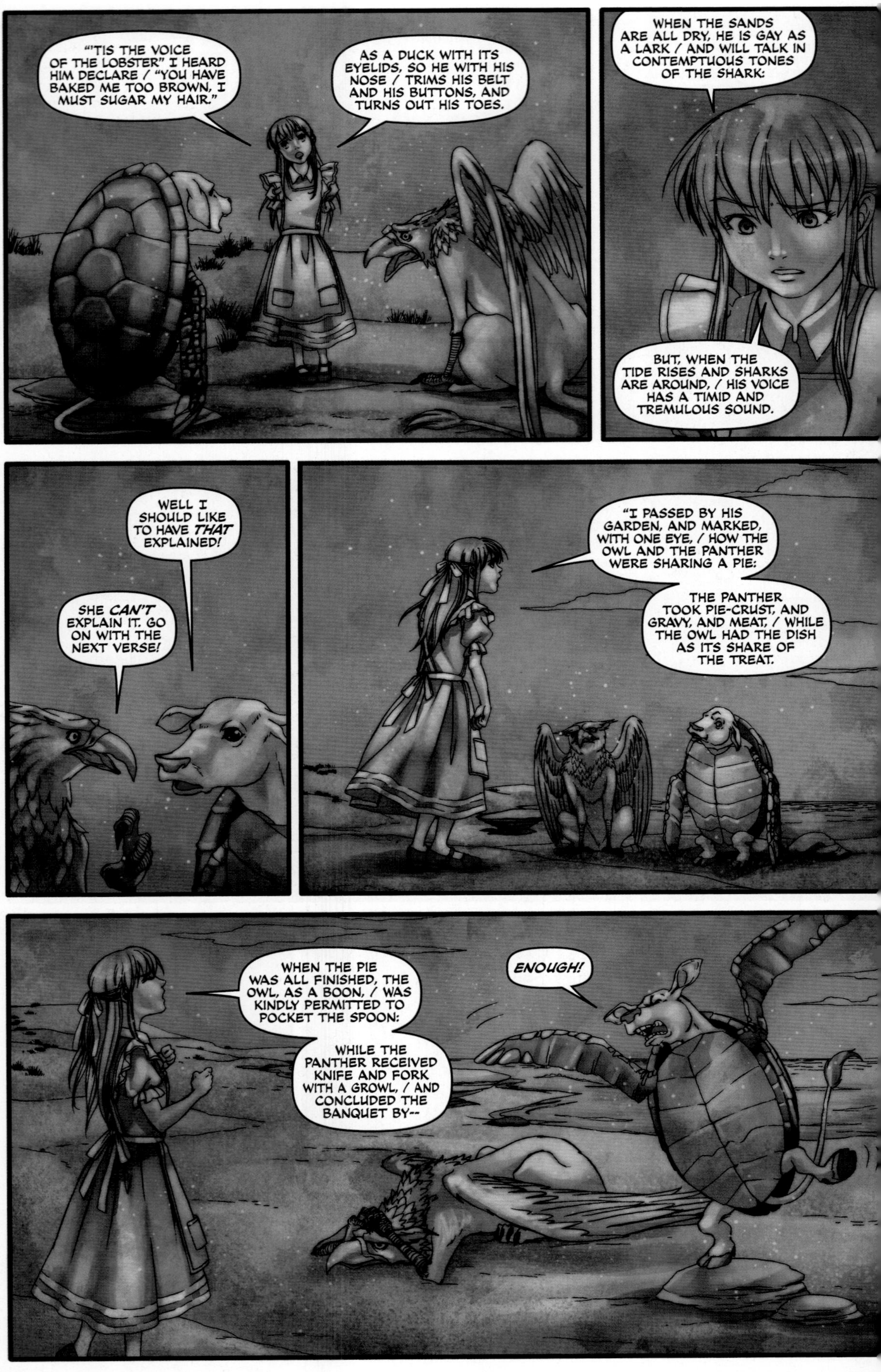
"'TIS THE VOICE OF THE LOBSTER" I HEARD HIM DECLARE / "YOU HAVE BAKED ME TOO BROWN, I MUST SUGAR MY HAIR."
AS A DUCK WITH ITS EYELIDS, SO HE WITH HIS NOSE / TRIMS HIS BELT AND HIS BUTTONS, AND TURNS OUT HIS TOES.
WHEN THE SANDS ARE ALL DRY, HE IS GAY AS A LARK / AND WILL TALK IN CONTEMPTUOUS TONES OF THE SHARK:
BUT, WHEN THE TIDE RISES AND SHARKS ARE AROUND, / HIS VOICE HAS A TIMID AND TREMULOUS SOUND.
WELL I SHOULD LIKE TO HAVE *THAT* EXPLAINED!
SHE *CAN'T* EXPLAIN IT. GO ON WITH THE NEXT VERSE!
"I PASSED BY HIS GARDEN, AND MARKED, WITH ONE EYE, / HOW THE OWL AND THE PANTHER WERE SHARING A PIE:
THE PANTHER TOOK PIE-CRUST, AND GRAVY, AND MEAT, / WHILE THE OWL HAD THE DISH AS ITS SHARE OF THE TREAT.
WHEN THE PIE WAS ALL FINISHED, THE OWL, AS A BOON, / WAS KINDLY PERMITTED TO POCKET THE SPOON:
WHILE THE PANTHER RECEIVED KNIFE AND FORK WITH A GROWL, / AND CONCLUDED THE BANQUET BY--
ENOUGH!

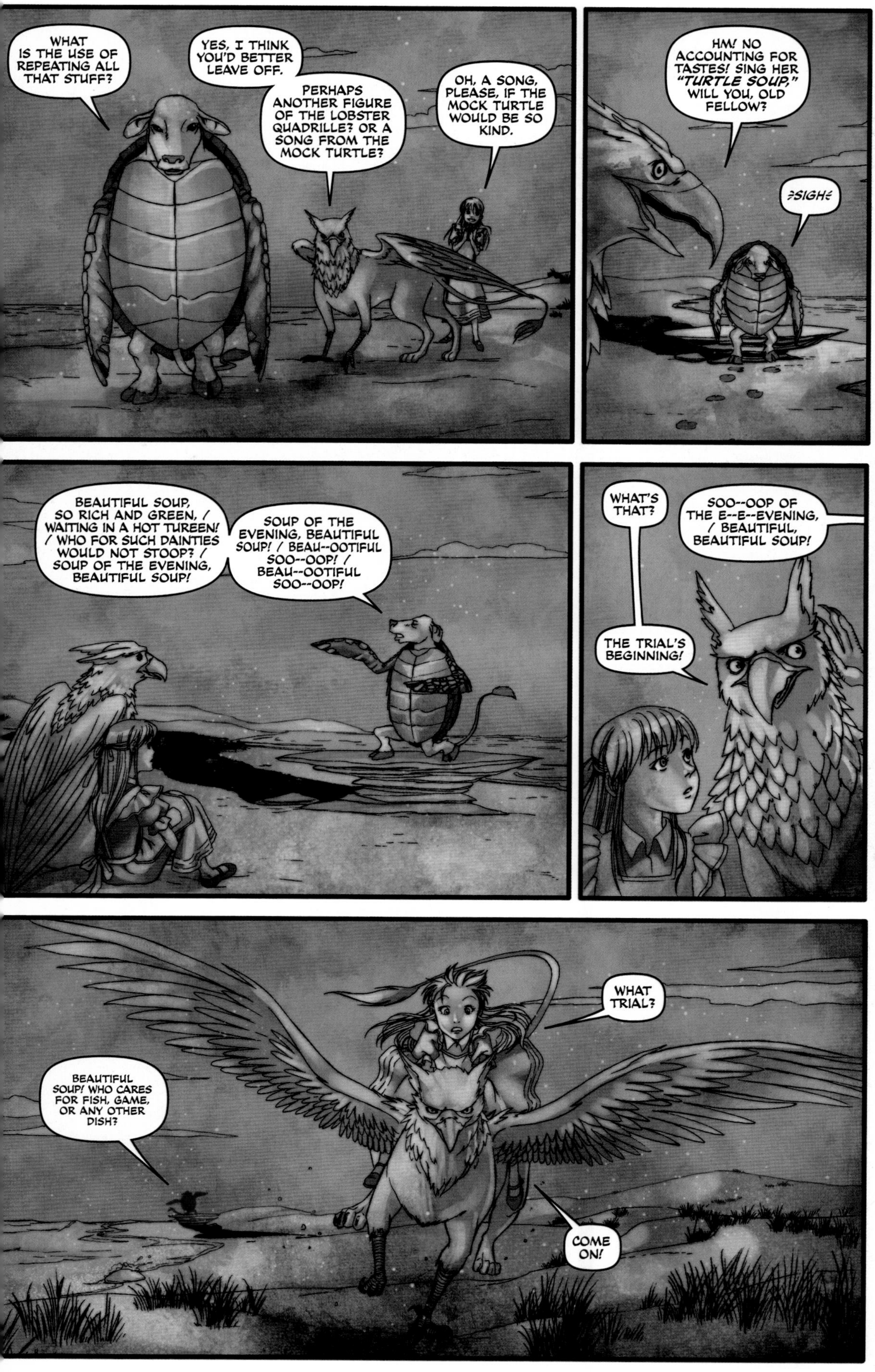
WHAT IS THE USE OF REPEATING ALL THAT STUFF?
YES, I THINK YOU'D BETTER LEAVE OFF.
PERHAPS ANOTHER FIGURE OF THE LOBSTER QUADRILLE? OR A SONG FROM THE MOCK TURTLE?
OH, A SONG, PLEASE, IF THE MOCK TURTLE WOULD BE SO KIND.
HM! NO ACCOUNTING FOR TASTES! SING HER "TURTLE SOUP," WILL YOU, OLD FELLOW?
SIGH
BEAUTIFUL SOUP, SO RICH AND GREEN, / WAITING IN A HOT TUREEN! / WHO FOR SUCH DAINTIES WOULD NOT STOOP? / SOUP OF THE EVENING, BEAUTIFUL SOUP!
SOUP OF THE EVENING, BEAUTIFUL SOUP! / BEAU--OOTIFUL SOO--OOP! / BEAU--OOTIFUL SOO--OOP!
WHAT'S THAT?
SOO--OOP OF THE E--E--EVENING, / BEAUTIFUL, BEAUTIFUL SOUP!
THE TRIAL'S BEGINNING!
WHAT TRIAL?
BEAUTIFUL SOUP! WHO CARES FOR FISH, GAME, OR ANY OTHER DISH?
COME ON!

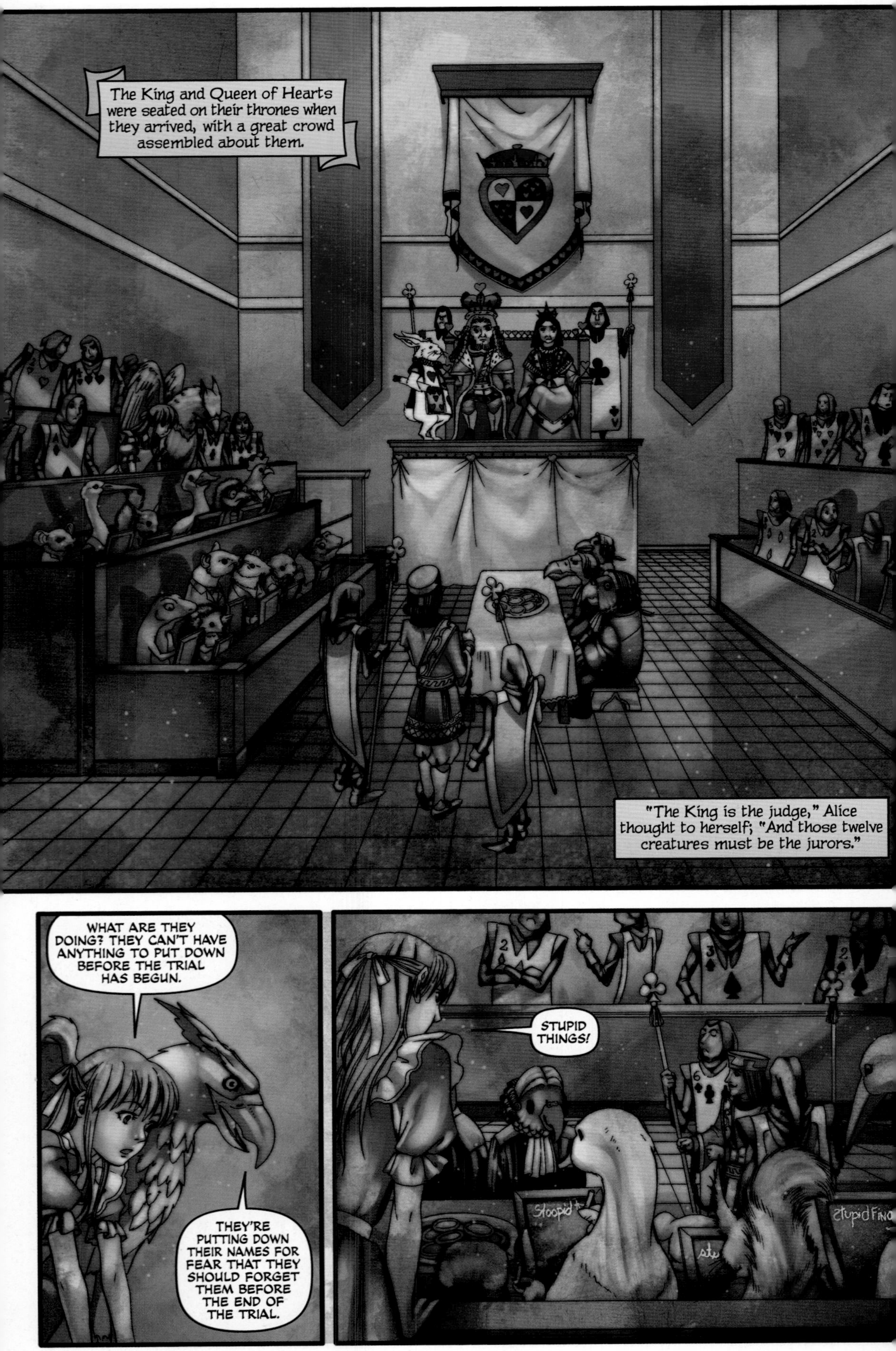

The King and Queen of Hearts were seated on their thrones when they arrived, with a great crowd assembled about them.
"The King is the judge," Alice thought to herself; "And those twelve creatures must be the jurors."
WHAT ARE THEY DOING? THEY CAN'T HAVE ANYTHING TO PUT DOWN BEFORE THE TRIAL HAS BEGUN.
THEY'RE PUTTING DOWN THEIR NAMES FOR FEAR THAT THEY SHOULD FORGET THEM BEFORE THE END OF THE TRIAL.
STUPID THINGS!

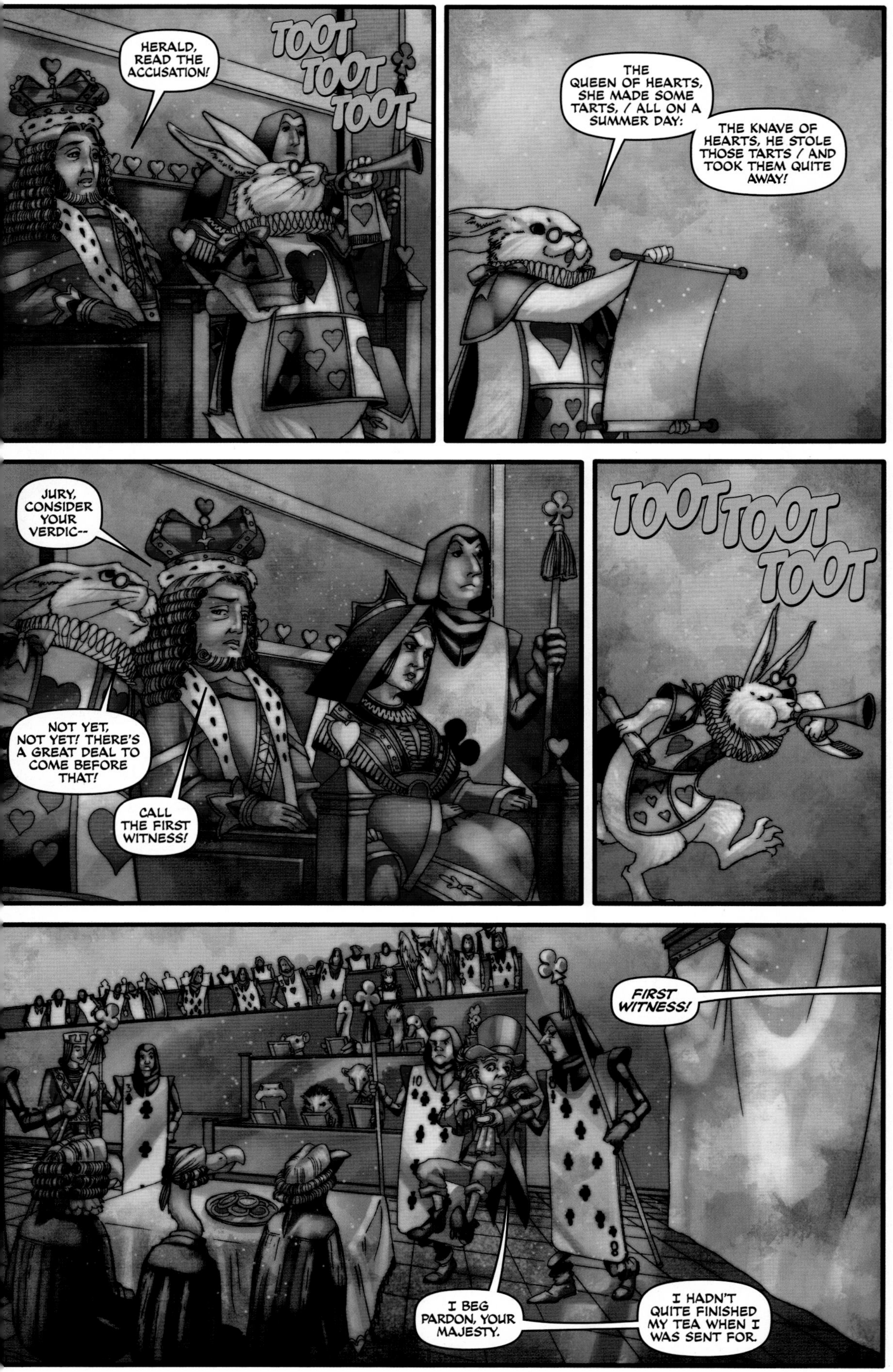
HERALD, READ THE ACCUSATION!
TOOT TOOT TOOT
THE QUEEN OF HEARTS, SHE MADE SOME TARTS, / ALL ON A SUMMER DAY:
THE KNAVE OF HEARTS, HE STOLE THOSE TARTS / AND TOOK THEM QUITE AWAY!
JURY, CONSIDER YOUR VERDIC--
NOT YET, NOT YET! THERE'S A GREAT DEAL TO COME BEFORE THAT!
CALL THE FIRST WITNESS!
TOOT TOOT TOOT
FIRST WITNESS!
I BEG PARDON, YOUR MAJESTY.
I HADN'T QUITE FINISHED MY TEA WHEN I WAS SENT FOR.

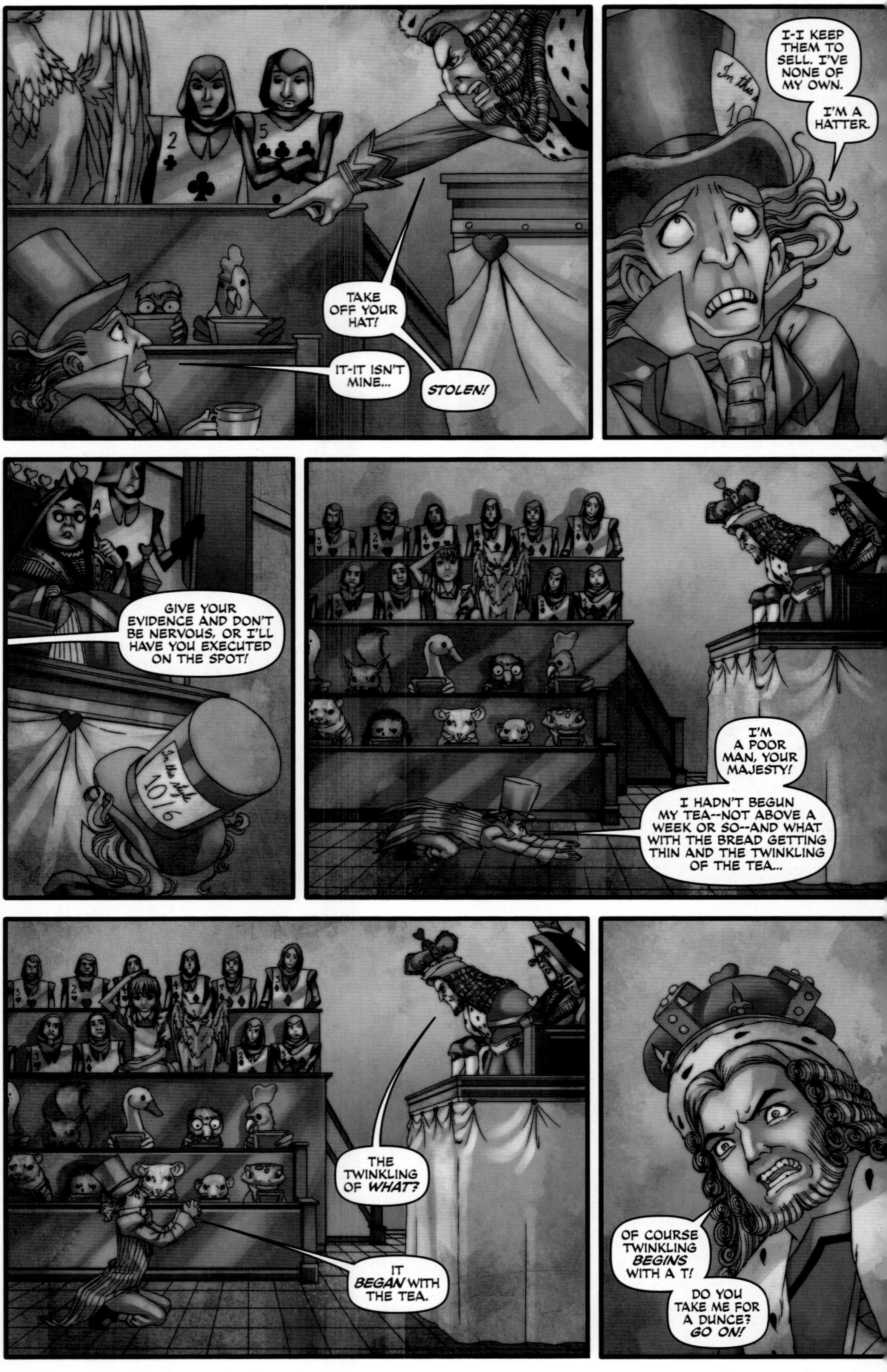
TAKE OFF YOUR HAT!
IT-IT ISN'T MINE...
STOLEN!
I-I KEEP THEM TO SELL. I'VE NONE OF MY OWN.
I'M A HATTER.
GIVE YOUR EVIDENCE AND DON'T BE NERVOUS, OR I'LL HAVE YOU EXECUTED ON THE SPOT!
I'M A POOR MAN, YOUR MAJESTY!
I HADN'T BEGUN MY TEA--NOT ABOVE A WEEK OR SO--AND WHAT WITH THE BREAD GETTING THIN AND THE TWINKLING OF THE TEA...
THE TWINKLING OF WHAT?
IT BEGAN WITH THE TEA.
OF COURSE TWINKLING BEGINS WITH A T!
DO YOU TAKE ME FOR A DUNCE? GO ON!

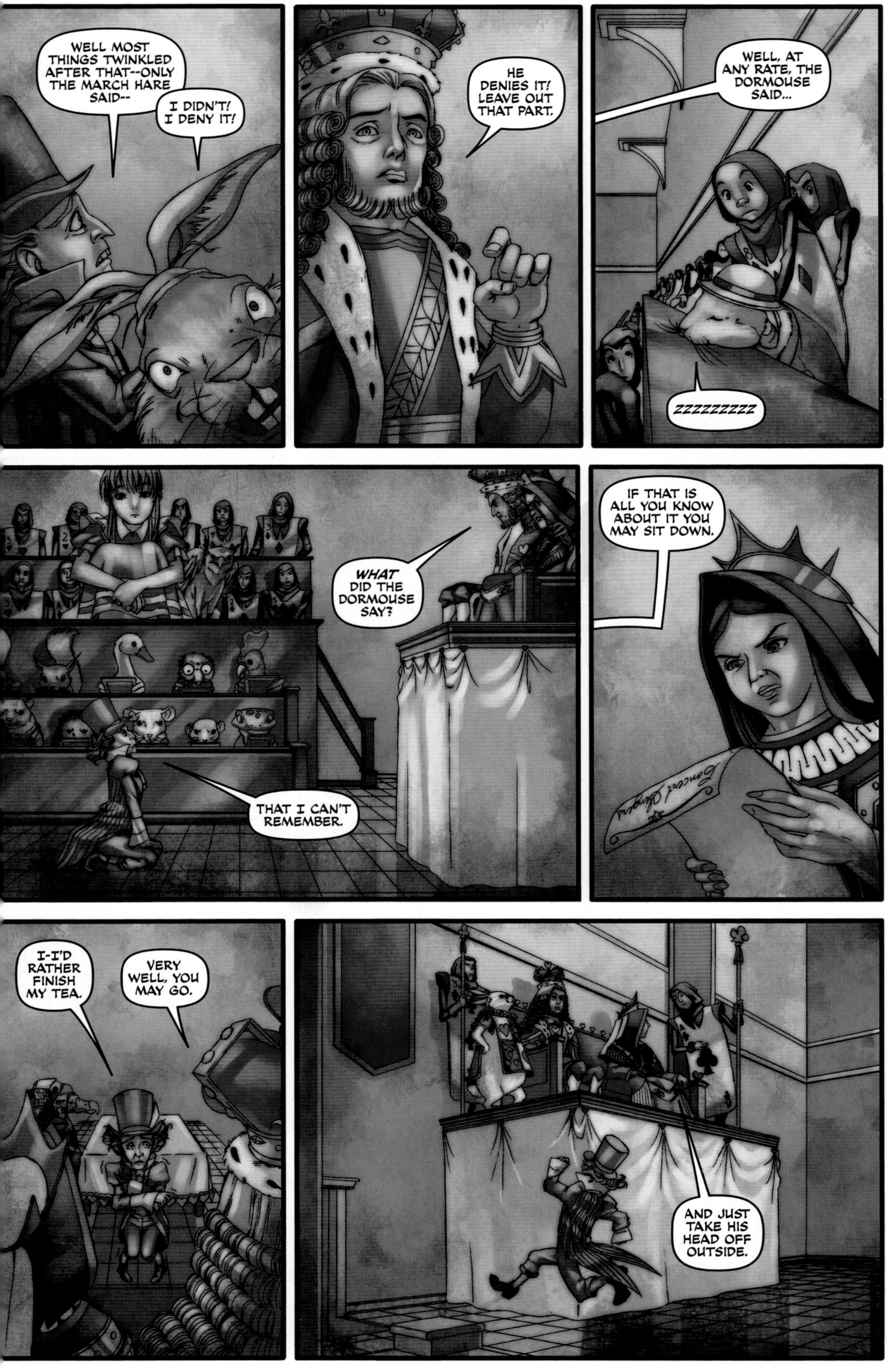
WELL MOST THINGS TWINKLED AFTER THAT--ONLY THE MARCH HARE SAID--
I DIDN'T! I DENY IT!
HE DENIES IT! LEAVE OUT THAT PART.
WELL, AT ANY RATE, THE DORMOUSE SAID...
ZZZZZZZZZ
WHAT DID THE DORMOUSE SAY?
THAT I CAN'T REMEMBER.
IF THAT IS ALL YOU KNOW ABOUT IT YOU MAY SIT DOWN.
I-I'D RATHER FINISH MY TEA.
VERY WELL, YOU MAY GO.
AND JUST TAKE HIS HEAD OFF OUTSIDE.

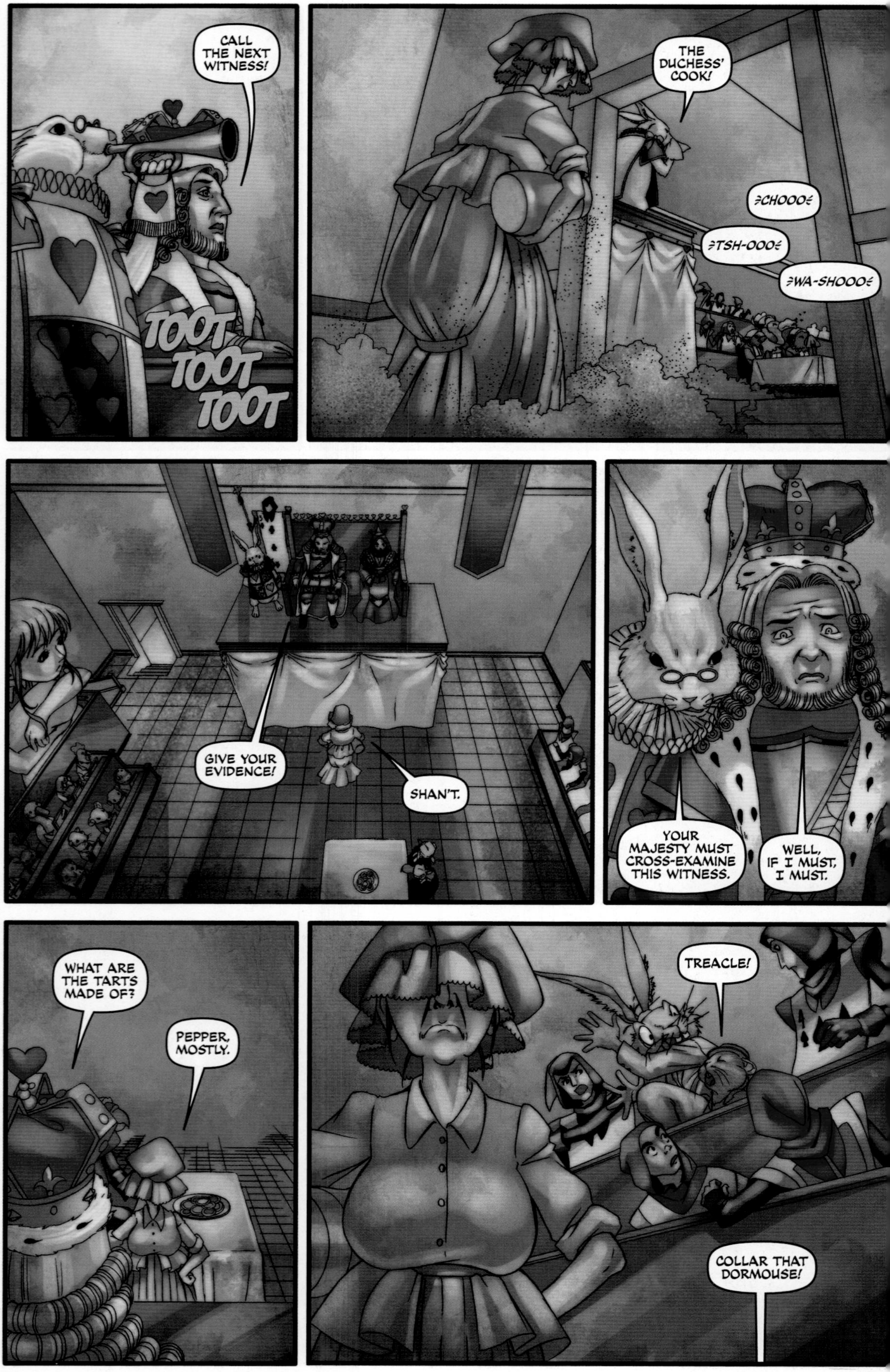
CALL THE NEXT WITNESS!
TOOT TOOT TOOT
THE DUCHESS' COOK!
CHOOO
TSH-OOO
WA-SHOOO
GIVE YOUR EVIDENCE!
SHAN'T.
YOUR MAJESTY MUST CROSS-EXAMINE THIS WITNESS.
WELL, IF I MUST, I MUST.
WHAT ARE THE TARTS MADE OF?
PEPPER, MOSTLY.
TREACLE!
COLLAR THAT DORMOUSE!

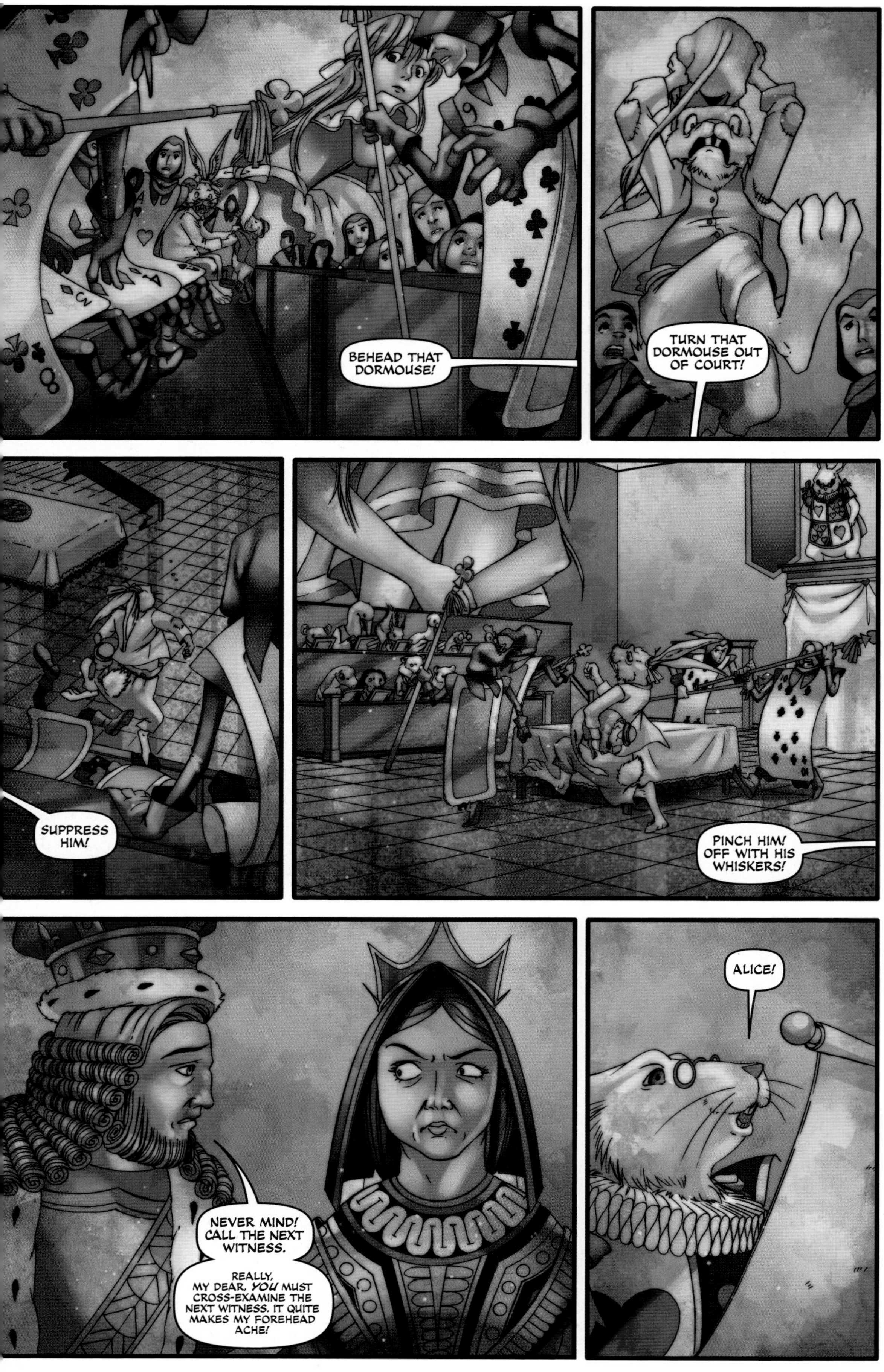
BEHEAD THAT DORMOUSE!
TURN THAT DORMOUSE OUT OF COURT!
SUPPRESS HIM!
PINCH HIM! OFF WITH HIS WHISKERS!
NEVER MIND! CALL THE NEXT WITNESS.
REALLY, MY DEAR, YOU MUST CROSS-EXAMINE THE NEXT WITNESS. IT QUITE MAKES MY FOREHEAD ACHE!
ALICE!

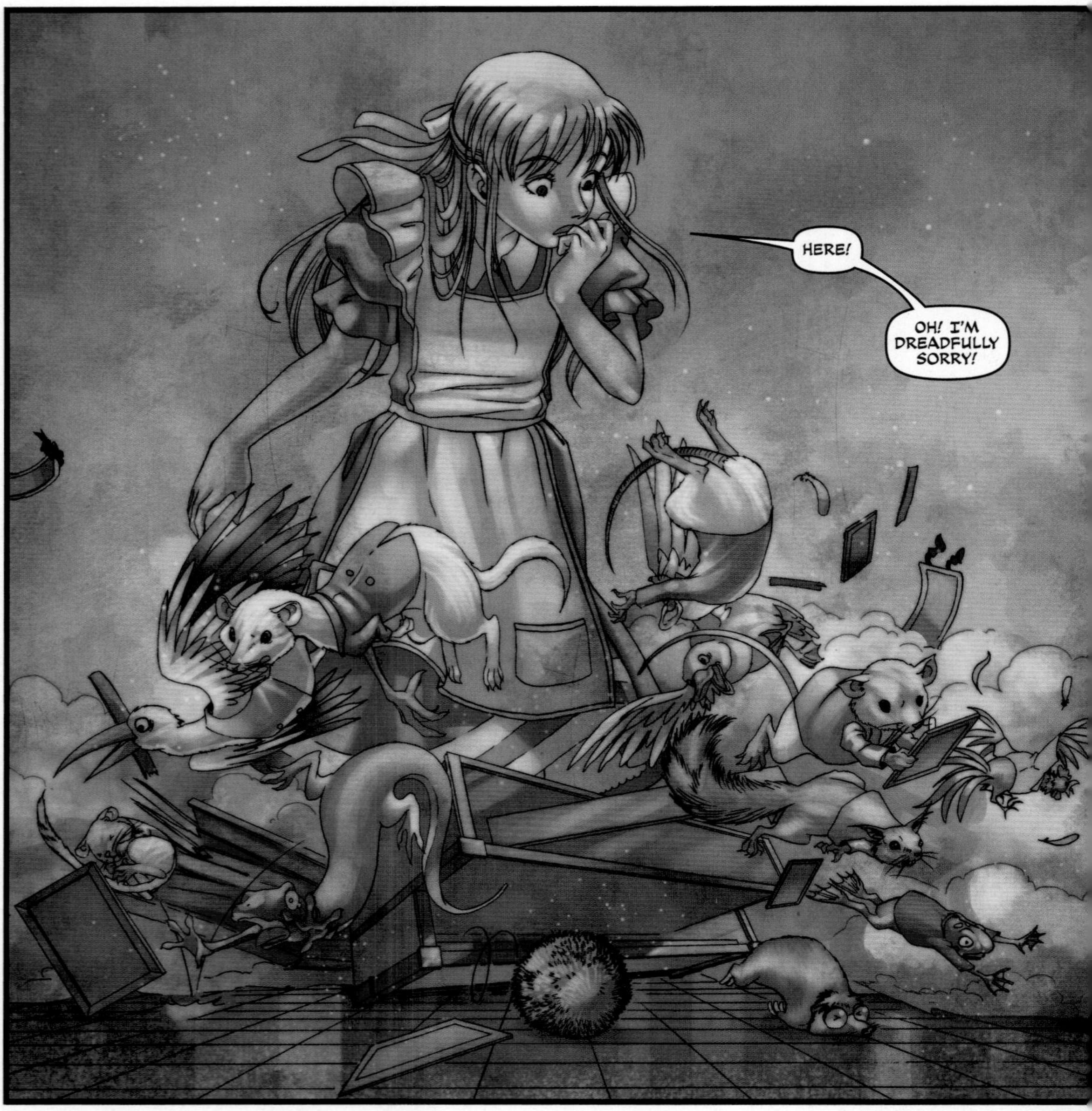
HERE!
OH! I'M DREADFULLY SORRY!

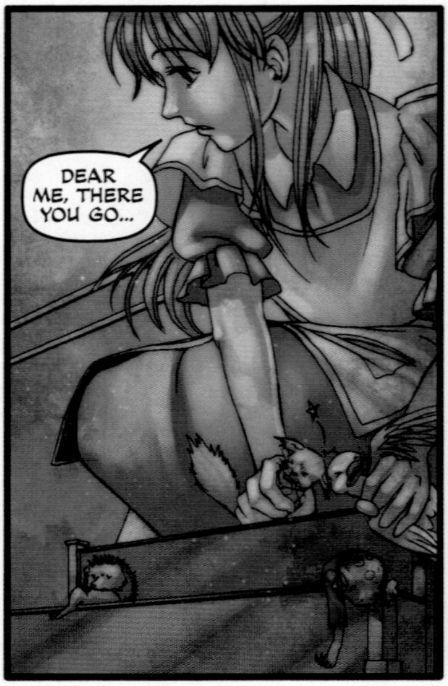
DEAR ME, THERE YOU GO...

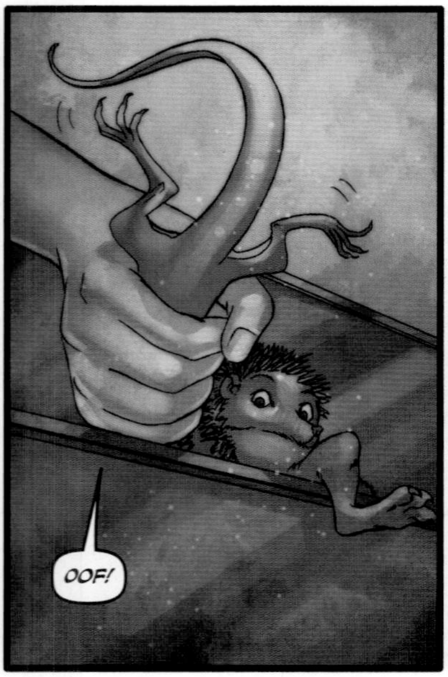
OOF!

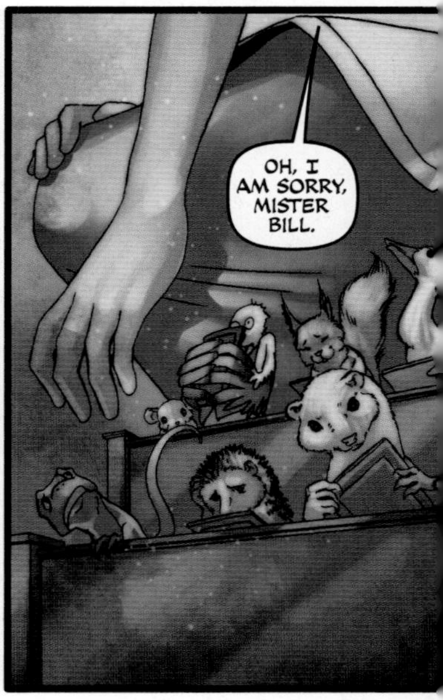
OH, I AM SORRY, MISTER BILL.

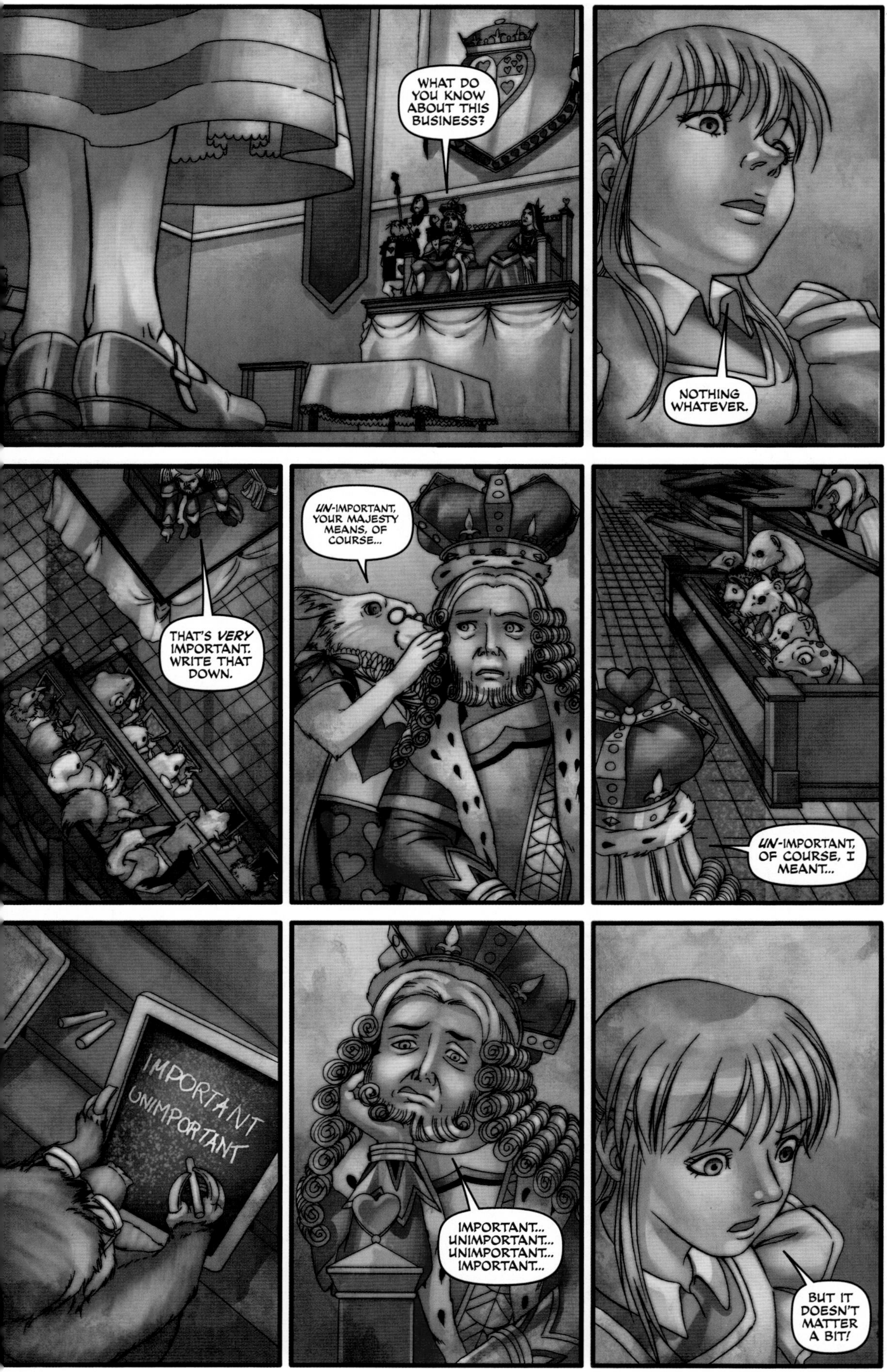
WHAT DO YOU KNOW ABOUT THIS BUSINESS?
NOTHING WHATEVER.
THAT'S VERY IMPORTANT. WRITE THAT DOWN.
UN-IMPORTANT, YOUR MAJESTY MEANS, OF COURSE...
UN-IMPORTANT, OF COURSE, I MEANT...
IMPORTANT
UNIMPORTANT
IMPORTANT... UNIMPORTANT... UNIMPORTANT... IMPORTANT...
BUT IT DOESN'T MATTER A BIT!

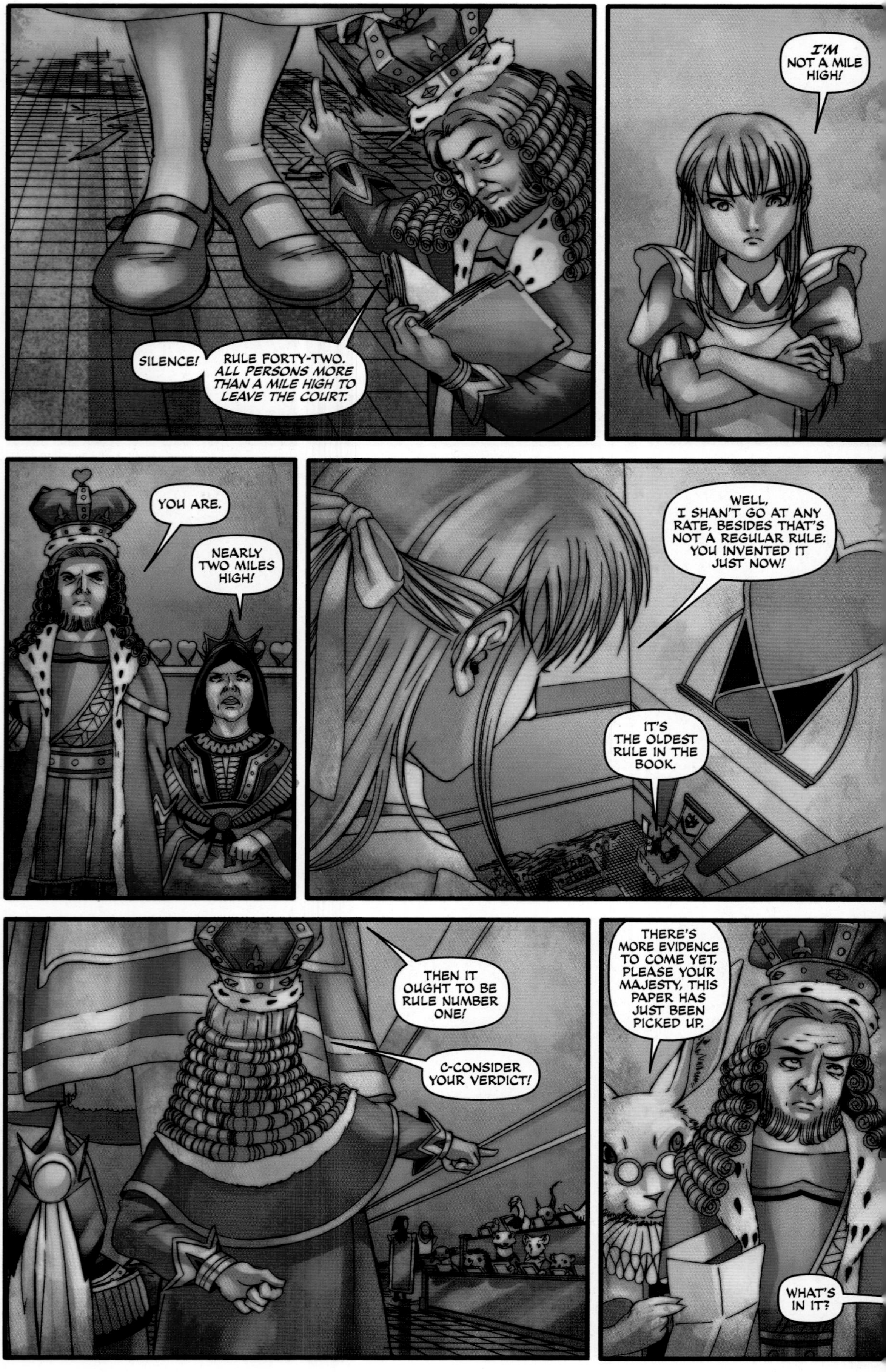
SILENCE!
RULE FORTY-TWO. ALL PERSONS MORE THAN A MILE HIGH TO LEAVE THE COURT.
I'M NOT A MILE HIGH!
YOU ARE.
NEARLY TWO MILES HIGH!
WELL, I SHAN'T GO AT ANY RATE, BESIDES THAT'S NOT A REGULAR RULE: YOU INVENTED IT JUST NOW!
IT'S THE OLDEST RULE IN THE BOOK.
THEN IT OUGHT TO BE RULE NUMBER ONE!
C-CONSIDER YOUR VERDICT!
THERE'S MORE EVIDENCE TO COME YET, PLEASE YOUR MAJESTY, THIS PAPER HAS JUST BEEN PICKED UP.
WHAT'S IN IT?

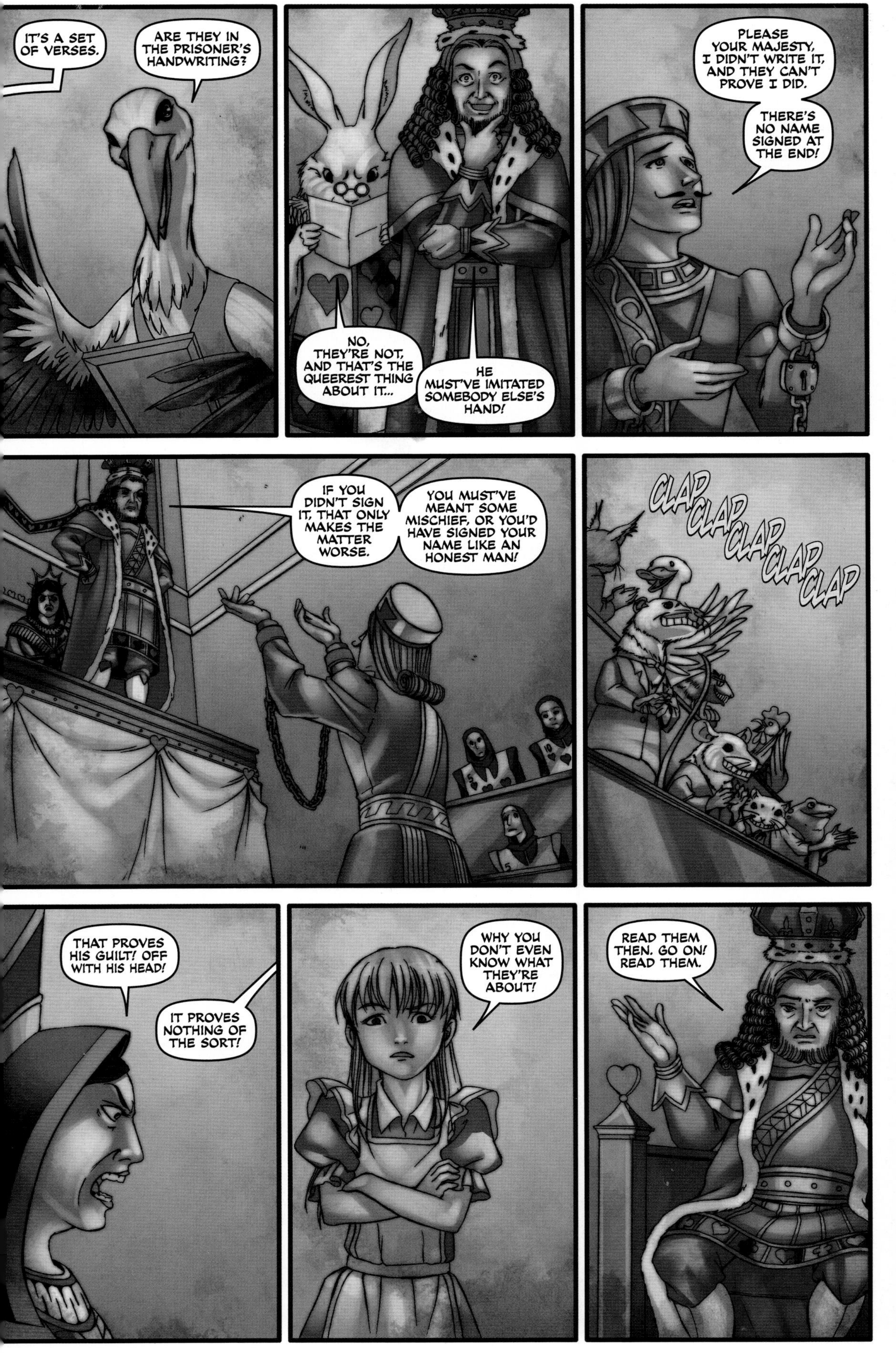
IT'S A SET OF VERSES.
ARE THEY IN THE PRISONER'S HANDWRITING?
NO, THEY'RE NOT, AND THAT'S THE QUEEREST THING ABOUT IT...
HE MUST'VE IMITATED SOMEBODY ELSE'S HAND!
PLEASE YOUR MAJESTY, I DIDN'T WRITE IT, AND THEY CAN'T PROVE I DID.
THERE'S NO NAME SIGNED AT THE END!
IF YOU DIDN'T SIGN IT, THAT ONLY MAKES THE MATTER WORSE.
YOU MUST'VE MEANT SOME MISCHIEF, OR YOU'D HAVE SIGNED YOUR NAME LIKE AN HONEST MAN!
CLAP CLAP CLAP CLAP CLAP
THAT PROVES HIS GUILT! OFF WITH HIS HEAD!
IT PROVES NOTHING OF THE SORT!
WHY YOU DON'T EVEN KNOW WHAT THEY'RE ABOUT!
READ THEM THEN. GO ON! READ THEM.

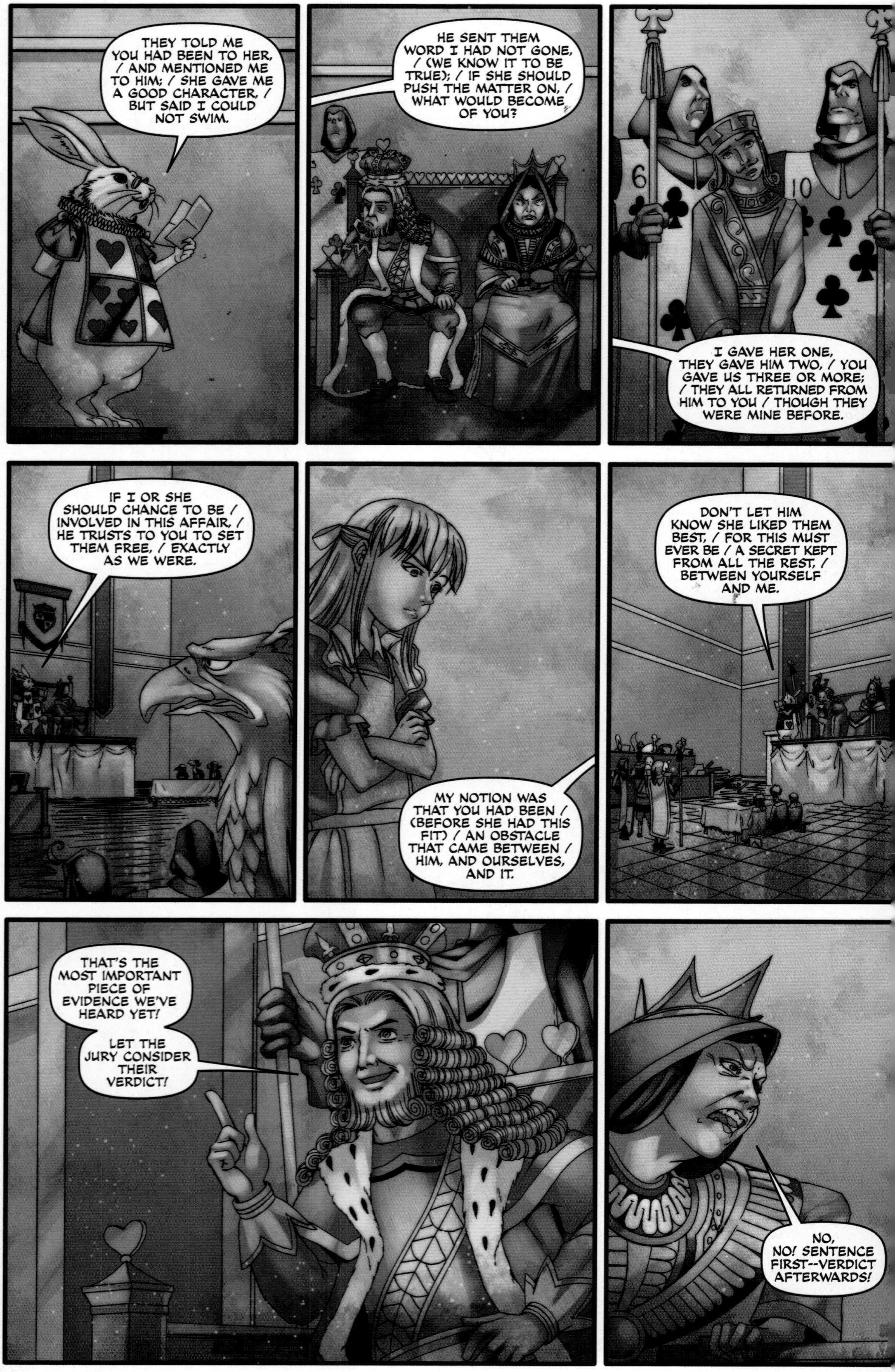
THEY TOLD ME YOU HAD BEEN TO HER, / AND MENTIONED ME TO HIM; / SHE GAVE ME A GOOD CHARACTER, / BUT SAID I COULD NOT SWIM.
HE SENT THEM WORD I HAD NOT GONE, / (WE KNOW IT TO BE TRUE); / IF SHE SHOULD PUSH THE MATTER ON, / WHAT WOULD BECOME OF YOU?
I GAVE HER ONE, THEY GAVE HIM TWO, / YOU GAVE US THREE OR MORE; / THEY ALL RETURNED FROM HIM TO YOU / THOUGH THEY WERE MINE BEFORE.
IF I OR SHE SHOULD CHANCE TO BE / INVOLVED IN THIS AFFAIR, / HE TRUSTS TO YOU TO SET THEM FREE, / EXACTLY AS WE WERE.
MY NOTION WAS THAT YOU HAD BEEN / (BEFORE SHE HAD THIS FIT) / AN OBSTACLE THAT CAME BETWEEN / HIM, AND OURSELVES, AND IT.
DON'T LET HIM KNOW SHE LIKED THEM BEST, / FOR THIS MUST EVER BE / A SECRET KEPT FROM ALL THE REST, / BETWEEN YOURSELF AND ME.
THAT'S THE MOST IMPORTANT PIECE OF EVIDENCE WE'VE HEARD YET!
LET THE JURY CONSIDER THEIR VERDICT!
NO, NO! SENTENCE FIRST--VERDICT AFTERWARDS!

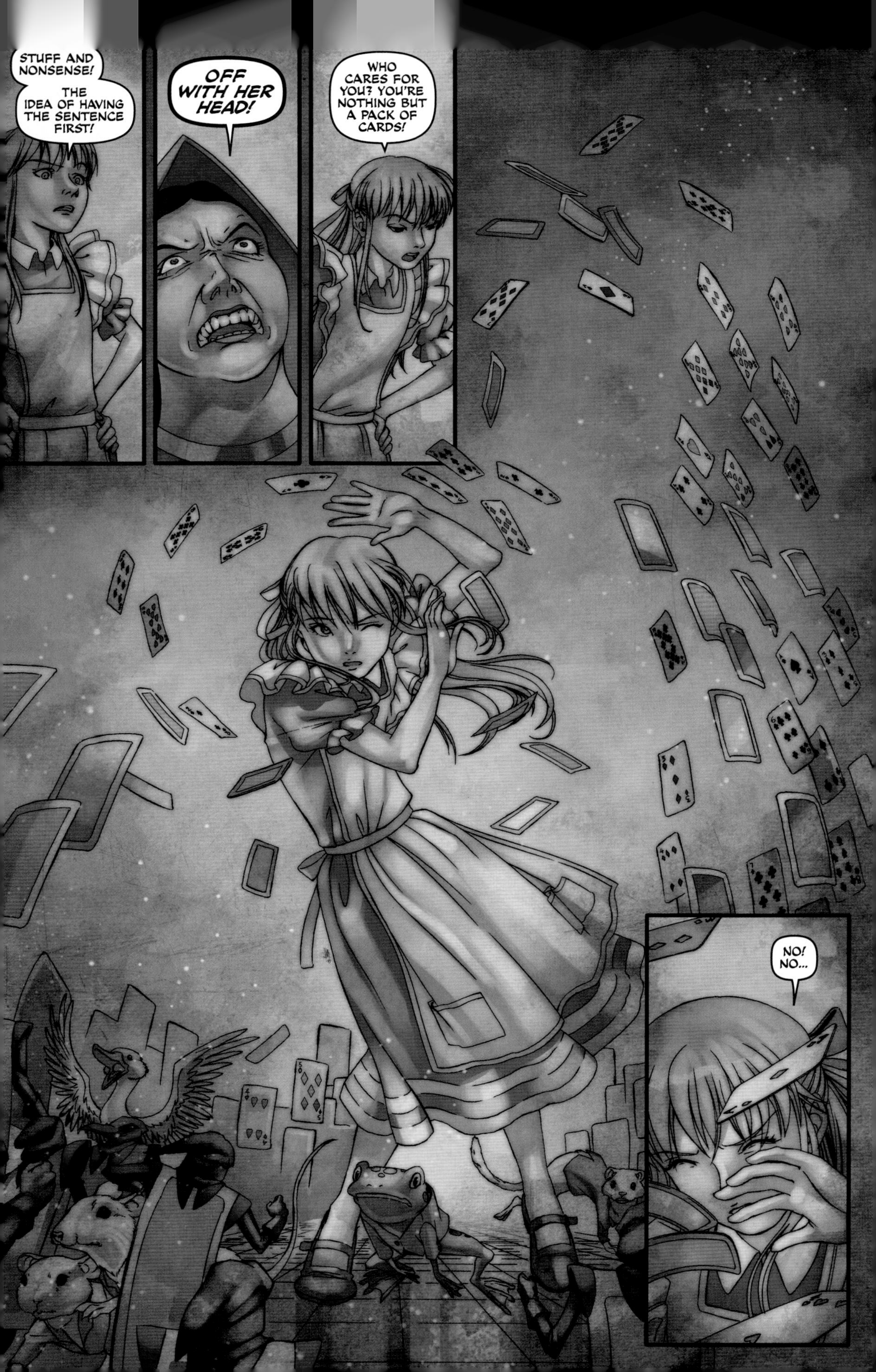
STUFF AND NONSENSE!
THE IDEA OF HAVING THE SENTENCE FIRST!
OFF WITH HER HEAD!
WHO CARES FOR YOU? YOU'RE NOTHING BUT A PACK OF CARDS!
NO! NO...

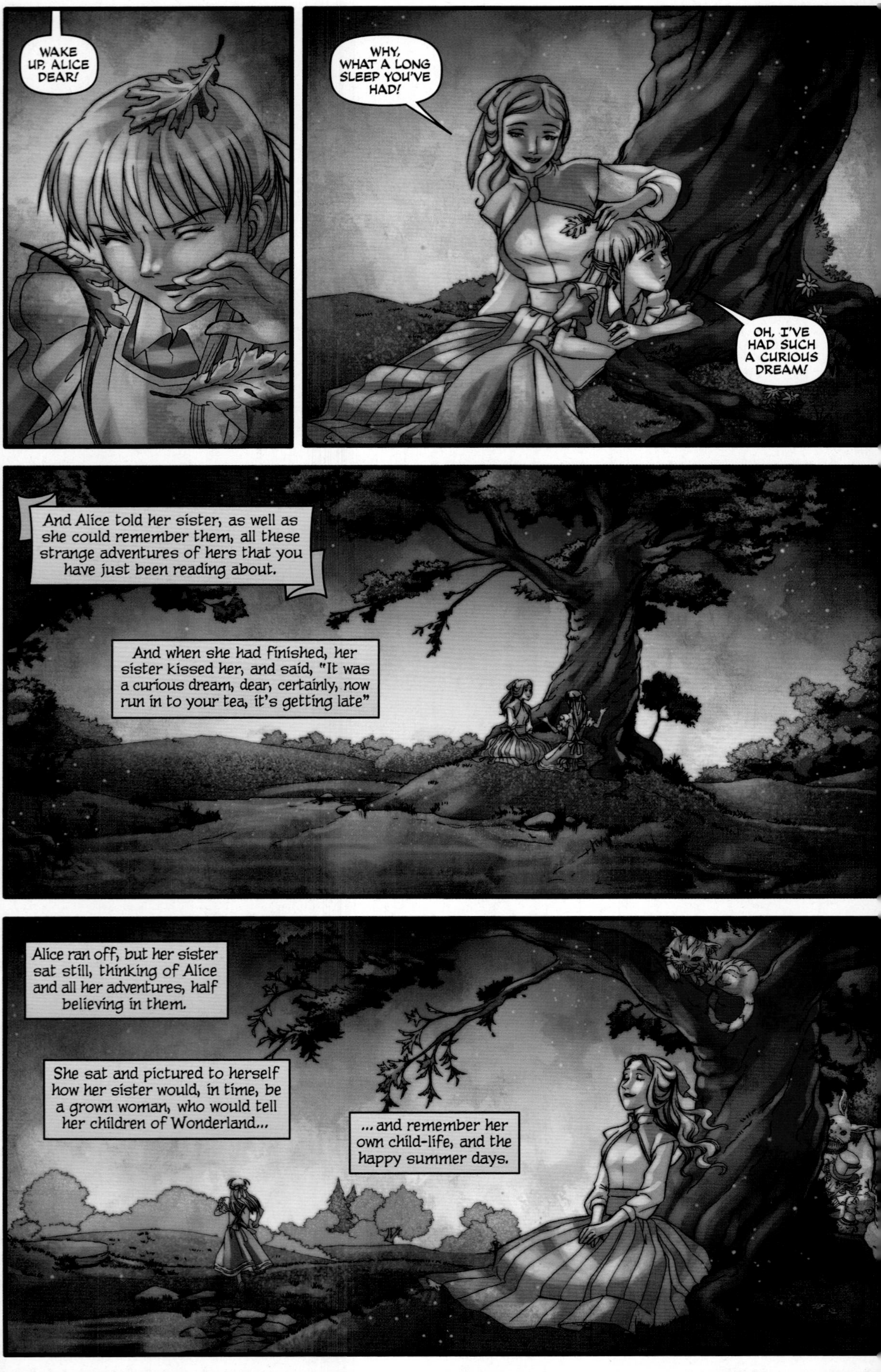
WAKE UP, ALICE DEAR!
WHY, WHAT A LONG SLEEP YOU'VE HAD!
OH, I'VE HAD SUCH A CURIOUS DREAM!
And Alice told her sister, as well as she could remember them, all these strange adventures of hers that you have just been reading about.
And when she had finished, her sister kissed her, and said, "It was a curious dream, dear, certainly, now run in to your tea, it's getting late"
Alice ran off, but her sister sat still, thinking of Alice and all her adventures, half believing in them.
She sat and pictured to herself how her sister would, in time, be a grown woman, who would tell her children of Wonderland...
...and remember her own child-life, and the happy summer days.

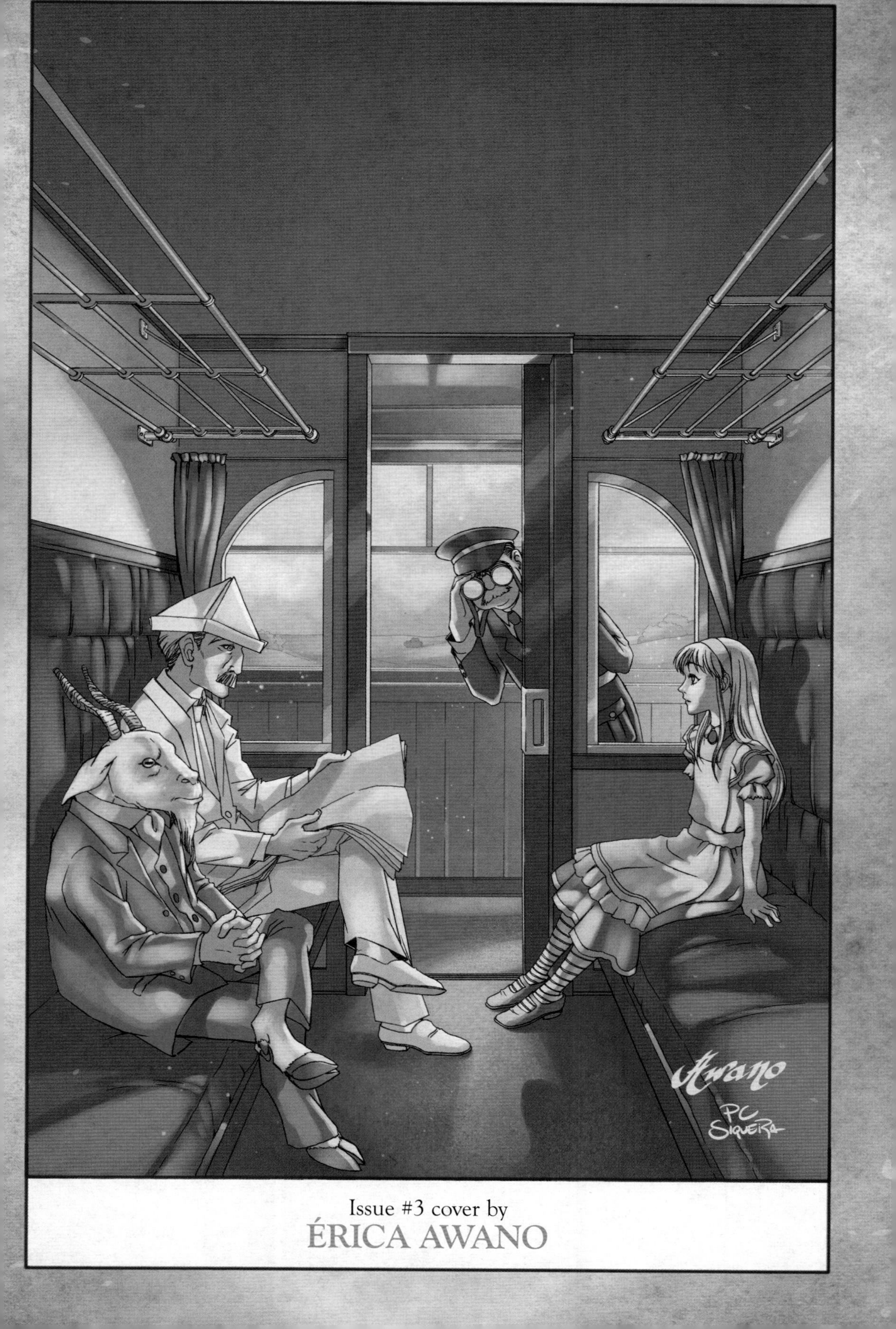
Awano
PC
Siqueira

Issue #3 cover by
ÉRICA AWANO

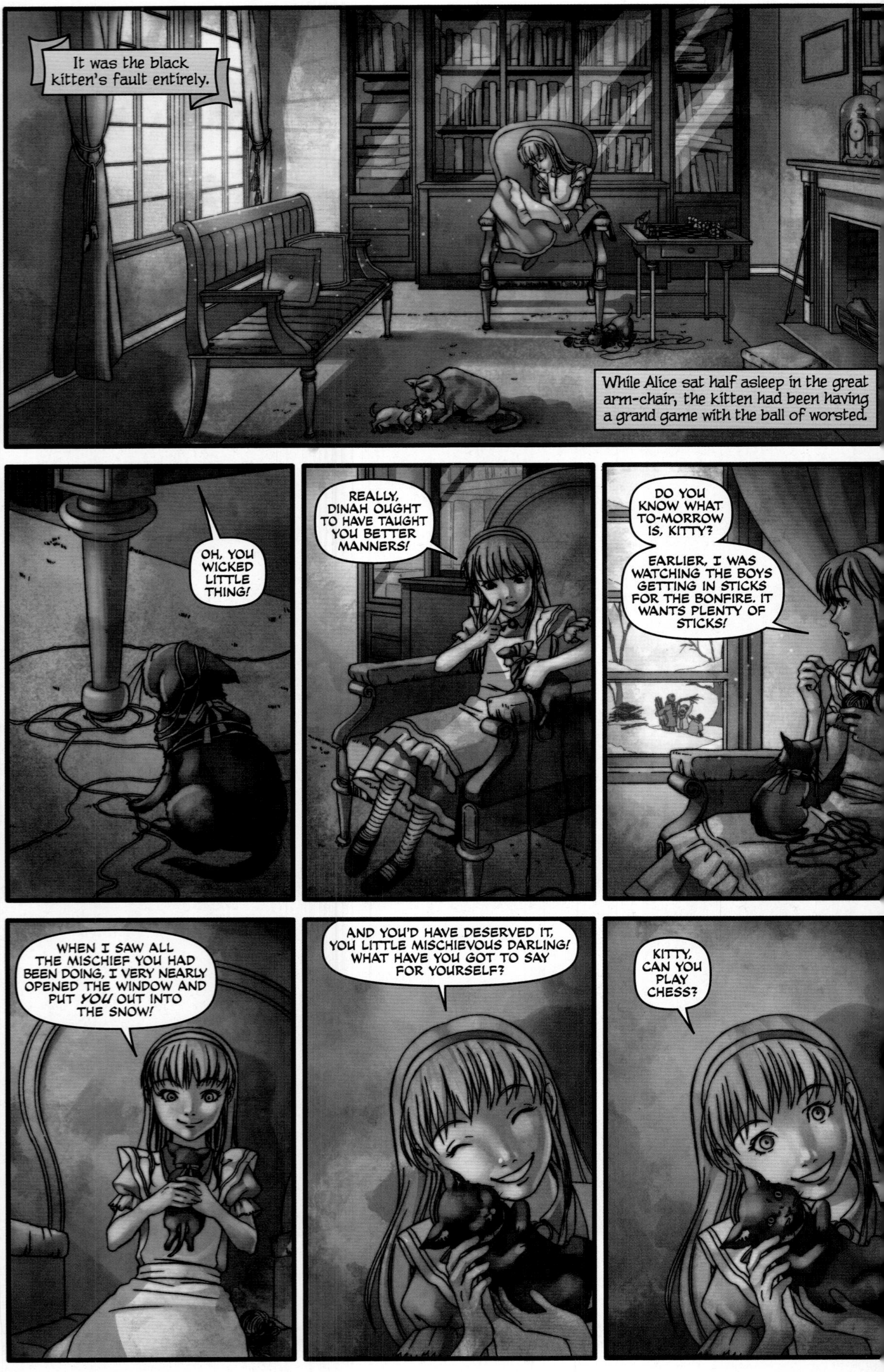
It was the black kitten's fault entirely.
While Alice sat half asleep in the great arm-chair, the kitten had been having a grand game with the ball of worsted.
OH, YOU WICKED LITTLE THING!
REALLY, DINAH OUGHT TO HAVE TAUGHT YOU BETTER MANNERS!
DO YOU KNOW WHAT TO-MORROW IS, KITTY?
EARLIER, I WAS WATCHING THE BOYS GETTING IN STICKS FOR THE BONFIRE. IT WANTS PLENTY OF STICKS!
WHEN I SAW ALL THE MISCHIEF YOU HAD BEEN DOING, I VERY NEARLY OPENED THE WINDOW AND PUT YOU OUT INTO THE SNOW!
AND YOU'D HAVE DESERVED IT, YOU LITTLE MISCHIEVOUS DARLING! WHAT HAVE YOU GOT TO SAY FOR YOURSELF?
KITTY, CAN YOU PLAY CHESS?

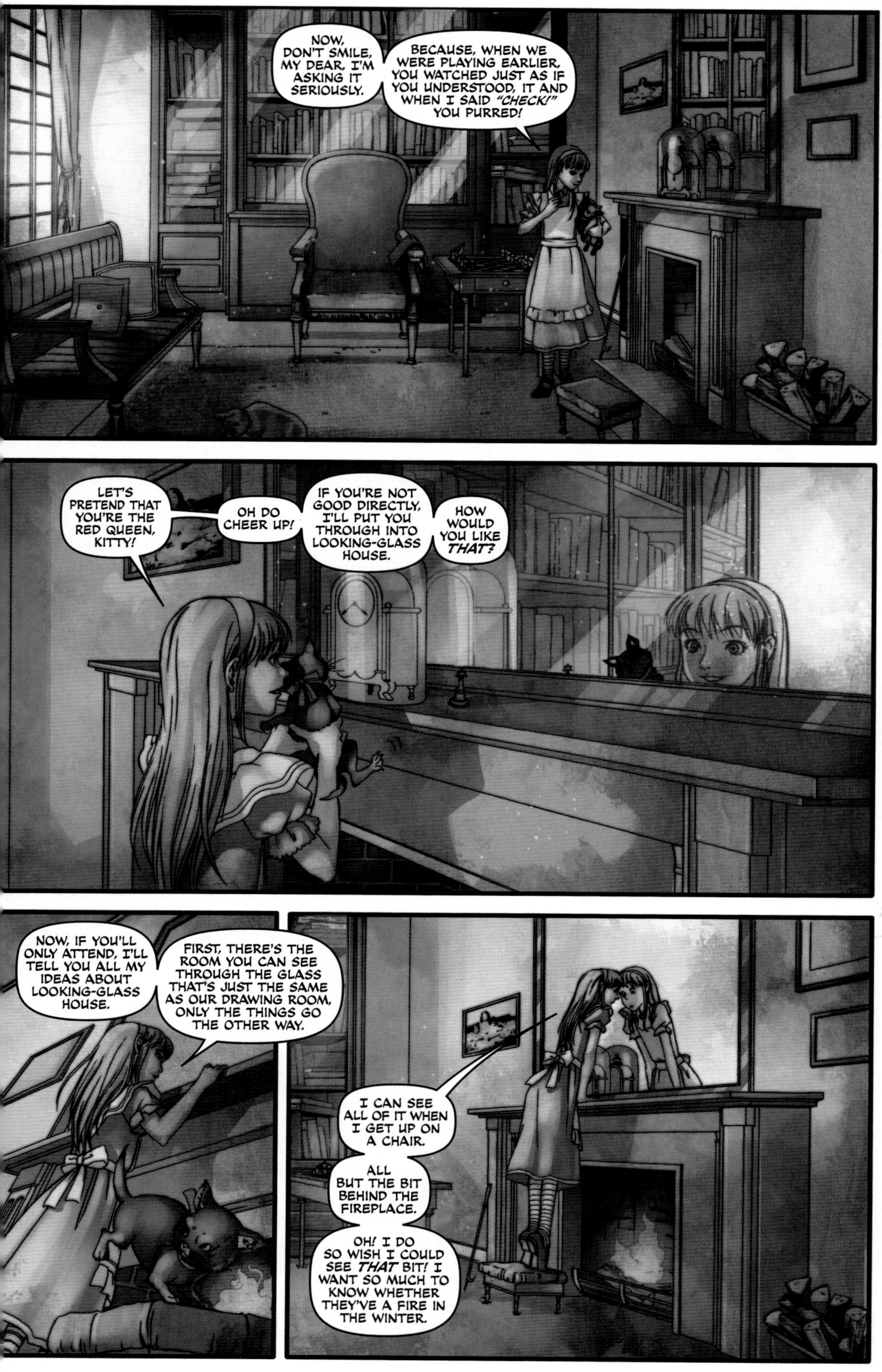
NOW, DON'T SMILE, MY DEAR, I'M ASKING IT SERIOUSLY.
BECAUSE, WHEN WE WERE PLAYING EARLIER, YOU WATCHED JUST AS IF YOU UNDERSTOOD, IT AND WHEN I SAID "CHECK!" YOU PURRED!
LET'S PRETEND THAT YOU'RE THE RED QUEEN, KITTY!
OH DO CHEER UP!
IF YOU'RE NOT GOOD DIRECTLY, I'LL PUT YOU THROUGH INTO LOOKING-GLASS HOUSE.
HOW WOULD YOU LIKE *THAT*?
NOW, IF YOU'LL ONLY ATTEND, I'LL TELL YOU ALL MY IDEAS ABOUT LOOKING-GLASS HOUSE.
FIRST, THERE'S THE ROOM YOU CAN SEE THROUGH THE GLASS THAT'S JUST THE SAME AS OUR DRAWING ROOM, ONLY THE THINGS GO THE OTHER WAY.
I CAN SEE ALL OF IT WHEN I GET UP ON A CHAIR.
ALL BUT THE BIT BEHIND THE FIREPLACE.
OH! I DO SO WISH I COULD SEE *THAT* BIT! I WANT SO MUCH TO KNOW WHETHER THEY'VE A FIRE IN THE WINTER.

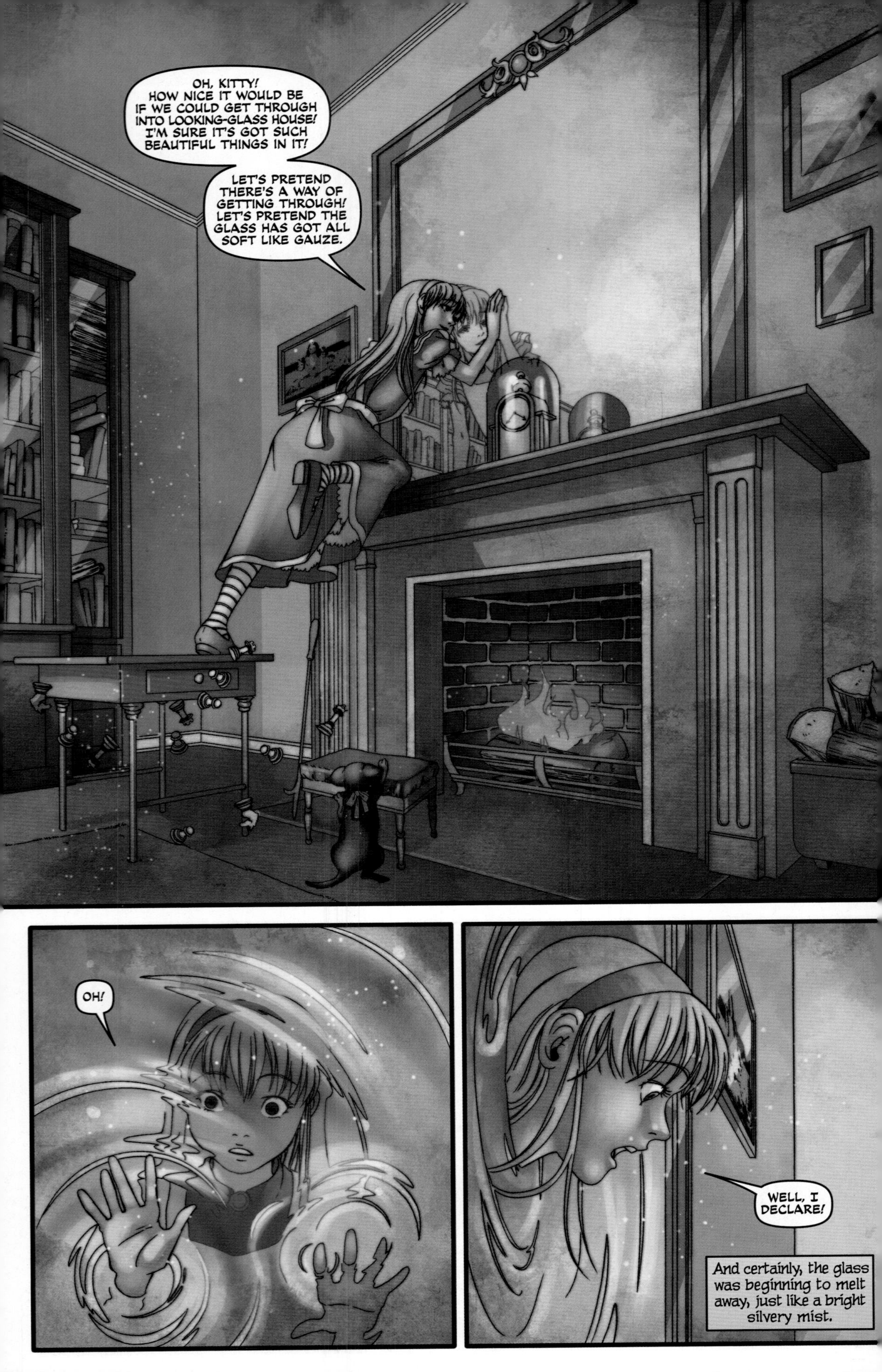
OH, KITTY! HOW NICE IT WOULD BE IF WE COULD GET THROUGH INTO LOOKING-GLASS HOUSE! I'M SURE IT'S GOT SUCH BEAUTIFUL THINGS IN IT!
LET'S PRETEND THERE'S A WAY OF GETTING THROUGH! LET'S PRETEND THE GLASS HAS GOT ALL SOFT LIKE GAUZE.
OH!
WELL, I DECLARE!
And certainly, the glass was beginning to melt away, just like a bright silvery mist.

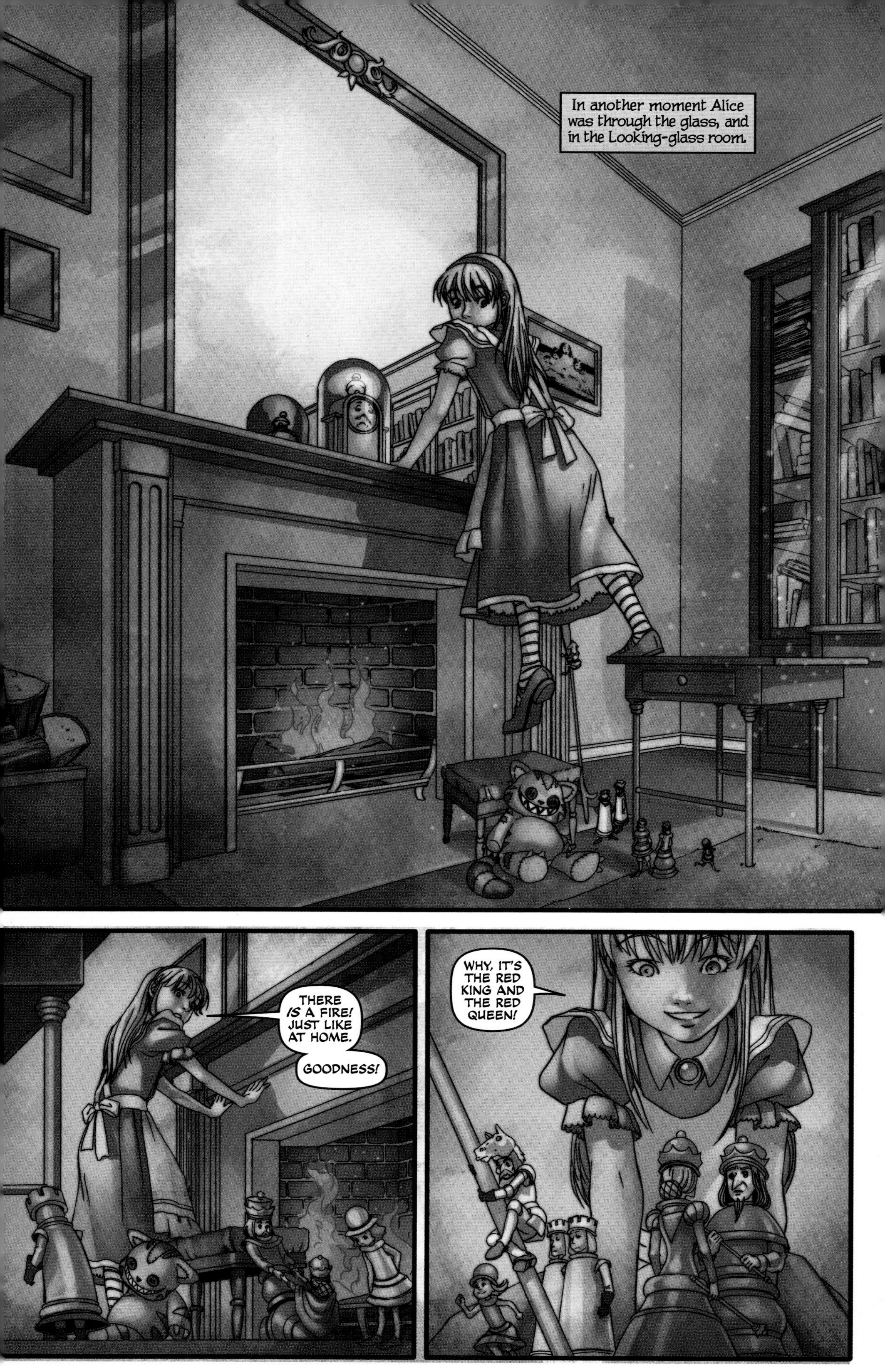
In another moment Alice was through the glass, and in the Looking-glass room.
THERE *IS* A FIRE! JUST LIKE AT HOME.
GOODNESS!
WHY, IT'S THE RED KING AND THE RED QUEEN!

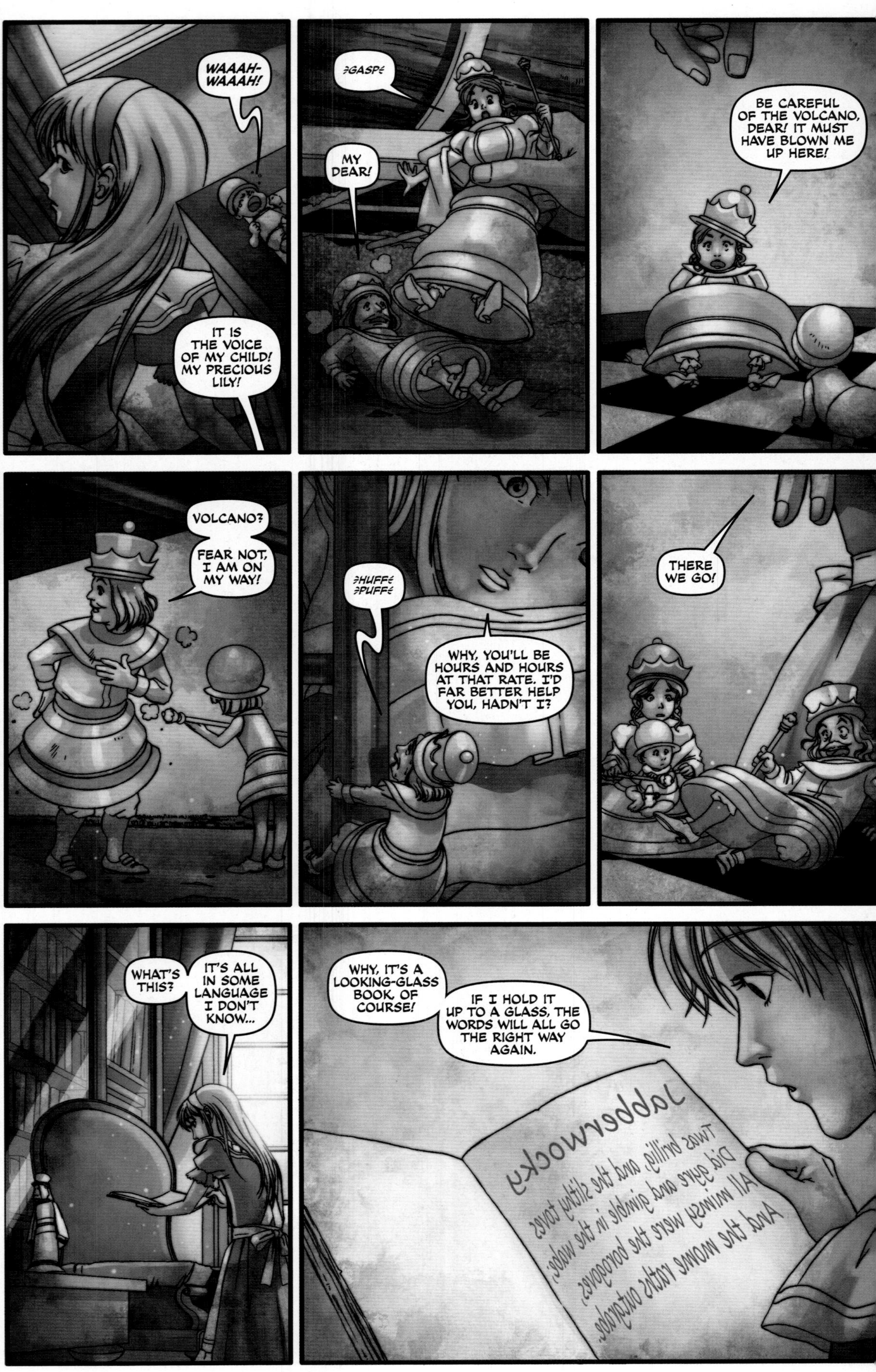
WAAAH-WAAAH!
IT IS THE VOICE OF MY CHILD! MY PRECIOUS LILY!
GASP
MY DEAR!
BE CAREFUL OF THE VOLCANO, DEAR! IT MUST HAVE BLOWN ME UP HERE!
VOLCANO?
FEAR NOT, I AM ON MY WAY!
HUFF PUFF
WHY, YOU'LL BE HOURS AND HOURS AT THAT RATE. I'D FAR BETTER HELP YOU, HADN'T I?
THERE WE GO!
WHAT'S THIS?
IT'S ALL IN SOME LANGUAGE I DON'T KNOW...
WHY, IT'S A LOOKING-GLASS BOOK, OF COURSE!
IF I HOLD IT UP TO A GLASS, THE WORDS WILL ALL GO THE RIGHT WAY AGAIN.
Jabberwocky
Twas brillig, and the slithy toves
Did gyre and gimble in the wabe;
All mimsy were the borogoves,
And the mome raths outgrabe.

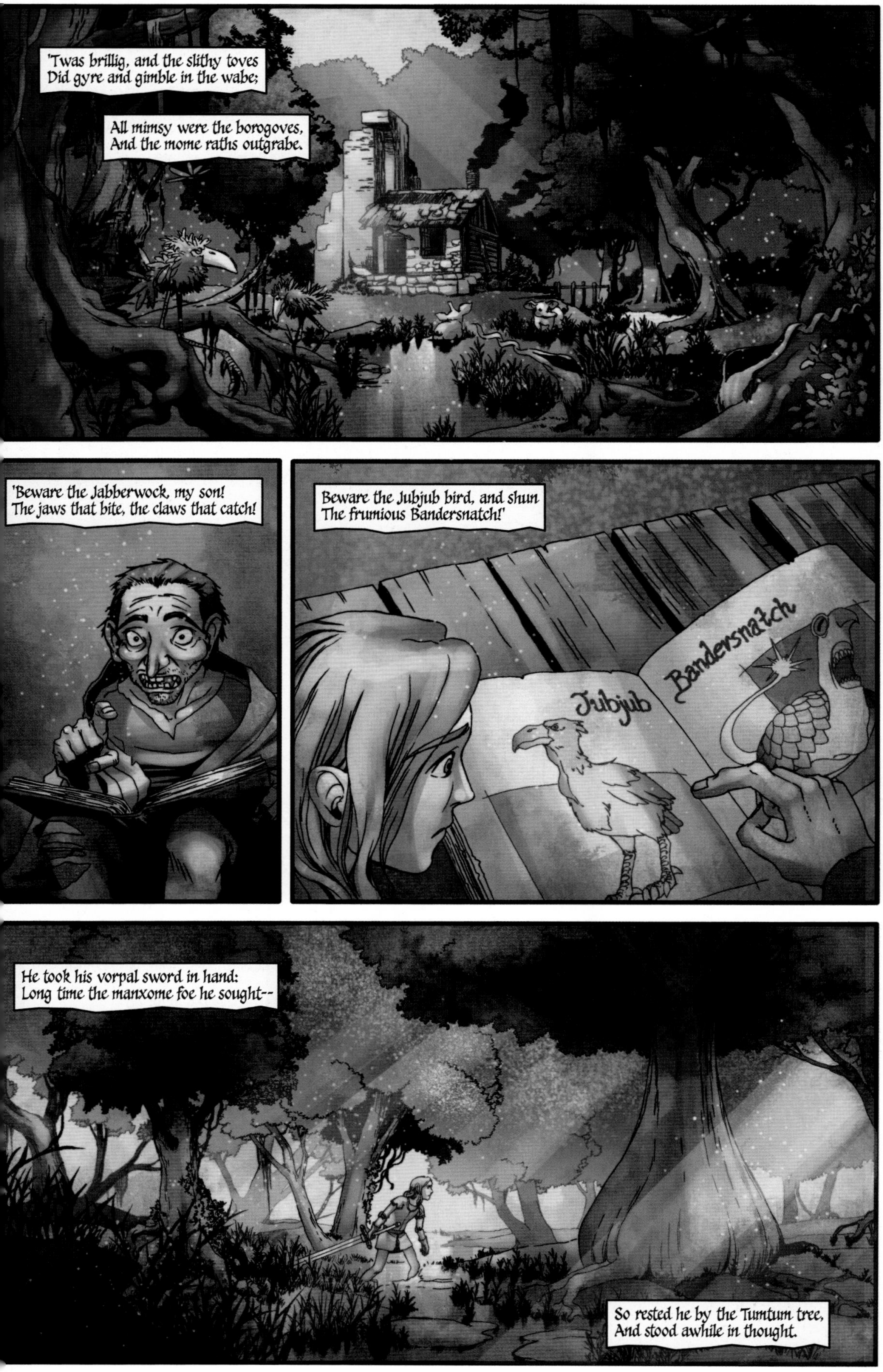
'Twas brillig, and the slithy toves
Did gyre and gimble in the wabe;
All mimsy were the borogoves,
And the mome raths outgrabe.
'Beware the Jabberwock, my son!
The jaws that bite, the claws that catch!
Beware the Jubjub bird, and shun
The frumious Bandersnatch!'
Jubjub
Bandersnatch
He took his vorpal sword in hand:
Long time the manxome foe he sought--
So rested he by the Tumtum tree,
And stood awhile in thought.

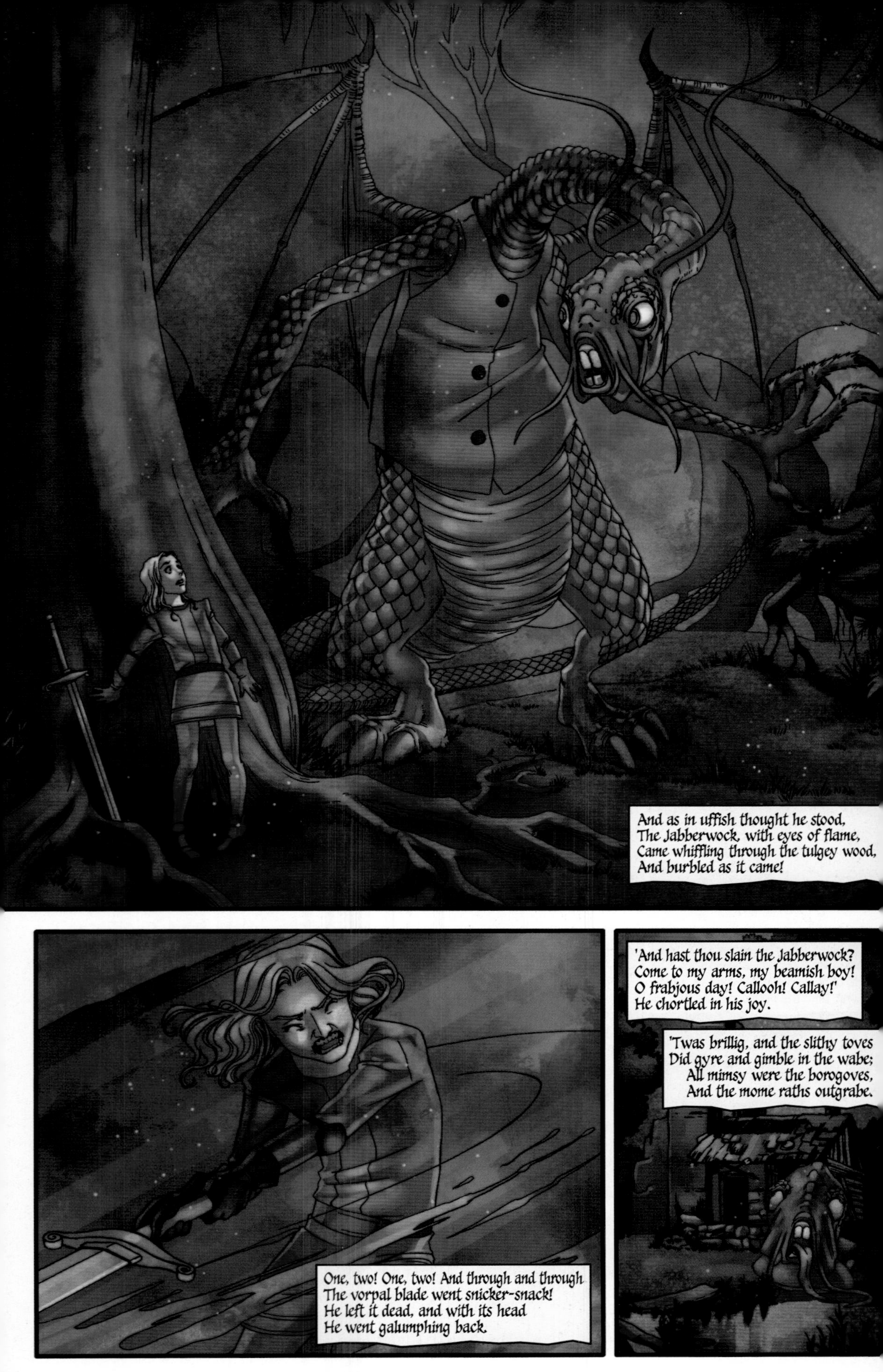
And as in uffish thought he stood,
The Jabberwock, with eyes of flame,
Came whiffling through the tulgey wood,
And burbled as it came!
One, two! One, two! And through and through
The vorpal blade went snicker-snack!
He left it dead, and with its head
He went galumphing back.
'And hast thou slain the Jabberwock?
Come to my arms, my beamish boy!
O frabjous day! Callooh! Callay!'
He chortled in his joy.
'Twas brillig, and the slithy toves
Did gyre and gimble in the wabe;
All mimsy were the borogoves,
And the mome raths outgrabe.

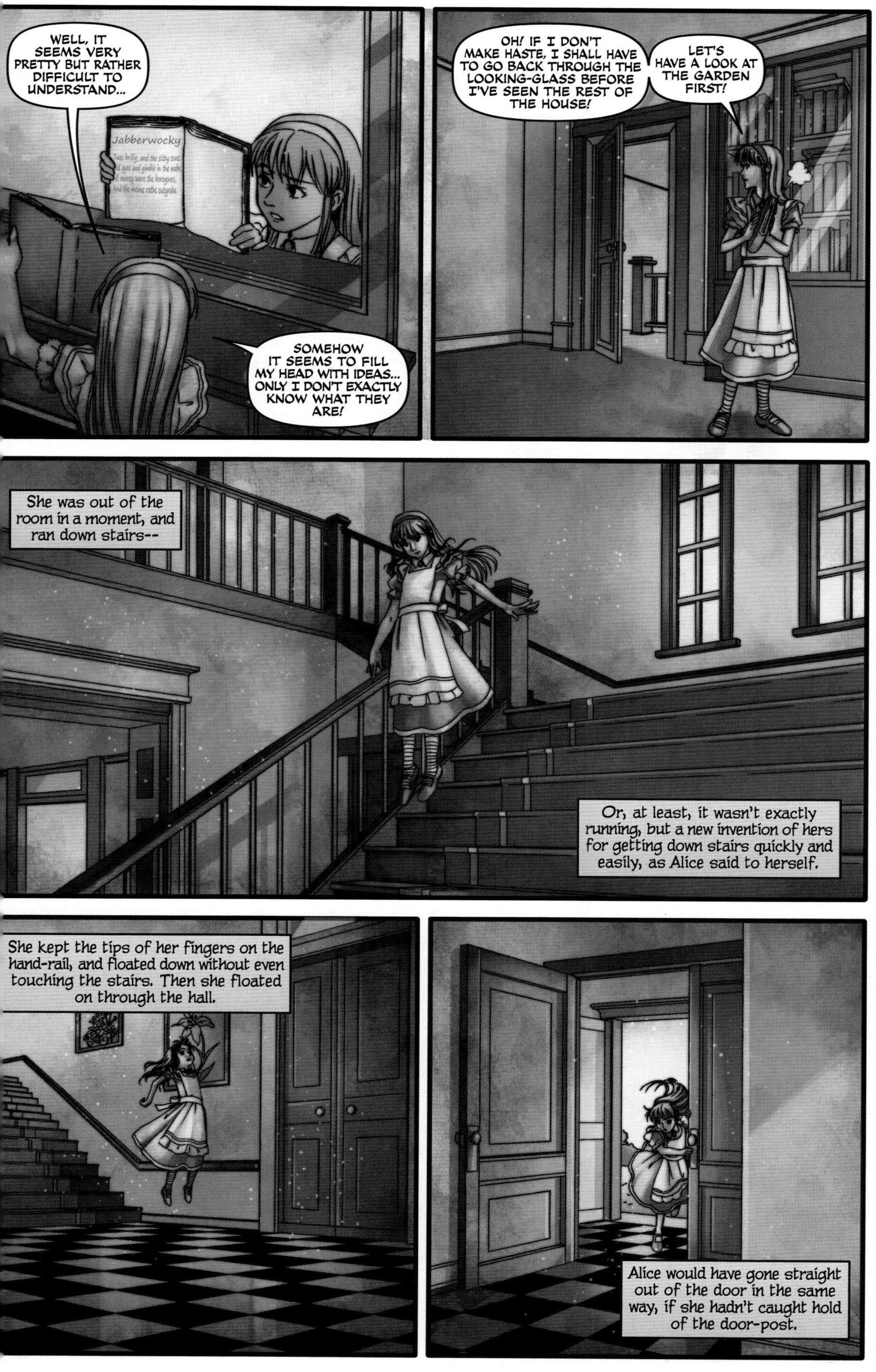
WELL, IT SEEMS VERY PRETTY BUT RATHER DIFFICULT TO UNDERSTAND...
Jabberwocky
SOMEHOW IT SEEMS TO FILL MY HEAD WITH IDEAS... ONLY I DON'T EXACTLY KNOW WHAT THEY ARE!
OH! IF I DON'T MAKE HASTE, I SHALL HAVE TO GO BACK THROUGH THE LOOKING-GLASS BEFORE I'VE SEEN THE REST OF THE HOUSE!
LET'S HAVE A LOOK AT THE GARDEN FIRST!
She was out of the room in a moment, and ran down stairs--
Or, at least, it wasn't exactly running, but a new invention of hers for getting down stairs quickly and easily, as Alice said to herself.
She kept the tips of her fingers on the hand-rail, and floated down without even touching the stairs. Then she floated on through the hall.
Alice would have gone straight out of the door in the same way, if she hadn't caught hold of the door-post.

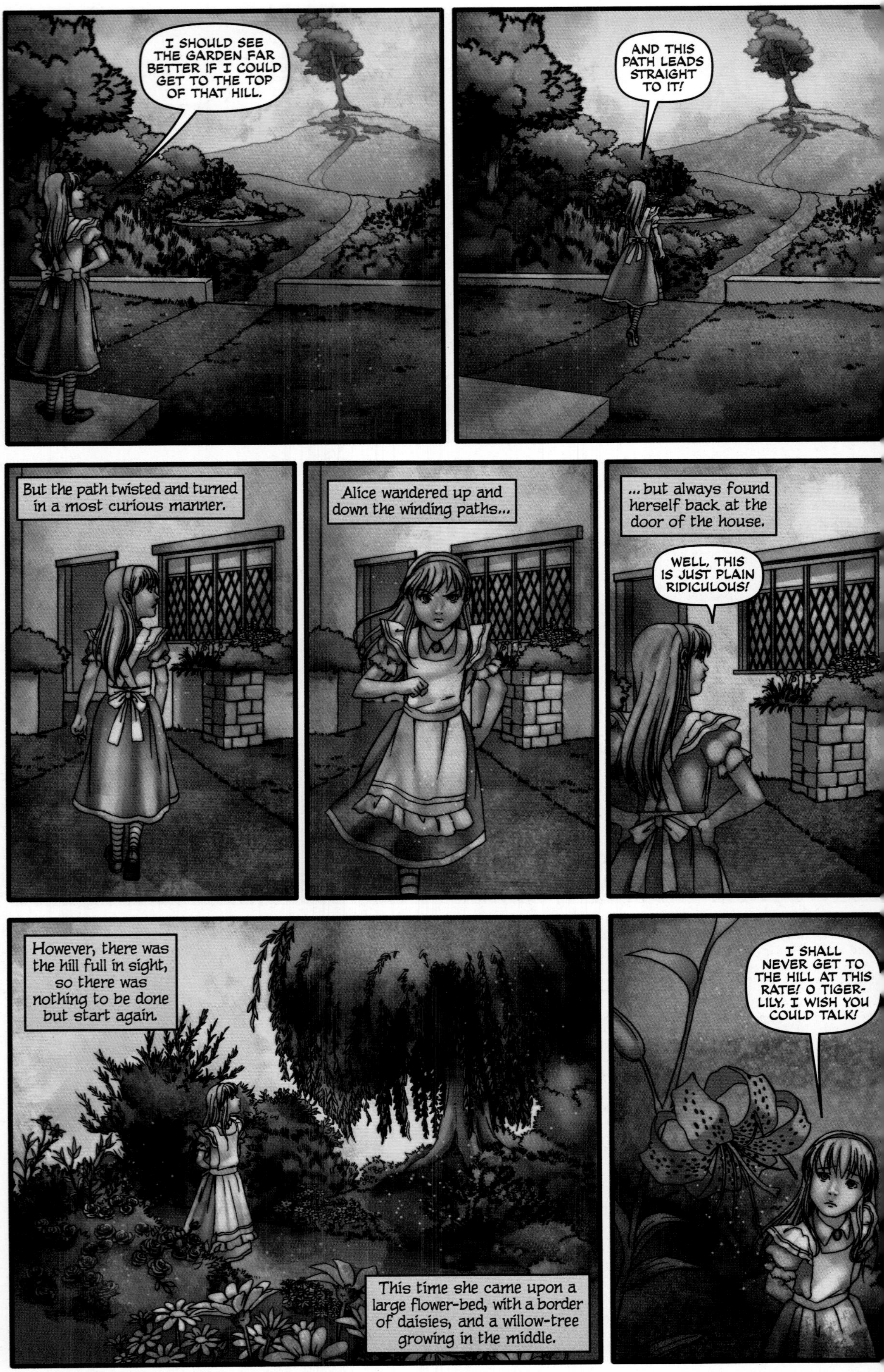
I SHOULD SEE THE GARDEN FAR BETTER IF I COULD GET TO THE TOP OF THAT HILL.
AND THIS PATH LEADS STRAIGHT TO IT!
But the path twisted and turned in a most curious manner.
Alice wandered up and down the winding paths...
...but always found herself back at the door of the house.
WELL, THIS IS JUST PLAIN RIDICULOUS!
However, there was the hill full in sight, so there was nothing to be done but start again.
This time she came upon a large flower-bed, with a border of daisies, and a willow-tree growing in the middle.
I SHALL NEVER GET TO THE HILL AT THIS RATE! O TIGER-LILY, I WISH YOU COULD TALK!

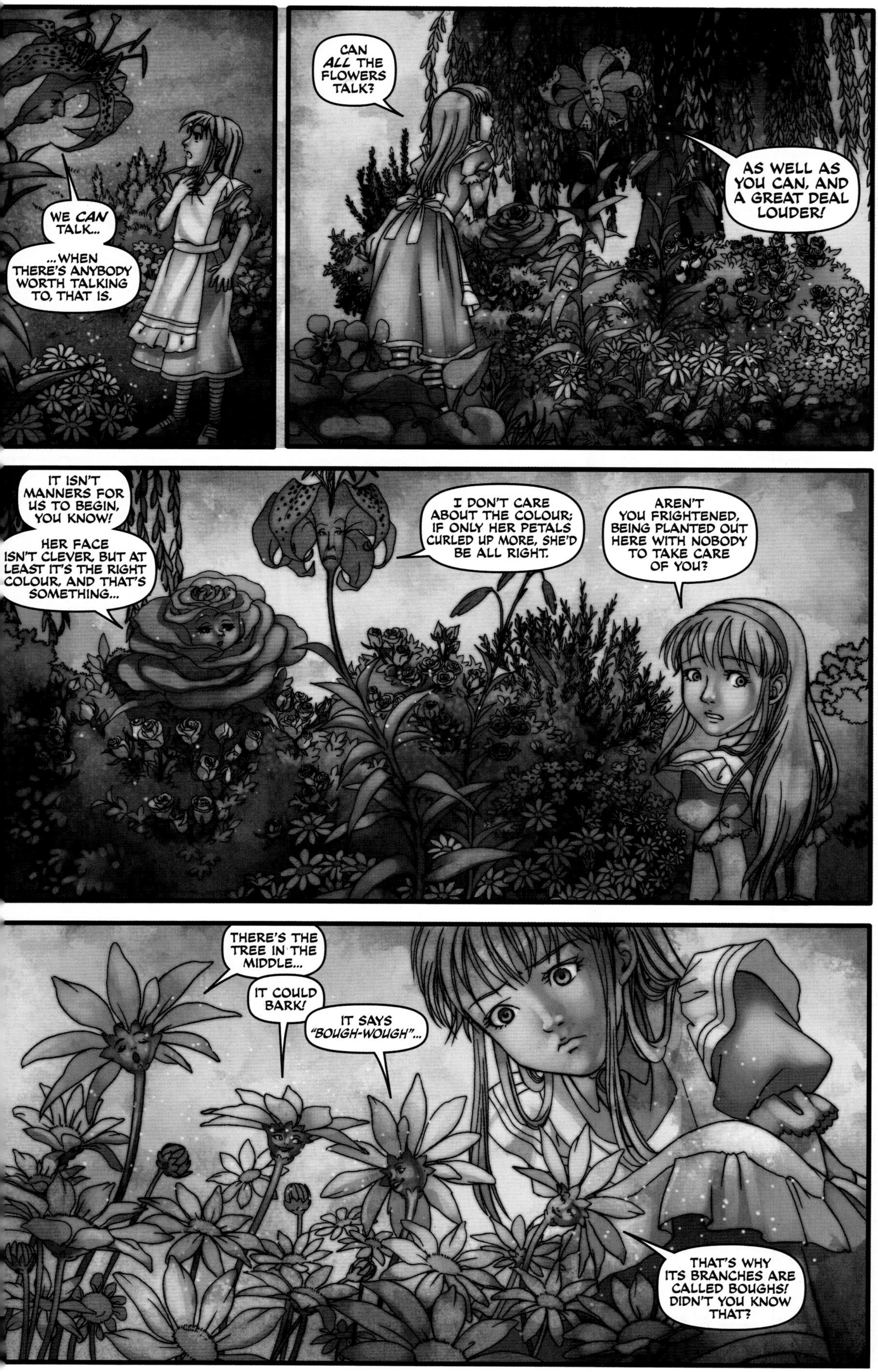

WE *CAN* TALK...
...WHEN THERE'S ANYBODY WORTH TALKING TO, THAT IS.
CAN *ALL* THE FLOWERS TALK?
AS WELL AS YOU CAN, AND A GREAT DEAL LOUDER!
IT ISN'T MANNERS FOR US TO BEGIN, YOU KNOW!
HER FACE ISN'T CLEVER, BUT AT LEAST IT'S THE RIGHT COLOUR, AND THAT'S SOMETHING...
I DON'T CARE ABOUT THE COLOUR; IF ONLY HER PETALS CURLED UP MORE, SHE'D BE ALL RIGHT.
AREN'T YOU FRIGHTENED, BEING PLANTED OUT HERE WITH NOBODY TO TAKE CARE OF YOU?
THERE'S THE TREE IN THE MIDDLE...
IT COULD BARK!
IT SAYS *"BOUGH-WOUGH"*...
THAT'S WHY ITS BRANCHES ARE CALLED BOUGHS! DIDN'T YOU KNOW THAT?

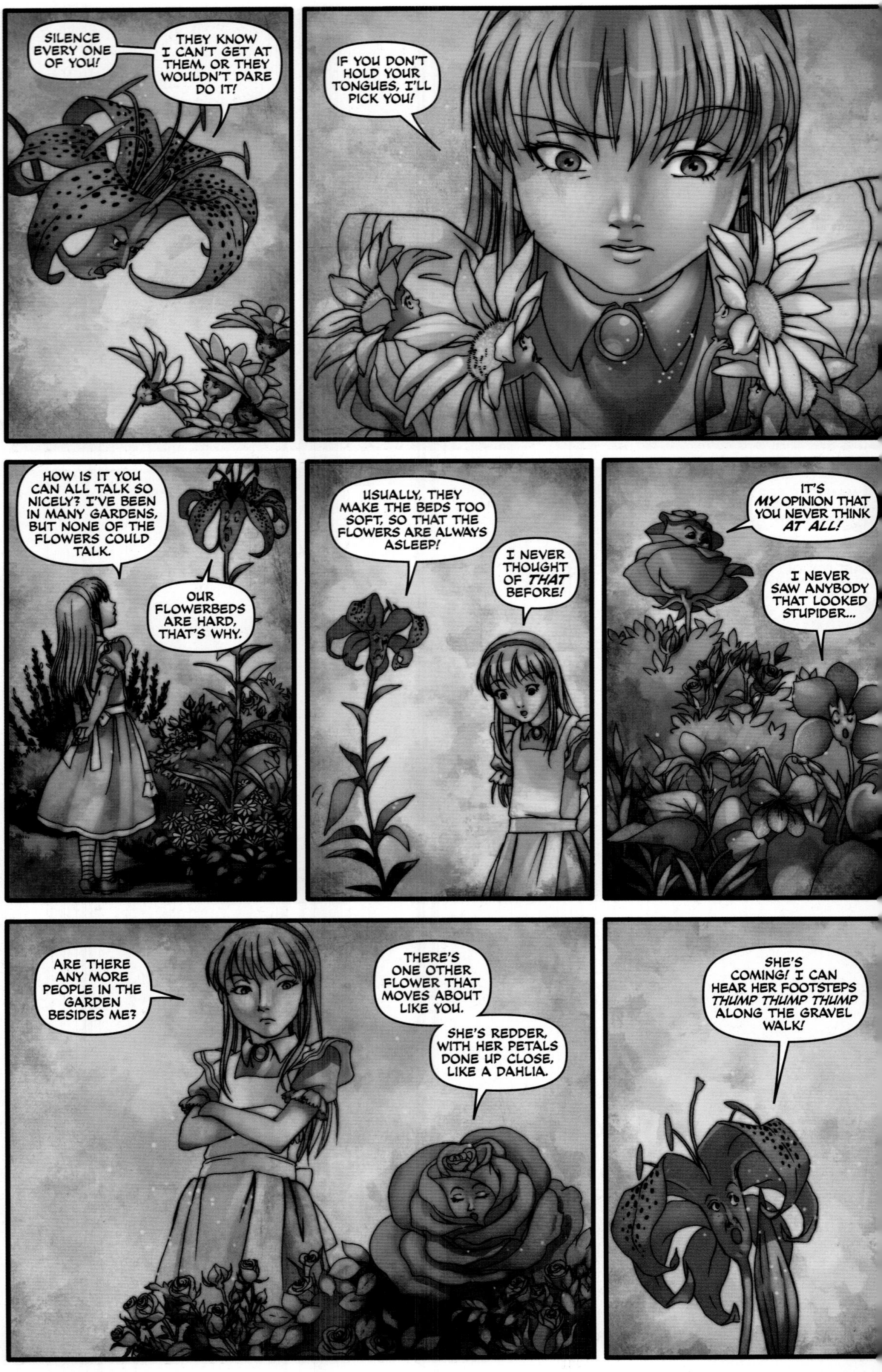
SILENCE EVERY ONE OF YOU!
THEY KNOW I CAN'T GET AT THEM, OR THEY WOULDN'T DARE DO IT!
IF YOU DON'T HOLD YOUR TONGUES, I'LL PICK YOU!
HOW IS IT YOU CAN ALL TALK SO NICELY? I'VE BEEN IN MANY GARDENS, BUT NONE OF THE FLOWERS COULD TALK.
OUR FLOWERBEDS ARE HARD, THAT'S WHY.
USUALLY, THEY MAKE THE BEDS TOO SOFT, SO THAT THE FLOWERS ARE ALWAYS ASLEEP!
I NEVER THOUGHT OF THAT BEFORE!
IT'S MY OPINION THAT YOU NEVER THINK AT ALL!
I NEVER SAW ANYBODY THAT LOOKED STUPIDER...
ARE THERE ANY MORE PEOPLE IN THE GARDEN BESIDES ME?
THERE'S ONE OTHER FLOWER THAT MOVES ABOUT LIKE YOU.
SHE'S REDDER, WITH HER PETALS DONE UP CLOSE, LIKE A DAHLIA.
SHE'S COMING! I CAN HEAR HER FOOTSTEPS THUMP THUMP THUMP ALONG THE GRAVEL WALK!

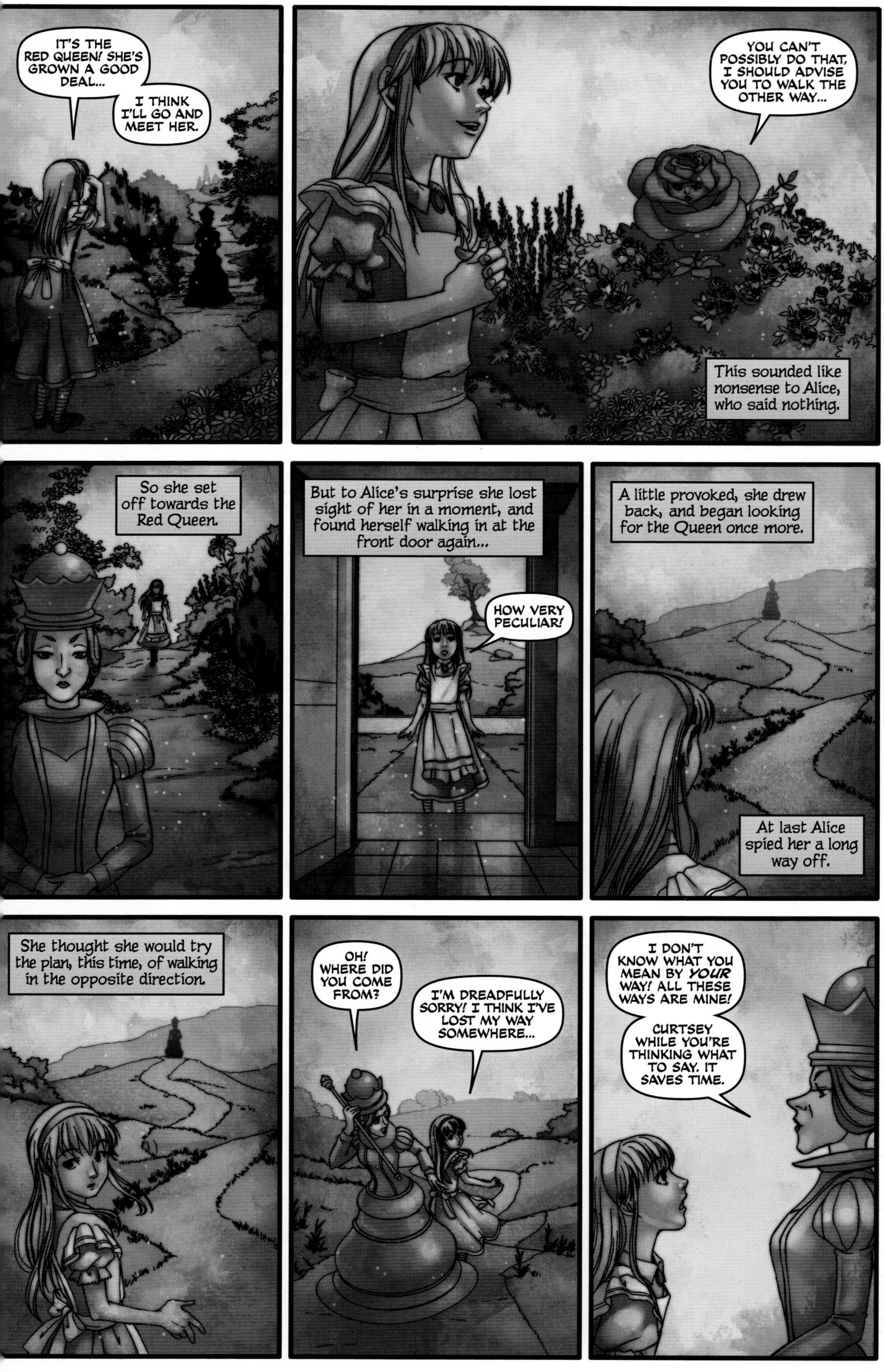
IT'S THE RED QUEEN! SHE'S GROWN A GOOD DEAL...
I THINK I'LL GO AND MEET HER.
YOU CAN'T POSSIBLY DO THAT, I SHOULD ADVISE YOU TO WALK THE OTHER WAY...
This sounded like nonsense to Alice, who said nothing.
So she set off towards the Red Queen.
But to Alice's surprise she lost sight of her in a moment, and found herself walking in at the front door again...
HOW VERY PECULIAR!
A little provoked, she drew back, and began looking for the Queen once more.
At last Alice spied her a long way off.
She thought she would try the plan, this time, of walking in the opposite direction.
OH! WHERE DID YOU COME FROM?
I'M DREADFULLY SORRY! I THINK I'VE LOST MY WAY SOMEWHERE...
I DON'T KNOW WHAT YOU MEAN BY *YOUR* WAY! ALL THESE WAYS ARE MINE!
CURTSEY WHILE YOU'RE THINKING WHAT TO SAY. IT SAVES TIME.

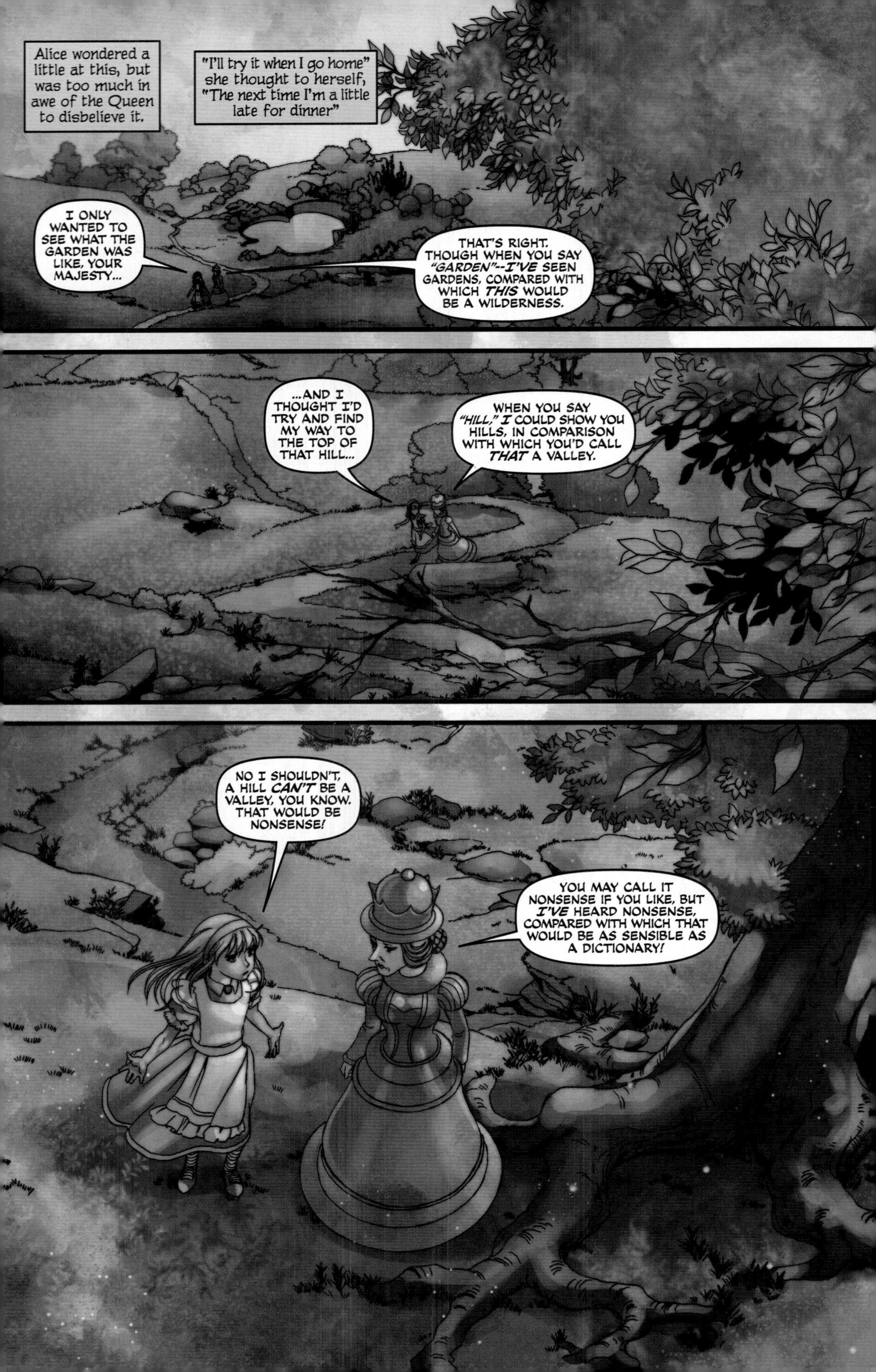
Alice wondered a little at this, but was too much in awe of the Queen to disbelieve it.
"I'll try it when I go home" she thought to herself, "The next time I'm a little late for dinner"
I ONLY WANTED TO SEE WHAT THE GARDEN WAS LIKE, YOUR MAJESTY...
THAT'S RIGHT. THOUGH WHEN YOU SAY "GARDEN"--I'VE SEEN GARDENS, COMPARED WITH WHICH THIS WOULD BE A WILDERNESS.
...AND I THOUGHT I'D TRY AND FIND MY WAY TO THE TOP OF THAT HILL...
WHEN YOU SAY "HILL," I COULD SHOW YOU HILLS, IN COMPARISON WITH WHICH YOU'D CALL THAT A VALLEY.
NO I SHOULDN'T, A HILL CAN'T BE A VALLEY, YOU KNOW. THAT WOULD BE NONSENSE!
YOU MAY CALL IT NONSENSE IF YOU LIKE, BUT I'VE HEARD NONSENSE, COMPARED WITH WHICH THAT WOULD BE AS SENSIBLE AS A DICTIONARY!

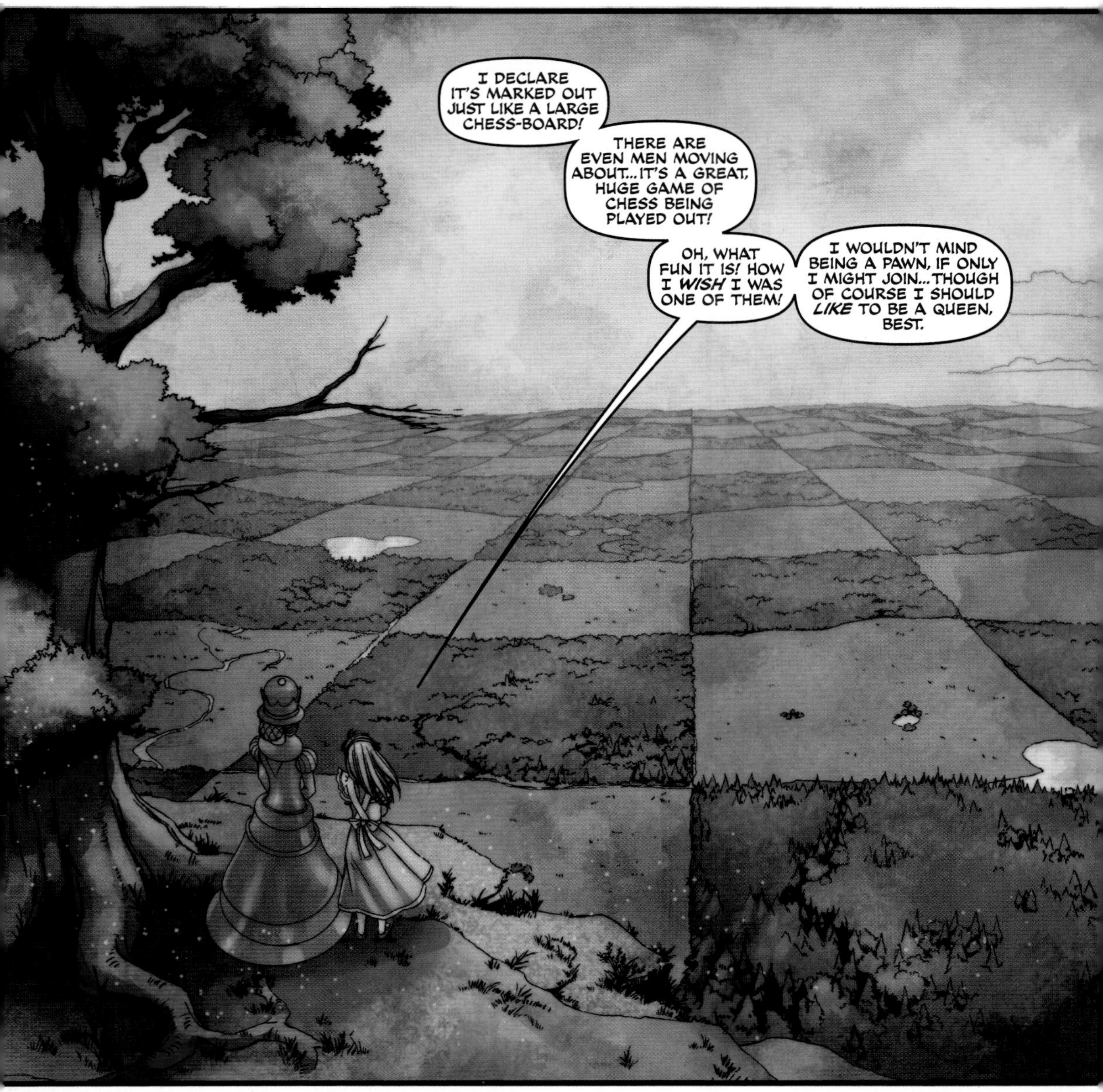
I DECLARE IT'S MARKED OUT JUST LIKE A LARGE CHESS-BOARD!
THERE ARE EVEN MEN MOVING ABOUT... IT'S A GREAT, HUGE GAME OF CHESS BEING PLAYED OUT!
OH, WHAT FUN IT IS! HOW I *WISH* I WAS ONE OF THEM!
I WOULDN'T MIND BEING A PAWN, IF ONLY I MIGHT JOIN... THOUGH OF COURSE I SHOULD *LIKE* TO BE A QUEEN, BEST.

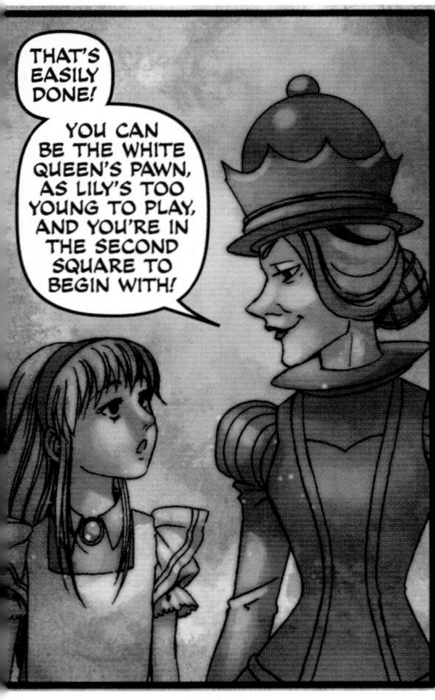
THAT'S EASILY DONE!
YOU CAN BE THE WHITE QUEEN'S PAWN, AS LILY'S TOO YOUNG TO PLAY, AND YOU'RE IN THE SECOND SQUARE TO BEGIN WITH!

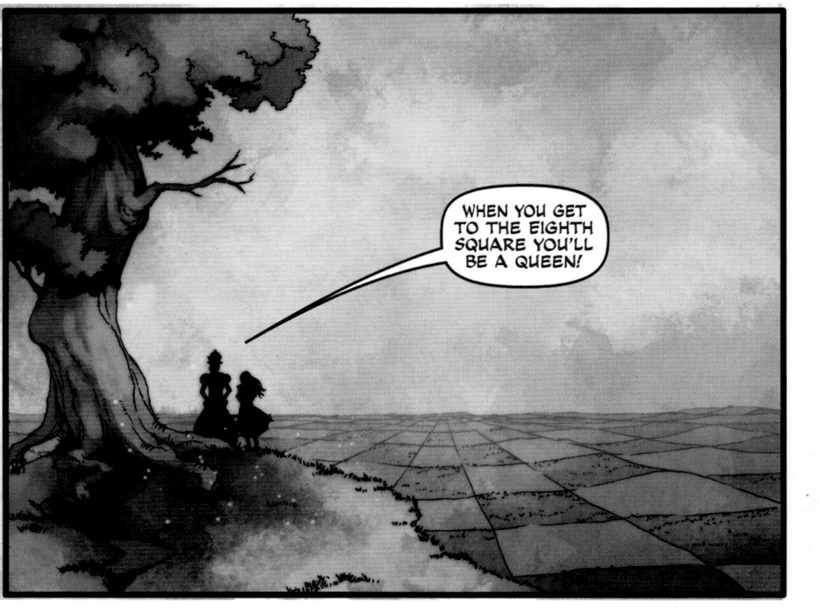
WHEN YOU GET TO THE EIGHTH SQUARE YOU'LL BE A QUEEN!

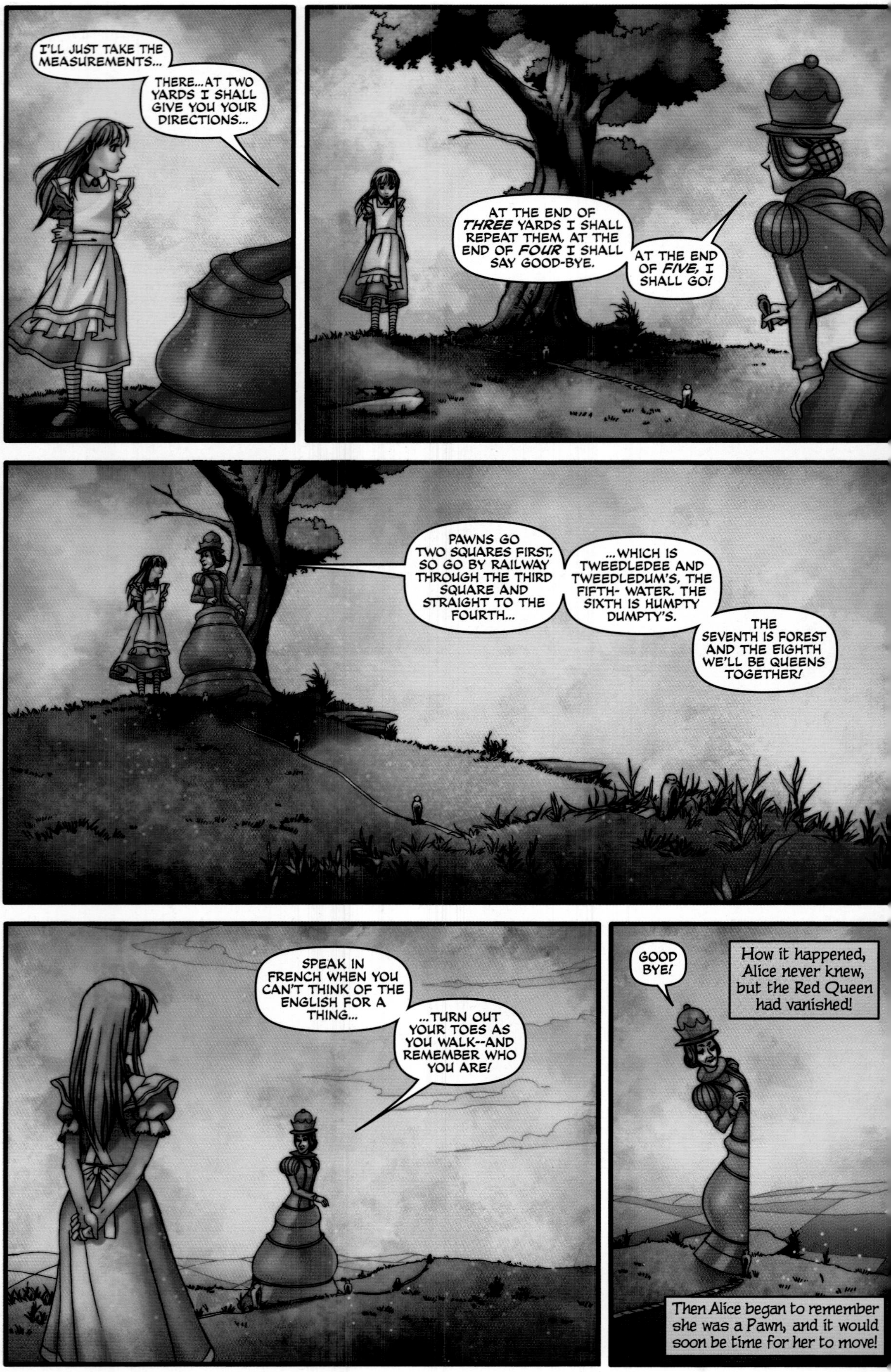
I'LL JUST TAKE THE MEASUREMENTS...
THERE...AT TWO YARDS I SHALL GIVE YOU YOUR DIRECTIONS...
AT THE END OF THREE YARDS I SHALL REPEAT THEM, AT THE END OF FOUR I SHALL SAY GOOD-BYE.
AT THE END OF FIVE, I SHALL GO!
PAWNS GO TWO SQUARES FIRST, SO GO BY RAILWAY THROUGH THE THIRD SQUARE AND STRAIGHT TO THE FOURTH...
...WHICH IS TWEEDLEDEE AND TWEEDLEDUM'S, THE FIFTH- WATER. THE SIXTH IS HUMPTY DUMPTY'S.
THE SEVENTH IS FOREST AND THE EIGHTH WE'LL BE QUEENS TOGETHER!
SPEAK IN FRENCH WHEN YOU CAN'T THINK OF THE ENGLISH FOR A THING...
...TURN OUT YOUR TOES AS YOU WALK--AND REMEMBER WHO YOU ARE!
GOOD BYE!
How it happened, Alice never knew, but the Red Queen had vanished!
Then Alice began to remember she was a Pawn, and it would soon be time for her to move!

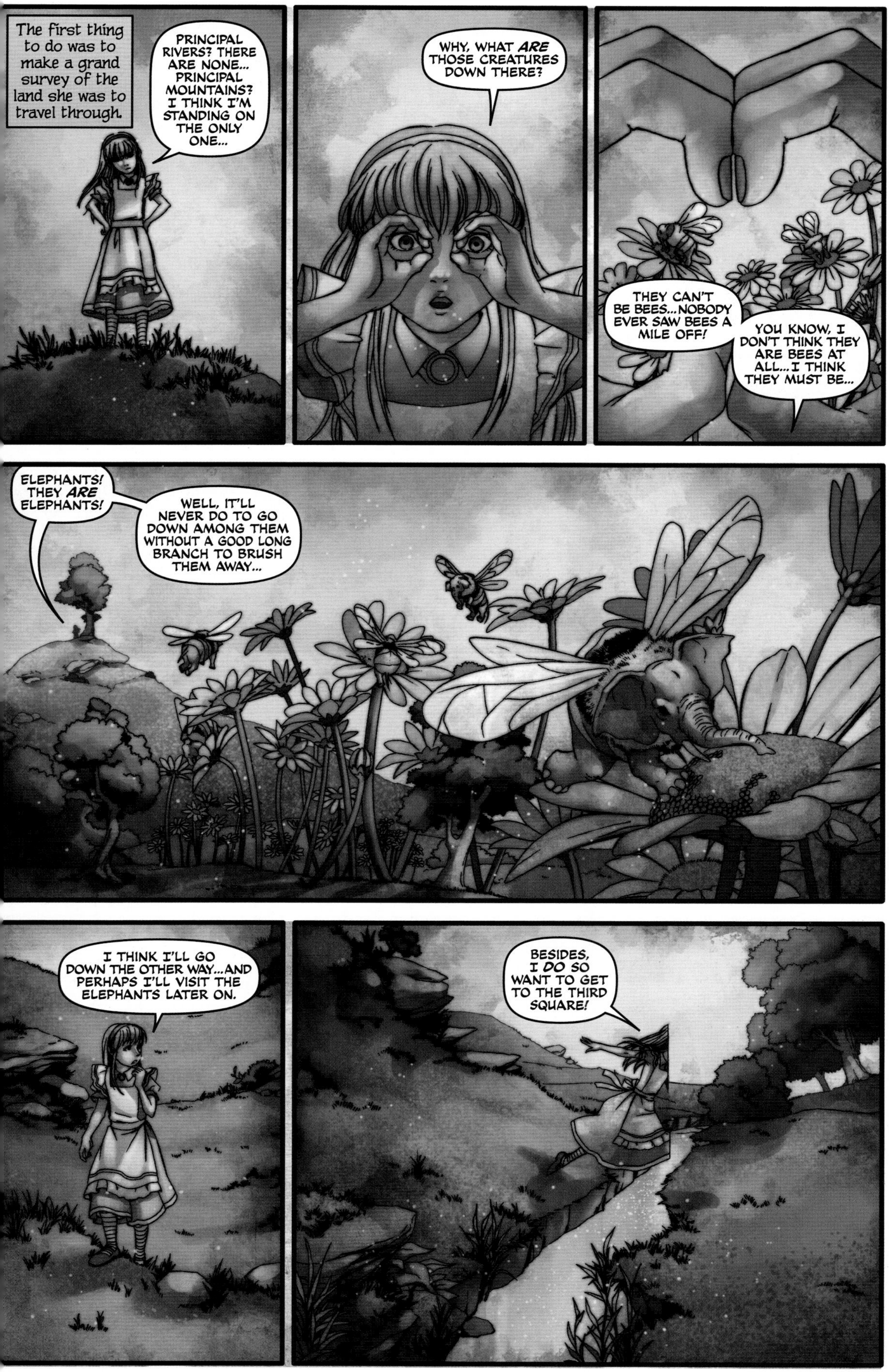
The first thing to do was to make a grand survey of the land she was to travel through.
PRINCIPAL RIVERS? THERE ARE NONE... PRINCIPAL MOUNTAINS? I THINK I'M STANDING ON THE ONLY ONE...
WHY, WHAT ARE THOSE CREATURES DOWN THERE?
THEY CAN'T BE BEES...NOBODY EVER SAW BEES A MILE OFF!
YOU KNOW, I DON'T THINK THEY ARE BEES AT ALL...I THINK THEY MUST BE...
ELEPHANTS! THEY ARE ELEPHANTS!
WELL, IT'LL NEVER DO TO GO DOWN AMONG THEM WITHOUT A GOOD LONG BRANCH TO BRUSH THEM AWAY...
I THINK I'LL GO DOWN THE OTHER WAY...AND PERHAPS I'LL VISIT THE ELEPHANTS LATER ON.
BESIDES, I DO SO WANT TO GET TO THE THIRD SQUARE!

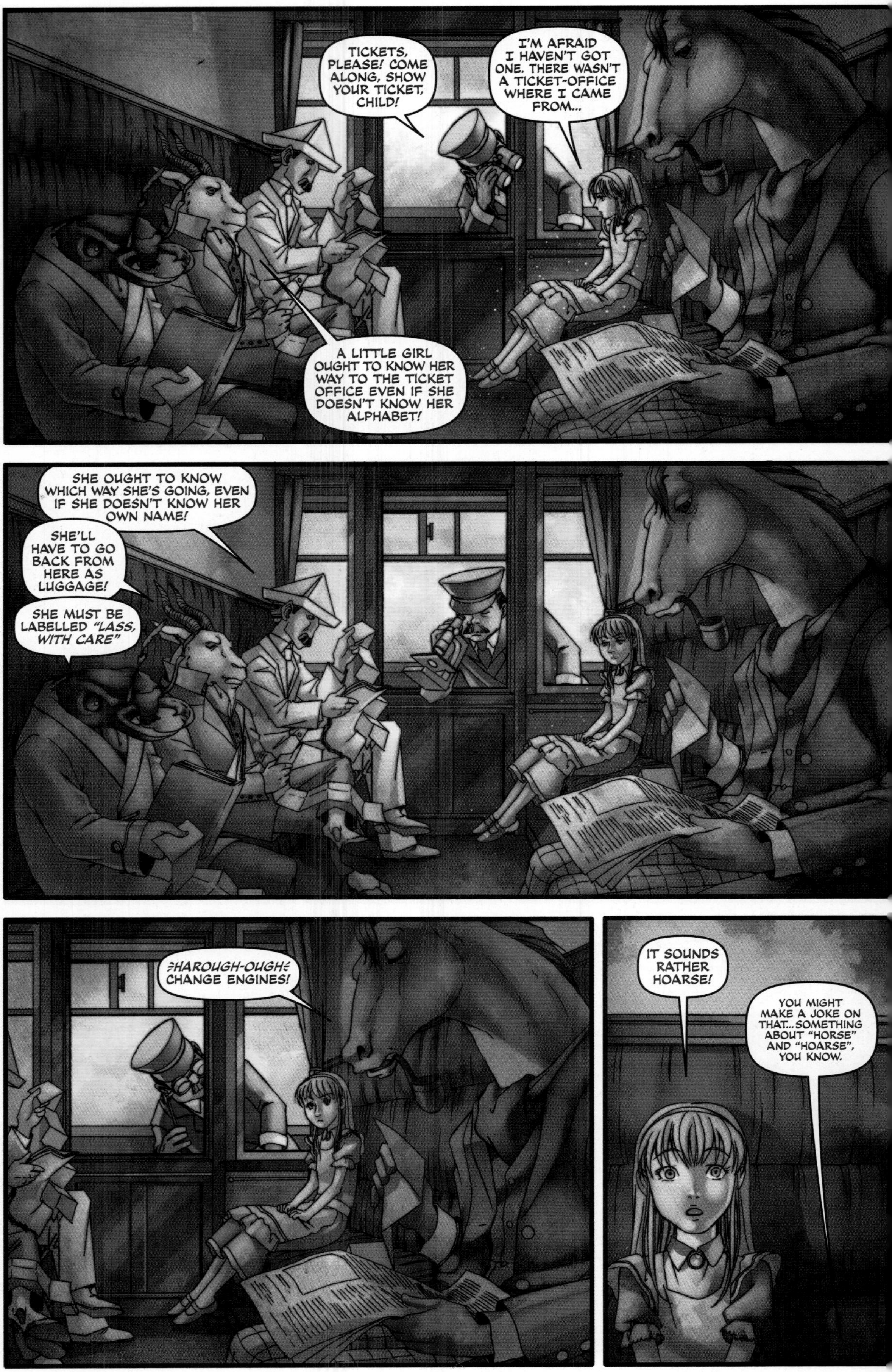

TICKETS, PLEASE! COME ALONG, SHOW YOUR TICKET, CHILD!
I'M AFRAID I HAVEN'T GOT ONE. THERE WASN'T A TICKET-OFFICE WHERE I CAME FROM...
A LITTLE GIRL OUGHT TO KNOW HER WAY TO THE TICKET OFFICE EVEN IF SHE DOESN'T KNOW HER ALPHABET!
SHE OUGHT TO KNOW WHICH WAY SHE'S GOING, EVEN IF SHE DOESN'T KNOW HER OWN NAME!
SHE'LL HAVE TO GO BACK FROM HERE AS LUGGAGE!
SHE MUST BE LABELLED "LASS, WITH CARE"
HAROUGH-OUGH CHANGE ENGINES!
IT SOUNDS RATHER HOARSE!
YOU MIGHT MAKE A JOKE ON THAT...SOMETHING ABOUT "HORSE" AND "HOARSE", YOU KNOW.

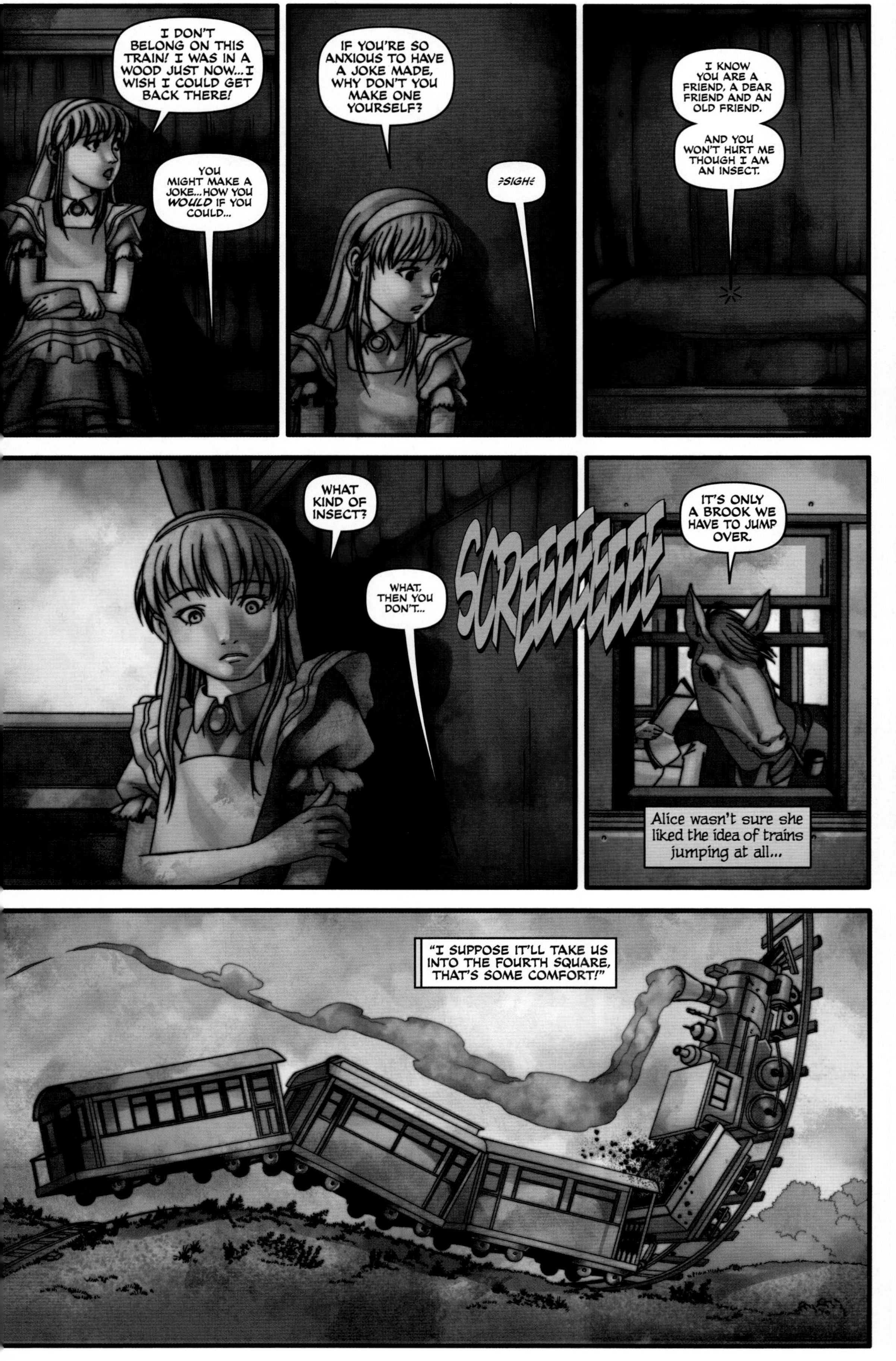
I DON'T BELONG ON THIS TRAIN! I WAS IN A WOOD JUST NOW...I WISH I COULD GET BACK THERE!
YOU MIGHT MAKE A JOKE...HOW YOU *WOULD* IF YOU COULD...
IF YOU'RE SO ANXIOUS TO HAVE A JOKE MADE, WHY DON'T YOU MAKE ONE YOURSELF?
SIGH
I KNOW YOU ARE A FRIEND, A DEAR FRIEND AND AN OLD FRIEND.
AND YOU WON'T HURT ME THOUGH I AM AN INSECT.
WHAT KIND OF INSECT?
WHAT, THEN YOU DON'T...
SCREEEEEEEE
IT'S ONLY A BROOK WE HAVE TO JUMP OVER.
Alice wasn't sure she liked the idea of trains jumping at all...
"I SUPPOSE IT'LL TAKE US INTO THE FOURTH SQUARE, THAT'S SOME COMFORT!"

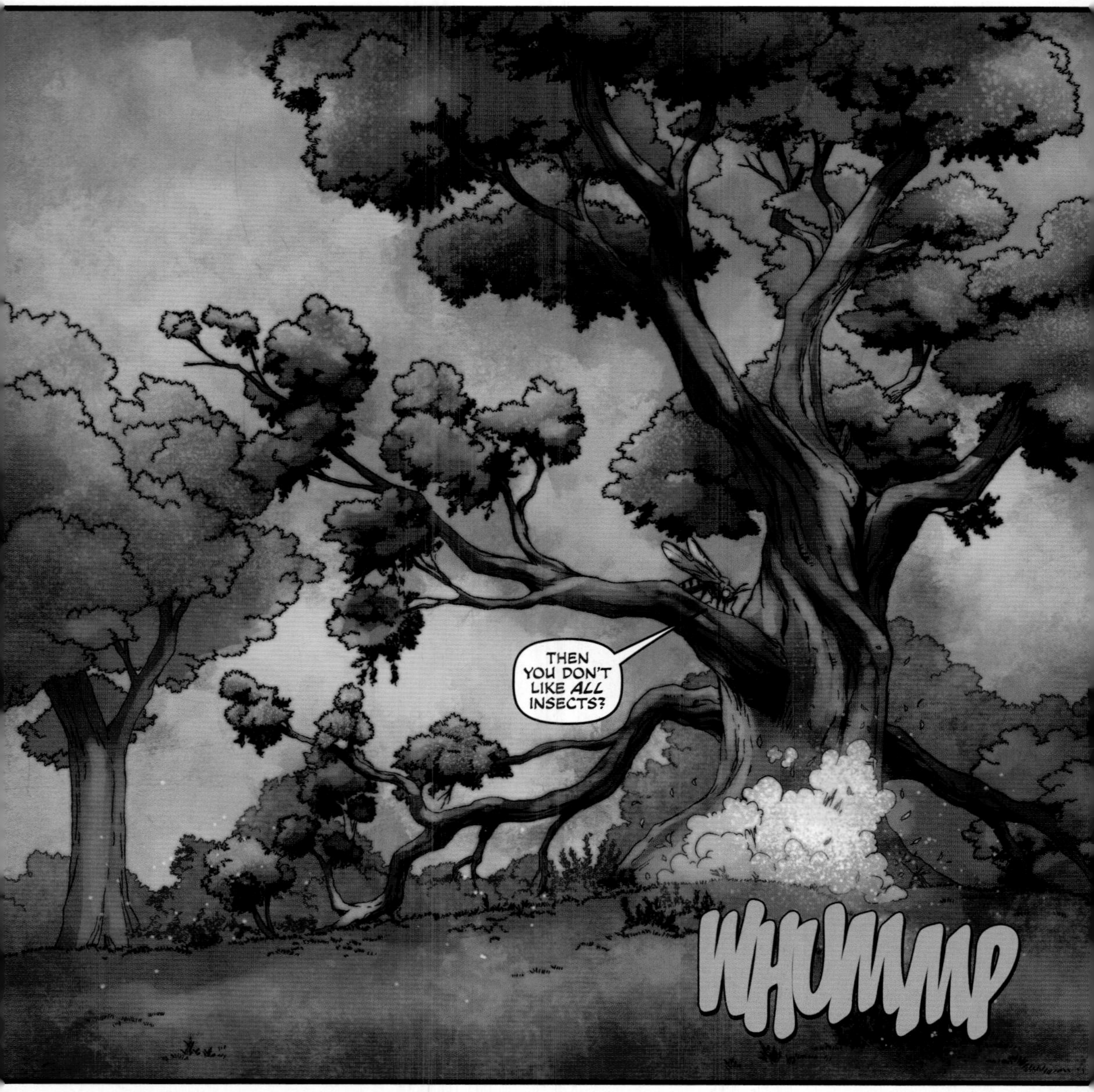
THEN YOU DON'T LIKE *ALL* INSECTS?
WHUMMP
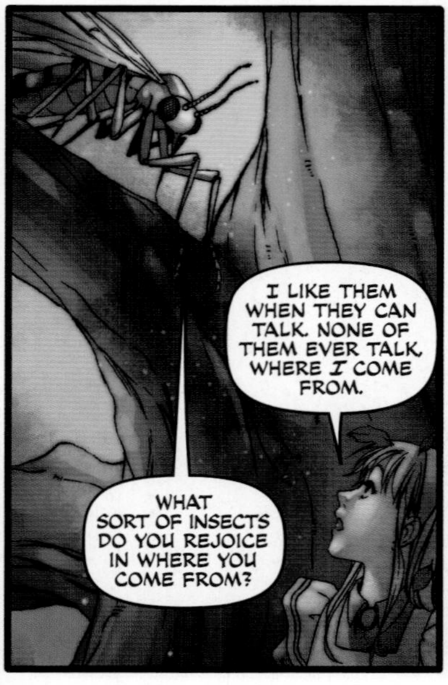
I LIKE THEM WHEN THEY CAN TALK. NONE OF THEM EVER TALK, WHERE *I* COME FROM.
WHAT SORT OF INSECTS DO YOU REJOICE IN WHERE YOU COME FROM?
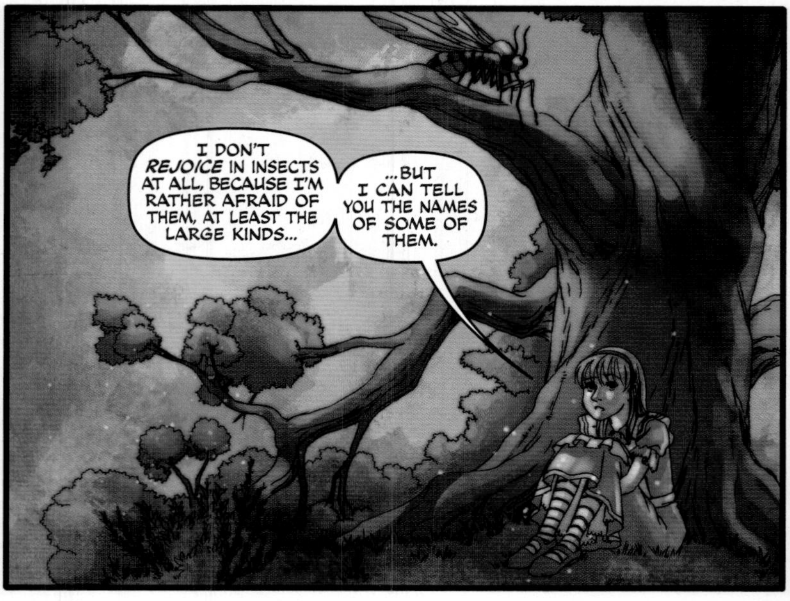
I DON'T *REJOICE* IN INSECTS AT ALL, BECAUSE I'M RATHER AFRAID OF THEM, AT LEAST THE LARGE KINDS...
...BUT I CAN TELL YOU THE NAMES OF SOME OF THEM.

OF COURSE THEY ANSWER TO THEIR NAMES?

I-I NEVER KNEW THEM TO.

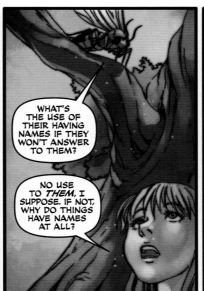

WHAT'S THE USE OF THEIR HAVING NAMES IF THEY WON'T ANSWER TO THEM?

NO USE TO *THEM*, I SUPPOSE. IF NOT, WHY DO THINGS HAVE NAMES AT ALL?

I CAN'T SAY.

FURTHER ON, IN THE WOOD DOWN THERE, THEY'VE GOT NO NAMES--HOWEVER, GO ON WITH YOUR LIST OF INSECTS. YOU'RE WASTING TIME!

LET ME SEE, THERE'S THE HORSE-FLY...

ALL RIGHT, HALF WAY UP THAT BUSH YOU'LL SEE A ROCKING HORSE FLY IF YOU LOOK.

WHAT DOES IT LIVE ON?

SAP AND SAWDUST. GO ON WITH THE LIST!

WELL, THERE'S A DRAGON-FLY.

LOOK ON THE BRANCH ABOVE YOUR HEAD AND THERE YOU'LL FIND A SNAP-DRAGON-FLY.

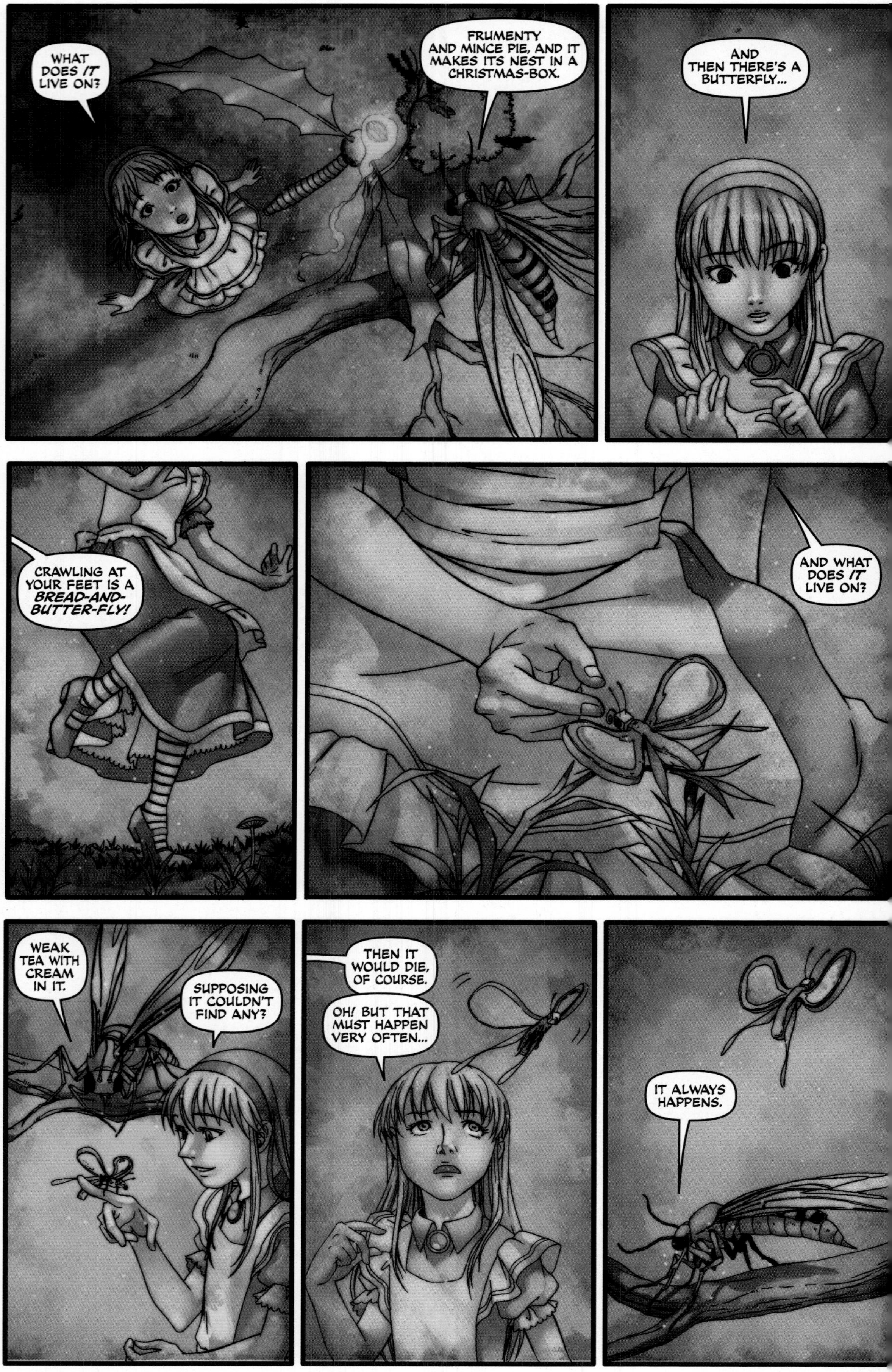
WHAT DOES *IT* LIVE ON?
FRUMENTY AND MINCE PIE, AND IT MAKES ITS NEST IN A CHRISTMAS-BOX.
AND THEN THERE'S A BUTTERFLY...
CRAWLING AT YOUR FEET IS A *BREAD-AND-BUTTER-FLY!*
AND WHAT DOES *IT* LIVE ON?
WEAK TEA WITH CREAM IN IT.
SUPPOSING IT COULDN'T FIND ANY?
THEN IT WOULD DIE, OF COURSE.
OH! BUT THAT MUST HAPPEN VERY OFTEN...
IT ALWAYS HAPPENS.

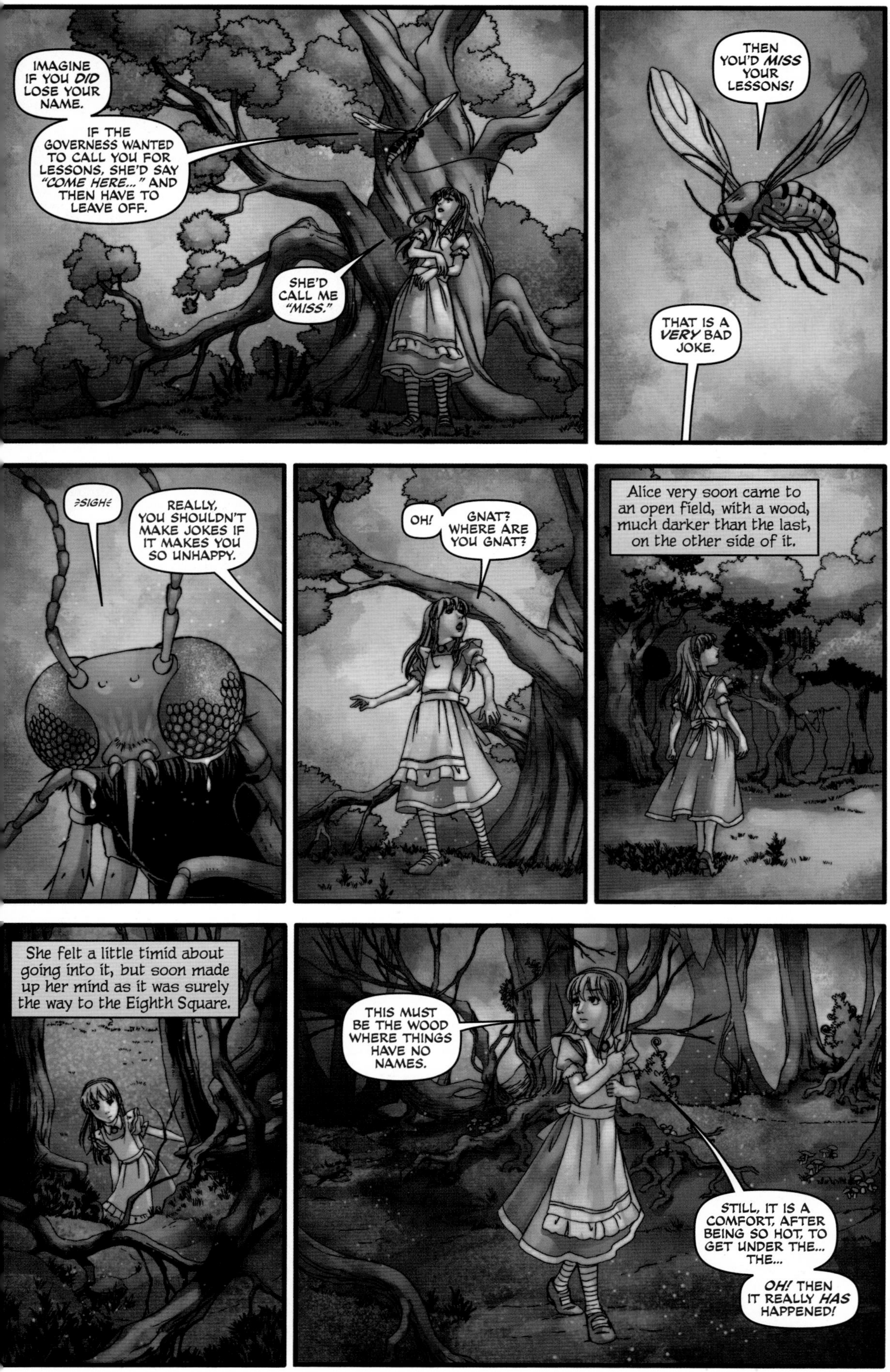
IMAGINE IF YOU *DID* LOSE YOUR NAME.
IF THE GOVERNESS WANTED TO CALL YOU FOR LESSONS, SHE'D SAY *"COME HERE..."* AND THEN HAVE TO LEAVE OFF.
SHE'D CALL ME *"MISS."*
THEN YOU'D *MISS* YOUR LESSONS!
THAT IS A *VERY* BAD JOKE.
SIGH
REALLY, YOU SHOULDN'T MAKE JOKES IF IT MAKES YOU SO UNHAPPY.
OH!
GNAT? WHERE ARE YOU GNAT?
Alice very soon came to an open field, with a wood, much darker than the last, on the other side of it.
She felt a little timid about going into it, but soon made up her mind as it was surely the way to the Eighth Square.
THIS MUST BE THE WOOD WHERE THINGS HAVE NO NAMES.
STILL, IT IS A COMFORT, AFTER BEING SO HOT, TO GET UNDER THE... THE...
OH! THEN IT REALLY *HAS* HAPPENED!

WHO AM I? I WILL REMEMBER IF I CAN! I'M DETERMINED TO DO IT!

...

L! I'M SURE IT BEGINS WITH L!

OH! HELLO THERE.

WHAT DO YOU CALL YOURSELF?

I-I WISH I KNEW! NOTHING JUST NOW.

PLEASE WON'T YOU TELL ME WHAT *YOU* CALL YOURSELF? I THINK THAT MIGHT HELP.

I'LL TELL YOU A LITTLE FARTHER ON. I CAN'T REMEMBER *HERE*.

So they walked on together through the wood, Alice with her arms clasped lovingly round the fawn's soft neck.

Until at last they came to another open field.

I'M A FAWN!

AND, DEAR ME, YOU'RE A HUMAN CHILD!

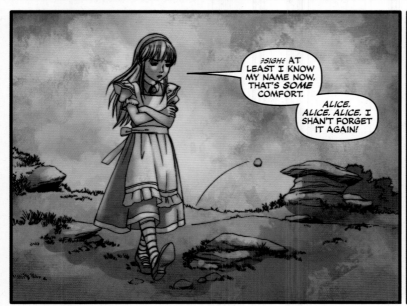

≈SIGH≈ AT LEAST I KNOW MY NAME NOW, THAT'S *SOME* COMFORT.

ALICE. ALICE. ALICE. I SHAN'T FORGET IT AGAIN!

WHICH TO FOLLOW? I EXPECT THE PATH DIVIDES FARTHER ON.

TO TWEEDLEDUM'S HOUSE

TO THE HOUSE OF TWEEDLEDEE

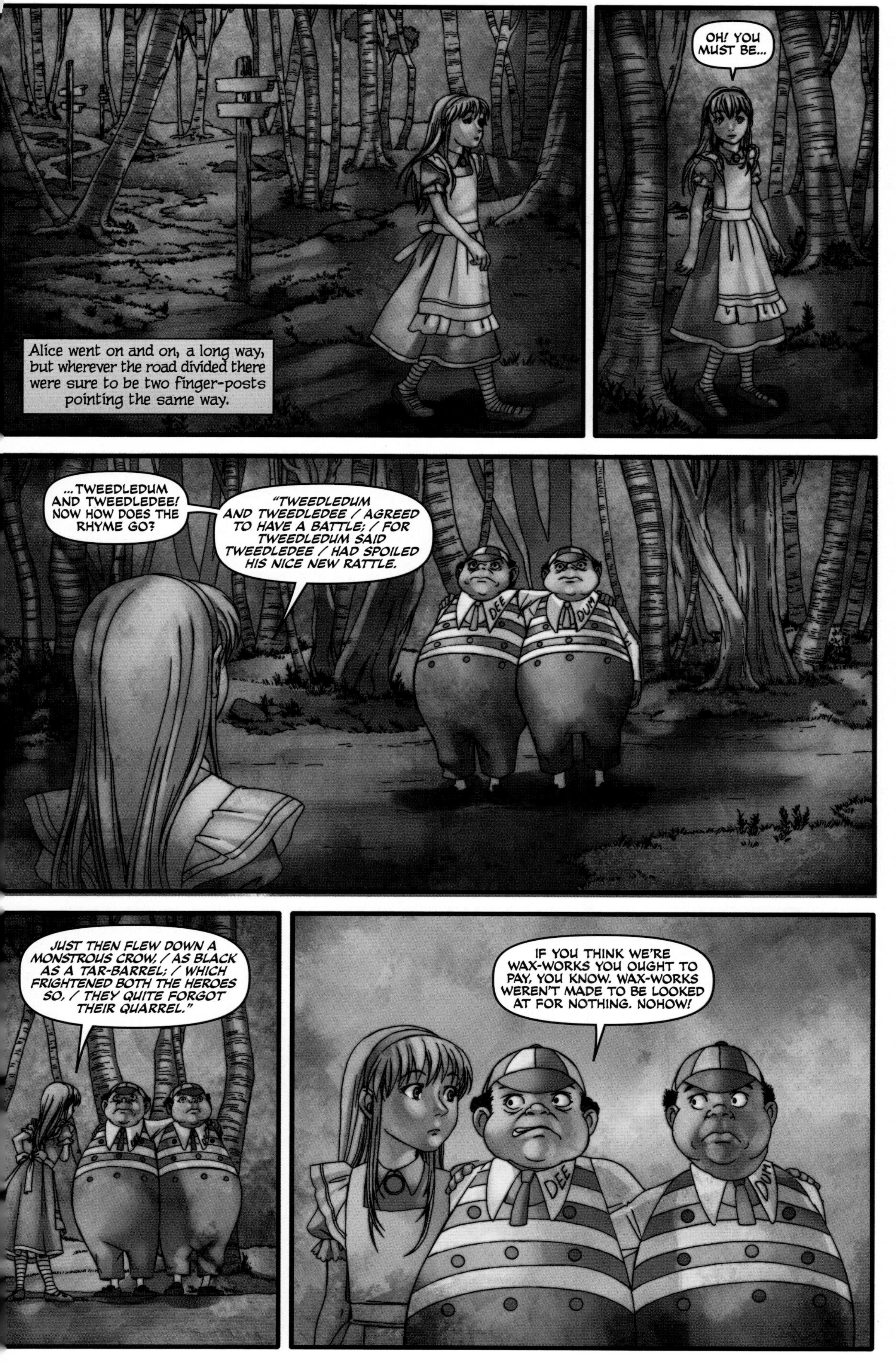
Alice went on and on, a long way, but wherever the road divided there were sure to be two finger-posts pointing the same way.
OH! YOU MUST BE...
...TWEEDLEDUM AND TWEEDLEDEE! NOW HOW DOES THE RHYME GO?
"TWEEDLEDUM AND TWEEDLEDEE / AGREED TO HAVE A BATTLE; / FOR TWEEDLEDUM SAID TWEEDLEDEE / HAD SPOILED HIS NICE NEW RATTLE.
DEE
DUM
JUST THEN FLEW DOWN A MONSTROUS CROW, / AS BLACK AS A TAR-BARREL; / WHICH FRIGHTENED BOTH THE HEROES SO, / THEY QUITE FORGOT THEIR QUARREL."
IF YOU THINK WE'RE WAX-WORKS YOU OUGHT TO PAY, YOU KNOW. WAX-WORKS WEREN'T MADE TO BE LOOKED AT FOR NOTHING. NOHOW!
DEE
DUM

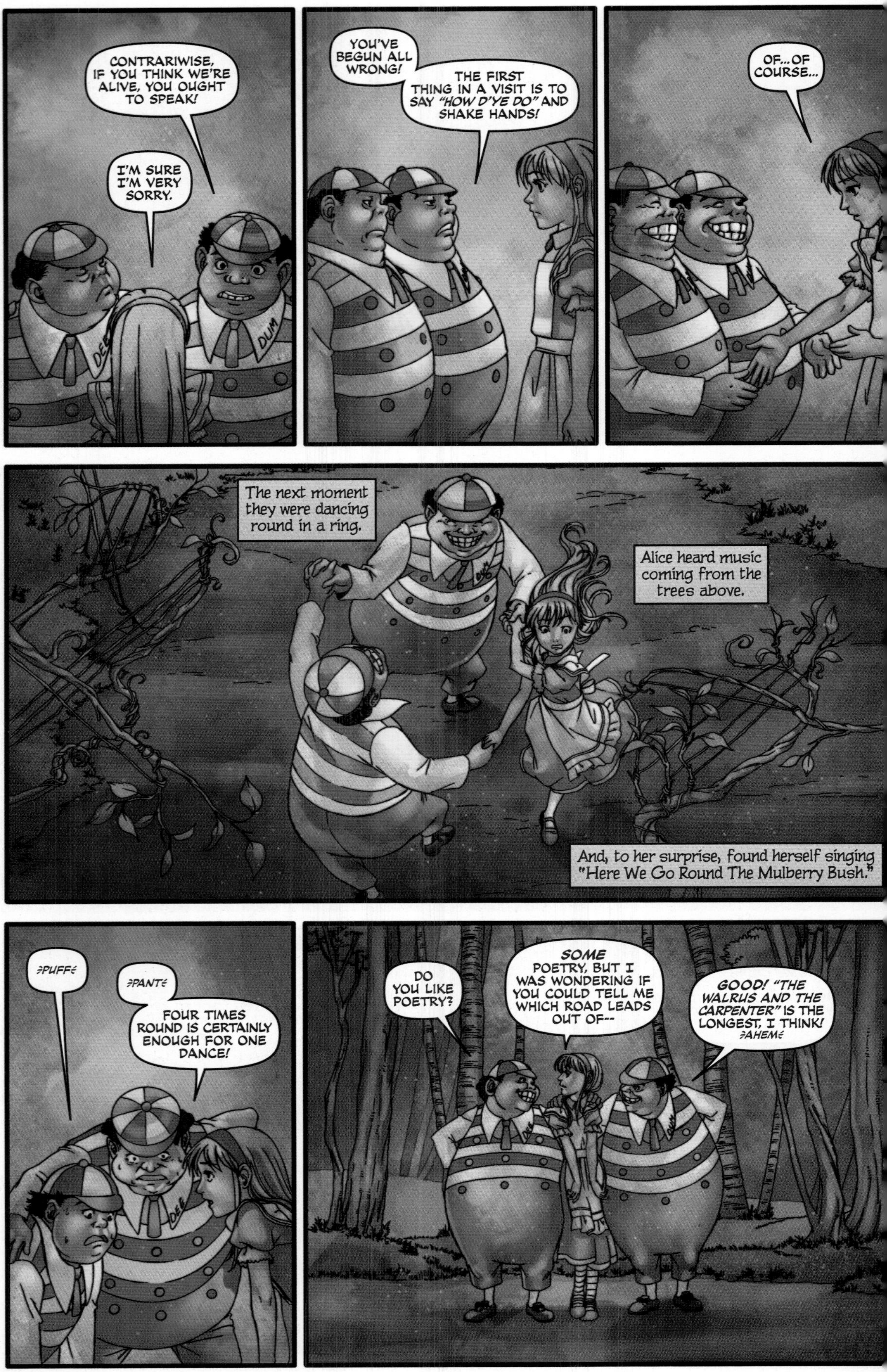
CONTRARIWISE, IF YOU THINK WE'RE ALIVE, YOU OUGHT TO SPEAK!
I'M SURE I'M VERY SORRY.
DEE
DUM
YOU'VE BEGUN ALL WRONG!
THE FIRST THING IN A VISIT IS TO SAY "HOW D'YE DO" AND SHAKE HANDS!
OF...OF COURSE...
The next moment they were dancing round in a ring.
Alice heard music coming from the trees above.
And, to her surprise, found herself singing "Here We Go Round The Mulberry Bush."
PUFF
PANT
FOUR TIMES ROUND IS CERTAINLY ENOUGH FOR ONE DANCE!
DO YOU LIKE POETRY?
SOME POETRY, BUT I WAS WONDERING IF YOU COULD TELL ME WHICH ROAD LEADS OUT OF--
GOOD! "THE WALRUS AND THE CARPENTER" IS THE LONGEST, I THINK!
AHEM

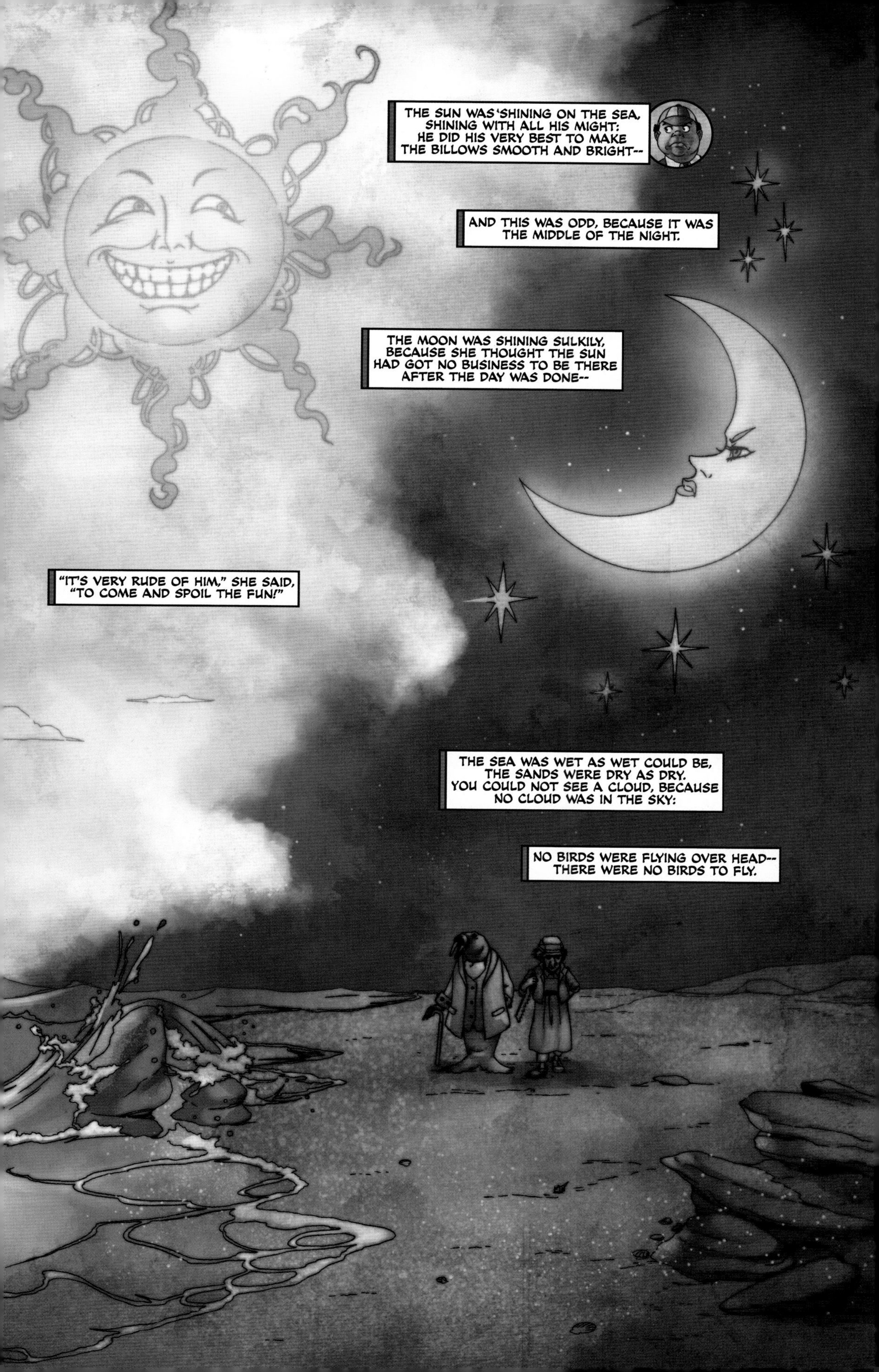
THE SUN WAS 'SHINING ON THE SEA, SHINING WITH ALL HIS MIGHT: HE DID HIS VERY BEST TO MAKE THE BILLOWS SMOOTH AND BRIGHT--
AND THIS WAS ODD, BECAUSE IT WAS THE MIDDLE OF THE NIGHT.
THE MOON WAS SHINING SULKILY, BECAUSE SHE THOUGHT THE SUN HAD GOT NO BUSINESS TO BE THERE AFTER THE DAY WAS DONE--
"IT'S VERY RUDE OF HIM," SHE SAID, "TO COME AND SPOIL THE FUN!"
THE SEA WAS WET AS WET COULD BE, THE SANDS WERE DRY AS DRY. YOU COULD NOT SEE A CLOUD, BECAUSE NO CLOUD WAS IN THE SKY:
NO BIRDS WERE FLYING OVER HEAD-- THERE WERE NO BIRDS TO FLY.

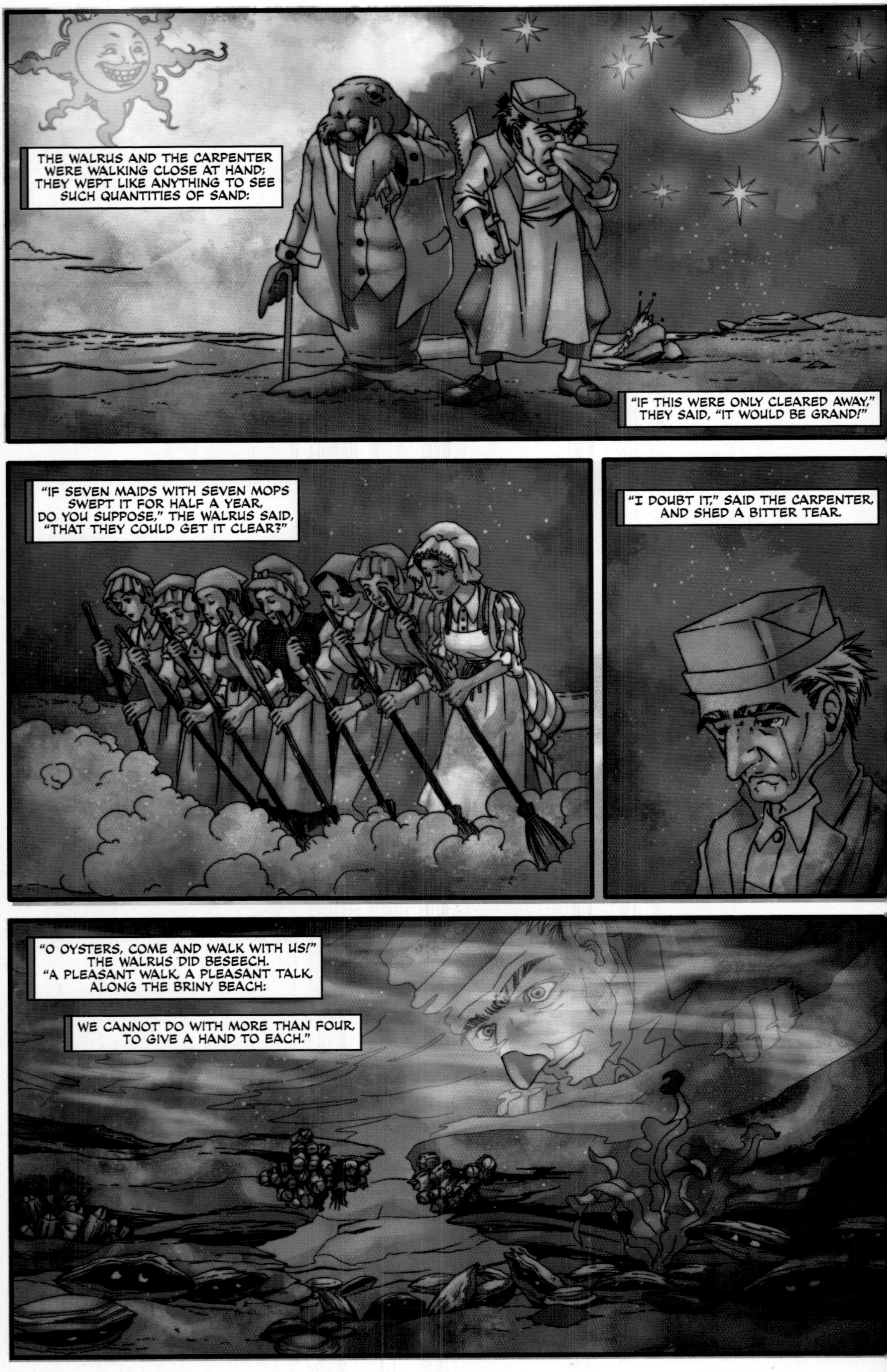
THE WALRUS AND THE CARPENTER WERE WALKING CLOSE AT HAND; THEY WEPT LIKE ANYTHING TO SEE SUCH QUANTITIES OF SAND:
"IF THIS WERE ONLY CLEARED AWAY," THEY SAID, "IT WOULD BE GRAND!"
"IF SEVEN MAIDS WITH SEVEN MOPS SWEPT IT FOR HALF A YEAR, DO YOU SUPPOSE," THE WALRUS SAID, "THAT THEY COULD GET IT CLEAR?"
"I DOUBT IT," SAID THE CARPENTER, AND SHED A BITTER TEAR.
"O OYSTERS, COME AND WALK WITH US!" THE WALRUS DID BESEECH. "A PLEASANT WALK, A PLEASANT TALK, ALONG THE BRINY BEACH:
WE CANNOT DO WITH MORE THAN FOUR, TO GIVE A HAND TO EACH."

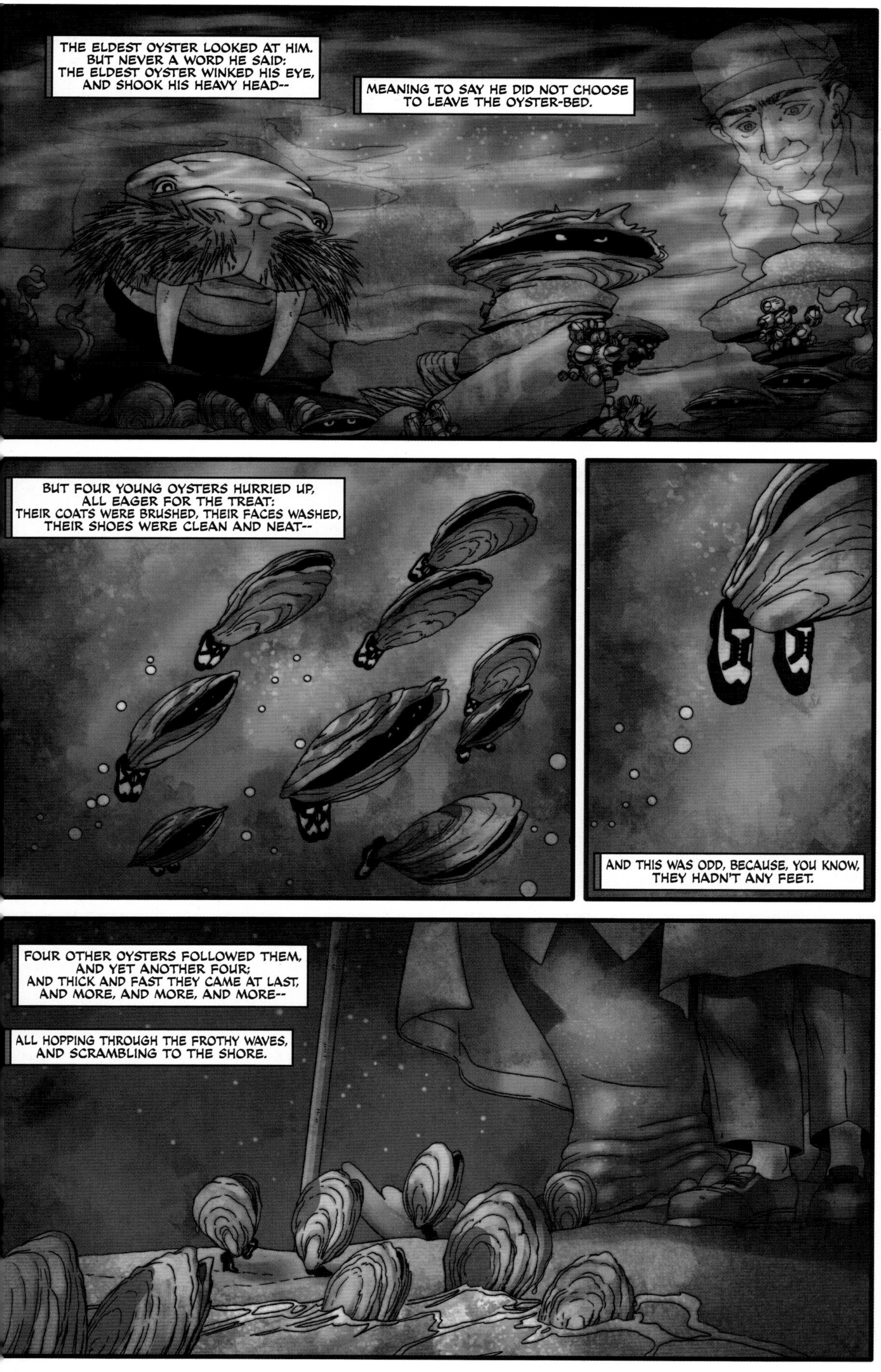
THE ELDEST OYSTER LOOKED AT HIM.
BUT NEVER A WORD HE SAID:
THE ELDEST OYSTER WINKED HIS EYE,
AND SHOOK HIS HEAVY HEAD--
MEANING TO SAY HE DID NOT CHOOSE
TO LEAVE THE OYSTER-BED.
BUT FOUR YOUNG OYSTERS HURRIED UP,
ALL EAGER FOR THE TREAT:
THEIR COATS WERE BRUSHED, THEIR FACES WASHED,
THEIR SHOES WERE CLEAN AND NEAT--
AND THIS WAS ODD, BECAUSE, YOU KNOW,
THEY HADN'T ANY FEET.
FOUR OTHER OYSTERS FOLLOWED THEM,
AND YET ANOTHER FOUR;
AND THICK AND FAST THEY CAME AT LAST,
AND MORE, AND MORE, AND MORE--
ALL HOPPING THROUGH THE FROTHY WAVES,
AND SCRAMBLING TO THE SHORE.

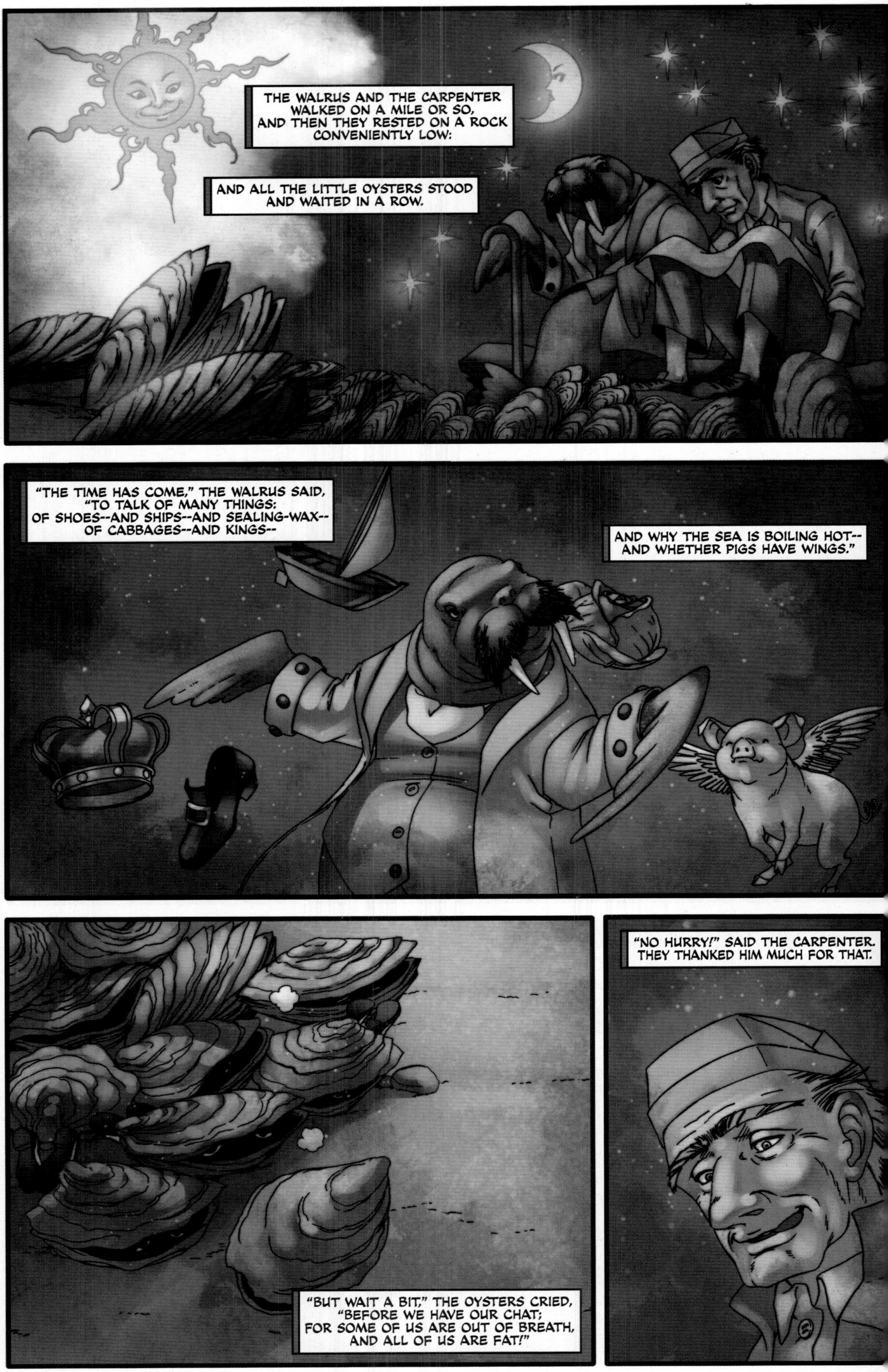
THE WALRUS AND THE CARPENTER WALKED ON A MILE OR SO, AND THEN THEY RESTED ON A ROCK CONVENIENTLY LOW:
AND ALL THE LITTLE OYSTERS STOOD AND WAITED IN A ROW.
"THE TIME HAS COME," THE WALRUS SAID, "TO TALK OF MANY THINGS: OF SHOES--AND SHIPS--AND SEALING-WAX-- OF CABBAGES--AND KINGS--
AND WHY THE SEA IS BOILING HOT-- AND WHETHER PIGS HAVE WINGS."
"BUT WAIT A BIT," THE OYSTERS CRIED, "BEFORE WE HAVE OUR CHAT; FOR SOME OF US ARE OUT OF BREATH, AND ALL OF US ARE FAT!"
"NO HURRY!" SAID THE CARPENTER. THEY THANKED HIM MUCH FOR THAT.

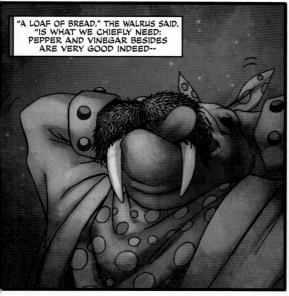

"A LOAF OF BREAD," THE WALRUS SAID, "IS WHAT WE CHIEFLY NEED: PEPPER AND VINEGAR BESIDES ARE VERY GOOD INDEED--

NOW IF YOU'RE READY OYSTERS DEAR, WE CAN BEGIN TO FEED."

"BUT NOT ON US!" THE OYSTERS CRIED, TURNING A LITTLE BLUE, "AFTER SUCH KINDNESS, THAT WOULD BE A DISMAL THING TO DO!"

"THE NIGHT IS FINE," THE WALRUS SAID. "DO YOU ADMIRE THE VIEW?

"IT WAS SO KIND OF YOU TO COME! AND YOU ARE VERY NICE!" THE CARPENTER SAID NOTHING BUT "CUT US ANOTHER SLICE:

I WISH YOU WERE NOT QUITE SO DEAF-- I'VE HAD TO ASK YOU TWICE!"

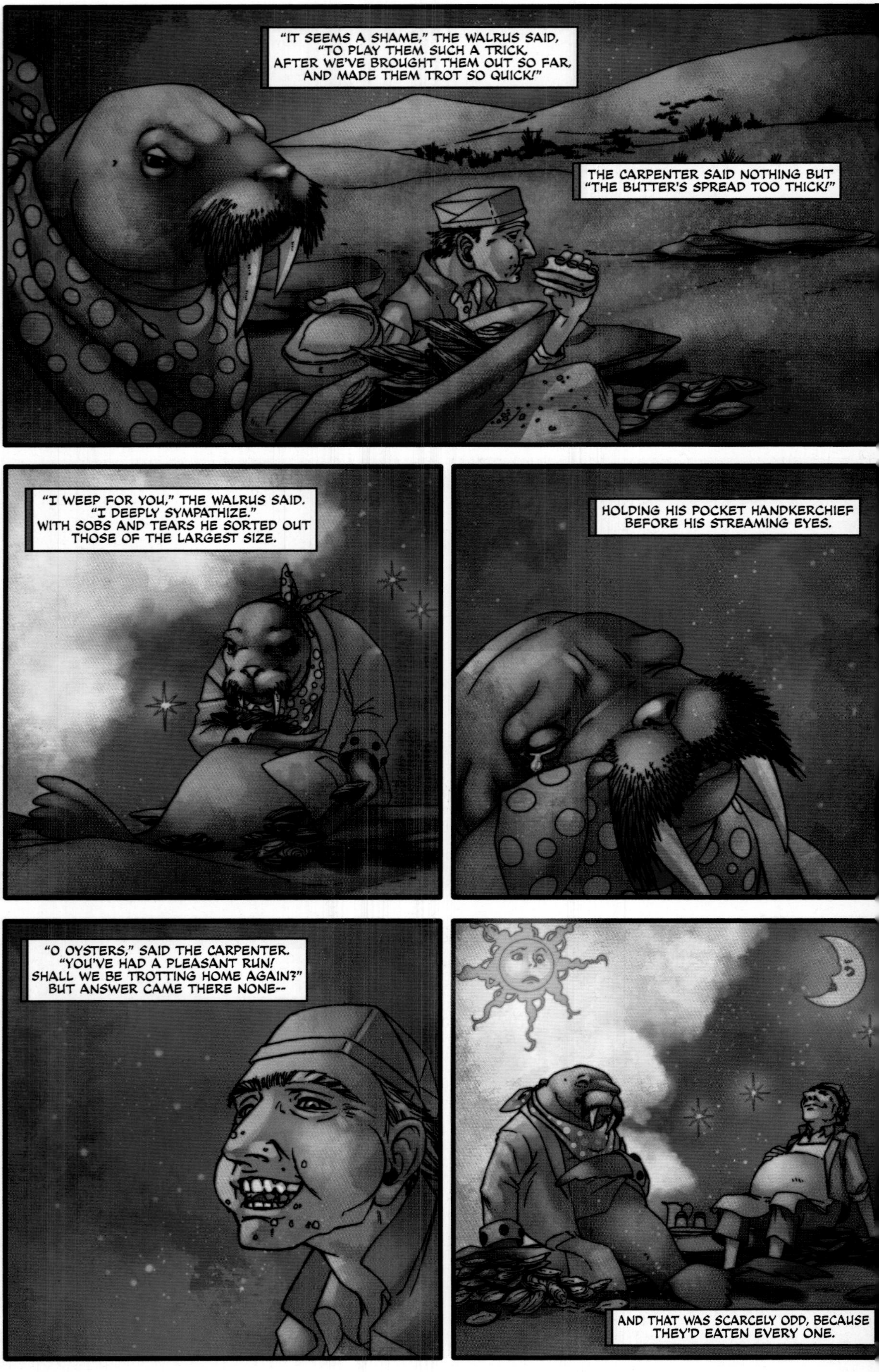
"IT SEEMS A SHAME," THE WALRUS SAID, "TO PLAY THEM SUCH A TRICK, AFTER WE'VE BROUGHT THEM OUT SO FAR, AND MADE THEM TROT SO QUICK!"
THE CARPENTER SAID NOTHING BUT "THE BUTTER'S SPREAD TOO THICK!"
"I WEEP FOR YOU," THE WALRUS SAID. "I DEEPLY SYMPATHIZE." WITH SOBS AND TEARS HE SORTED OUT THOSE OF THE LARGEST SIZE.
HOLDING HIS POCKET HANDKERCHIEF BEFORE HIS STREAMING EYES.
"O OYSTERS," SAID THE CARPENTER. "YOU'VE HAD A PLEASANT RUN! SHALL WE BE TROTTING HOME AGAIN?" BUT ANSWER CAME THERE NONE--
AND THAT WAS SCARCELY ODD, BECAUSE THEY'D EATEN EVERY ONE.

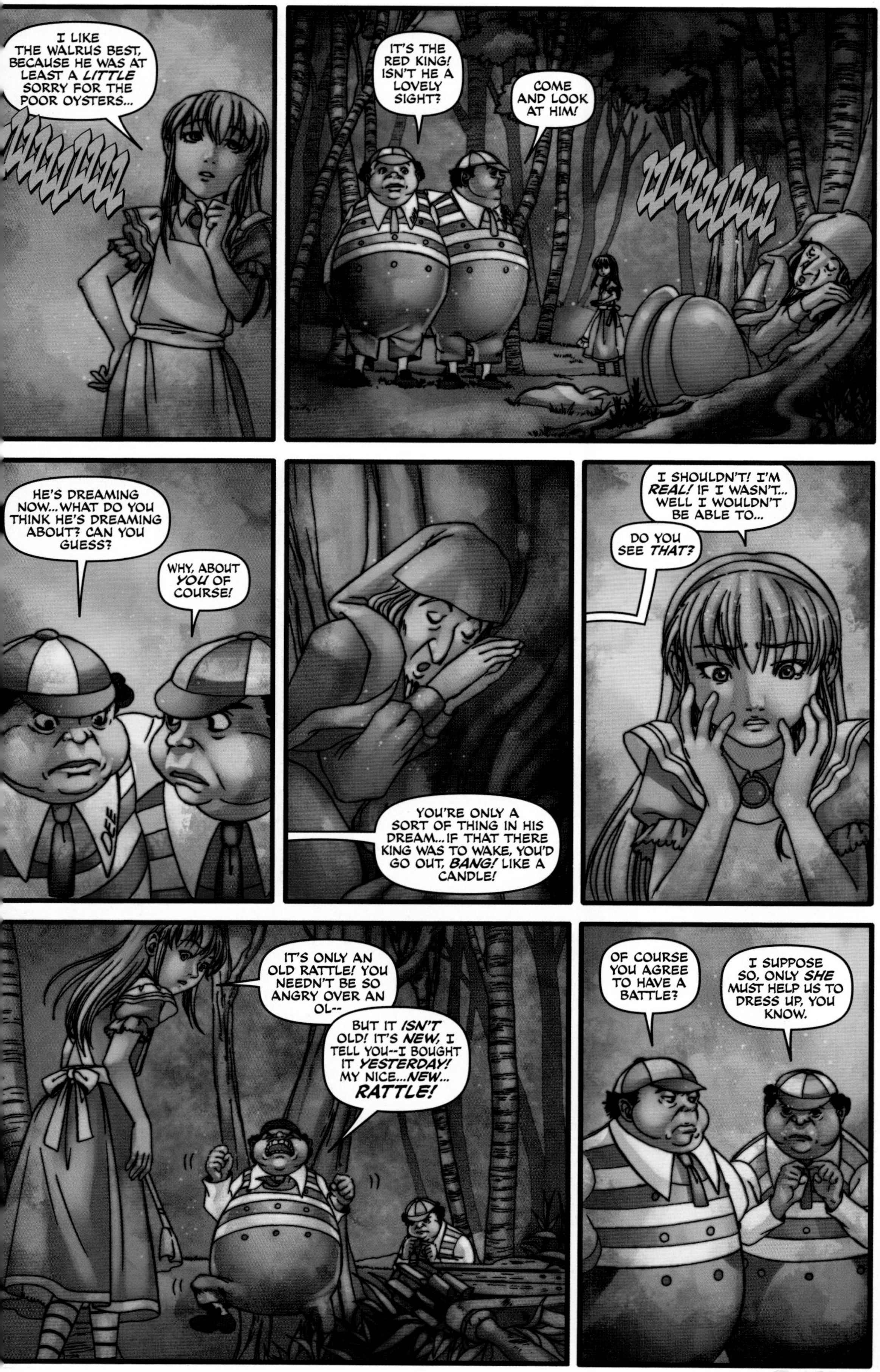
I LIKE THE WALRUS BEST, BECAUSE HE WAS AT LEAST A *LITTLE* SORRY FOR THE POOR OYSTERS...
ZZZZZZZZ
IT'S THE RED KING! ISN'T HE A LOVELY SIGHT?
COME AND LOOK AT HIM!
ZZZZZZZZZZZ
HE'S DREAMING NOW...WHAT DO YOU THINK HE'S DREAMING ABOUT? CAN YOU GUESS?
WHY, ABOUT *YOU* OF COURSE!
DEE
YOU'RE ONLY A SORT OF THING IN HIS DREAM...IF THAT THERE KING WAS TO WAKE, YOU'D GO OUT, *BANG!* LIKE A CANDLE!
I SHOULDN'T! I'M *REAL!* IF I WASN'T... WELL I WOULDN'T BE ABLE TO...
DO YOU SEE *THAT?*
IT'S ONLY AN OLD RATTLE! YOU NEEDN'T BE SO ANGRY OVER AN OL--
BUT IT *ISN'T* OLD! IT'S *NEW,* I TELL YOU--I BOUGHT IT *YESTERDAY!* MY NICE...*NEW*... ***RATTLE!***
OF COURSE YOU AGREE TO HAVE A BATTLE?
I SUPPOSE SO, ONLY *SHE* MUST HELP US TO DRESS UP, YOU KNOW.

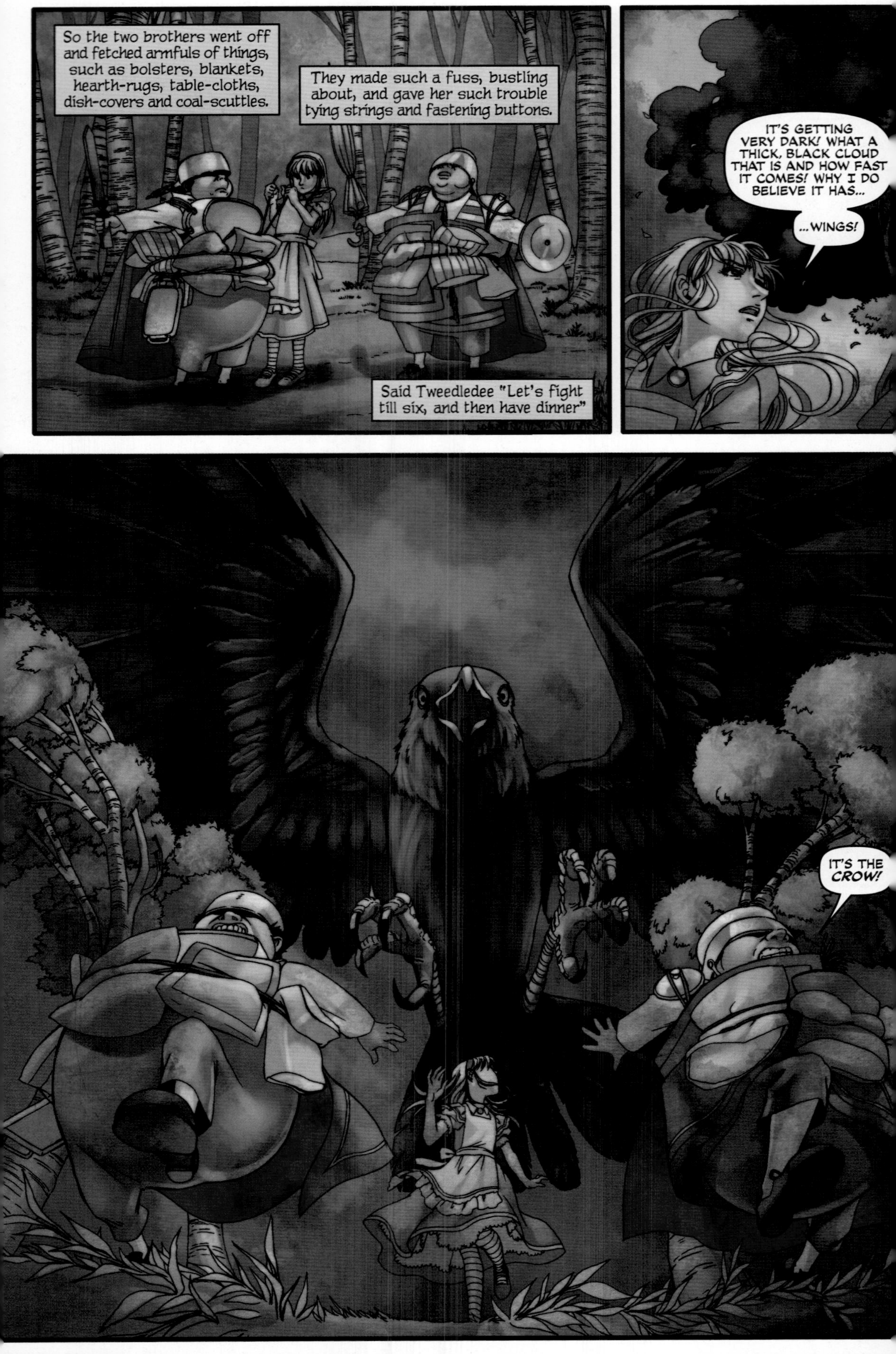
So the two brothers went off and fetched armfuls of things, such as bolsters, blankets, hearth-rugs, table-cloths, dish-covers and coal-scuttles.
They made such a fuss, bustling about, and gave her such trouble tying strings and fastening buttons.
Said Tweedledee "Let's fight till six, and then have dinner"
IT'S GETTING VERY DARK! WHAT A THICK, BLACK CLOUD THAT IS AND HOW FAST IT COMES! WHY I DO BELIEVE IT HAS...
...WINGS!
IT'S THE CROW!

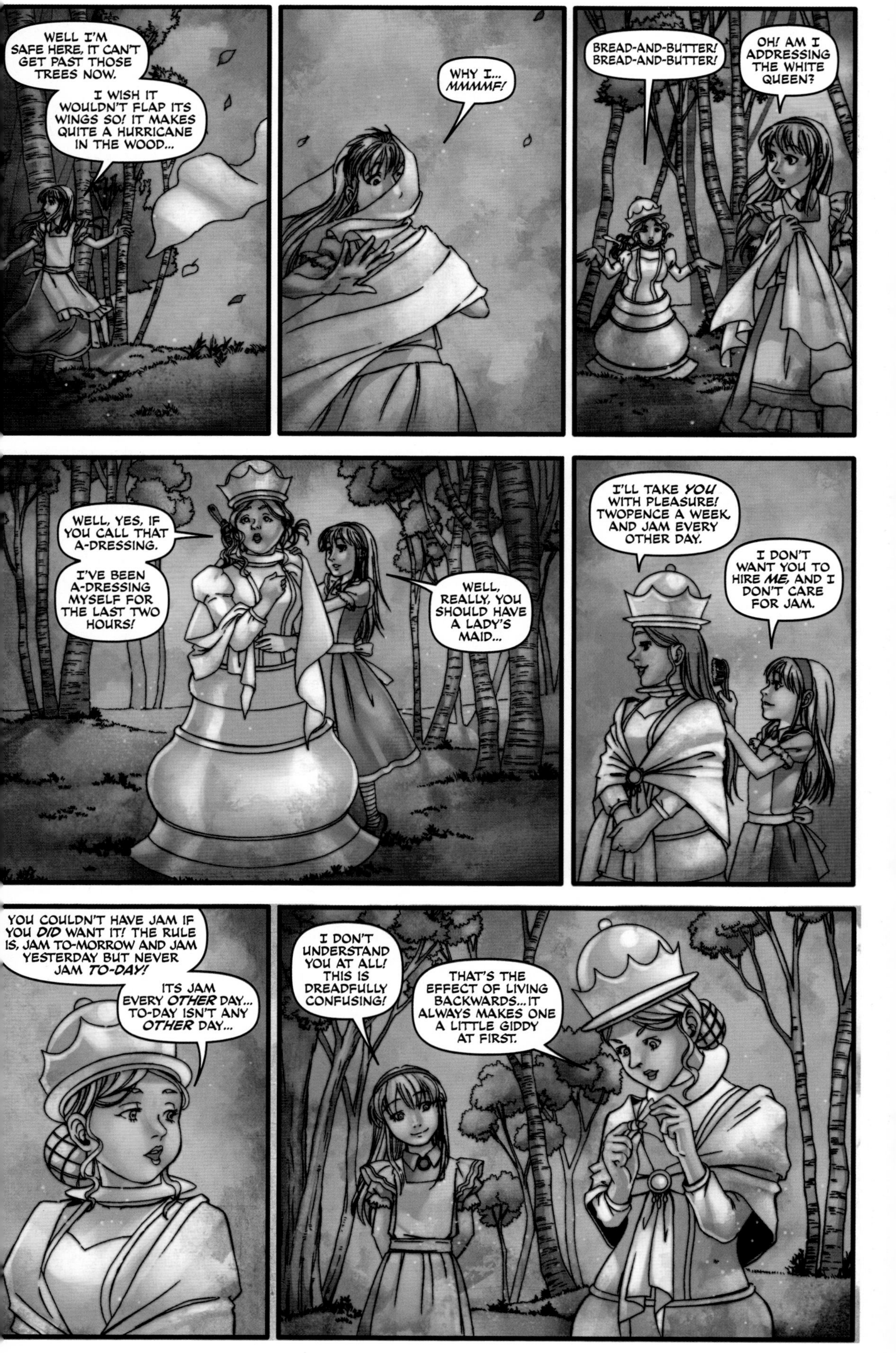
WELL I'M SAFE HERE, IT CAN'T GET PAST THOSE TREES NOW.
I WISH IT WOULDN'T FLAP ITS WINGS SO! IT MAKES QUITE A HURRICANE IN THE WOOD...
WHY I... MMMMF!
BREAD-AND-BUTTER! BREAD-AND-BUTTER!
OH! AM I ADDRESSING THE WHITE QUEEN?
WELL, YES, IF YOU CALL THAT A-DRESSING.
I'VE BEEN A-DRESSING MYSELF FOR THE LAST TWO HOURS!
WELL, REALLY, YOU SHOULD HAVE A LADY'S MAID...
I'LL TAKE YOU WITH PLEASURE! TWOPENCE A WEEK, AND JAM EVERY OTHER DAY.
I DON'T WANT YOU TO HIRE ME, AND I DON'T CARE FOR JAM.
YOU COULDN'T HAVE JAM IF YOU DID WANT IT! THE RULE IS, JAM TO-MORROW AND JAM YESTERDAY BUT NEVER JAM TO-DAY!
ITS JAM EVERY OTHER DAY... TO-DAY ISN'T ANY OTHER DAY...
I DON'T UNDERSTAND YOU AT ALL! THIS IS DREADFULLY CONFUSING!
THAT'S THE EFFECT OF LIVING BACKWARDS... IT ALWAYS MAKES ONE A LITTLE GIDDY AT FIRST.

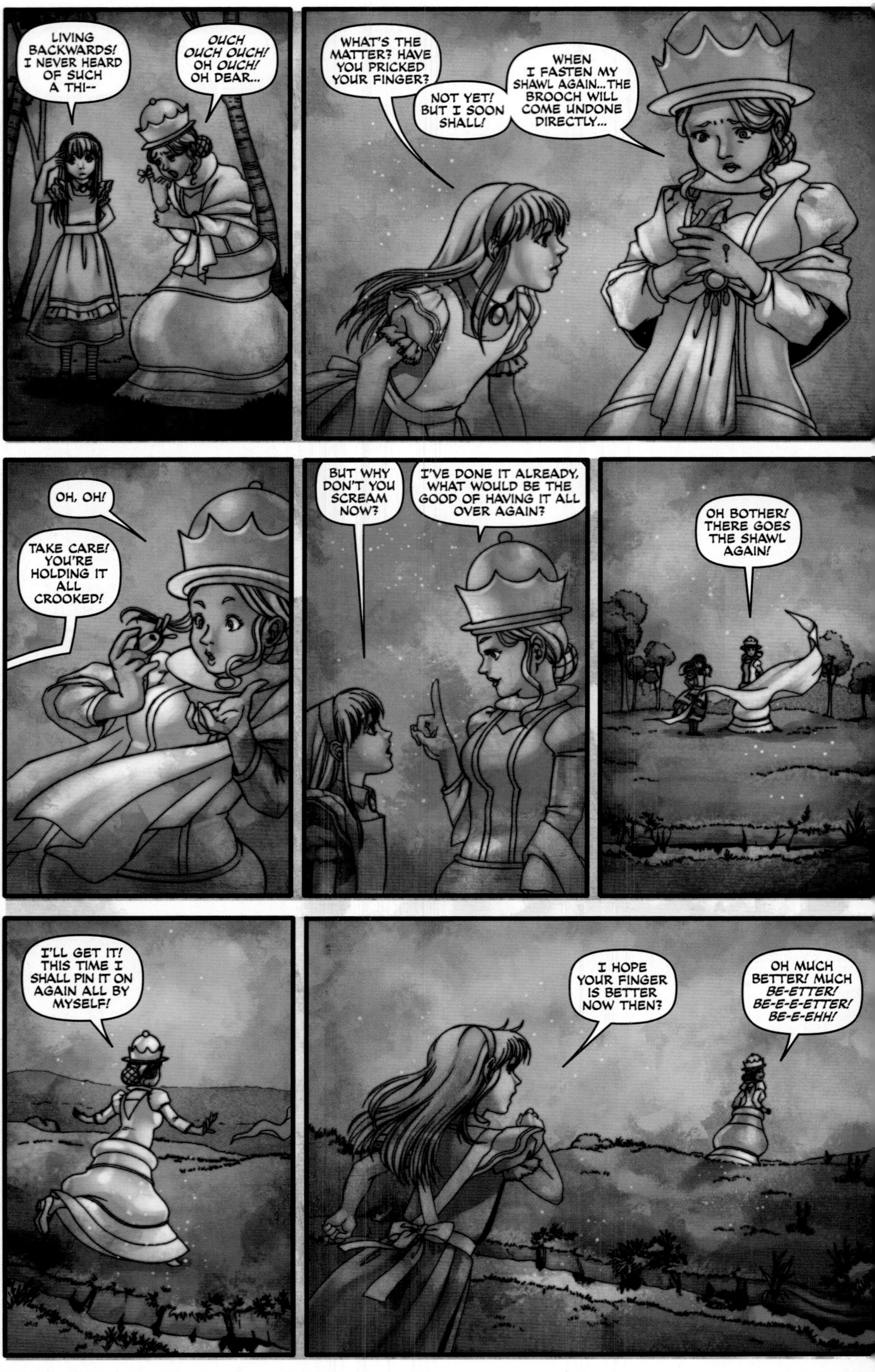
LIVING BACKWARDS! I NEVER HEARD OF SUCH A THI--
OUCH OUCH OUCH! OH OUCH! OH DEAR...
WHAT'S THE MATTER? HAVE YOU PRICKED YOUR FINGER?
NOT YET! BUT I SOON SHALL!
WHEN I FASTEN MY SHAWL AGAIN...THE BROOCH WILL COME UNDONE DIRECTLY...
OH, OH!
TAKE CARE! YOU'RE HOLDING IT ALL CROOKED!
BUT WHY DON'T YOU SCREAM NOW?
I'VE DONE IT ALREADY, WHAT WOULD BE THE GOOD OF HAVING IT ALL OVER AGAIN?
OH BOTHER! THERE GOES THE SHAWL AGAIN!
I'LL GET IT! THIS TIME I SHALL PIN IT ON AGAIN ALL BY MYSELF!
I HOPE YOUR FINGER IS BETTER NOW THEN?
OH MUCH BETTER! MUCH BE-ETTER! BE-E-E-ETTER! BE-E-EHH!

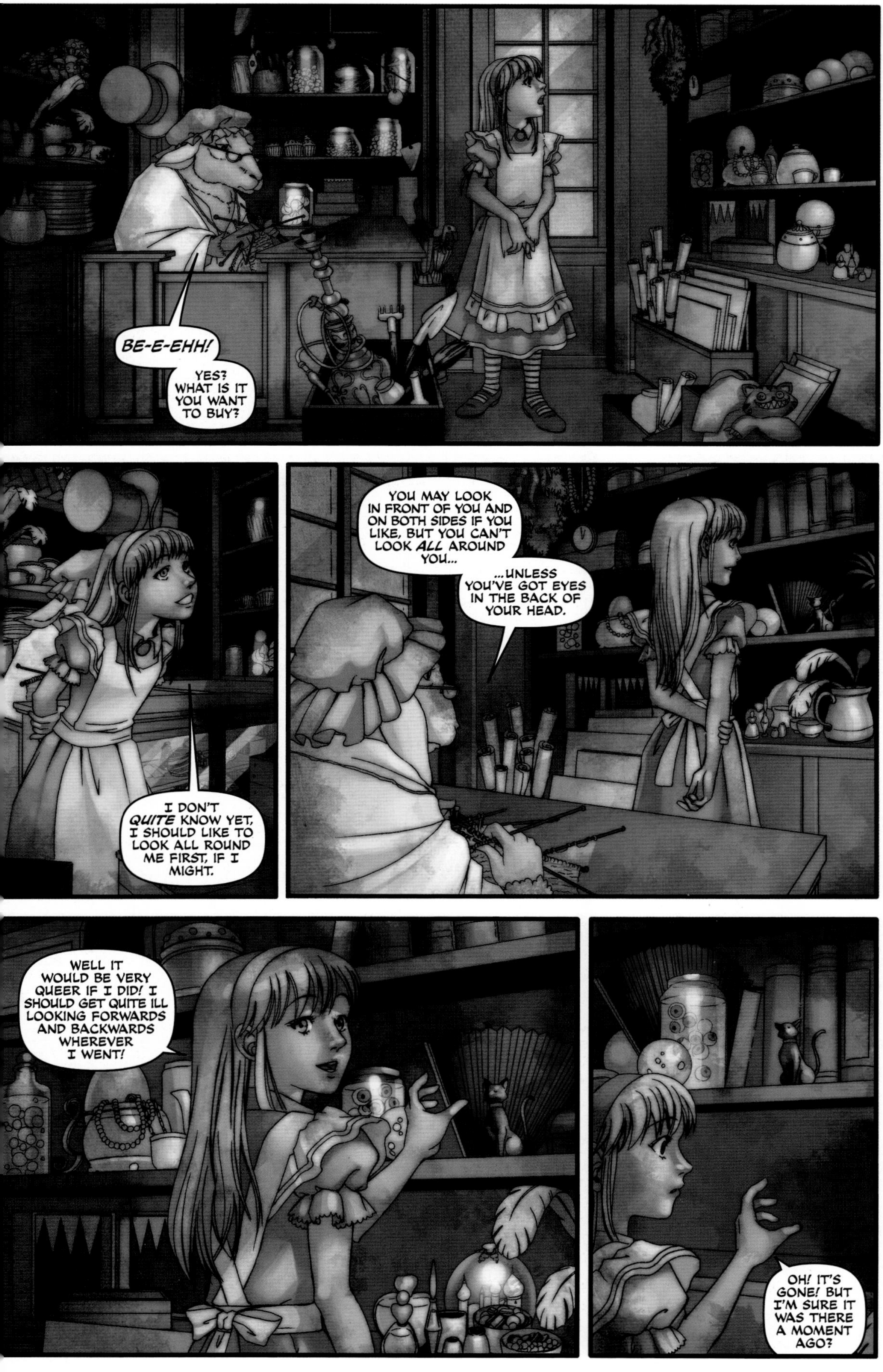
BE-E-EHH!
YES? WHAT IS IT YOU WANT TO BUY?
I DON'T *QUITE* KNOW YET, I SHOULD LIKE TO LOOK ALL ROUND ME FIRST, IF I MIGHT.
YOU MAY LOOK IN FRONT OF YOU AND ON BOTH SIDES IF YOU LIKE, BUT YOU CAN'T LOOK *ALL* AROUND YOU...
...UNLESS YOU'VE GOT EYES IN THE BACK OF YOUR HEAD.
WELL IT WOULD BE VERY QUEER IF I DID! I SHOULD GET QUITE ILL LOOKING FORWARDS AND BACKWARDS WHEREVER I WENT!
OH! IT'S GONE! BUT I'M SURE IT WAS THERE A MOMENT AGO?

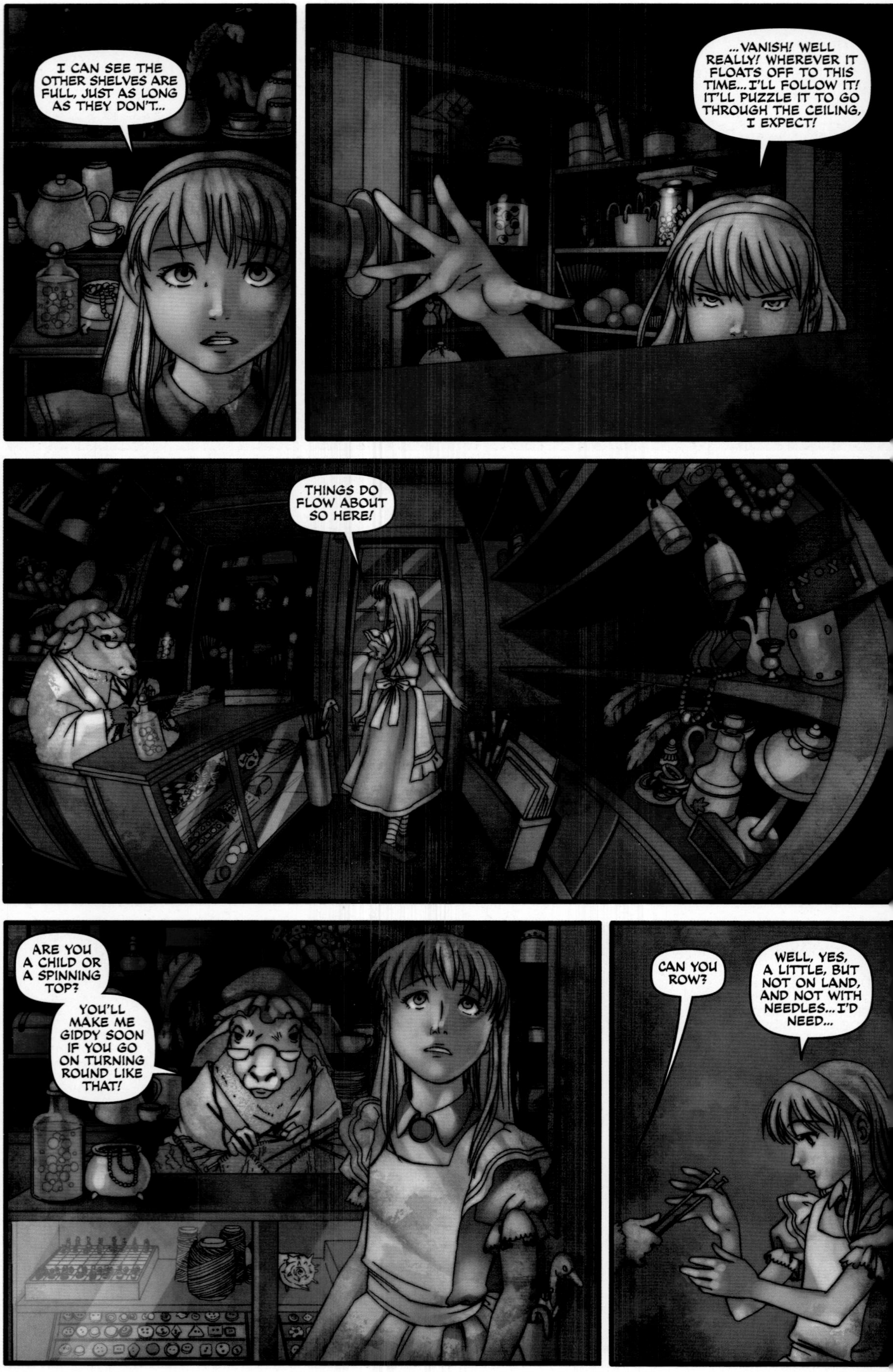
I CAN SEE THE OTHER SHELVES ARE FULL, JUST AS LONG AS THEY DON'T...
...VANISH! WELL REALLY! WHEREVER IT FLOATS OFF TO THIS TIME... I'LL FOLLOW IT! IT'LL PUZZLE IT TO GO THROUGH THE CEILING, I EXPECT!
THINGS DO FLOW ABOUT SO HERE!
ARE YOU A CHILD OR A SPINNING TOP?
YOU'LL MAKE ME GIDDY SOON IF YOU GO ON TURNING ROUND LIKE THAT!
CAN YOU ROW?
WELL, YES, A LITTLE, BUT NOT ON LAND, AND NOT WITH NEEDLES... I'D NEED...

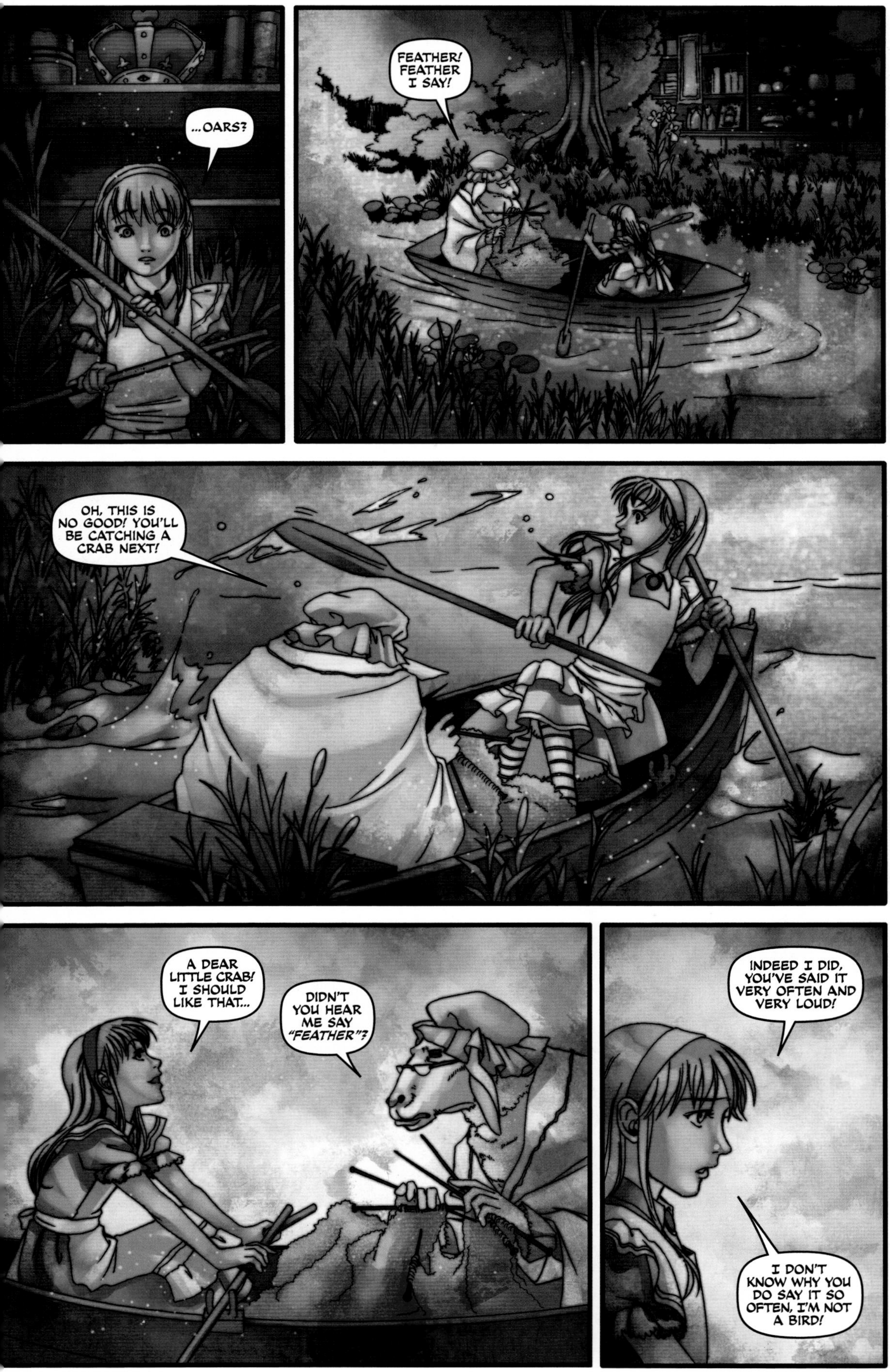
...OARS?
FEATHER! FEATHER I SAY!
OH, THIS IS NO GOOD! YOU'LL BE CATCHING A CRAB NEXT!
A DEAR LITTLE CRAB! I SHOULD LIKE THAT...
DIDN'T YOU HEAR ME SAY "FEATHER"?
INDEED I DID, YOU'VE SAID IT VERY OFTEN AND VERY LOUD!
I DON'T KNOW WHY YOU DO SAY IT SO OFTEN, I'M NOT A BIRD!

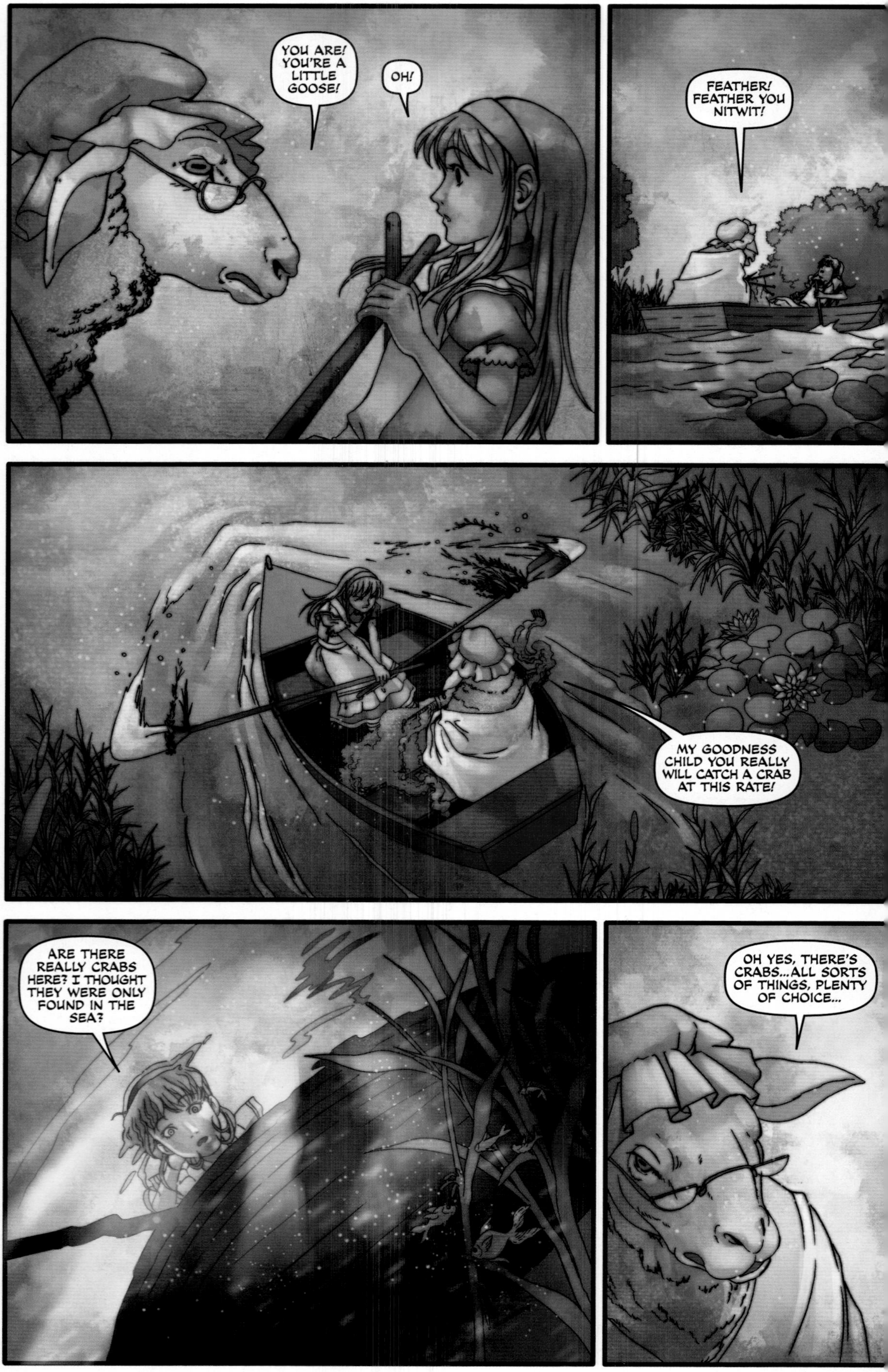
YOU ARE! YOU'RE A LITTLE GOOSE!
OH!
FEATHER! FEATHER YOU NITWIT!
MY GOODNESS CHILD YOU REALLY WILL CATCH A CRAB AT THIS RATE!
ARE THERE REALLY CRABS HERE? I THOUGHT THEY WERE ONLY FOUND IN THE SEA?
OH YES, THERE'S CRABS...ALL SORTS OF THINGS, PLENTY OF CHOICE...

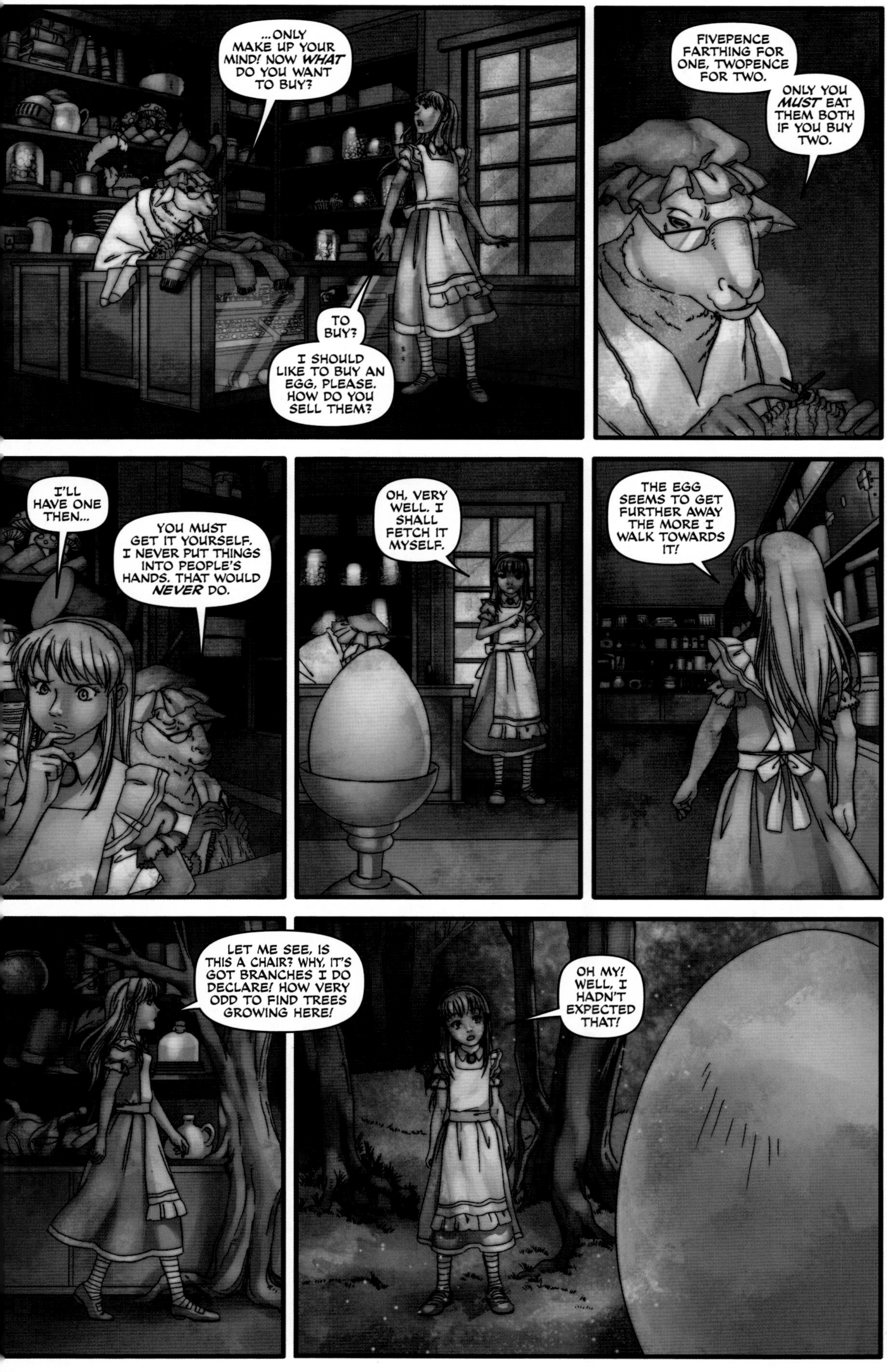
...ONLY MAKE UP YOUR MIND! NOW WHAT DO YOU WANT TO BUY?
TO BUY?
I SHOULD LIKE TO BUY AN EGG, PLEASE. HOW DO YOU SELL THEM?
FIVEPENCE FARTHING FOR ONE, TWOPENCE FOR TWO.
ONLY YOU MUST EAT THEM BOTH IF YOU BUY TWO.
I'LL HAVE ONE THEN...
YOU MUST GET IT YOURSELF. I NEVER PUT THINGS INTO PEOPLE'S HANDS. THAT WOULD NEVER DO.
OH, VERY WELL. I SHALL FETCH IT MYSELF.
THE EGG SEEMS TO GET FURTHER AWAY THE MORE I WALK TOWARDS IT!
LET ME SEE, IS THIS A CHAIR? WHY, IT'S GOT BRANCHES I DO DECLARE! HOW VERY ODD TO FIND TREES GROWING HERE!
OH MY! WELL, I HADN'T EXPECTED THAT!

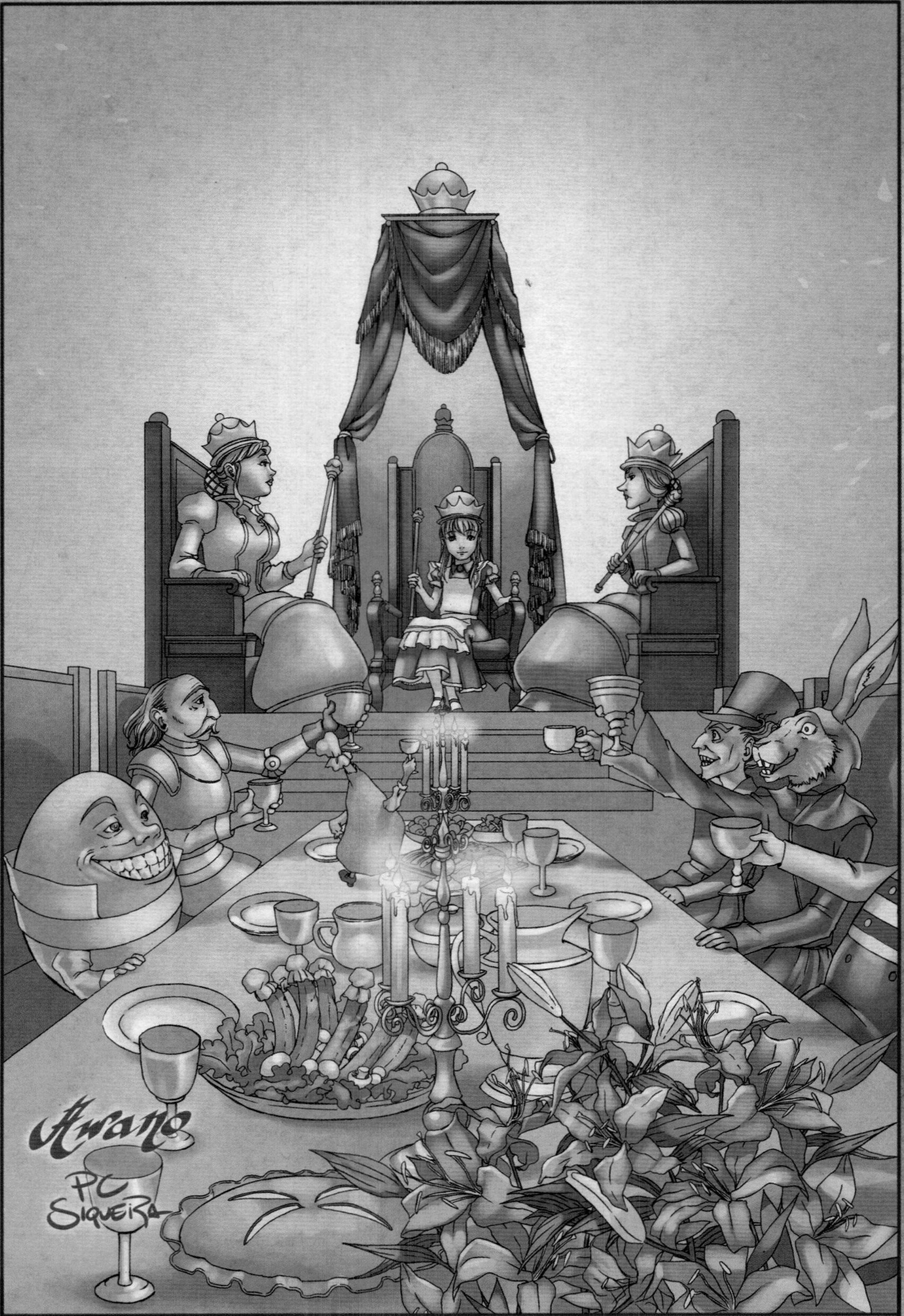
Awano
PC
SIQUEIRA

Issue #4 cover by
ÉRICA AWANO

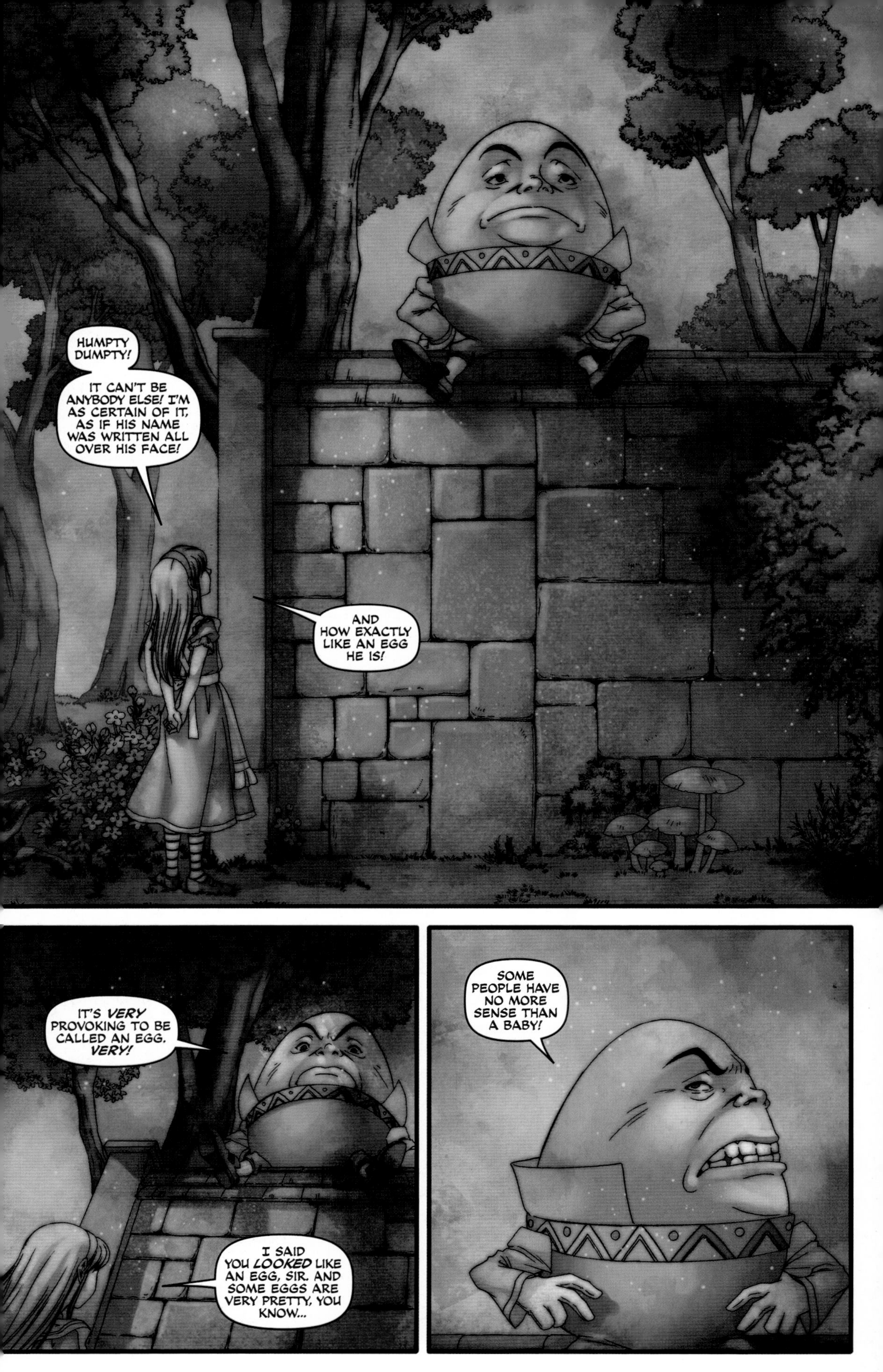
HUMPTY DUMPTY!
IT CAN'T BE ANYBODY ELSE! I'M AS CERTAIN OF IT, AS IF HIS NAME WAS WRITTEN ALL OVER HIS FACE!
AND HOW EXACTLY LIKE AN EGG HE IS!
IT'S *VERY* PROVOKING TO BE CALLED AN EGG. *VERY!*
I SAID YOU *LOOKED* LIKE AN EGG, SIR. AND SOME EGGS ARE VERY PRETTY, YOU KNOW...
SOME PEOPLE HAVE NO MORE SENSE THAN A BABY!

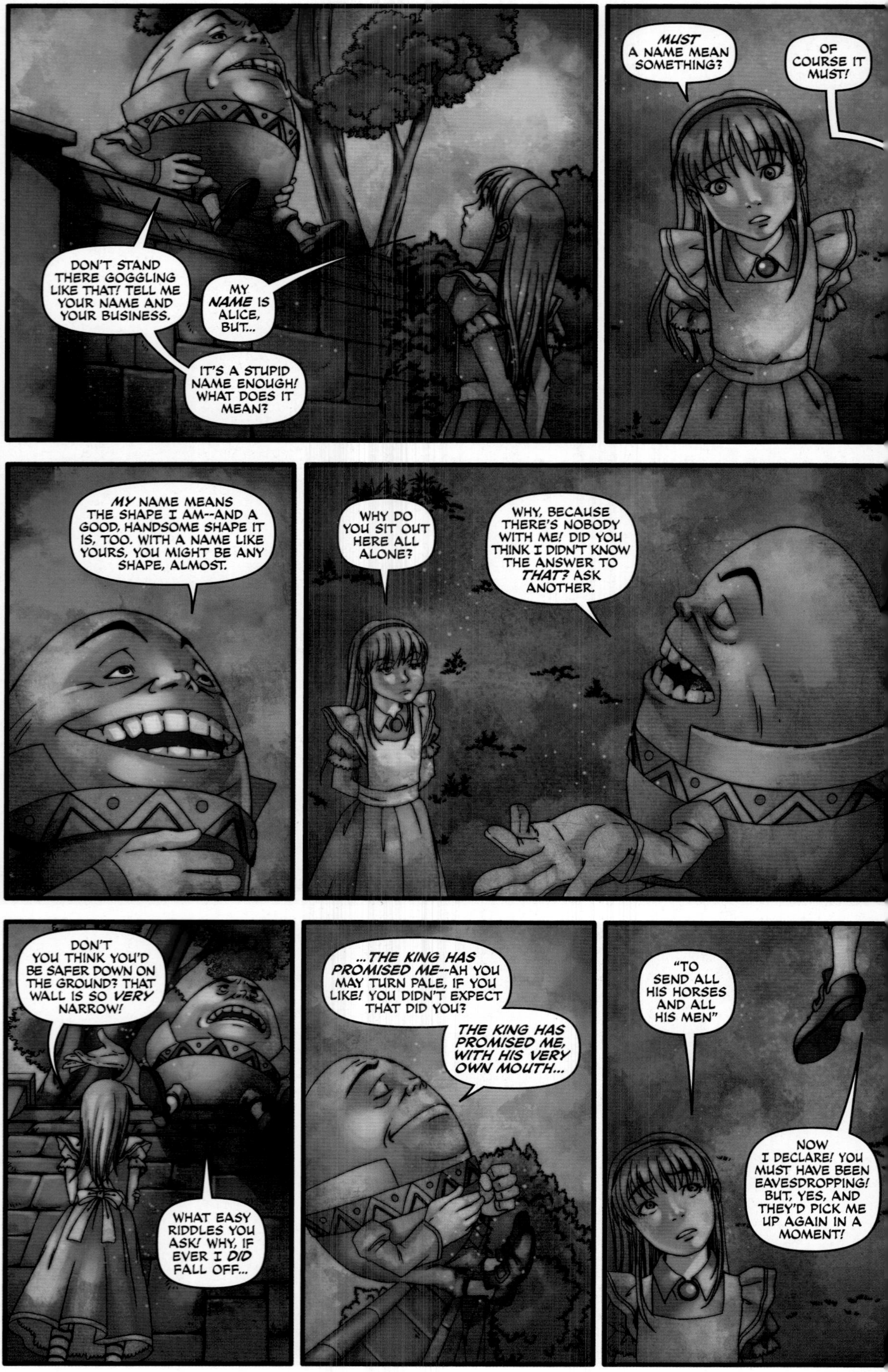
DON'T STAND THERE GOGGLING LIKE THAT! TELL ME YOUR NAME AND YOUR BUSINESS.
MY *NAME* IS ALICE, BUT...
IT'S A STUPID NAME ENOUGH! WHAT DOES IT MEAN?
MUST A NAME MEAN SOMETHING?
OF COURSE IT MUST!
MY NAME MEANS THE SHAPE I AM--AND A GOOD, HANDSOME SHAPE IT IS, TOO. WITH A NAME LIKE YOURS, YOU MIGHT BE ANY SHAPE, ALMOST.
WHY DO YOU SIT OUT HERE ALL ALONE?
WHY, BECAUSE THERE'S NOBODY WITH ME! DID YOU THINK I DIDN'T KNOW THE ANSWER TO *THAT?* ASK ANOTHER.
DON'T YOU THINK YOU'D BE SAFER DOWN ON THE GROUND? THAT WALL IS SO *VERY* NARROW!
WHAT EASY RIDDLES YOU ASK! WHY, IF EVER I *DID* FALL OFF...
...THE KING HAS PROMISED ME--AH YOU MAY TURN PALE, IF YOU LIKE! YOU DIDN'T EXPECT THAT DID YOU?
THE KING HAS PROMISED ME, WITH HIS VERY OWN MOUTH...
"TO SEND ALL HIS HORSES AND ALL HIS MEN"
NOW I DECLARE! YOU MUST HAVE BEEN EAVESDROPPING! BUT, YES, AND THEY'D PICK ME UP AGAIN IN A MOMENT!

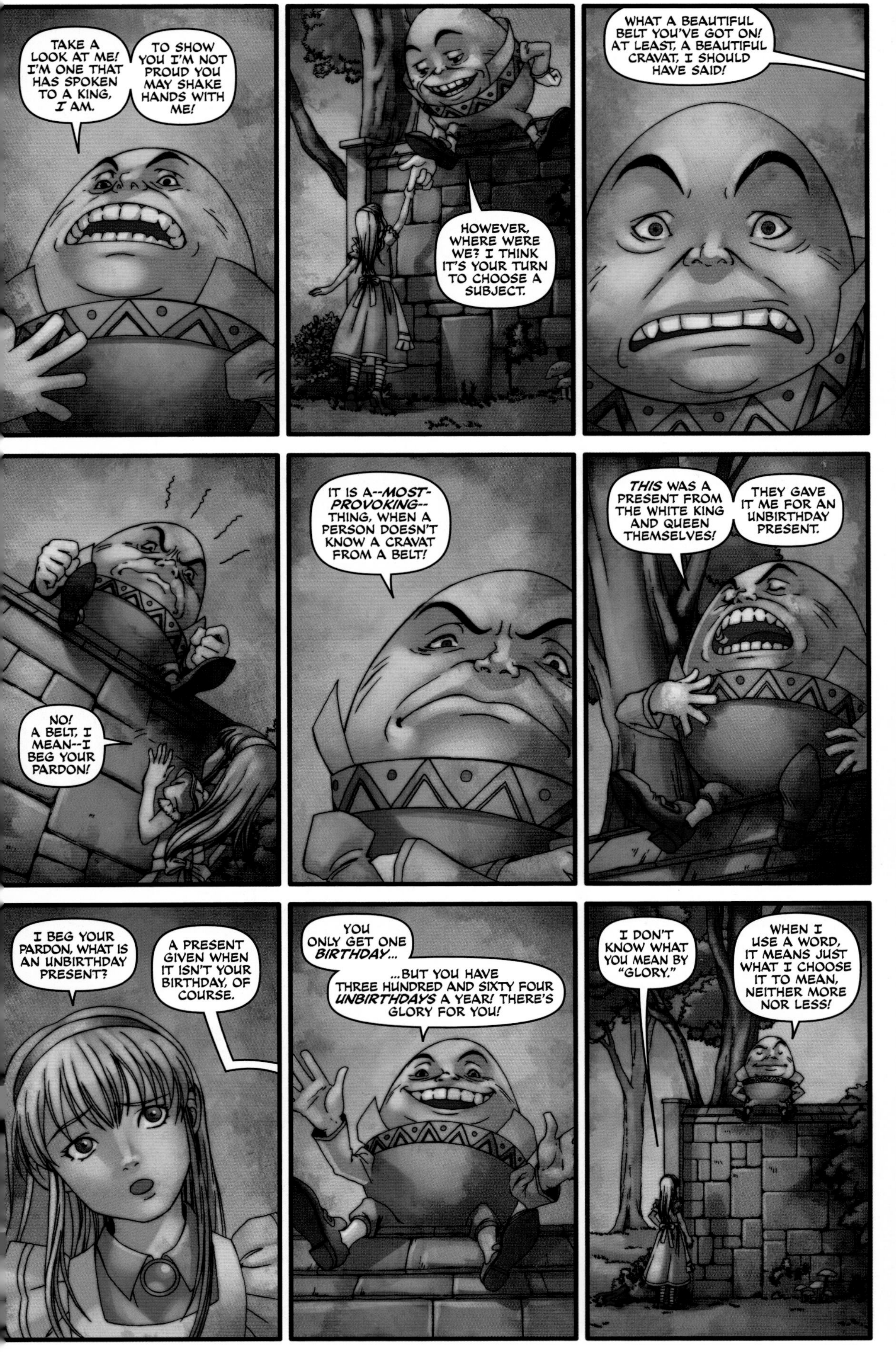
TAKE A LOOK AT ME! I'M ONE THAT HAS SPOKEN TO A KING, I AM.
TO SHOW YOU I'M NOT PROUD YOU MAY SHAKE HANDS WITH ME!
HOWEVER, WHERE WERE WE? I THINK IT'S YOUR TURN TO CHOOSE A SUBJECT.
WHAT A BEAUTIFUL BELT YOU'VE GOT ON! AT LEAST, A BEAUTIFUL CRAVAT, I SHOULD HAVE SAID!
NO! A BELT, I MEAN--I BEG YOUR PARDON!
IT IS A--MOST-PROVOKING--THING, WHEN A PERSON DOESN'T KNOW A CRAVAT FROM A BELT!
THIS WAS A PRESENT FROM THE WHITE KING AND QUEEN THEMSELVES!
THEY GAVE IT ME FOR AN UNBIRTHDAY PRESENT.
I BEG YOUR PARDON, WHAT IS AN UNBIRTHDAY PRESENT?
A PRESENT GIVEN WHEN IT ISN'T YOUR BIRTHDAY, OF COURSE.
YOU ONLY GET ONE BIRTHDAY...
...BUT YOU HAVE THREE HUNDRED AND SIXTY FOUR UNBIRTHDAYS A YEAR! THERE'S GLORY FOR YOU!
I DON'T KNOW WHAT YOU MEAN BY "GLORY."
WHEN I USE A WORD, IT MEANS JUST WHAT I CHOOSE IT TO MEAN, NEITHER MORE NOR LESS!

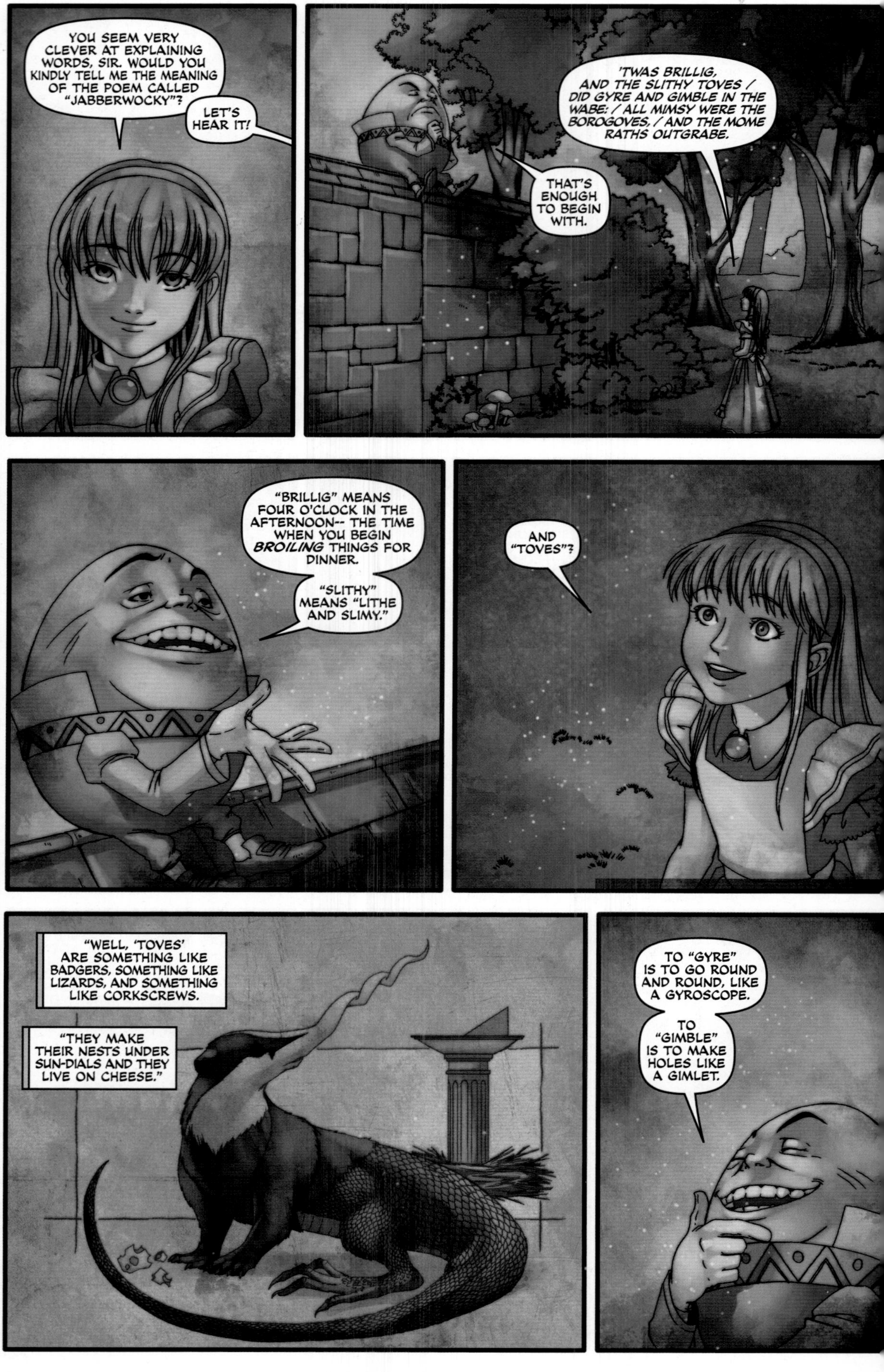

YOU SEEM VERY CLEVER AT EXPLAINING WORDS, SIR. WOULD YOU KINDLY TELL ME THE MEANING OF THE POEM CALLED "JABBERWOCKY"?
LET'S HEAR IT!
'TWAS BRILLIG, AND THE SLITHY TOVES / DID GYRE AND GIMBLE IN THE WABE: / ALL MIMSY WERE THE BOROGOVES, / AND THE MOME RATHS OUTGRABE.
THAT'S ENOUGH TO BEGIN WITH.
"BRILLIG" MEANS FOUR O'CLOCK IN THE AFTERNOON-- THE TIME WHEN YOU BEGIN *BROILING* THINGS FOR DINNER.
"SLITHY" MEANS "LITHE AND SLIMY."
AND "TOVES"?
"WELL, 'TOVES' ARE SOMETHING LIKE BADGERS, SOMETHING LIKE LIZARDS, AND SOMETHING LIKE CORKSCREWS.
"THEY MAKE THEIR NESTS UNDER SUN-DIALS AND THEY LIVE ON CHEESE."
TO "GYRE" IS TO GO ROUND AND ROUND, LIKE A GYROSCOPE.
TO "GIMBLE" IS TO MAKE HOLES LIKE A GIMLET.

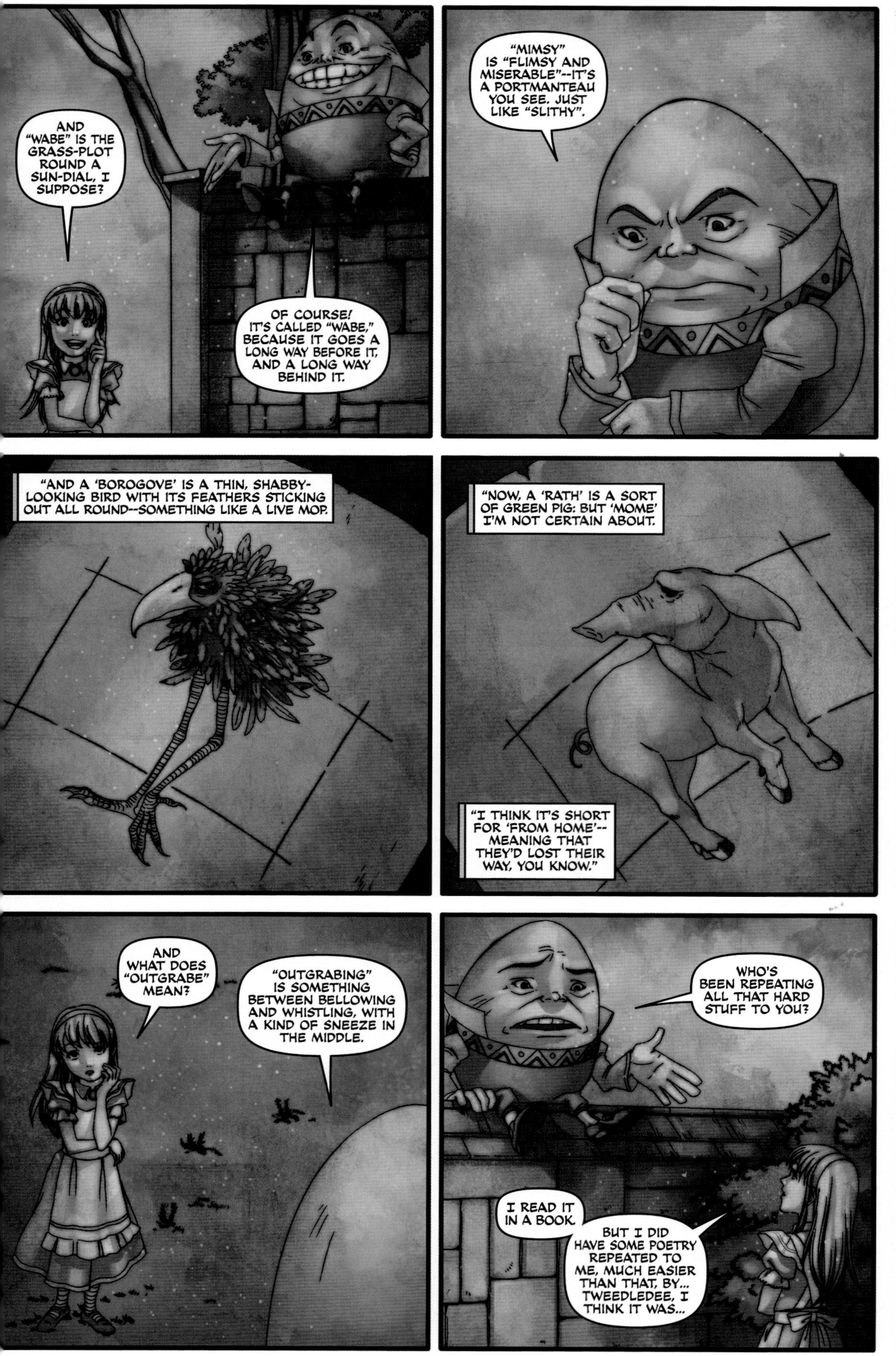
AND "WABE" IS THE GRASS-PLOT ROUND A SUN-DIAL, I SUPPOSE?
OF COURSE! IT'S CALLED "WABE," BECAUSE IT GOES A LONG WAY BEFORE IT, AND A LONG WAY BEHIND IT.
"MIMSY" IS "FLIMSY AND MISERABLE"--IT'S A PORTMANTEAU YOU SEE. JUST LIKE "SLITHY".
"AND A 'BOROGOVE' IS A THIN, SHABBY-LOOKING BIRD WITH ITS FEATHERS STICKING OUT ALL ROUND--SOMETHING LIKE A LIVE MOP.
"NOW, A 'RATH' IS A SORT OF GREEN PIG: BUT 'MOME' I'M NOT CERTAIN ABOUT.
"I THINK IT'S SHORT FOR 'FROM HOME'--MEANING THAT THEY'D LOST THEIR WAY, YOU KNOW."
AND WHAT DOES "OUTGRABE" MEAN?
"OUTGRABING" IS SOMETHING BETWEEN BELLOWING AND WHISTLING, WITH A KIND OF SNEEZE IN THE MIDDLE.
WHO'S BEEN REPEATING ALL THAT HARD STUFF TO YOU?
I READ IT IN A BOOK.
BUT I DID HAVE SOME POETRY REPEATED TO ME, MUCH EASIER THAN THAT, BY... TWEEDLEDEE, I THINK IT WAS...

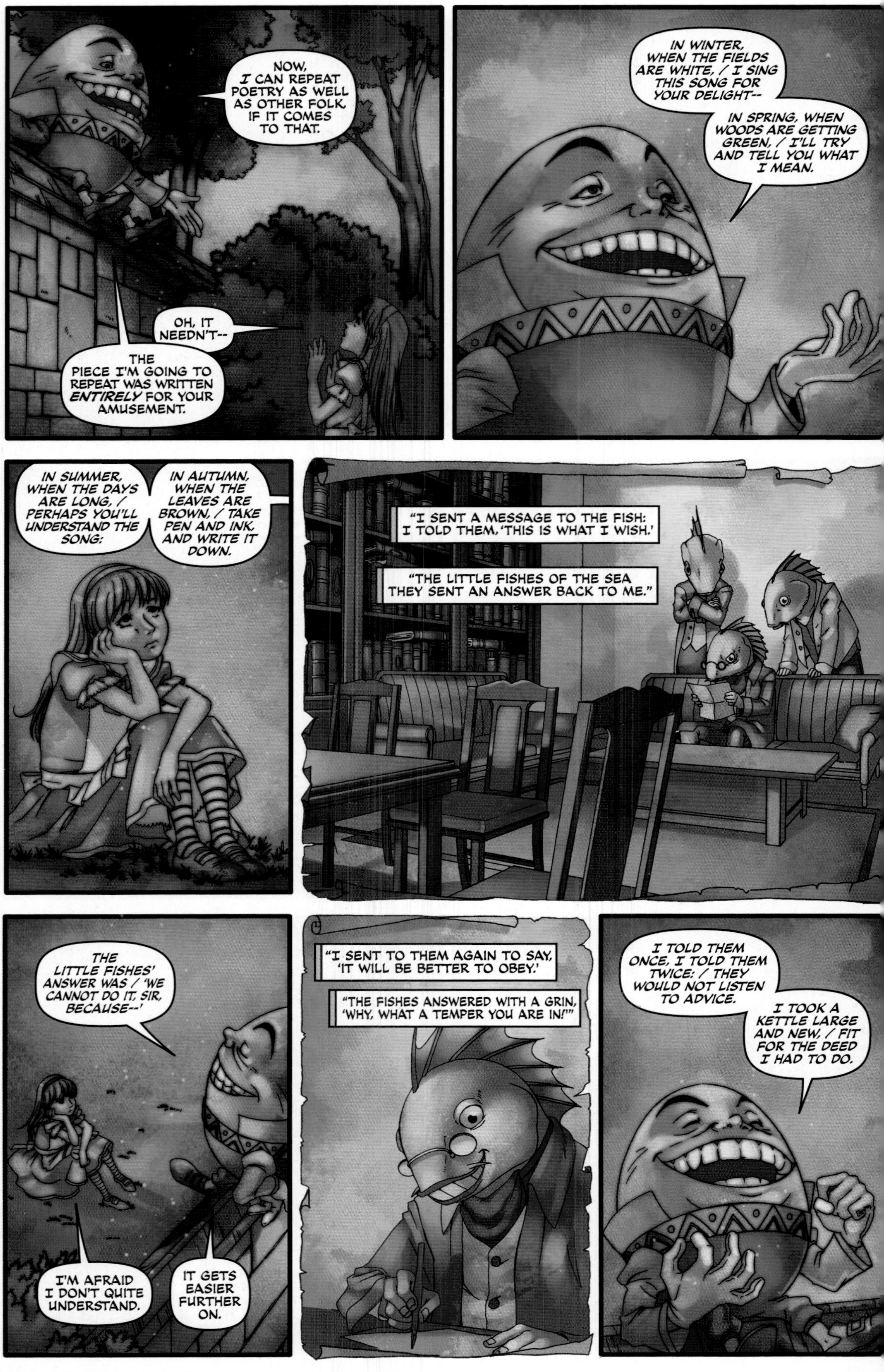
NOW, I CAN REPEAT POETRY AS WELL AS OTHER FOLK, IF IT COMES TO THAT.
OH, IT NEEDN'T--
THE PIECE I'M GOING TO REPEAT WAS WRITTEN ENTIRELY FOR YOUR AMUSEMENT.
IN WINTER, WHEN THE FIELDS ARE WHITE, / I SING THIS SONG FOR YOUR DELIGHT--
IN SPRING, WHEN WOODS ARE GETTING GREEN, / I'LL TRY AND TELL YOU WHAT I MEAN.
IN SUMMER, WHEN THE DAYS ARE LONG, / PERHAPS YOU'LL UNDERSTAND THE SONG:
IN AUTUMN, WHEN THE LEAVES ARE BROWN, / TAKE PEN AND INK, AND WRITE IT DOWN.
"I SENT A MESSAGE TO THE FISH: I TOLD THEM, 'THIS IS WHAT I WISH.'
"THE LITTLE FISHES OF THE SEA THEY SENT AN ANSWER BACK TO ME."
THE LITTLE FISHES' ANSWER WAS / 'WE CANNOT DO IT, SIR, BECAUSE--'
I'M AFRAID I DON'T QUITE UNDERSTAND.
IT GETS EASIER FURTHER ON.
"I SENT TO THEM AGAIN TO SAY, 'IT WILL BE BETTER TO OBEY.'
"THE FISHES ANSWERED WITH A GRIN, 'WHY, WHAT A TEMPER YOU ARE IN!'"
I TOLD THEM ONCE, I TOLD THEM TWICE: / THEY WOULD NOT LISTEN TO ADVICE.
I TOOK A KETTLE LARGE AND NEW, / FIT FOR THE DEED I HAD TO DO.

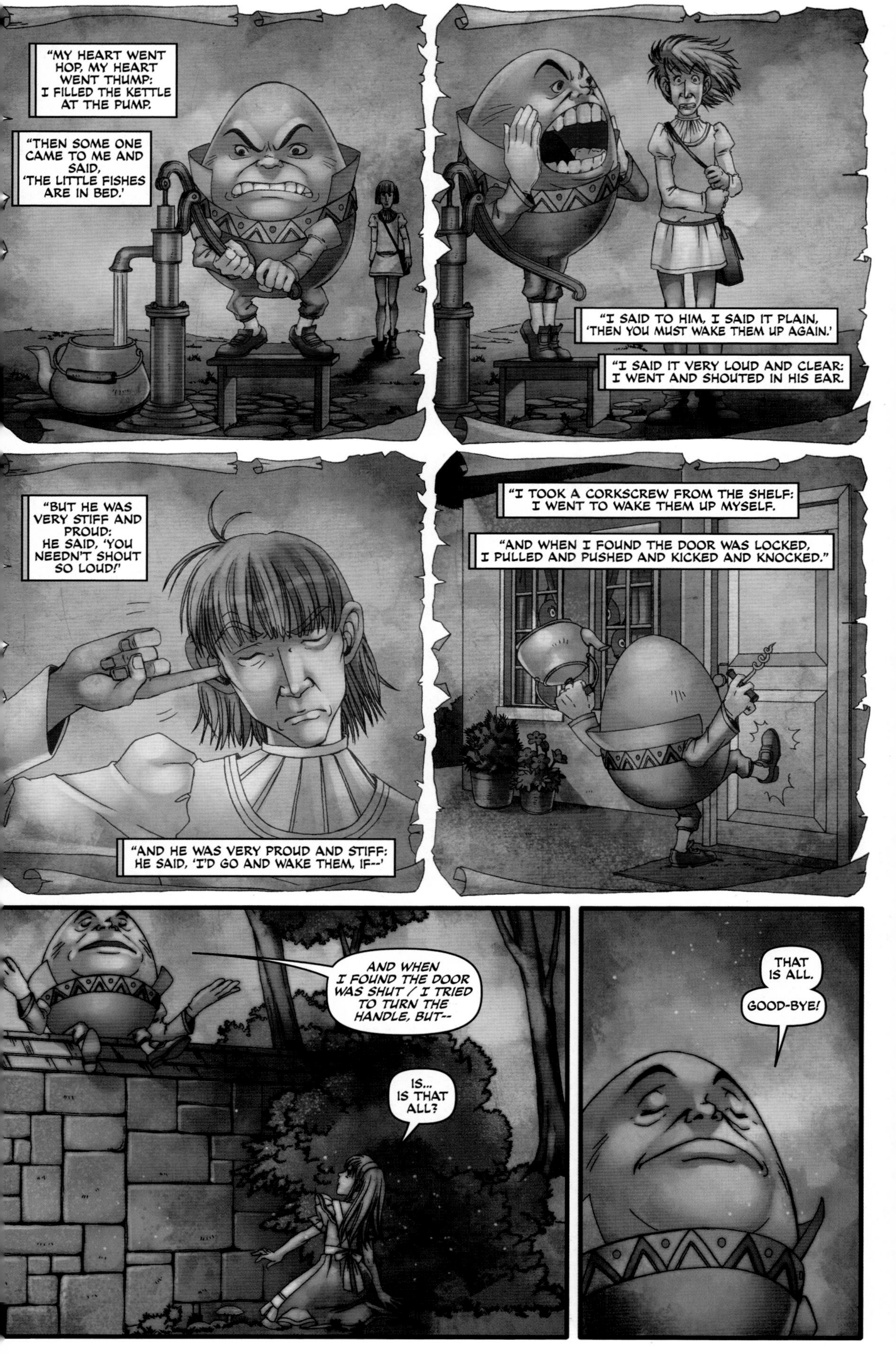
"MY HEART WENT HOP, MY HEART WENT THUMP: I FILLED THE KETTLE AT THE PUMP.
"THEN SOME ONE CAME TO ME AND SAID, 'THE LITTLE FISHES ARE IN BED.'
"I SAID TO HIM, I SAID IT PLAIN, 'THEN YOU MUST WAKE THEM UP AGAIN.'
"I SAID IT VERY LOUD AND CLEAR: I WENT AND SHOUTED IN HIS EAR.
"BUT HE WAS VERY STIFF AND PROUD: HE SAID, 'YOU NEEDN'T SHOUT SO LOUD!'
"AND HE WAS VERY PROUD AND STIFF: HE SAID, 'I'D GO AND WAKE THEM, IF--'
"I TOOK A CORKSCREW FROM THE SHELF: I WENT TO WAKE THEM UP MYSELF.
"AND WHEN I FOUND THE DOOR WAS LOCKED, I PULLED AND PUSHED AND KICKED AND KNOCKED."
AND WHEN I FOUND THE DOOR WAS SHUT / I TRIED TO TURN THE HANDLE, BUT--
IS... IS THAT ALL?
THAT IS ALL.
GOOD-BYE!

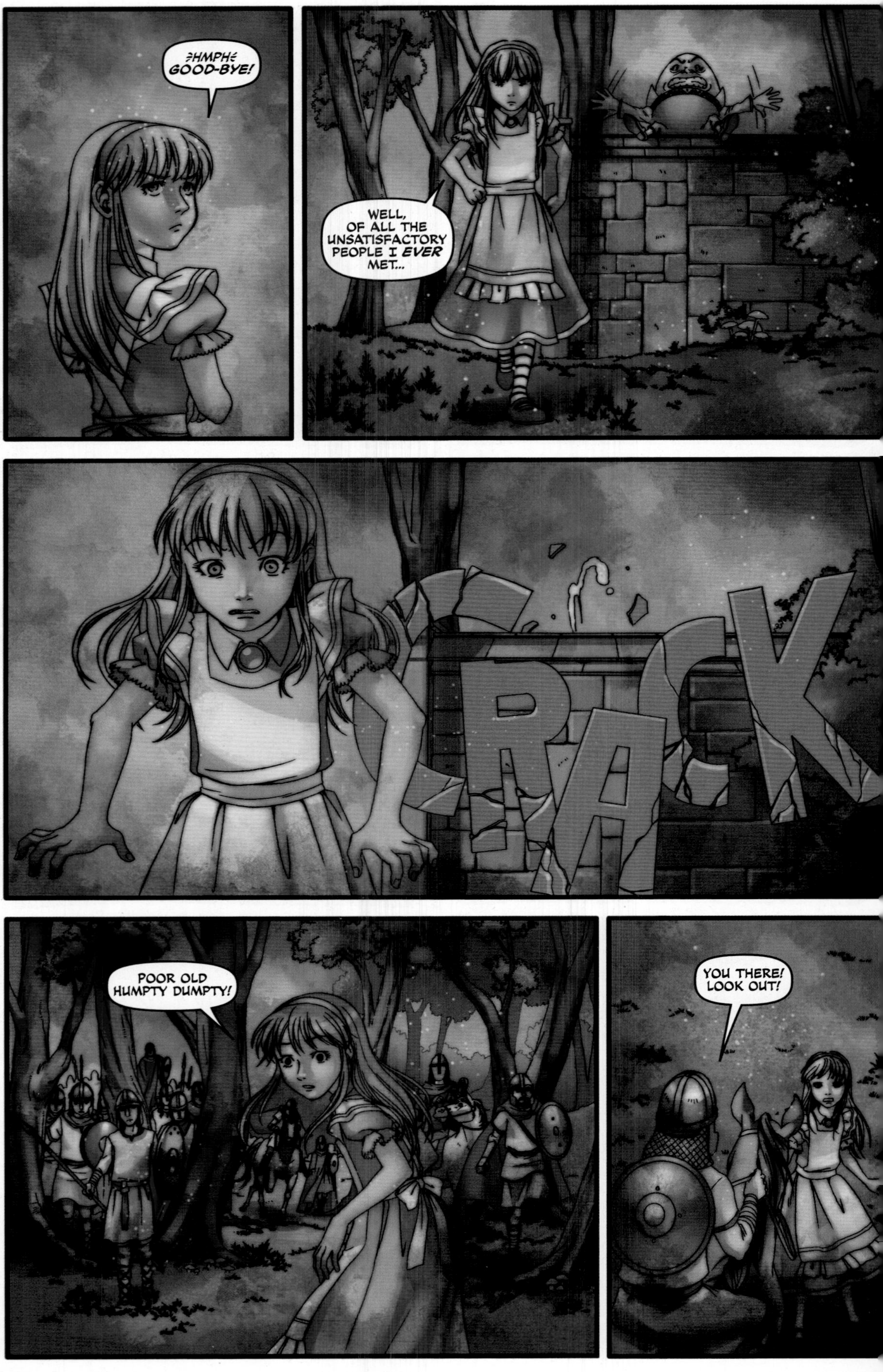

HMPH
GOOD-BYE!
WELL, OF ALL THE UNSATISFACTORY PEOPLE I EVER MET...
CRACK
POOR OLD HUMPTY DUMPTY!
YOU THERE! LOOK OUT!

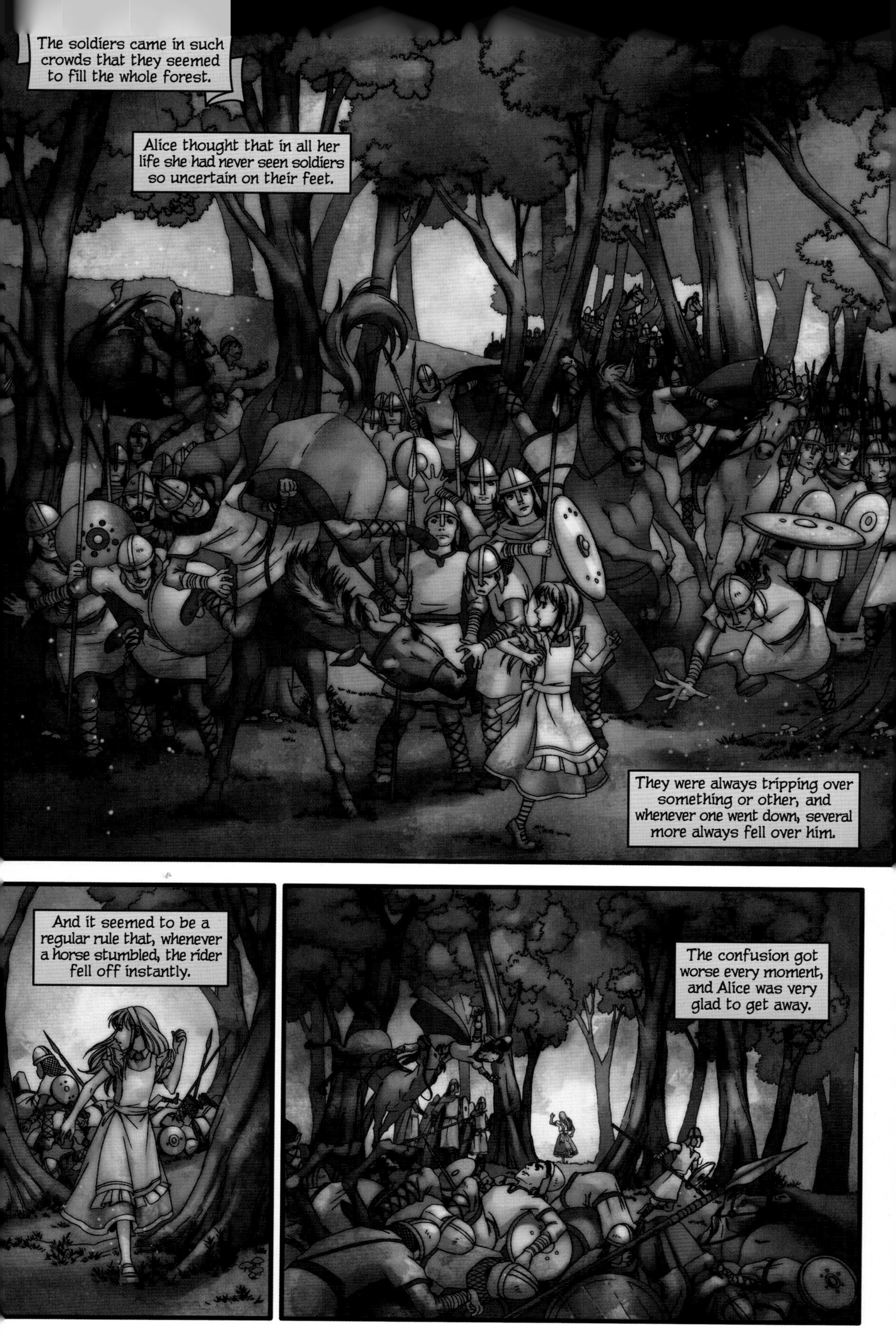
The soldiers came in such crowds that they seemed to fill the whole forest.
Alice thought that in all her life she had never seen soldiers so uncertain on their feet.
They were always tripping over something or other, and whenever one went down, several more always fell over him.
And it seemed to be a regular rule that, whenever a horse stumbled, the rider fell off instantly.
The confusion got worse every moment, and Alice was very glad to get away.

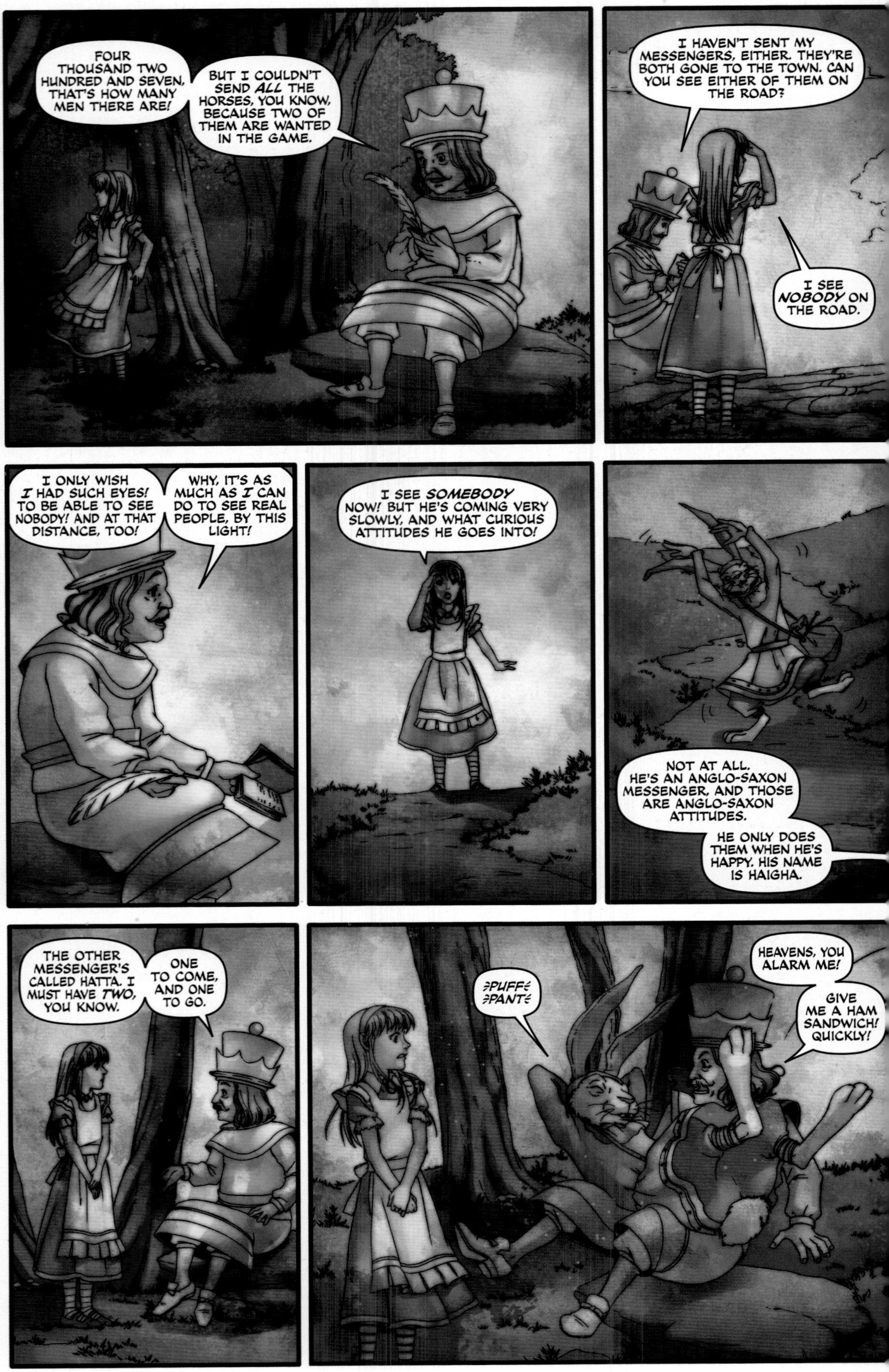
FOUR THOUSAND TWO HUNDRED AND SEVEN, THAT'S HOW MANY MEN THERE ARE!
BUT I COULDN'T SEND *ALL* THE HORSES, YOU KNOW, BECAUSE TWO OF THEM ARE WANTED IN THE GAME.
I HAVEN'T SENT MY MESSENGERS, EITHER. THEY'RE BOTH GONE TO THE TOWN. CAN YOU SEE EITHER OF THEM ON THE ROAD?
I SEE *NOBODY* ON THE ROAD.
I ONLY WISH *I* HAD SUCH EYES! TO BE ABLE TO SEE NOBODY! AND AT THAT DISTANCE, TOO!
WHY, IT'S AS MUCH AS *I* CAN DO TO SEE REAL PEOPLE, BY THIS LIGHT!
I SEE *SOMEBODY* NOW! BUT HE'S COMING VERY SLOWLY, AND WHAT CURIOUS ATTITUDES HE GOES INTO!
NOT AT ALL. HE'S AN ANGLO-SAXON MESSENGER, AND THOSE ARE ANGLO-SAXON ATTITUDES.
HE ONLY DOES THEM WHEN HE'S HAPPY. HIS NAME IS HAIGHA.
THE OTHER MESSENGER'S CALLED HATTA. I MUST HAVE *TWO*, YOU KNOW.
ONE TO COME, AND ONE TO GO.
PUFF
PANT
HEAVENS, YOU ALARM ME!
GIVE ME A HAM SANDWICH! QUICKLY!

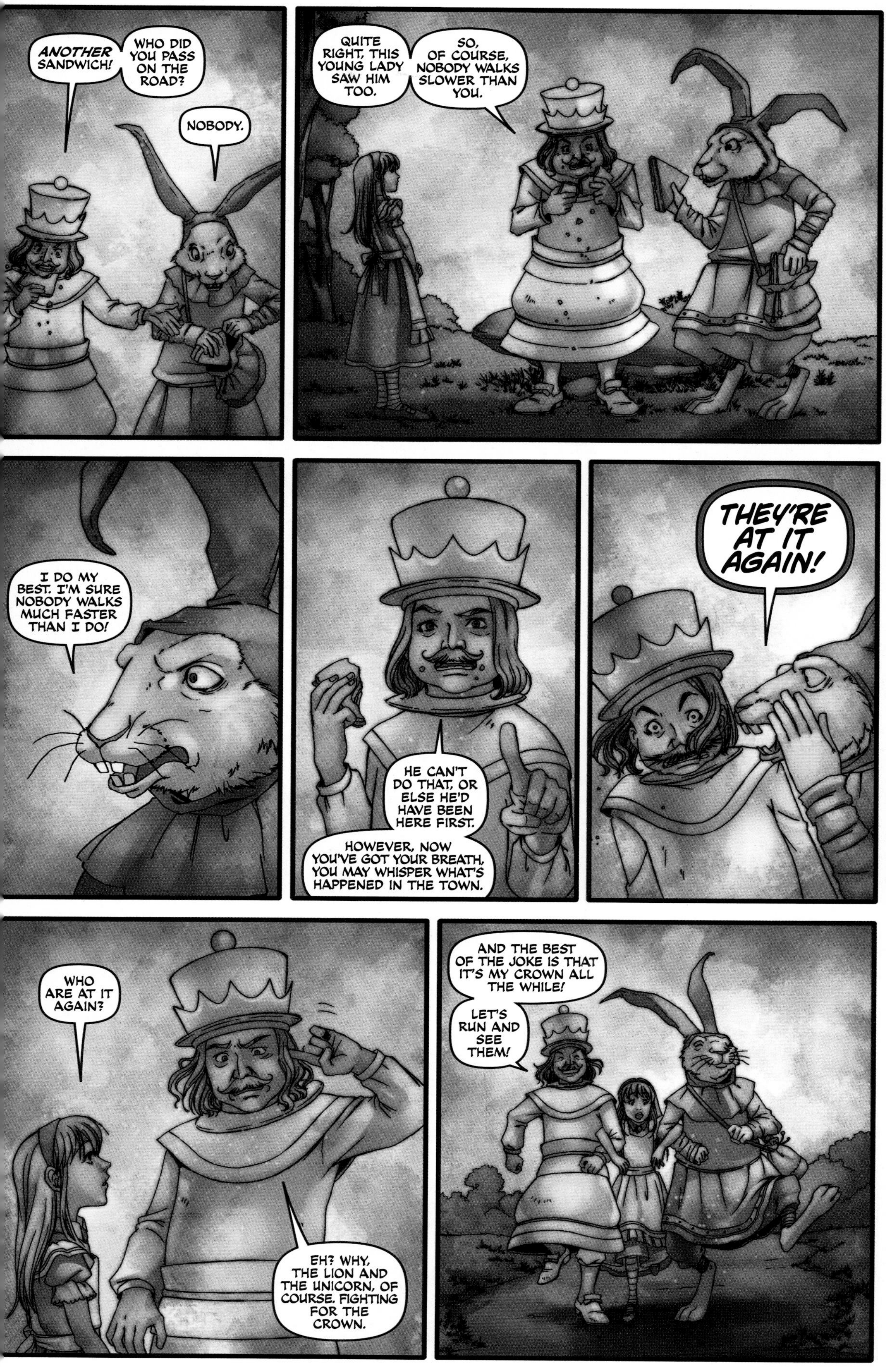
ANOTHER SANDWICH!
WHO DID YOU PASS ON THE ROAD?
NOBODY.
QUITE RIGHT, THIS YOUNG LADY SAW HIM TOO.
SO, OF COURSE, NOBODY WALKS SLOWER THAN YOU.
I DO MY BEST. I'M SURE NOBODY WALKS MUCH FASTER THAN I DO!
HE CAN'T DO THAT, OR ELSE HE'D HAVE BEEN HERE FIRST.
HOWEVER, NOW YOU'VE GOT YOUR BREATH, YOU MAY WHISPER WHAT'S HAPPENED IN THE TOWN.
THEY'RE AT IT AGAIN!
WHO ARE AT IT AGAIN?
EH? WHY, THE LION AND THE UNICORN, OF COURSE. FIGHTING FOR THE CROWN.
AND THE BEST OF THE JOKE IS THAT IT'S MY CROWN ALL THE WHILE!
LET'S RUN AND SEE THEM!

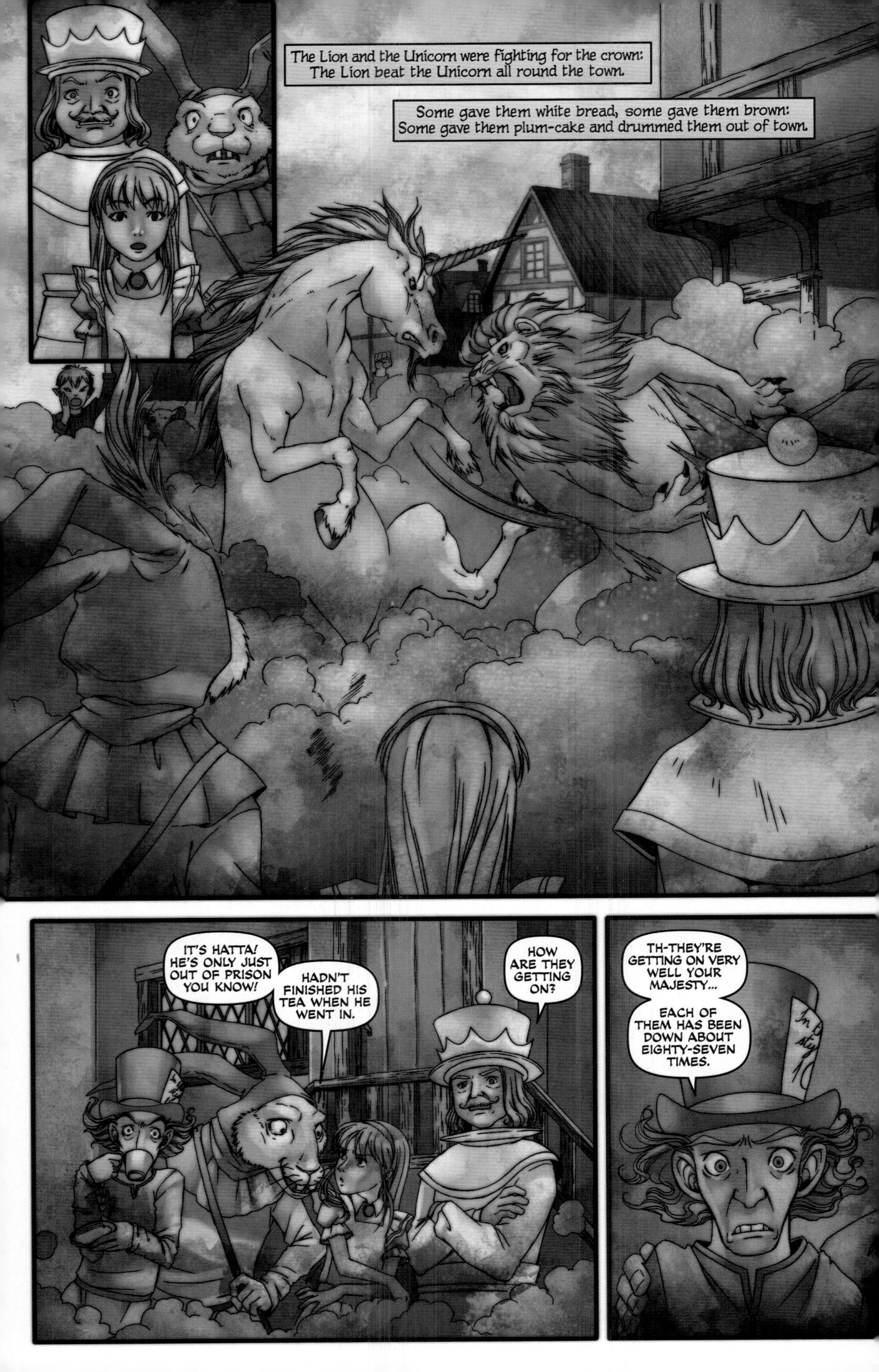

The Lion and the Unicorn were fighting for the crown:
The Lion beat the Unicorn all round the town.
Some gave them white bread, some gave them brown:
Some gave them plum-cake and drummed them out of town.
IT'S HATTA! HE'S ONLY JUST OUT OF PRISON YOU KNOW!
HADN'T FINISHED HIS TEA WHEN HE WENT IN.
HOW ARE THEY GETTING ON?
TH-THEY'RE GETTING ON VERY WELL YOUR MAJESTY...
EACH OF THEM HAS BEEN DOWN ABOUT EIGHTY-SEVEN TIMES.

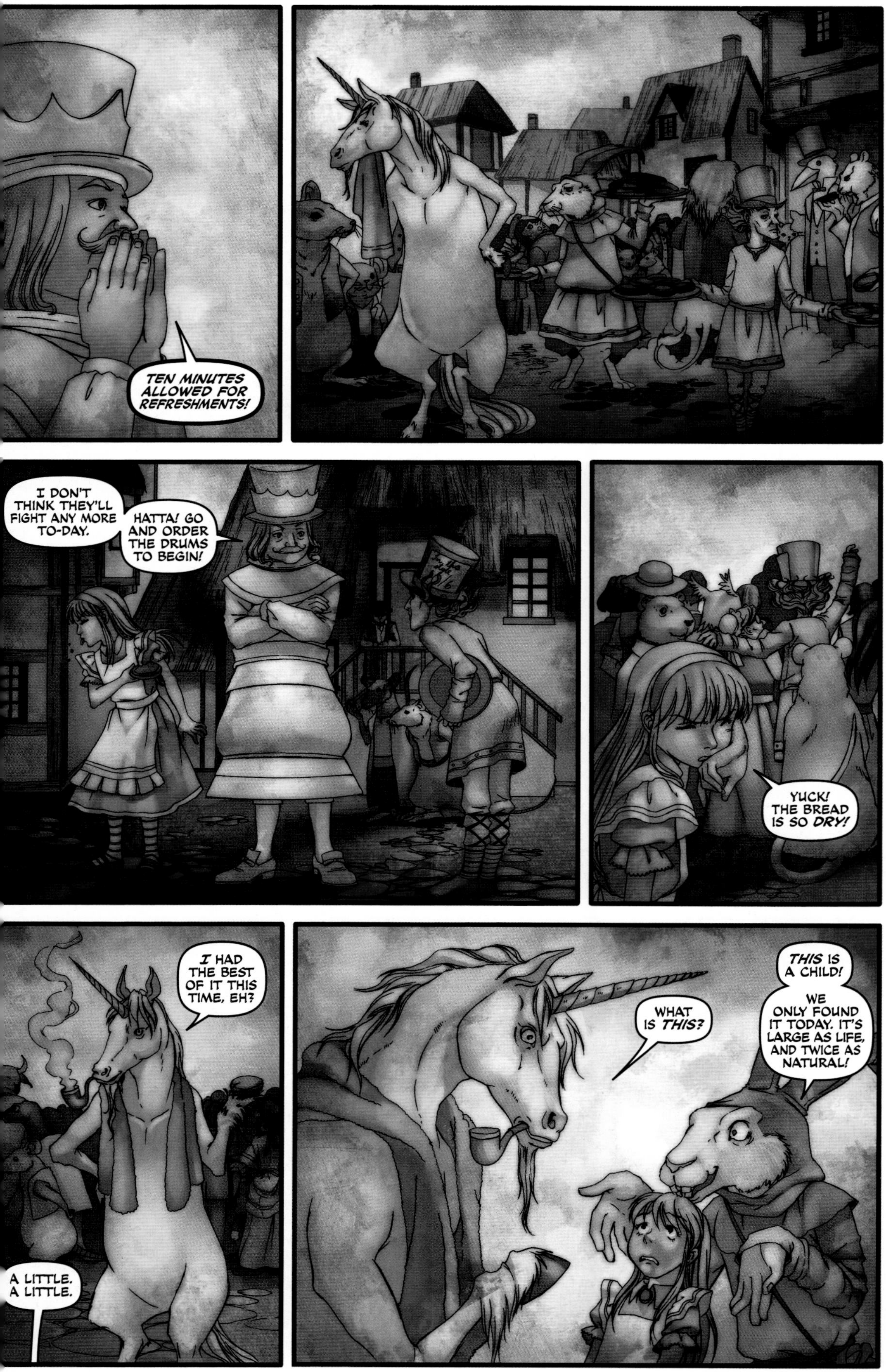

TEN MINUTES ALLOWED FOR REFRESHMENTS!
I DON'T THINK THEY'LL FIGHT ANY MORE TO-DAY.
HATTA! GO AND ORDER THE DRUMS TO BEGIN!
YUCK! THE BREAD IS SO DRY!
I HAD THE BEST OF IT THIS TIME, EH?
A LITTLE. A LITTLE.
WHAT IS THIS?
THIS IS A CHILD!
WE ONLY FOUND IT TODAY. IT'S LARGE AS LIFE, AND TWICE AS NATURAL!

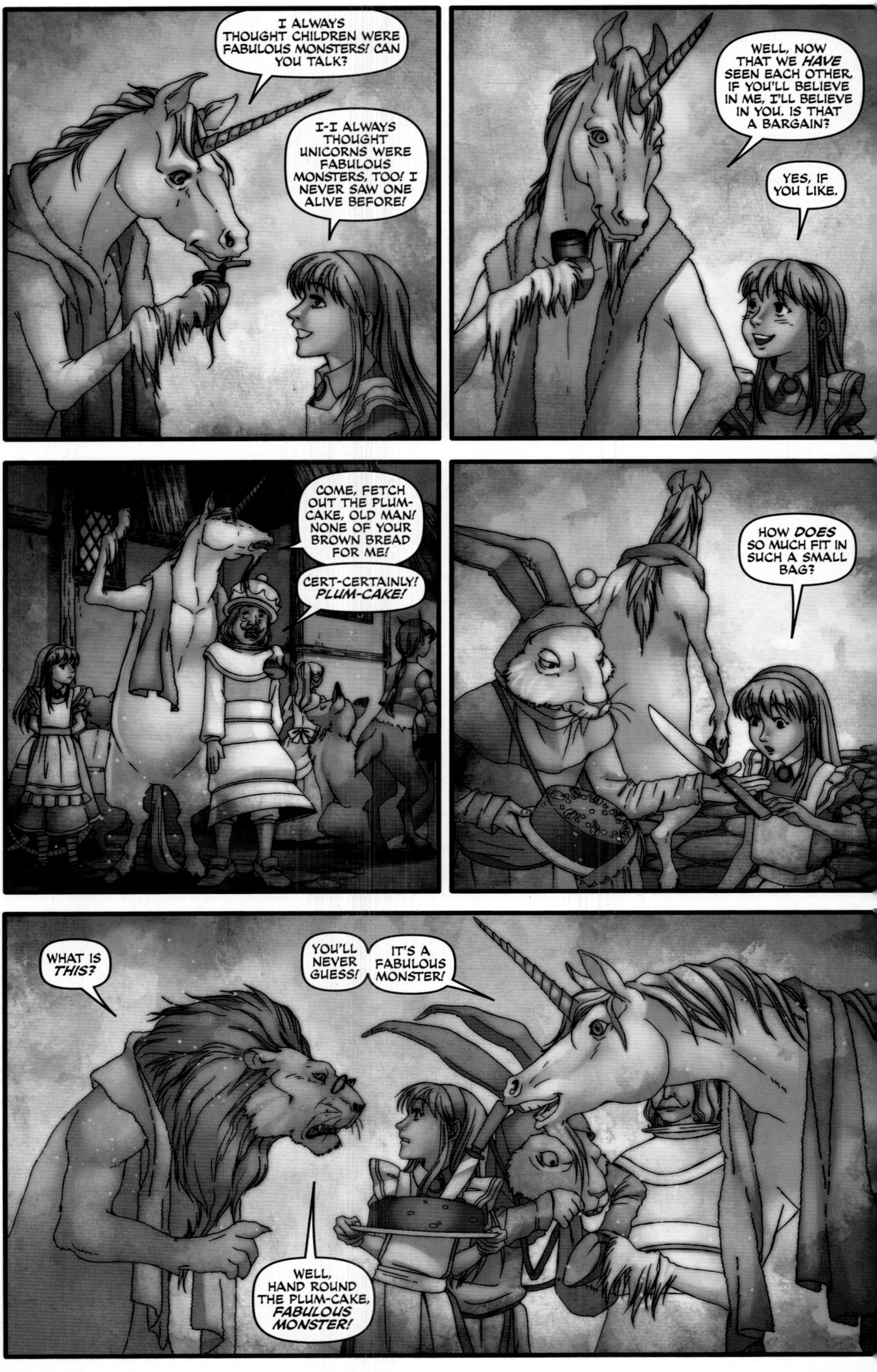
I ALWAYS THOUGHT CHILDREN WERE FABULOUS MONSTERS! CAN YOU TALK?
I-I ALWAYS THOUGHT UNICORNS WERE FABULOUS MONSTERS, TOO! I NEVER SAW ONE ALIVE BEFORE!
WELL, NOW THAT WE *HAVE* SEEN EACH OTHER, IF YOU'LL BELIEVE IN ME, I'LL BELIEVE IN YOU. IS THAT A BARGAIN?
YES, IF YOU LIKE.
COME, FETCH OUT THE PLUM-CAKE, OLD MAN! NONE OF YOUR BROWN BREAD FOR ME!
CERT-CERTAINLY! *PLUM-CAKE!*
HOW *DOES* SO MUCH FIT IN SUCH A SMALL BAG?
WHAT IS *THIS?*
YOU'LL NEVER GUESS!
IT'S A FABULOUS MONSTER!
WELL, HAND ROUND THE PLUM-CAKE, *FABULOUS MONSTER!*

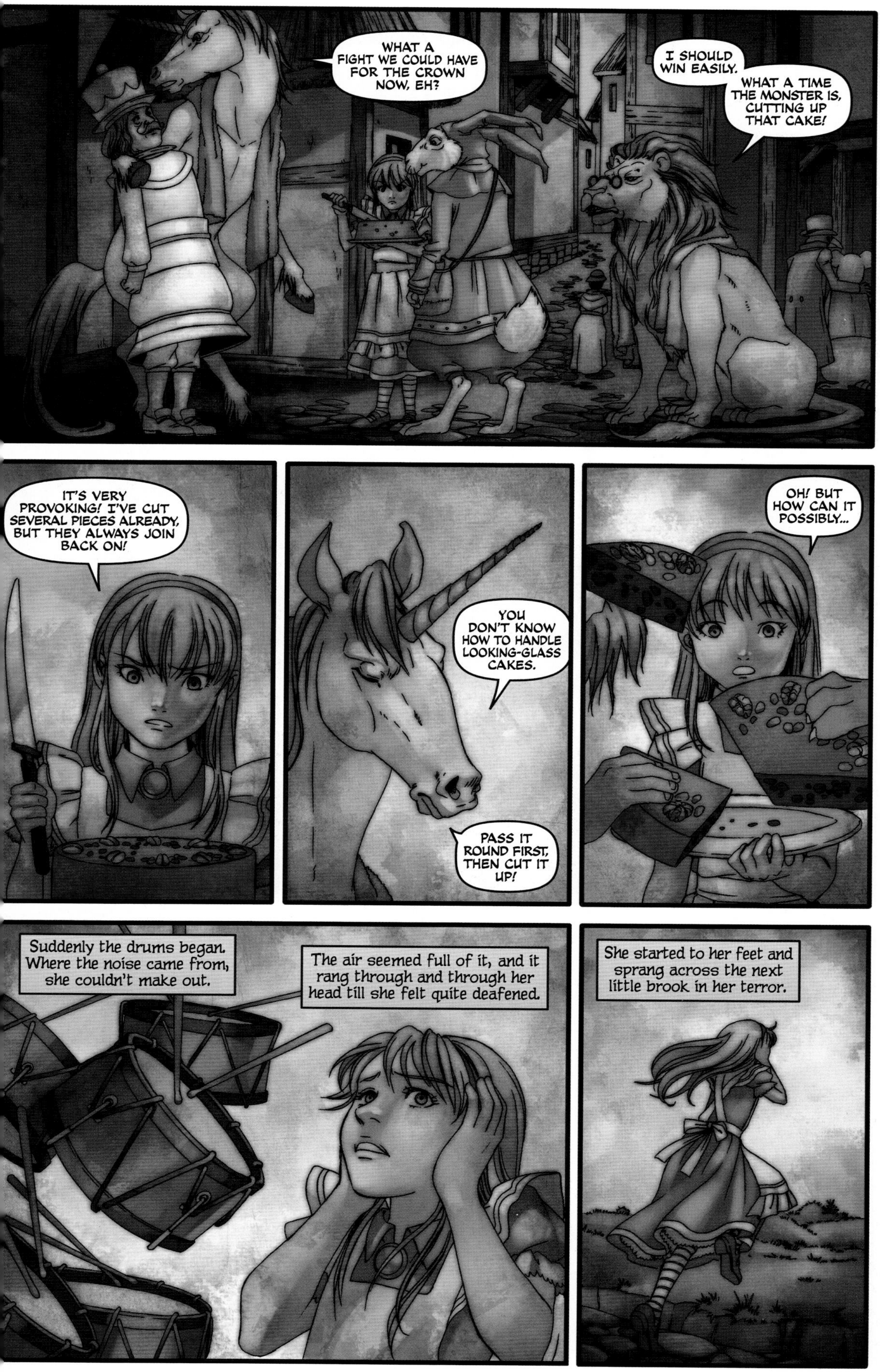
WHAT A FIGHT WE COULD HAVE FOR THE CROWN NOW, EH?
I SHOULD WIN EASILY.
WHAT A TIME THE MONSTER IS, CUTTING UP THAT CAKE!
IT'S VERY PROVOKING! I'VE CUT SEVERAL PIECES ALREADY, BUT THEY ALWAYS JOIN BACK ON!
YOU DON'T KNOW HOW TO HANDLE LOOKING-GLASS CAKES.
PASS IT ROUND FIRST, THEN CUT IT UP!
OH! BUT HOW CAN IT POSSIBLY...
Suddenly the drums began. Where the noise came from, she couldn't make out.
The air seemed full of it, and it rang through and through her head till she felt quite deafened.
She started to her feet and sprang across the next little brook in her terror.

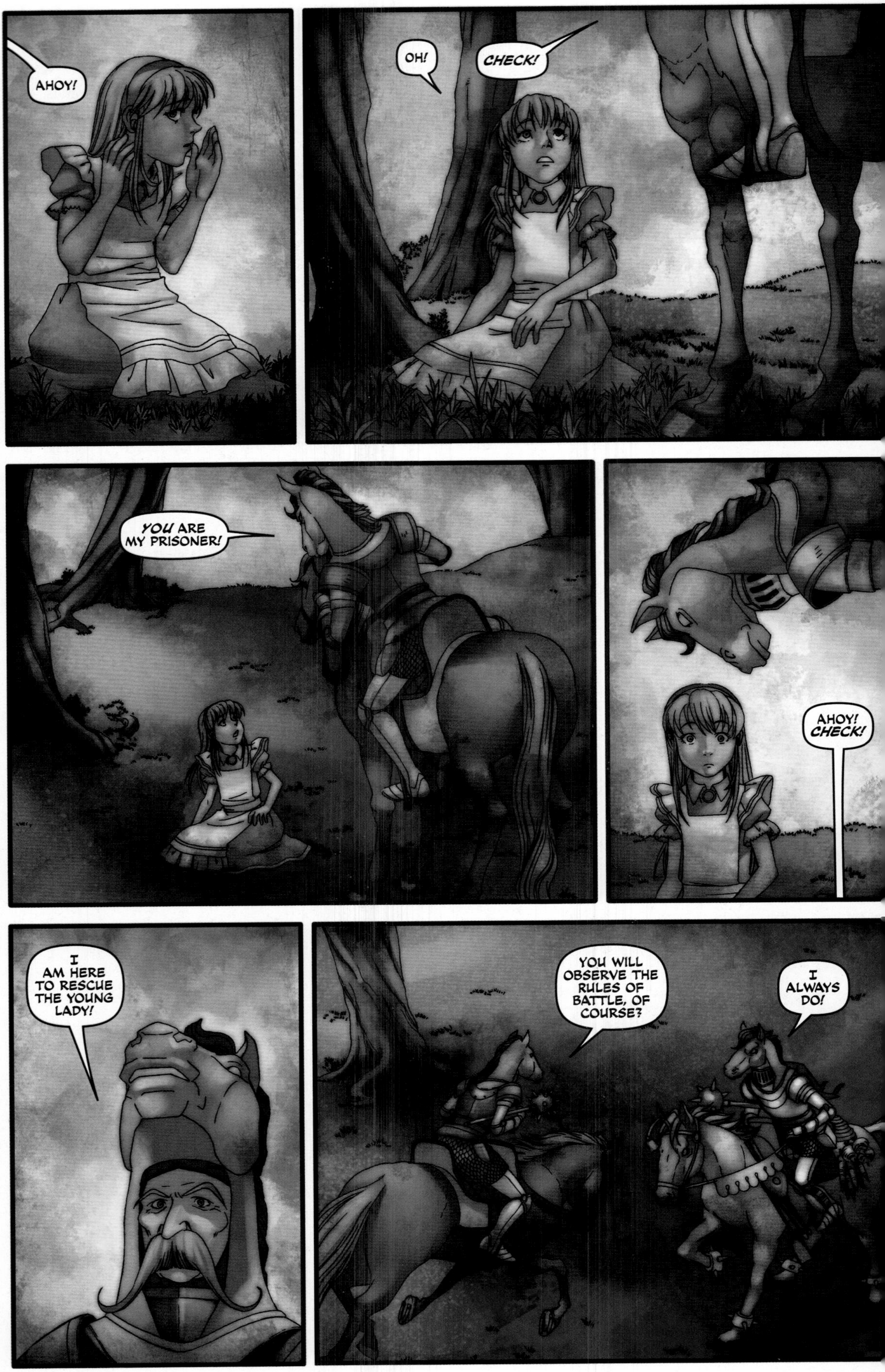
AHOY!
OH!
CHECK!
YOU ARE MY PRISONER!
AHOY! CHECK!
I AM HERE TO RESCUE THE YOUNG LADY!
YOU WILL OBSERVE THE RULES OF BATTLE, OF COURSE?
I ALWAYS DO!

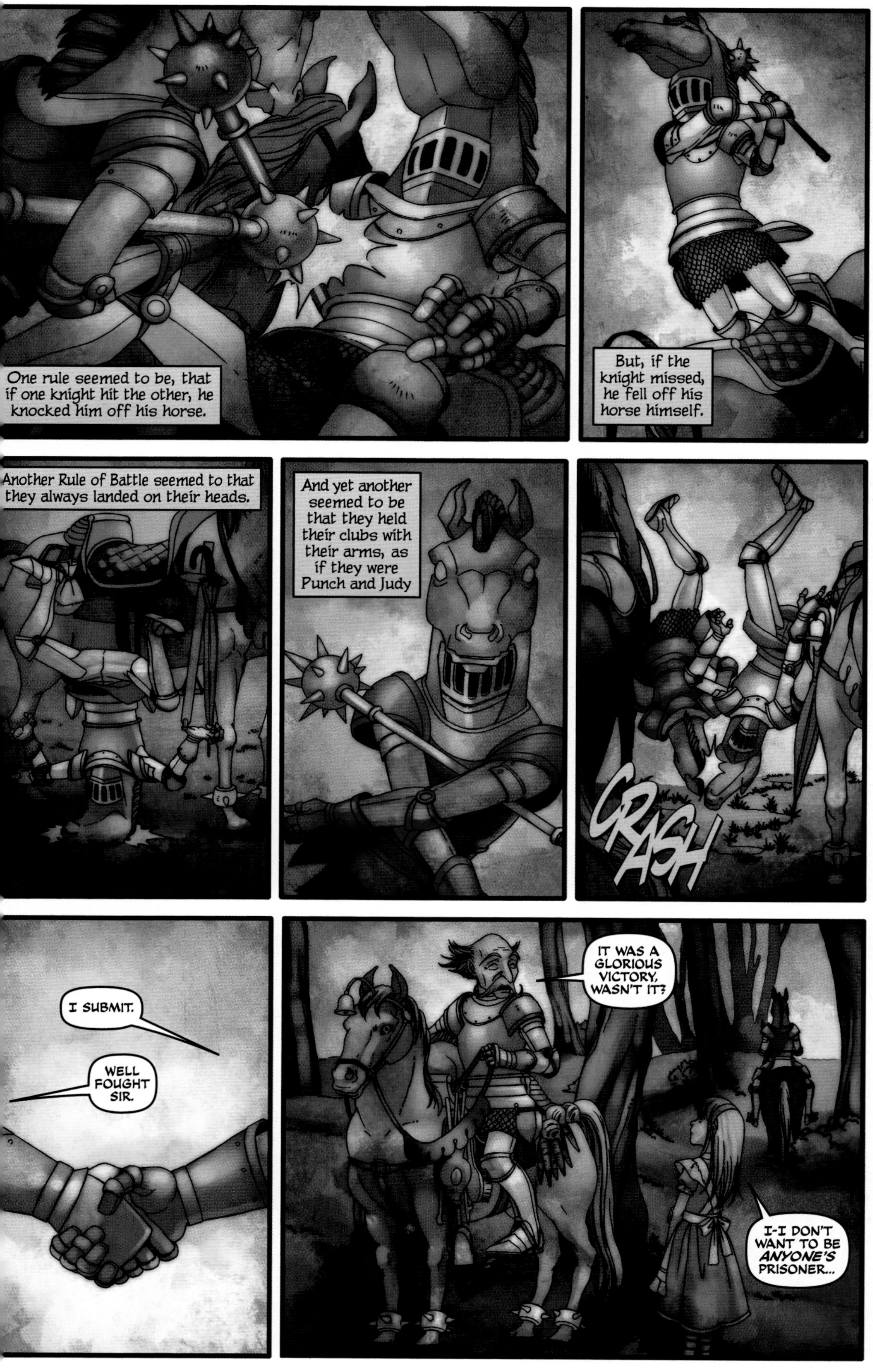
One rule seemed to be, that if one knight hit the other, he knocked him off his horse.
But, if the knight missed, he fell off his horse himself.
Another Rule of Battle seemed to that they always landed on their heads.
And yet another seemed to be that they held their clubs with their arms, as if they were Punch and Judy
CRASH
I SUBMIT.
WELL FOUGHT SIR.
IT WAS A GLORIOUS VICTORY, WASN'T IT?
I-I DON'T WANT TO BE *ANYONE'S* PRISONER...

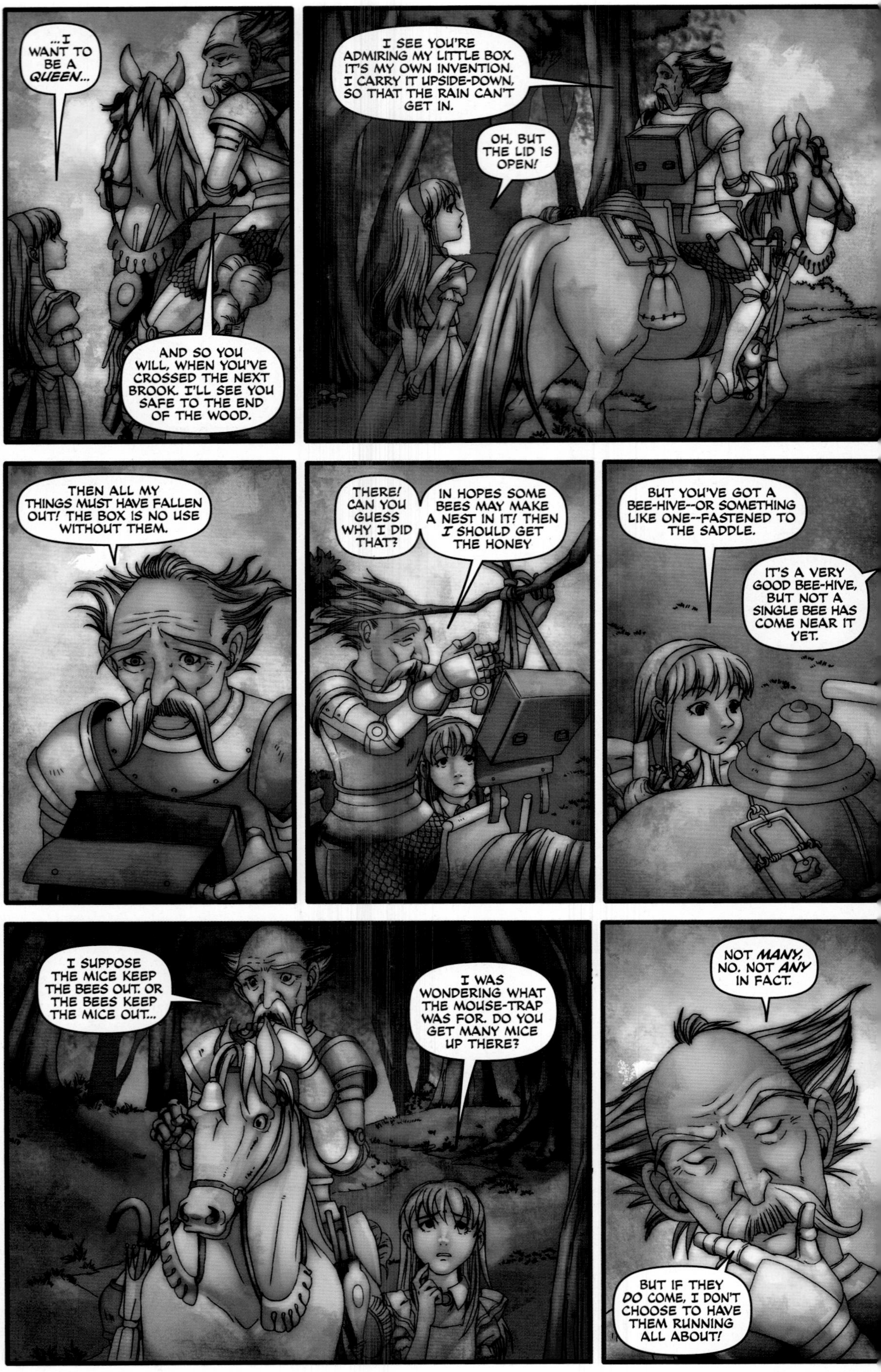
...I WANT TO BE A *QUEEN*...
AND SO YOU WILL, WHEN YOU'VE CROSSED THE NEXT BROOK. I'LL SEE YOU SAFE TO THE END OF THE WOOD.
I SEE YOU'RE ADMIRING MY LITTLE BOX. IT'S MY OWN INVENTION. I CARRY IT UPSIDE-DOWN, SO THAT THE RAIN CAN'T GET IN.
OH, BUT THE LID IS OPEN!
THEN ALL MY THINGS MUST HAVE FALLEN OUT! THE BOX IS NO USE WITHOUT THEM.
THERE! CAN YOU GUESS WHY I DID THAT?
IN HOPES SOME BEES MAY MAKE A NEST IN IT! THEN *I* SHOULD GET THE HONEY
BUT YOU'VE GOT A BEE-HIVE--OR SOMETHING LIKE ONE--FASTENED TO THE SADDLE.
IT'S A VERY GOOD BEE-HIVE, BUT NOT A SINGLE BEE HAS COME NEAR IT YET.
I SUPPOSE THE MICE KEEP THE BEES OUT. OR THE BEES KEEP THE MICE OUT...
I WAS WONDERING WHAT THE MOUSE-TRAP WAS FOR. DO YOU GET MANY MICE UP THERE?
NOT *MANY,* NO. NOT *ANY* IN FACT.
BUT IF THEY *DO* COME, I DON'T CHOOSE TO HAVE THEM RUNNING ALL ABOUT!

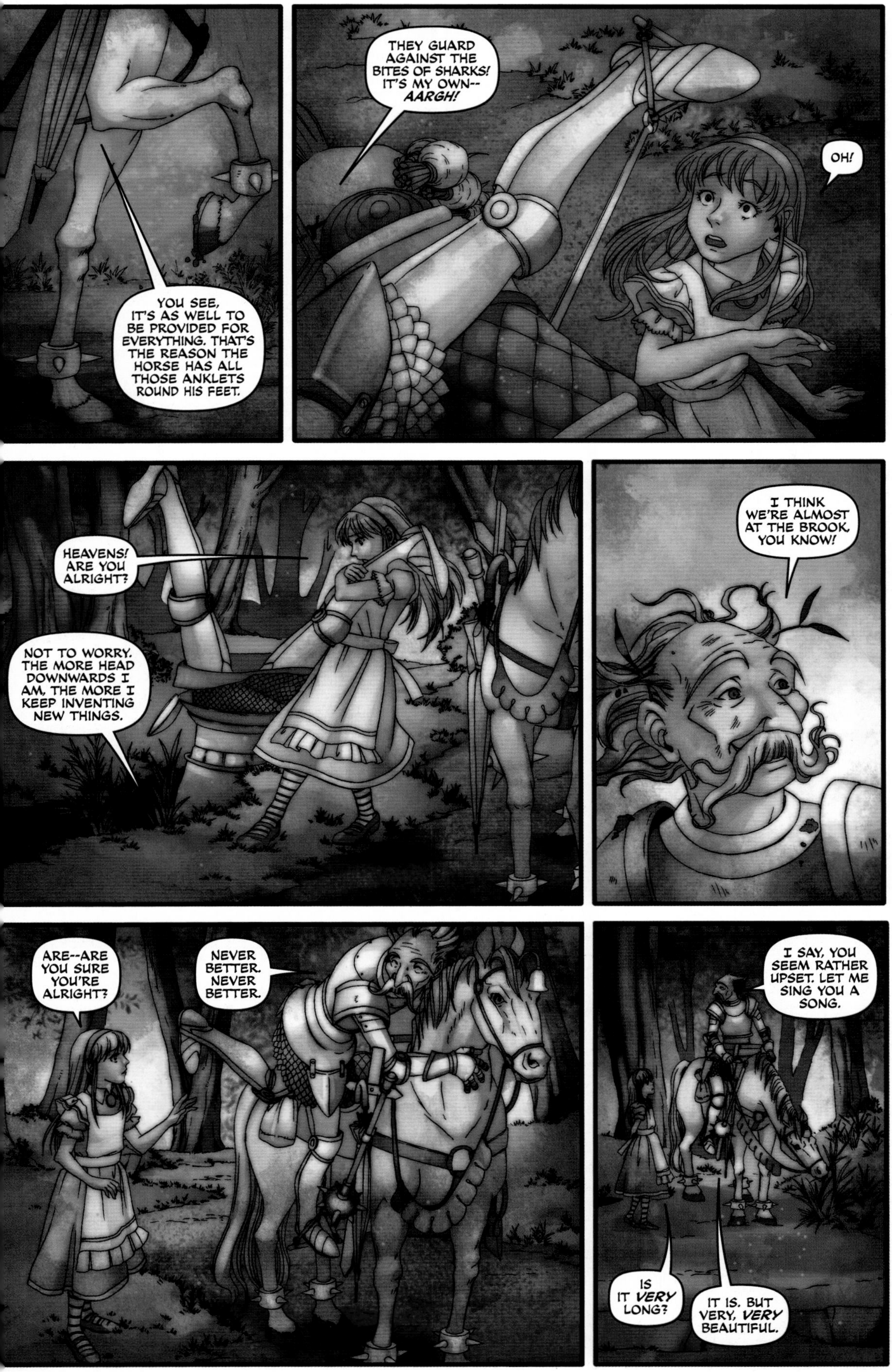

YOU SEE, IT'S AS WELL TO BE PROVIDED FOR EVERYTHING. THAT'S THE REASON THE HORSE HAS ALL THOSE ANKLETS ROUND HIS FEET.
THEY GUARD AGAINST THE BITES OF SHARKS! IT'S MY OWN-- *AARGH!*
OH!
HEAVENS! ARE YOU ALRIGHT?
NOT TO WORRY. THE MORE HEAD DOWNWARDS I AM, THE MORE I KEEP INVENTING NEW THINGS.
I THINK WE'RE ALMOST AT THE BROOK, YOU KNOW!
ARE--ARE YOU SURE YOU'RE ALRIGHT?
NEVER BETTER. NEVER BETTER.
I SAY, YOU SEEM RATHER UPSET. LET ME SING YOU A SONG.
IS IT *VERY* LONG?
IT IS. BUT VERY, *VERY* BEAUTIFUL.

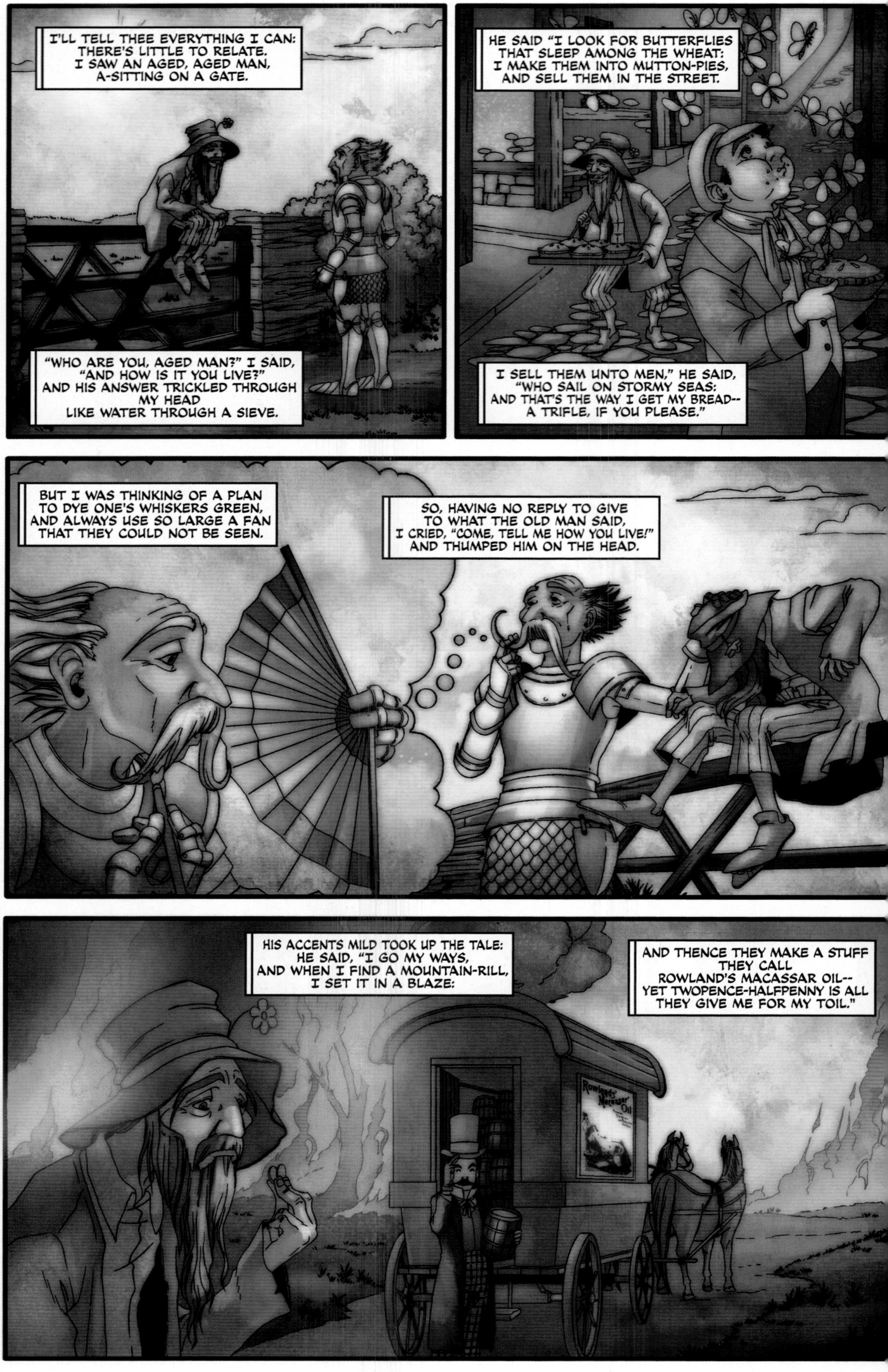
I'LL TELL THEE EVERYTHING I CAN: THERE'S LITTLE TO RELATE. I SAW AN AGED, AGED MAN, A-SITTING ON A GATE.
"WHO ARE YOU, AGED MAN?" I SAID, "AND HOW IS IT YOU LIVE?" AND HIS ANSWER TRICKLED THROUGH MY HEAD LIKE WATER THROUGH A SIEVE.
HE SAID "I LOOK FOR BUTTERFLIES THAT SLEEP AMONG THE WHEAT: I MAKE THEM INTO MUTTON-PIES, AND SELL THEM IN THE STREET.
I SELL THEM UNTO MEN," HE SAID, "WHO SAIL ON STORMY SEAS: AND THAT'S THE WAY I GET MY BREAD-- A TRIFLE, IF YOU PLEASE."
BUT I WAS THINKING OF A PLAN TO DYE ONE'S WHISKERS GREEN, AND ALWAYS USE SO LARGE A FAN THAT THEY COULD NOT BE SEEN.
SO, HAVING NO REPLY TO GIVE TO WHAT THE OLD MAN SAID, I CRIED, "COME, TELL ME HOW YOU LIVE!" AND THUMPED HIM ON THE HEAD.
HIS ACCENTS MILD TOOK UP THE TALE: HE SAID, "I GO MY WAYS, AND WHEN I FIND A MOUNTAIN-RILL, I SET IT IN A BLAZE:
AND THENCE THEY MAKE A STUFF THEY CALL ROWLAND'S MACASSAR OIL-- YET TWOPENCE-HALFPENNY IS ALL THEY GIVE ME FOR MY TOIL."
Rowlands' Macassar Oil

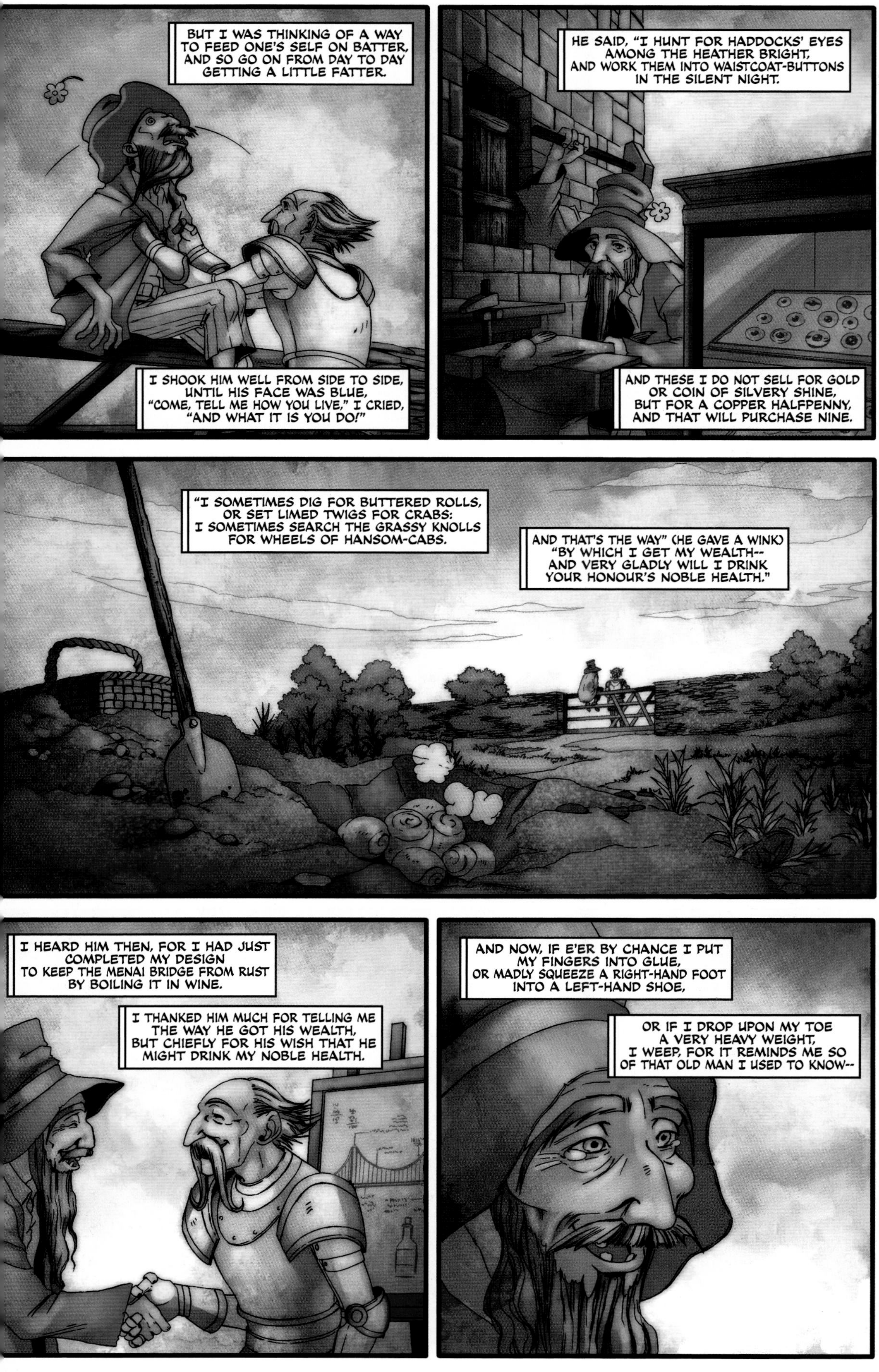
BUT I WAS THINKING OF A WAY TO FEED ONE'S SELF ON BATTER, AND SO GO ON FROM DAY TO DAY GETTING A LITTLE FATTER.
I SHOOK HIM WELL FROM SIDE TO SIDE, UNTIL HIS FACE WAS BLUE, "COME, TELL ME HOW YOU LIVE," I CRIED, "AND WHAT IT IS YOU DO!"
HE SAID, "I HUNT FOR HADDOCKS' EYES AMONG THE HEATHER BRIGHT, AND WORK THEM INTO WAISTCOAT-BUTTONS IN THE SILENT NIGHT.
AND THESE I DO NOT SELL FOR GOLD OR COIN OF SILVERY SHINE, BUT FOR A COPPER HALFPENNY, AND THAT WILL PURCHASE NINE.
"I SOMETIMES DIG FOR BUTTERED ROLLS, OR SET LIMED TWIGS FOR CRABS: I SOMETIMES SEARCH THE GRASSY KNOLLS FOR WHEELS OF HANSOM-CABS.
AND THAT'S THE WAY" (HE GAVE A WINK) "BY WHICH I GET MY WEALTH-- AND VERY GLADLY WILL I DRINK YOUR HONOUR'S NOBLE HEALTH."
I HEARD HIM THEN, FOR I HAD JUST COMPLETED MY DESIGN TO KEEP THE MENAI BRIDGE FROM RUST BY BOILING IT IN WINE.
I THANKED HIM MUCH FOR TELLING ME THE WAY HE GOT HIS WEALTH, BUT CHIEFLY FOR HIS WISH THAT HE MIGHT DRINK MY NOBLE HEALTH.
AND NOW, IF E'ER BY CHANCE I PUT MY FINGERS INTO GLUE, OR MADLY SQUEEZE A RIGHT-HAND FOOT INTO A LEFT-HAND SHOE,
OR IF I DROP UPON MY TOE A VERY HEAVY WEIGHT, I WEEP, FOR IT REMINDS ME SO OF THAT OLD MAN I USED TO KNOW--

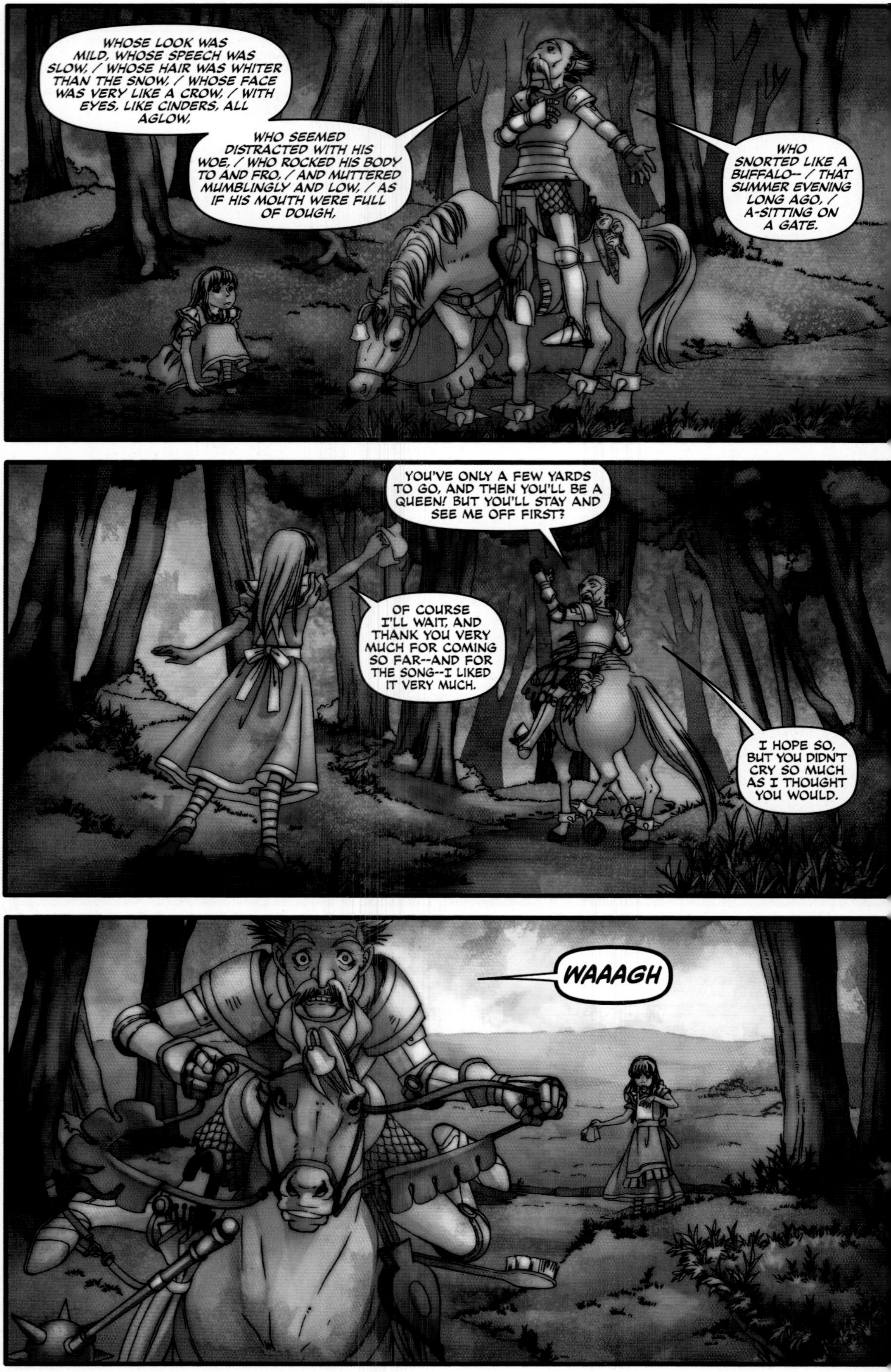
WHOSE LOOK WAS MILD, WHOSE SPEECH WAS SLOW, / WHOSE HAIR WAS WHITER THAN THE SNOW, / WHOSE FACE WAS VERY LIKE A CROW, / WITH EYES, LIKE CINDERS, ALL AGLOW,
WHO SEEMED DISTRACTED WITH HIS WOE, / WHO ROCKED HIS BODY TO AND FRO, / AND MUTTERED MUMBLINGLY AND LOW, / AS IF HIS MOUTH WERE FULL OF DOUGH,
WHO SNORTED LIKE A BUFFALO-- / THAT SUMMER EVENING LONG AGO, / A-SITTING ON A GATE.
YOU'VE ONLY A FEW YARDS TO GO, AND THEN YOU'LL BE A QUEEN! BUT YOU'LL STAY AND SEE ME OFF FIRST?
OF COURSE I'LL WAIT, AND THANK YOU VERY MUCH FOR COMING SO FAR--AND FOR THE SONG--I LIKED IT VERY MUCH.
I HOPE SO, BUT YOU DIDN'T CRY SO MUCH AS I THOUGHT YOU WOULD.
WAAAGH

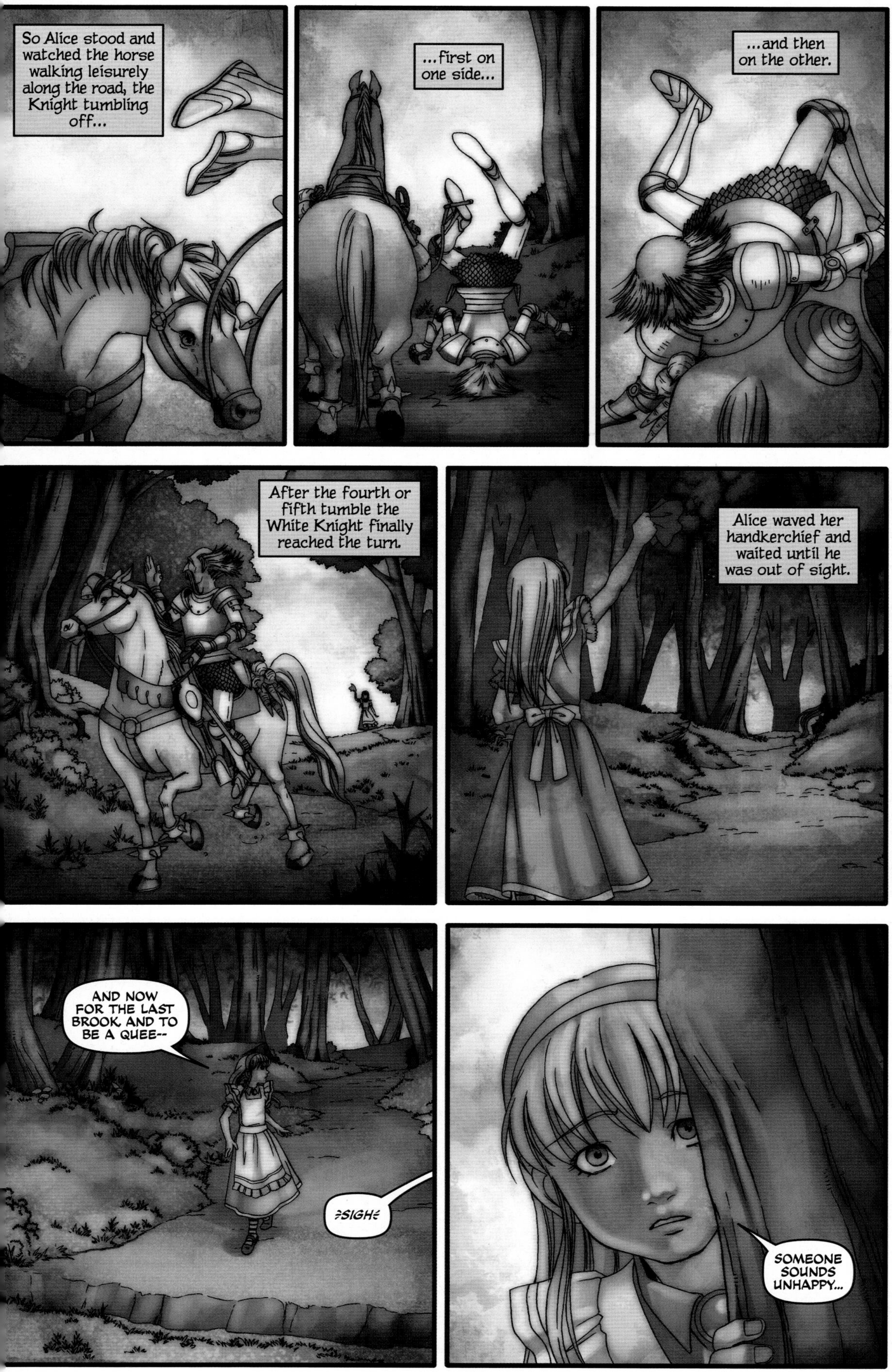
So Alice stood and watched the horse walking leisurely along the road, the Knight tumbling off...
...first on one side...
...and then on the other.
After the fourth or fifth tumble the White Knight finally reached the turn.
Alice waved her handkerchief and waited until he was out of sight.
AND NOW FOR THE LAST BROOK, AND TO BE A QUEE--
SIGH
SOMEONE SOUNDS UNHAPPY...

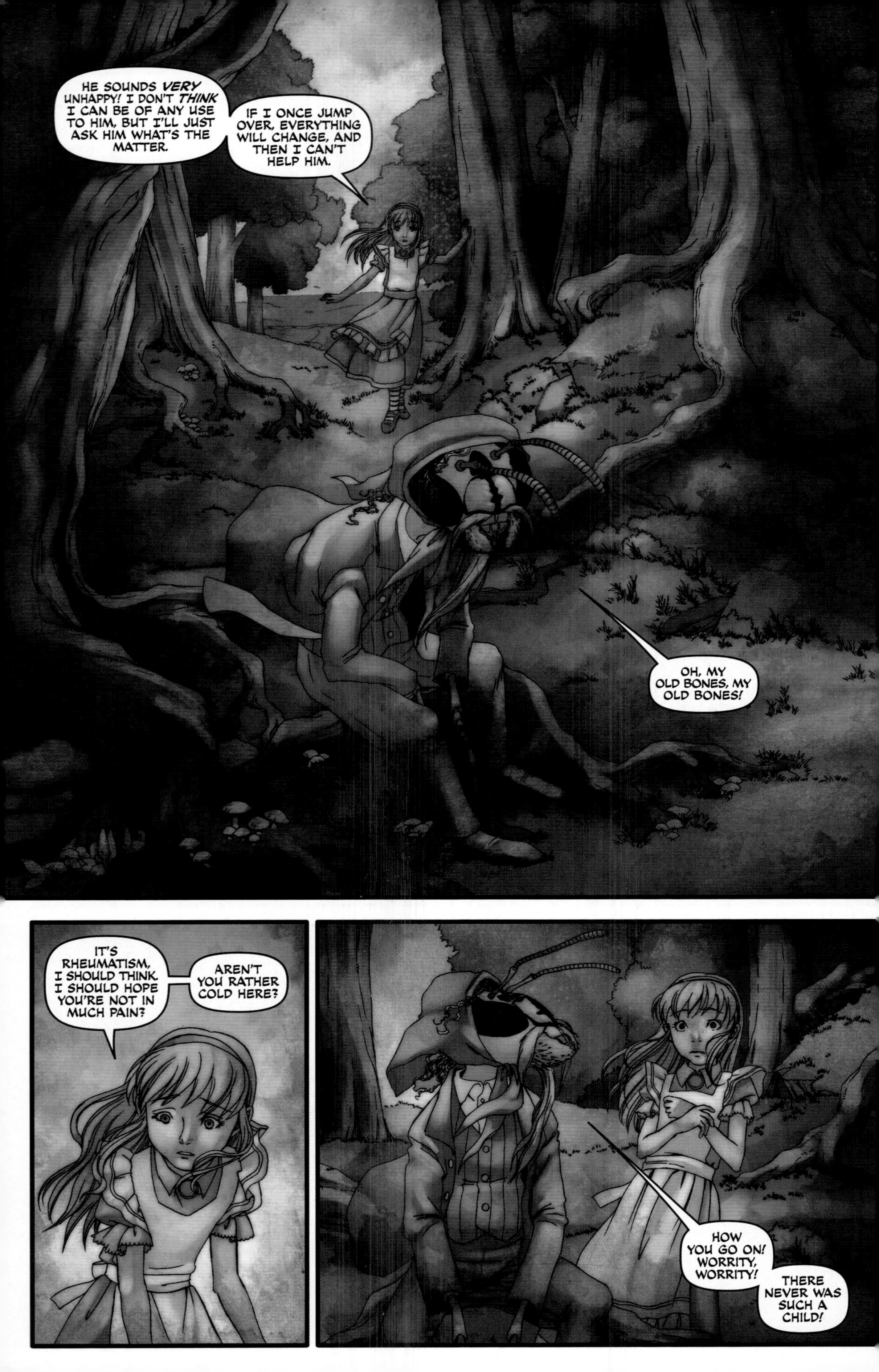
HE SOUNDS VERY UNHAPPY! I DON'T THINK I CAN BE OF ANY USE TO HIM, BUT I'LL JUST ASK HIM WHAT'S THE MATTER.
IF I ONCE JUMP OVER, EVERYTHING WILL CHANGE, AND THEN I CAN'T HELP HIM.
OH, MY OLD BONES, MY OLD BONES!
IT'S RHEUMATISM, I SHOULD THINK. I SHOULD HOPE YOU'RE NOT IN MUCH PAIN?
AREN'T YOU RATHER COLD HERE?
HOW YOU GO ON! WORRITY, WORRITY!
THERE NEVER WAS SUCH A CHILD!

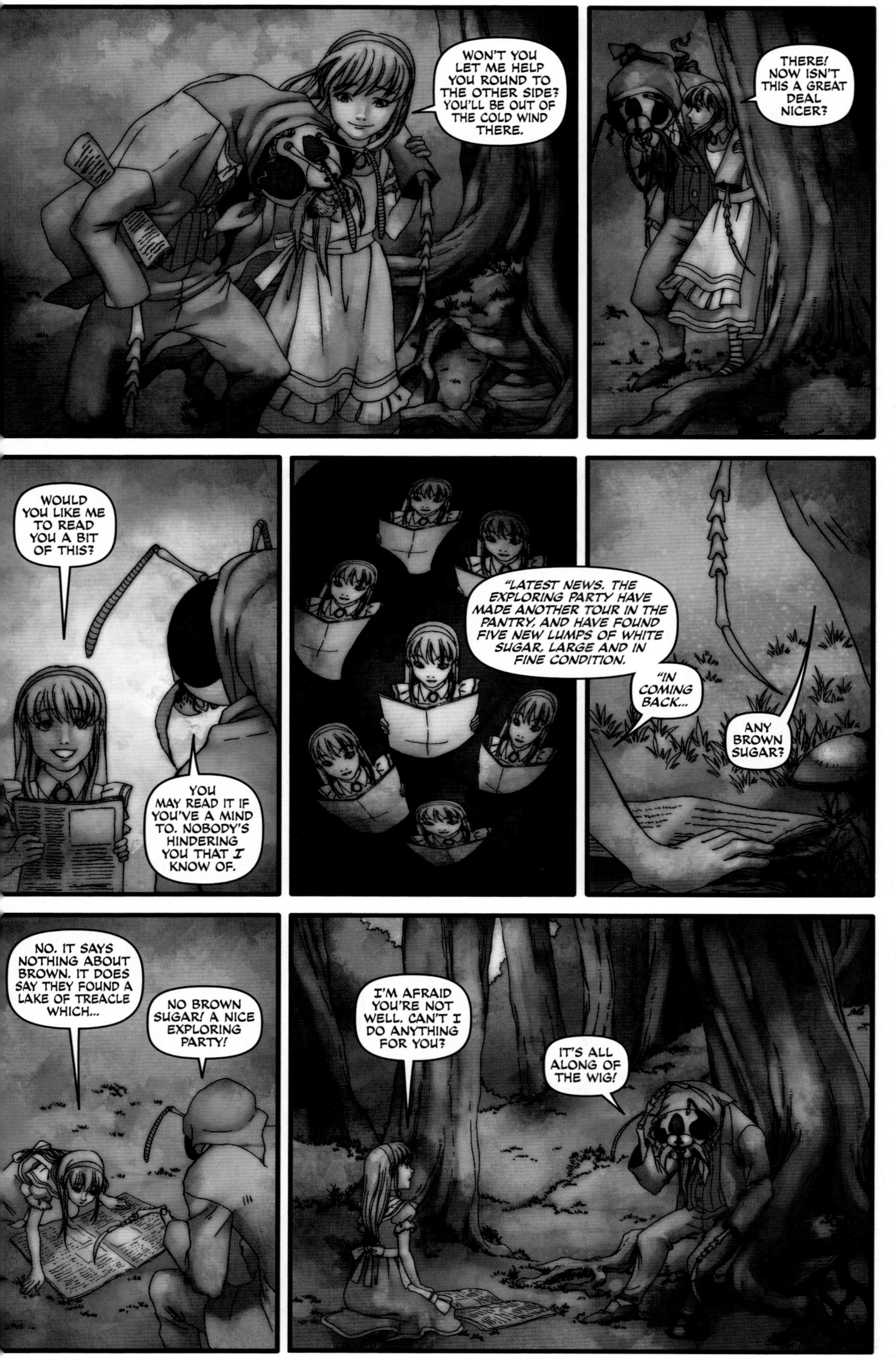
WON'T YOU LET ME HELP YOU ROUND TO THE OTHER SIDE? YOU'LL BE OUT OF THE COLD WIND THERE.
THERE! NOW ISN'T THIS A GREAT DEAL NICER?
WOULD YOU LIKE ME TO READ YOU A BIT OF THIS?
YOU MAY READ IT IF YOU'VE A MIND TO. NOBODY'S HINDERING YOU THAT *I* KNOW OF.
"LATEST NEWS. THE EXPLORING PARTY HAVE MADE ANOTHER TOUR IN THE PANTRY, AND HAVE FOUND FIVE NEW LUMPS OF WHITE SUGAR, LARGE AND IN FINE CONDITION.
"IN COMING BACK...
ANY BROWN SUGAR?
NO. IT SAYS NOTHING ABOUT BROWN. IT DOES SAY THEY FOUND A LAKE OF TREACLE WHICH...
NO BROWN SUGAR! A NICE EXPLORING PARTY!
I'M AFRAID YOU'RE NOT WELL. CAN'T I DO ANYTHING FOR YOU?
IT'S ALL ALONG OF THE WIG!

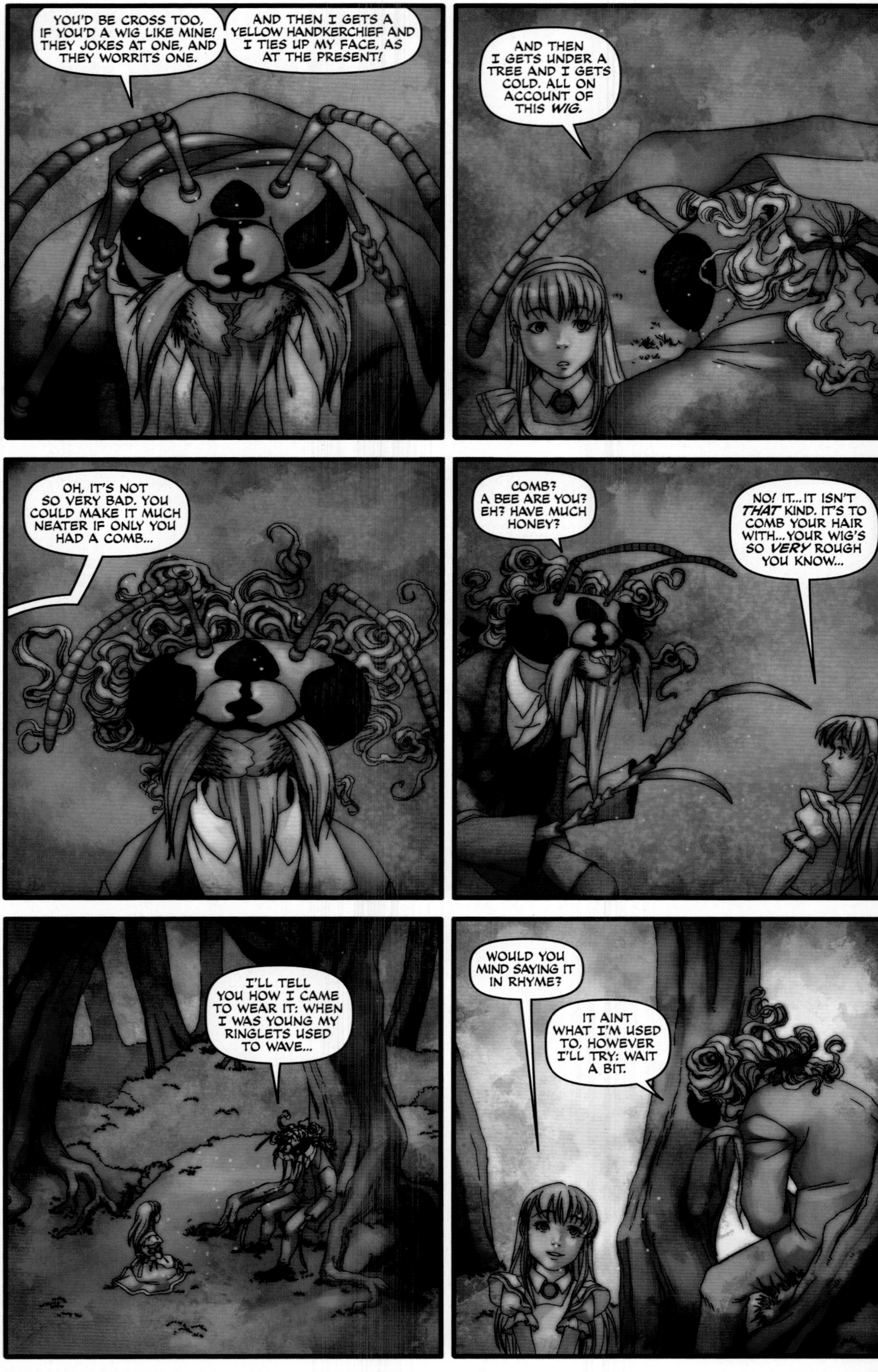
YOU'D BE CROSS TOO, IF YOU'D A WIG LIKE MINE! THEY JOKES AT ONE, AND THEY WORRITS ONE.
AND THEN I GETS A YELLOW HANDKERCHIEF AND I TIES UP MY FACE, AS AT THE PRESENT!
AND THEN I GETS UNDER A TREE AND I GETS COLD. ALL ON ACCOUNT OF THIS WIG.
OH, IT'S NOT SO VERY BAD. YOU COULD MAKE IT MUCH NEATER IF ONLY YOU HAD A COMB...
COMB? A BEE ARE YOU? EH? HAVE MUCH HONEY?
NO! IT... IT ISN'T THAT KIND. IT'S TO COMB YOUR HAIR WITH... YOUR WIG'S SO VERY ROUGH YOU KNOW...
I'LL TELL YOU HOW I CAME TO WEAR IT: WHEN I WAS YOUNG MY RINGLETS USED TO WAVE...
WOULD YOU MIND SAYING IT IN RHYME?
IT AINT WHAT I'M USED TO, HOWEVER I'LL TRY: WAIT A BIT.

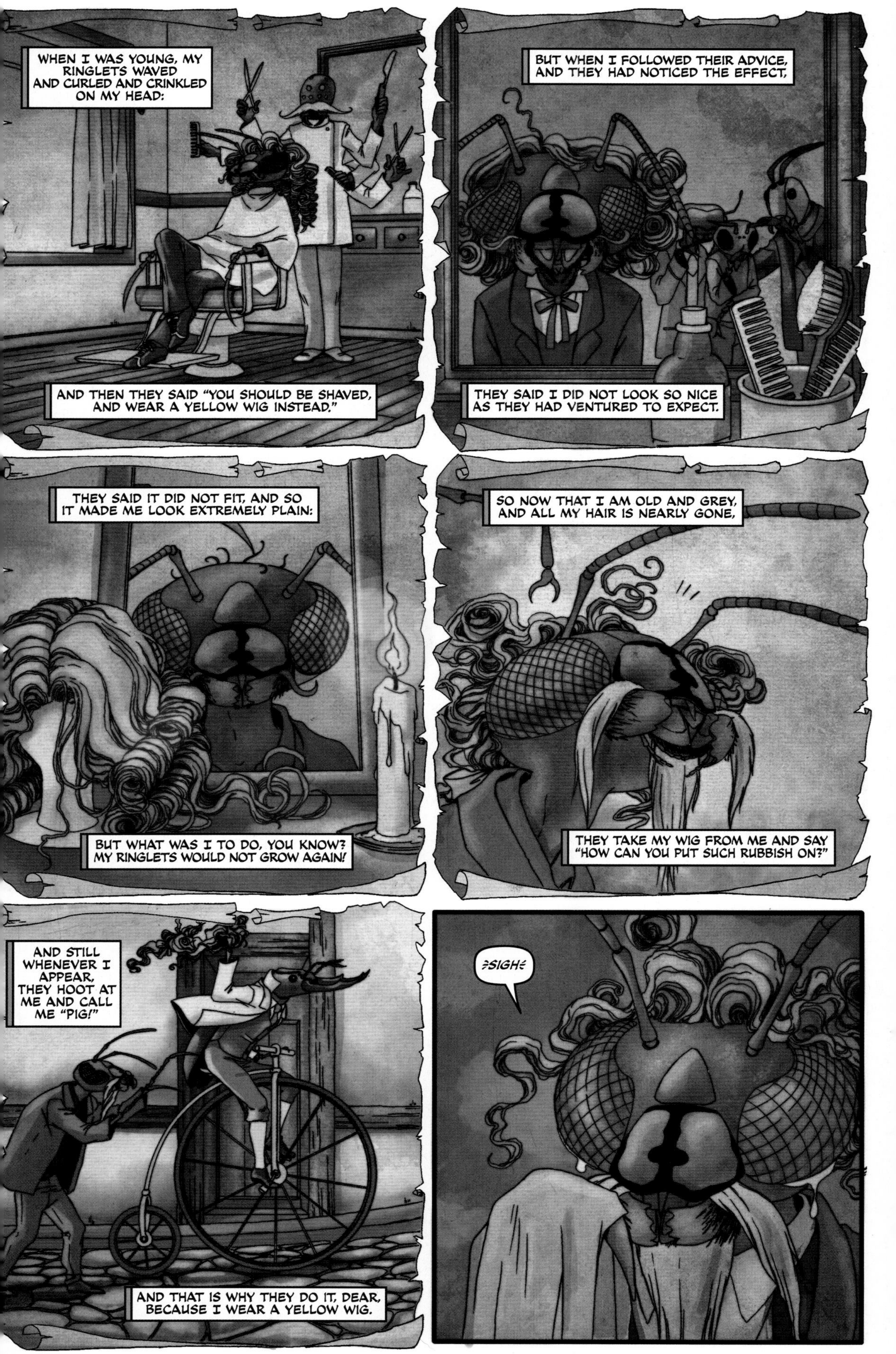
WHEN I WAS YOUNG, MY RINGLETS WAVED AND CURLED AND CRINKLED ON MY HEAD:
AND THEN THEY SAID "YOU SHOULD BE SHAVED, AND WEAR A YELLOW WIG INSTEAD."
BUT WHEN I FOLLOWED THEIR ADVICE, AND THEY HAD NOTICED THE EFFECT,
THEY SAID I DID NOT LOOK SO NICE AS THEY HAD VENTURED TO EXPECT.
THEY SAID IT DID NOT FIT, AND SO IT MADE ME LOOK EXTREMELY PLAIN:
BUT WHAT WAS I TO DO, YOU KNOW? MY RINGLETS WOULD NOT GROW AGAIN!
SO NOW THAT I AM OLD AND GREY, AND ALL MY HAIR IS NEARLY GONE,
THEY TAKE MY WIG FROM ME AND SAY "HOW CAN YOU PUT SUCH RUBBISH ON?"
AND STILL WHENEVER I APPEAR, THEY HOOT AT ME AND CALL ME "PIG!"
AND THAT IS WHY THEY DO IT, DEAR, BECAUSE I WEAR A YELLOW WIG.
SIGH

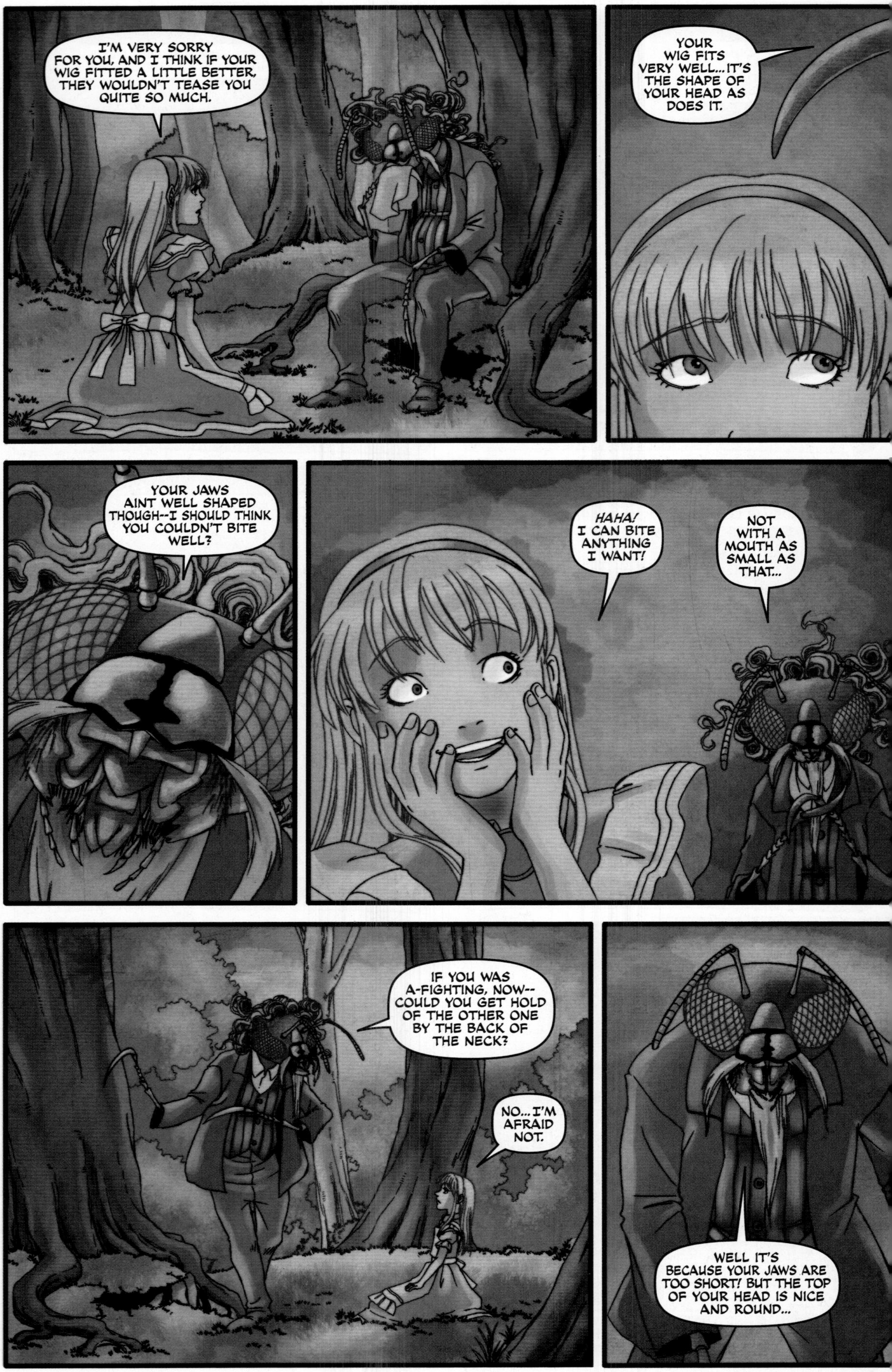
I'M VERY SORRY FOR YOU, AND I THINK IF YOUR WIG FITTED A LITTLE BETTER, THEY WOULDN'T TEASE YOU QUITE SO MUCH.
YOUR WIG FITS VERY WELL...IT'S THE SHAPE OF YOUR HEAD AS DOES IT.
YOUR JAWS AINT WELL SHAPED THOUGH--I SHOULD THINK YOU COULDN'T BITE WELL?
HAHA! I CAN BITE ANYTHING I WANT!
NOT WITH A MOUTH AS SMALL AS THAT...
IF YOU WAS A-FIGHTING, NOW--COULD YOU GET HOLD OF THE OTHER ONE BY THE BACK OF THE NECK?
NO...I'M AFRAID NOT.
WELL IT'S BECAUSE YOUR JAWS ARE TOO SHORT! BUT THE TOP OF YOUR HEAD IS NICE AND ROUND...

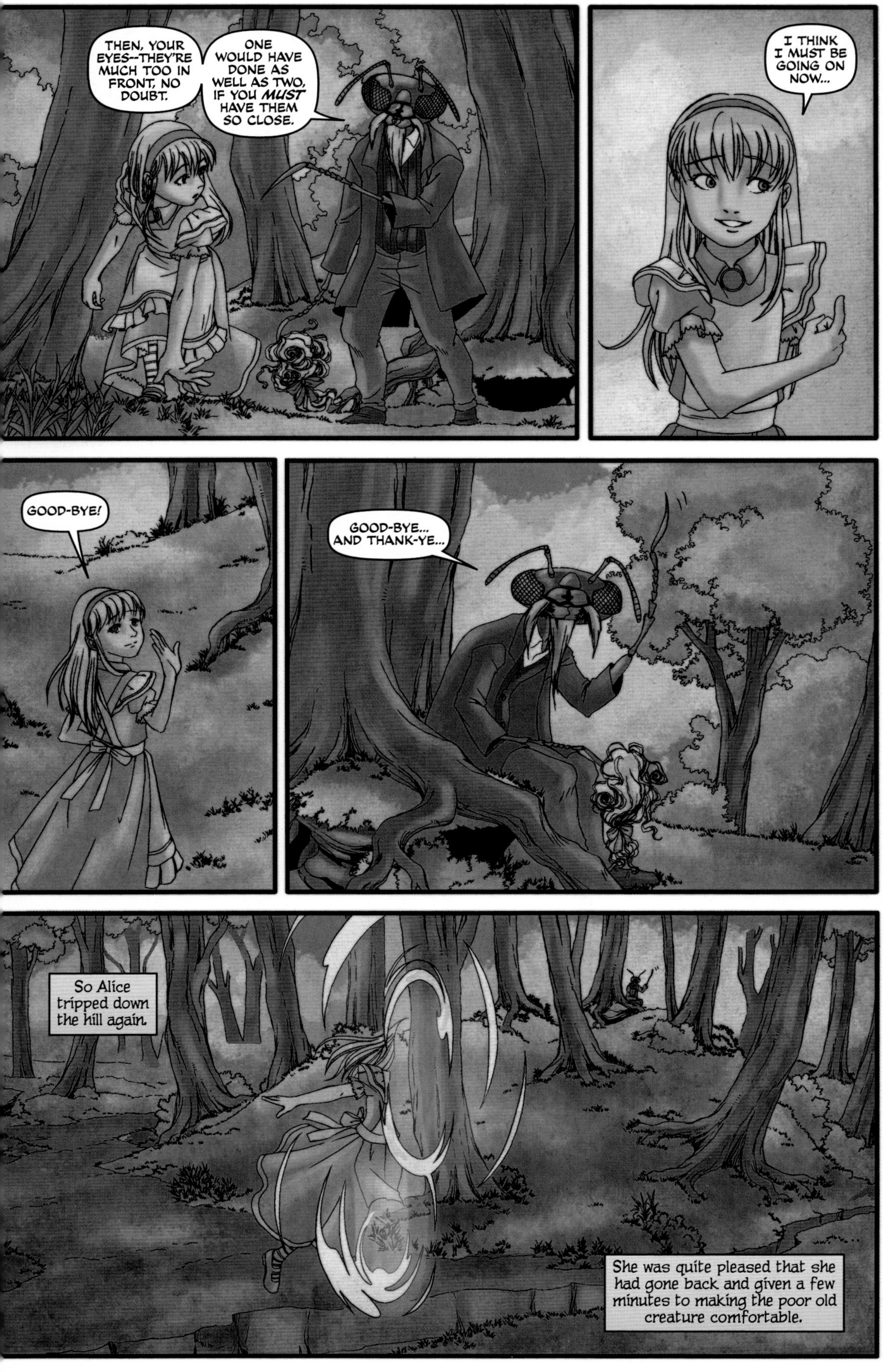
THEN, YOUR EYES--THEY'RE MUCH TOO IN FRONT, NO DOUBT.
ONE WOULD HAVE DONE AS WELL AS TWO, IF YOU *MUST* HAVE THEM SO CLOSE.
I THINK I MUST BE GOING ON NOW...
GOOD-BYE!
GOOD-BYE... AND THANK-YE...
So Alice tripped down the hill again.
She was quite pleased that she had gone back and given a few minutes to making the poor old creature comfortable.

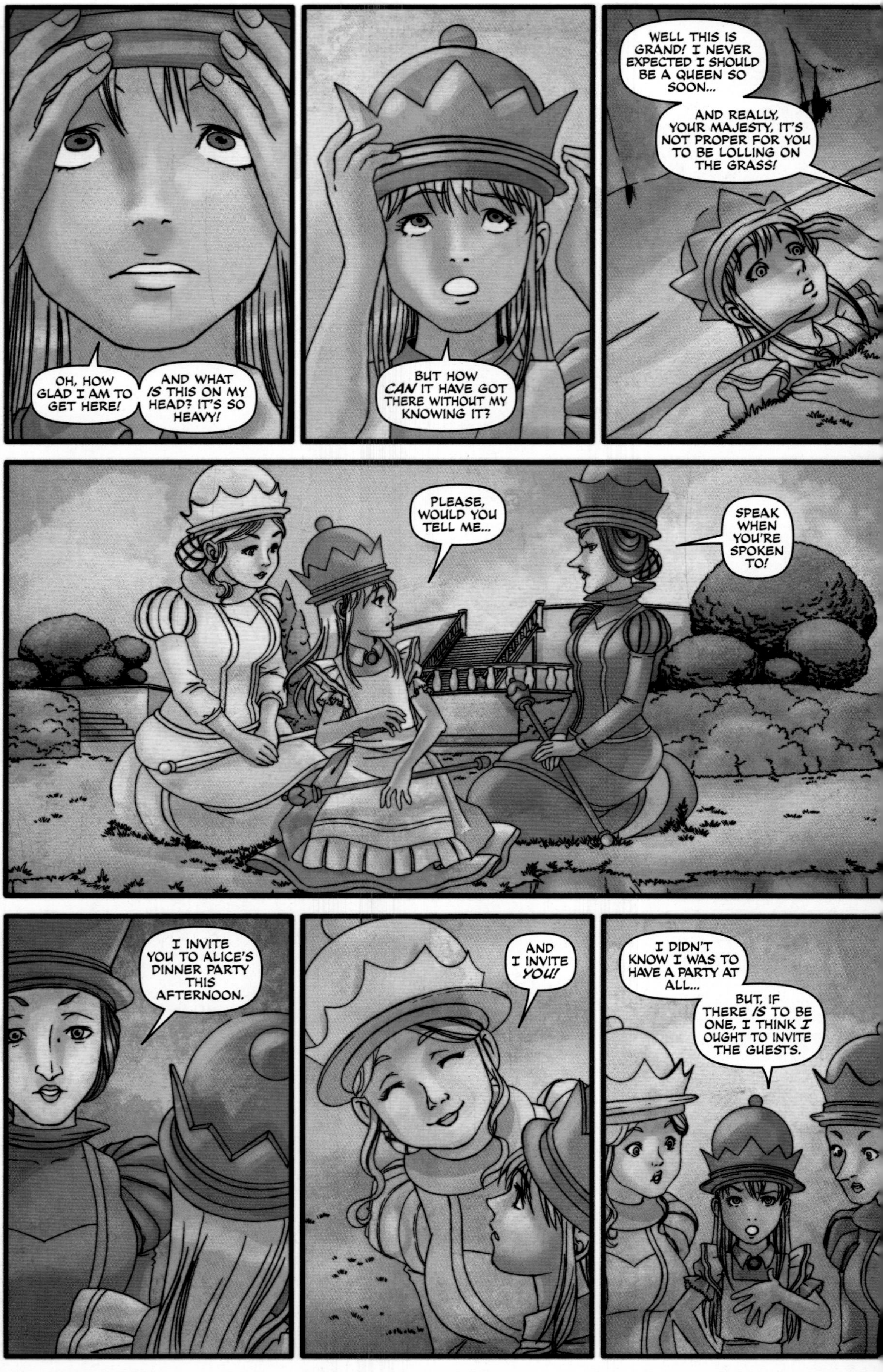
OH, HOW GLAD I AM TO GET HERE!
AND WHAT *IS* THIS ON MY HEAD? IT'S SO HEAVY!
BUT HOW *CAN* IT HAVE GOT THERE WITHOUT MY KNOWING IT?
WELL THIS IS GRAND! I NEVER EXPECTED I SHOULD BE A QUEEN SO SOON...
AND REALLY, YOUR MAJESTY, IT'S NOT PROPER FOR YOU TO BE LOLLING ON THE GRASS!
PLEASE, WOULD YOU TELL ME...
SPEAK WHEN YOU'RE SPOKEN TO!
I INVITE YOU TO ALICE'S DINNER PARTY THIS AFTERNOON.
AND I INVITE *YOU!*
I DIDN'T KNOW I WAS TO HAVE A PARTY AT ALL...
BUT, IF THERE *IS* TO BE ONE, I THINK *I* OUGHT TO INVITE THE GUESTS.

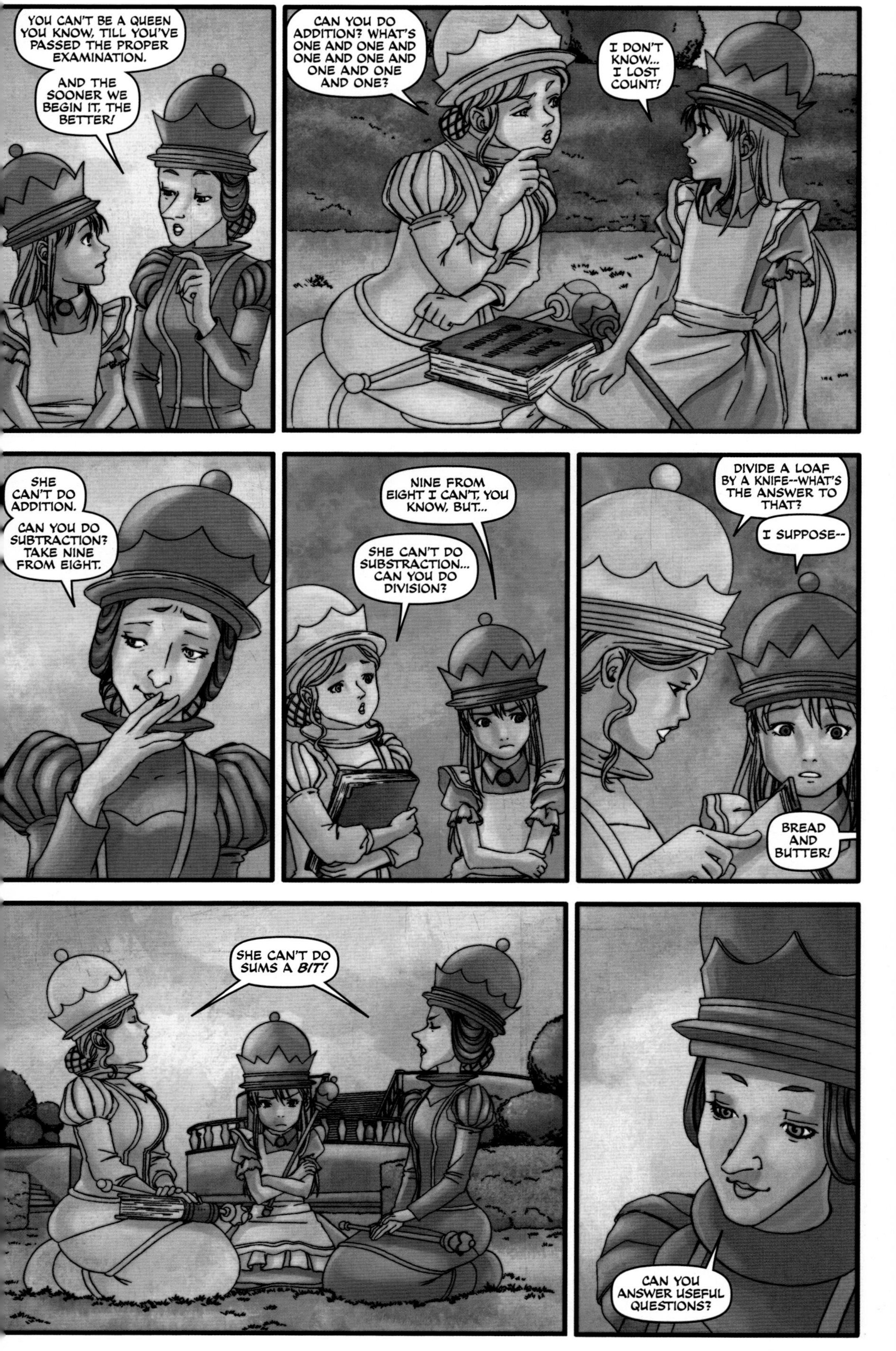
YOU CAN'T BE A QUEEN YOU KNOW, TILL YOU'VE PASSED THE PROPER EXAMINATION.
AND THE SOONER WE BEGIN IT, THE BETTER!
CAN YOU DO ADDITION? WHAT'S ONE AND ONE AND ONE AND ONE AND ONE AND ONE AND ONE?
I DON'T KNOW... I LOST COUNT!
SHE CAN'T DO ADDITION.
CAN YOU DO SUBTRACTION? TAKE NINE FROM EIGHT.
NINE FROM EIGHT I CAN'T, YOU KNOW, BUT...
SHE CAN'T DO SUBSTRACTION... CAN YOU DO DIVISION?
DIVIDE A LOAF BY A KNIFE--WHAT'S THE ANSWER TO THAT?
I SUPPOSE--
BREAD AND BUTTER!
SHE CAN'T DO SUMS A *BIT!*
CAN YOU ANSWER USEFUL QUESTIONS?

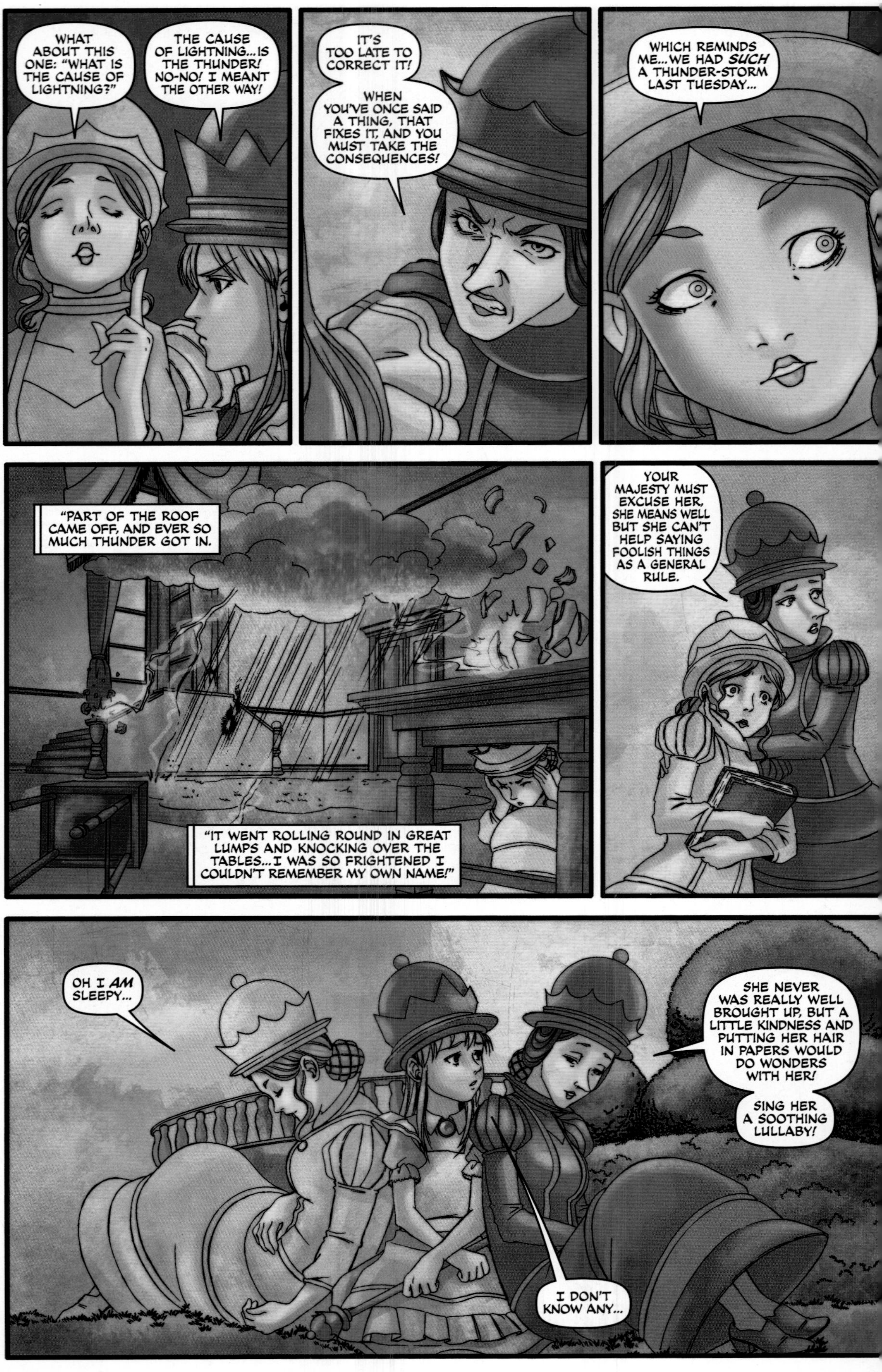
WHAT ABOUT THIS ONE: "WHAT IS THE CAUSE OF LIGHTNING?"
THE CAUSE OF LIGHTNING...IS THE THUNDER! NO-NO! I MEANT THE OTHER WAY!
IT'S TOO LATE TO CORRECT IT!
WHEN YOU'VE ONCE SAID A THING, THAT FIXES IT, AND YOU MUST TAKE THE CONSEQUENCES!
WHICH REMINDS ME...WE HAD SUCH A THUNDER-STORM LAST TUESDAY...
"PART OF THE ROOF CAME OFF, AND EVER SO MUCH THUNDER GOT IN.
"IT WENT ROLLING ROUND IN GREAT LUMPS AND KNOCKING OVER THE TABLES...I WAS SO FRIGHTENED I COULDN'T REMEMBER MY OWN NAME!"
YOUR MAJESTY MUST EXCUSE HER. SHE MEANS WELL BUT SHE CAN'T HELP SAYING FOOLISH THINGS AS A GENERAL RULE.
OH I AM SLEEPY...
SHE NEVER WAS REALLY WELL BROUGHT UP, BUT A LITTLE KINDNESS AND PUTTING HER HAIR IN PAPERS WOULD DO WONDERS WITH HER!
SING HER A SOOTHING LULLABY!
I DON'T KNOW ANY...

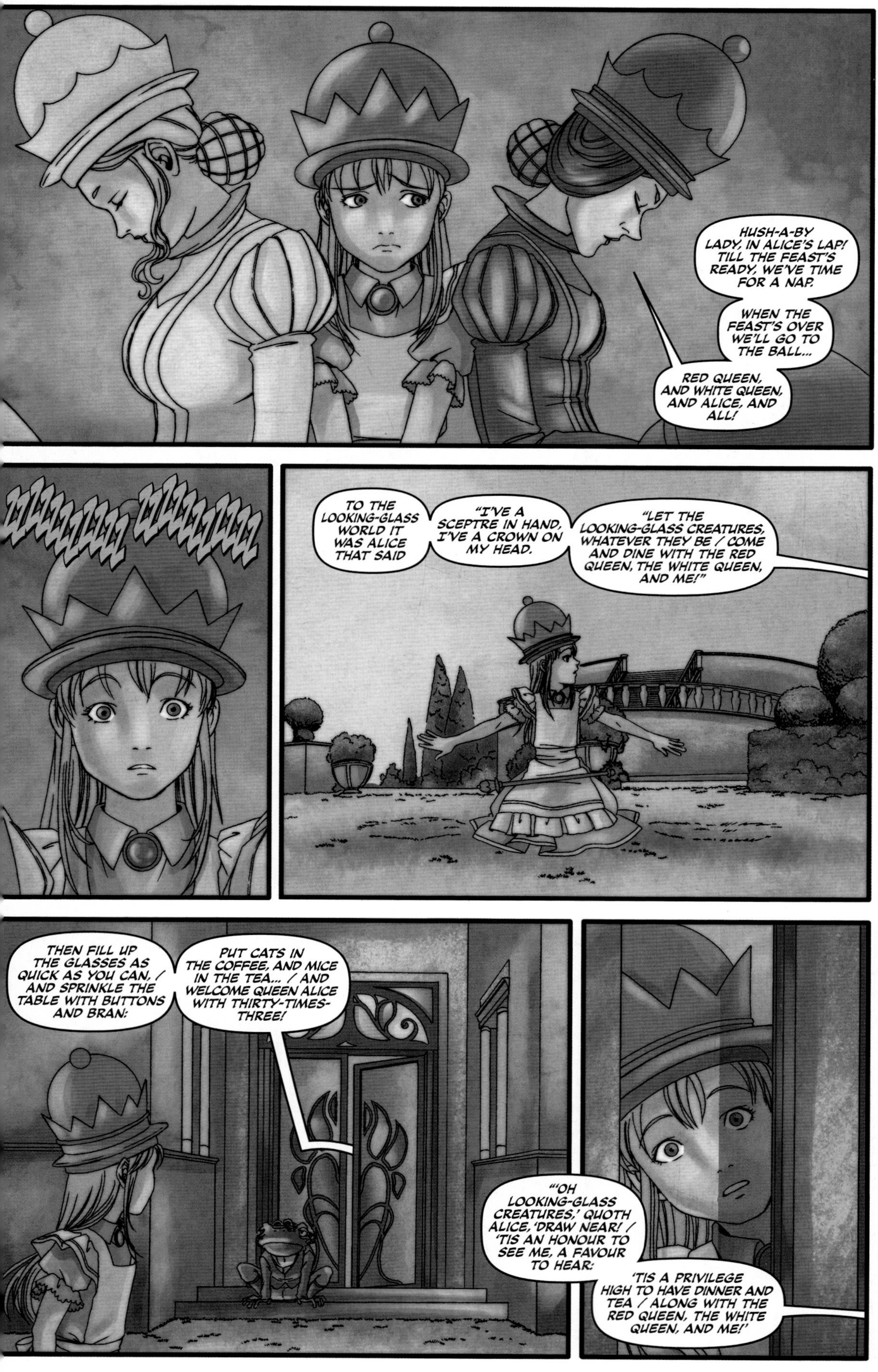
HUSH-A-BY LADY, IN ALICE'S LAP! TILL THE FEAST'S READY, WE'VE TIME FOR A NAP.
WHEN THE FEAST'S OVER WE'LL GO TO THE BALL...
RED QUEEN, AND WHITE QUEEN, AND ALICE, AND ALL!
ZZZZZZZZZ ZZZZZZZZZ
TO THE LOOKING-GLASS WORLD IT WAS ALICE THAT SAID
"I'VE A SCEPTRE IN HAND, I'VE A CROWN ON MY HEAD.
"LET THE LOOKING-GLASS CREATURES, WHATEVER THEY BE / COME AND DINE WITH THE RED QUEEN, THE WHITE QUEEN, AND ME!"
THEN FILL UP THE GLASSES AS QUICK AS YOU CAN, / AND SPRINKLE THE TABLE WITH BUTTONS AND BRAN:
PUT CATS IN THE COFFEE, AND MICE IN THE TEA... / AND WELCOME QUEEN ALICE WITH THIRTY-TIMES-THREE!
"'OH LOOKING-GLASS CREATURES,' QUOTH ALICE, 'DRAW NEAR! / 'TIS AN HONOUR TO SEE ME, A FAVOUR TO HEAR:
'TIS A PRIVILEGE HIGH TO HAVE DINNER AND TEA / ALONG WITH THE RED QUEEN, THE WHITE QUEEN, AND ME!'

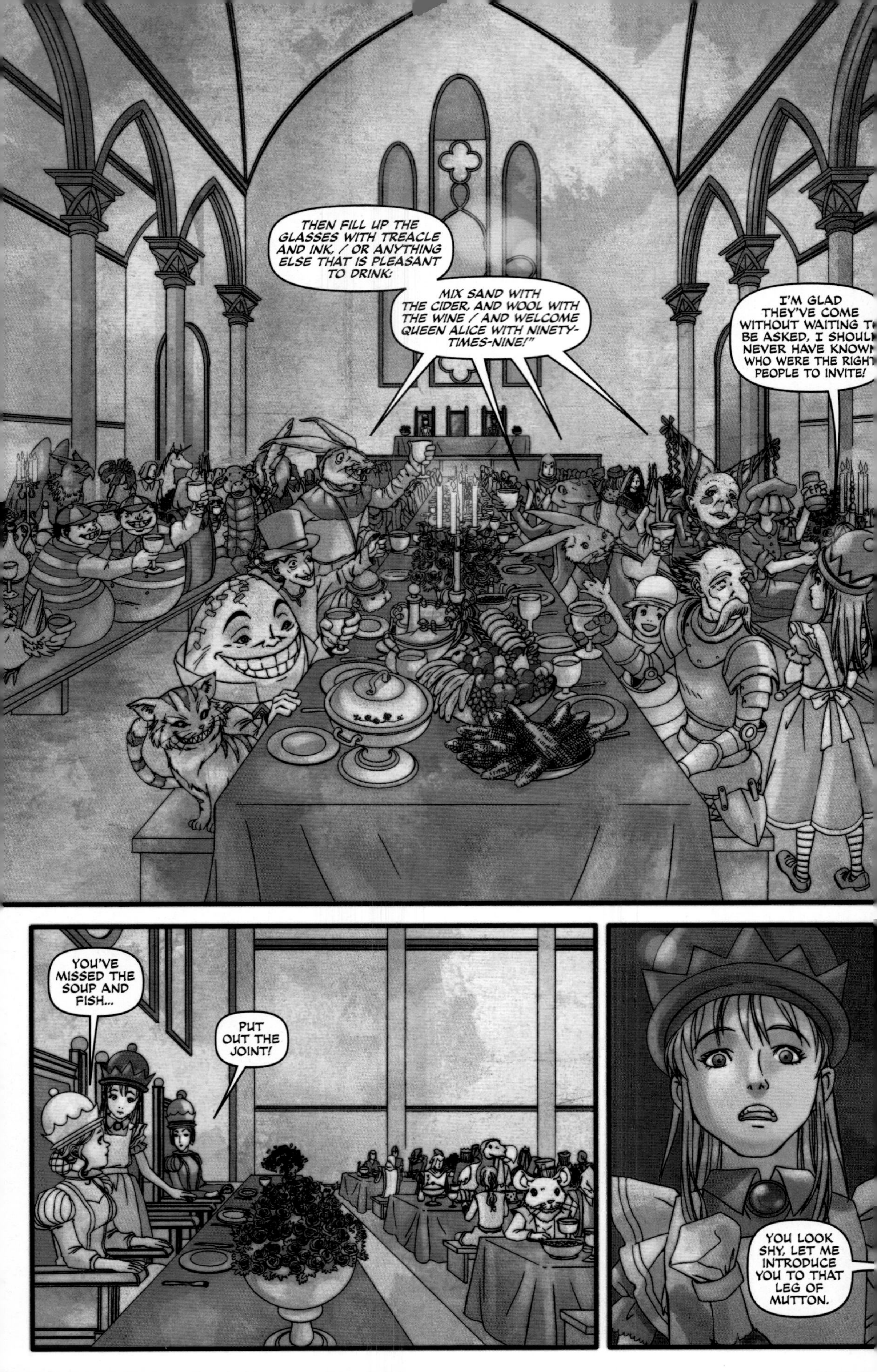
THEN FILL UP THE GLASSES WITH TREACLE AND INK, / OR ANYTHING ELSE THAT IS PLEASANT TO DRINK:
MIX SAND WITH THE CIDER, AND WOOL WITH THE WINE / AND WELCOME QUEEN ALICE WITH NINETY-TIMES-NINE!"
I'M GLAD THEY'VE COME WITHOUT WAITING TO BE ASKED, I SHOULD NEVER HAVE KNOWN WHO WERE THE RIGHT PEOPLE TO INVITE!
YOU'VE MISSED THE SOUP AND FISH...
PUT OUT THE JOINT!
YOU LOOK SHY, LET ME INTRODUCE YOU TO THAT LEG OF MUTTON.

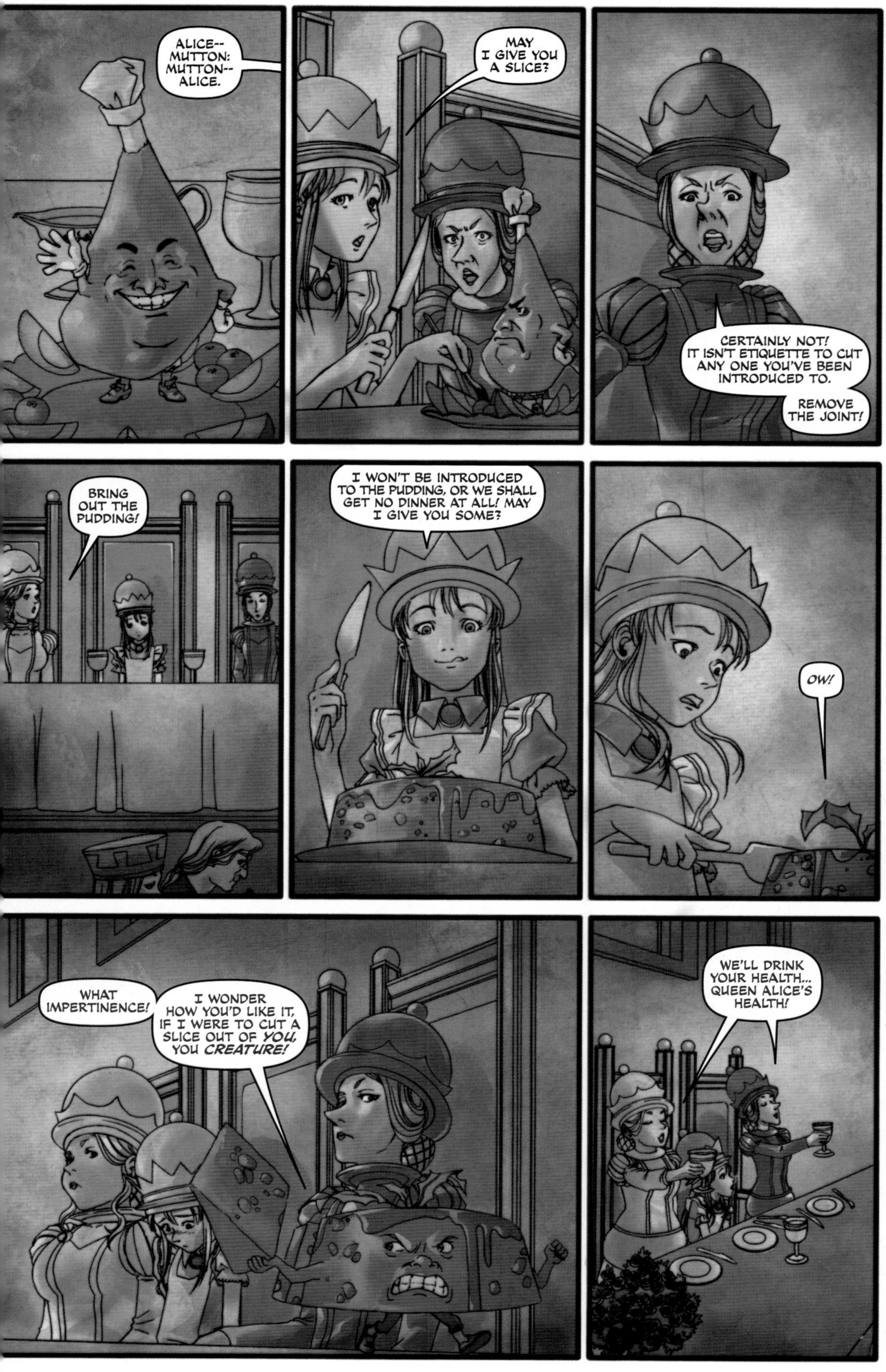
ALICE--MUTTON: MUTTON--ALICE.
MAY I GIVE YOU A SLICE?
CERTAINLY NOT! IT ISN'T ETIQUETTE TO CUT ANY ONE YOU'VE BEEN INTRODUCED TO.
REMOVE THE JOINT!
BRING OUT THE PUDDING!
I WON'T BE INTRODUCED TO THE PUDDING, OR WE SHALL GET NO DINNER AT ALL! MAY I GIVE YOU SOME?
OW!
WHAT IMPERTINENCE!
I WONDER HOW YOU'D LIKE IT, IF I WERE TO CUT A SLICE OUT OF *YOU*, YOU *CREATURE!*
WE'LL DRINK YOUR HEALTH... QUEEN ALICE'S HEALTH!

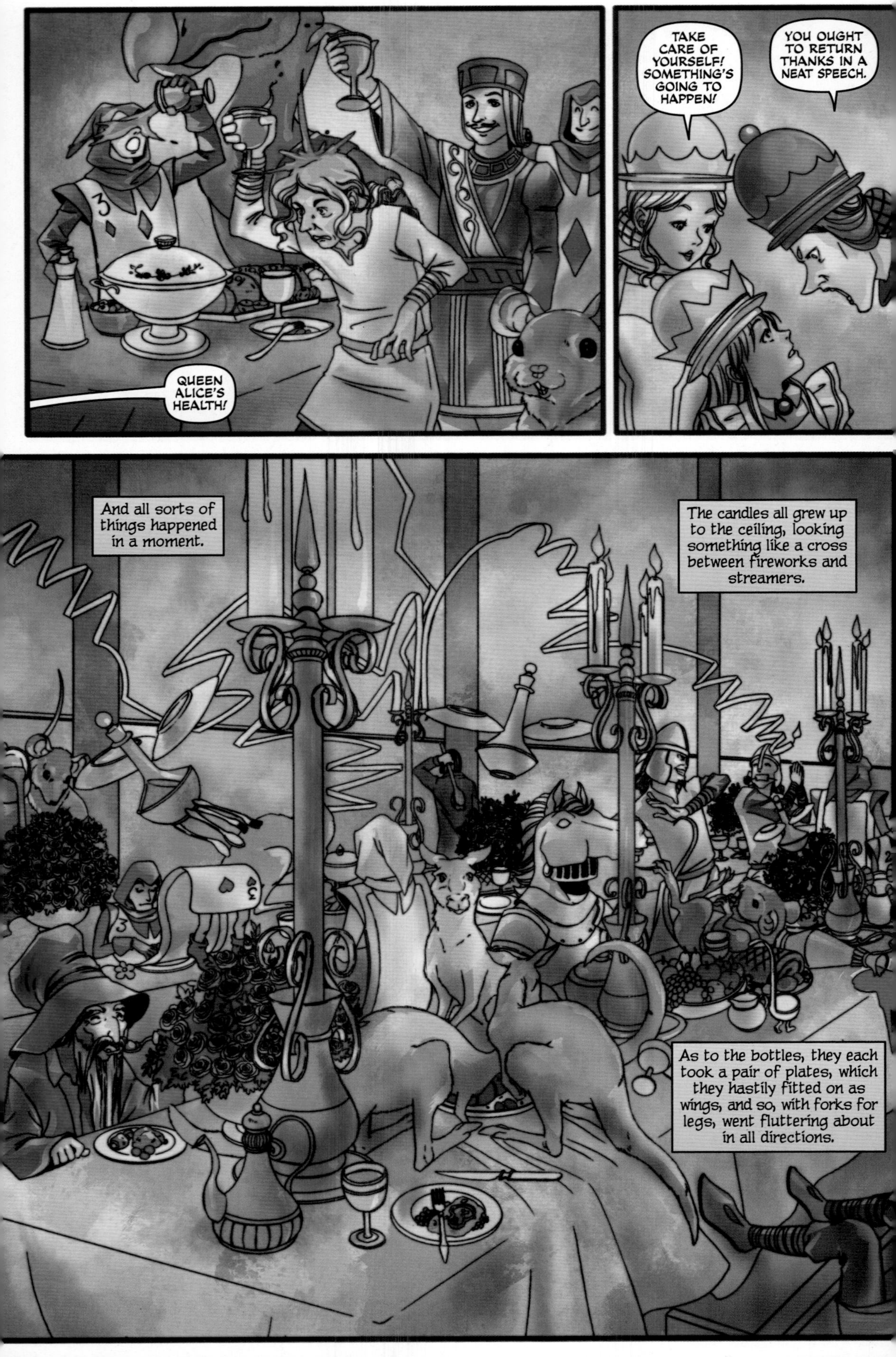
QUEEN ALICE'S HEALTH!
TAKE CARE OF YOURSELF! SOMETHING'S GOING TO HAPPEN!
YOU OUGHT TO RETURN THANKS IN A NEAT SPEECH.
And all sorts of things happened in a moment.
The candles all grew up to the ceiling, looking something like a cross between fireworks and streamers.
As to the bottles, they each took a pair of plates, which they hastily fitted on as wings, and so, with forks for legs, went fluttering about in all directions.

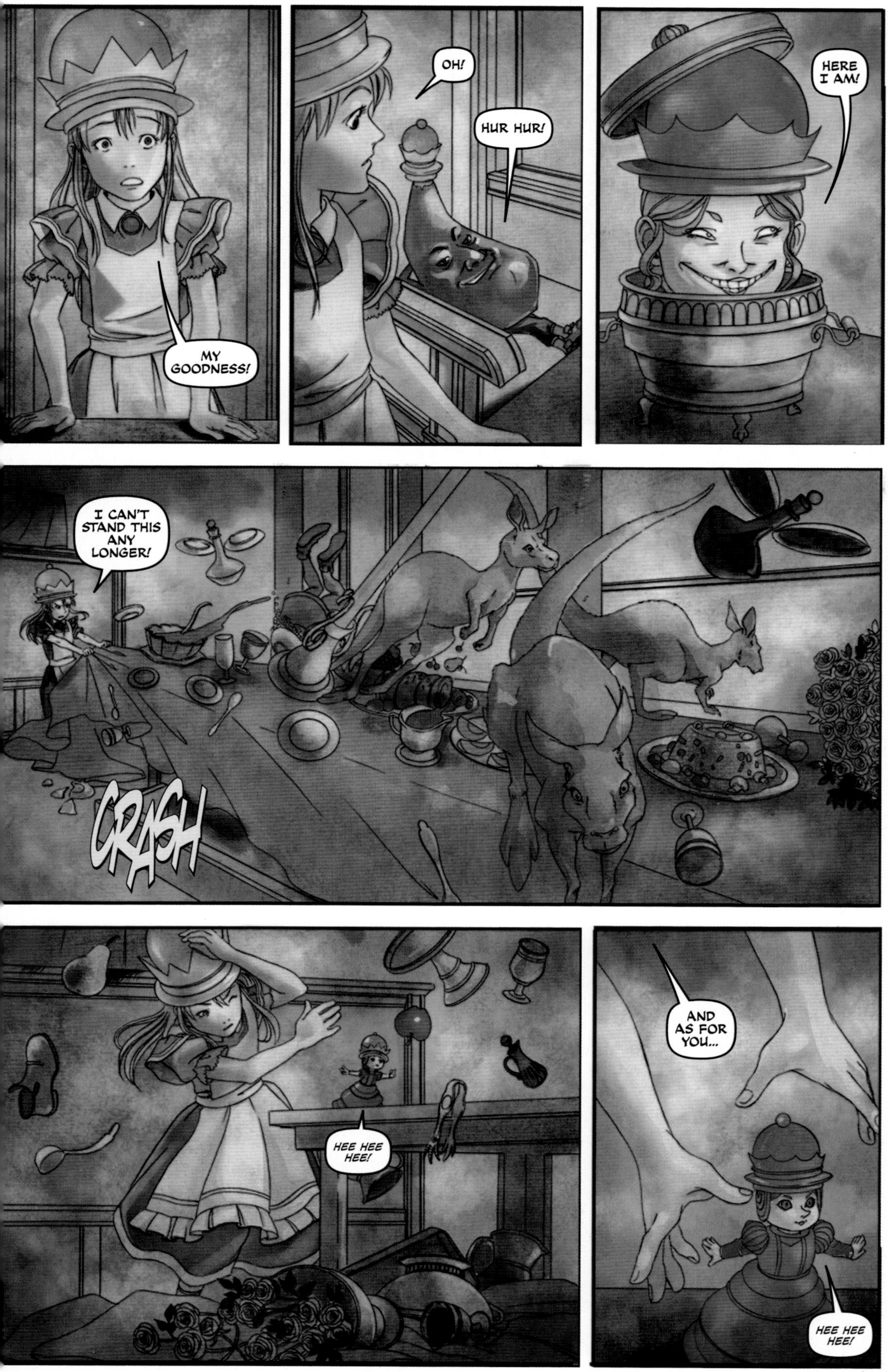
MY GOODNESS!
OH!
HUR HUR!
HERE I AM!
I CAN'T STAND THIS ANY LONGER!
CRASH
HEE HEE HEE!
AND AS FOR YOU...
HEE HEE HEE!

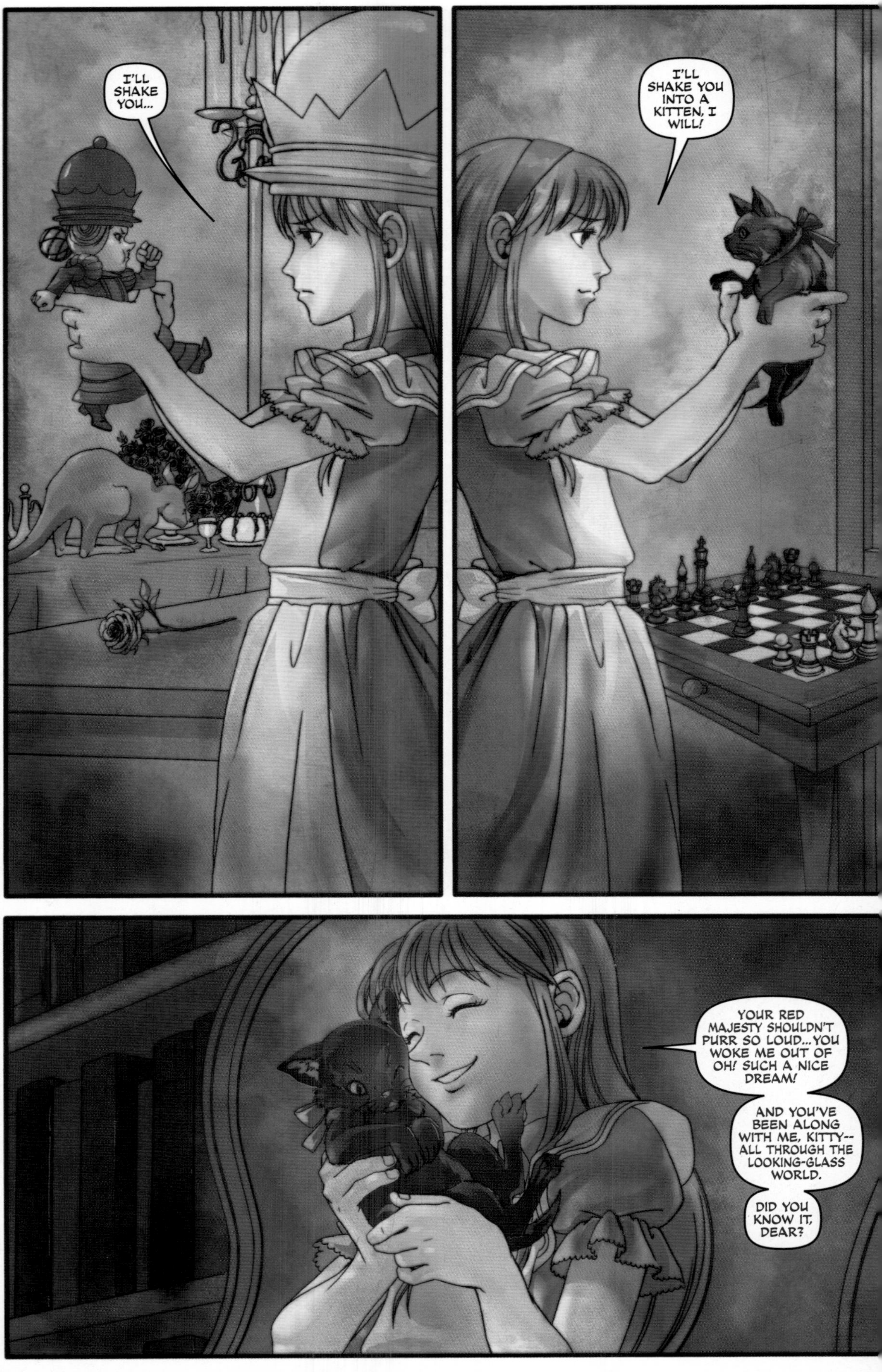
I'LL SHAKE YOU...
I'LL SHAKE YOU INTO A KITTEN, I WILL!
YOUR RED MAJESTY SHOULDN'T PURR SO LOUD...YOU WOKE ME OUT OF OH! SUCH A NICE DREAM!
AND YOU'VE BEEN ALONG WITH ME, KITTY-- ALL THROUGH THE LOOKING-GLASS WORLD.
DID YOU KNOW IT, DEAR?

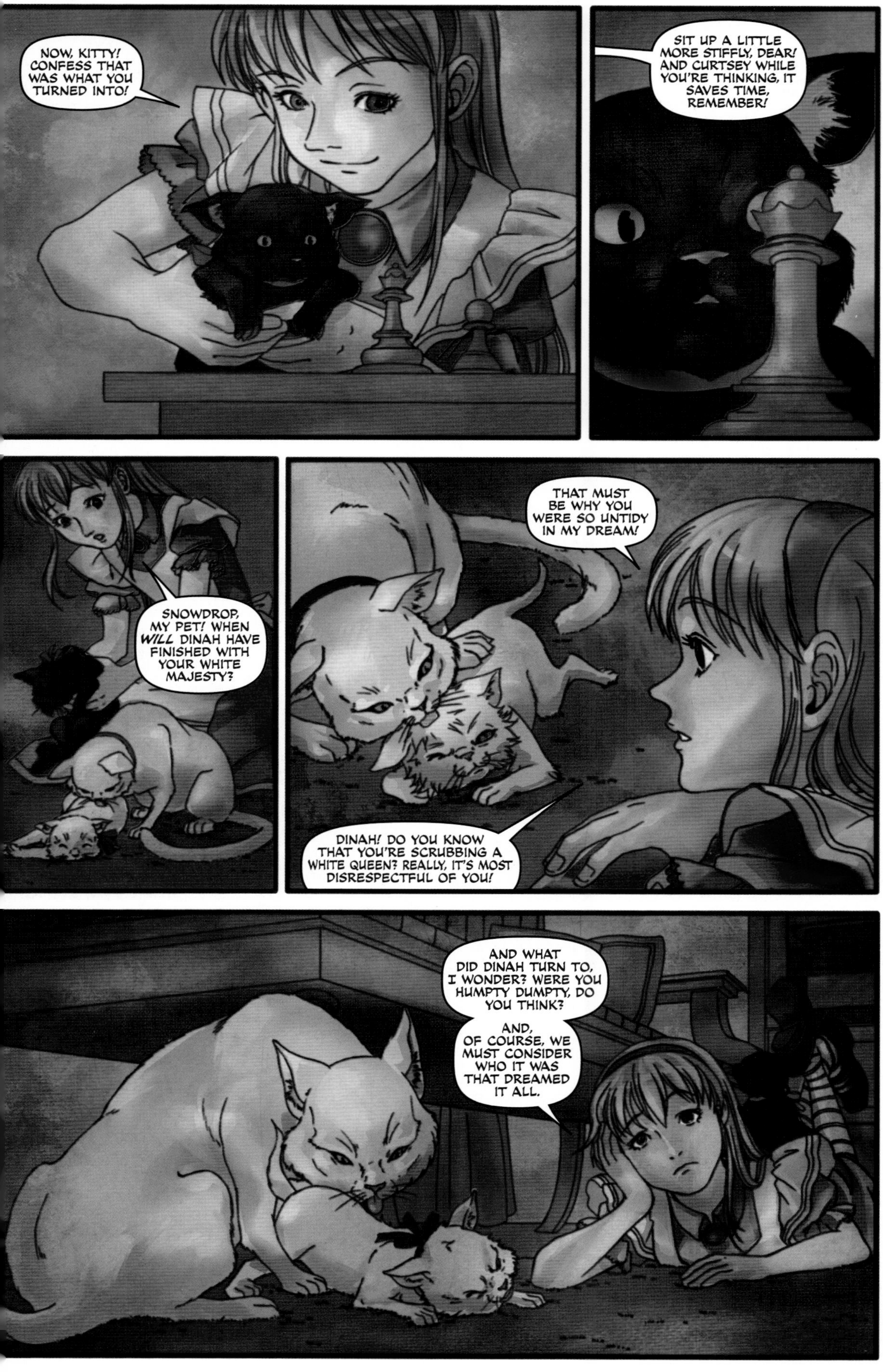
NOW, KITTY! CONFESS THAT WAS WHAT YOU TURNED INTO!
SIT UP A LITTLE MORE STIFFLY, DEAR! AND CURTSEY WHILE YOU'RE THINKING, IT SAVES TIME, REMEMBER!
SNOWDROP, MY PET! WHEN *WILL* DINAH HAVE FINISHED WITH YOUR WHITE MAJESTY?
THAT MUST BE WHY YOU WERE SO UNTIDY IN MY DREAM!
DINAH! DO YOU KNOW THAT YOU'RE SCRUBBING A WHITE QUEEN? REALLY, IT'S MOST DISRESPECTFUL OF YOU!
AND WHAT DID DINAH TURN TO, I WONDER? WERE YOU HUMPTY DUMPTY, DO YOU THINK?
AND, OF COURSE, WE MUST CONSIDER WHO IT WAS THAT DREAMED IT ALL.

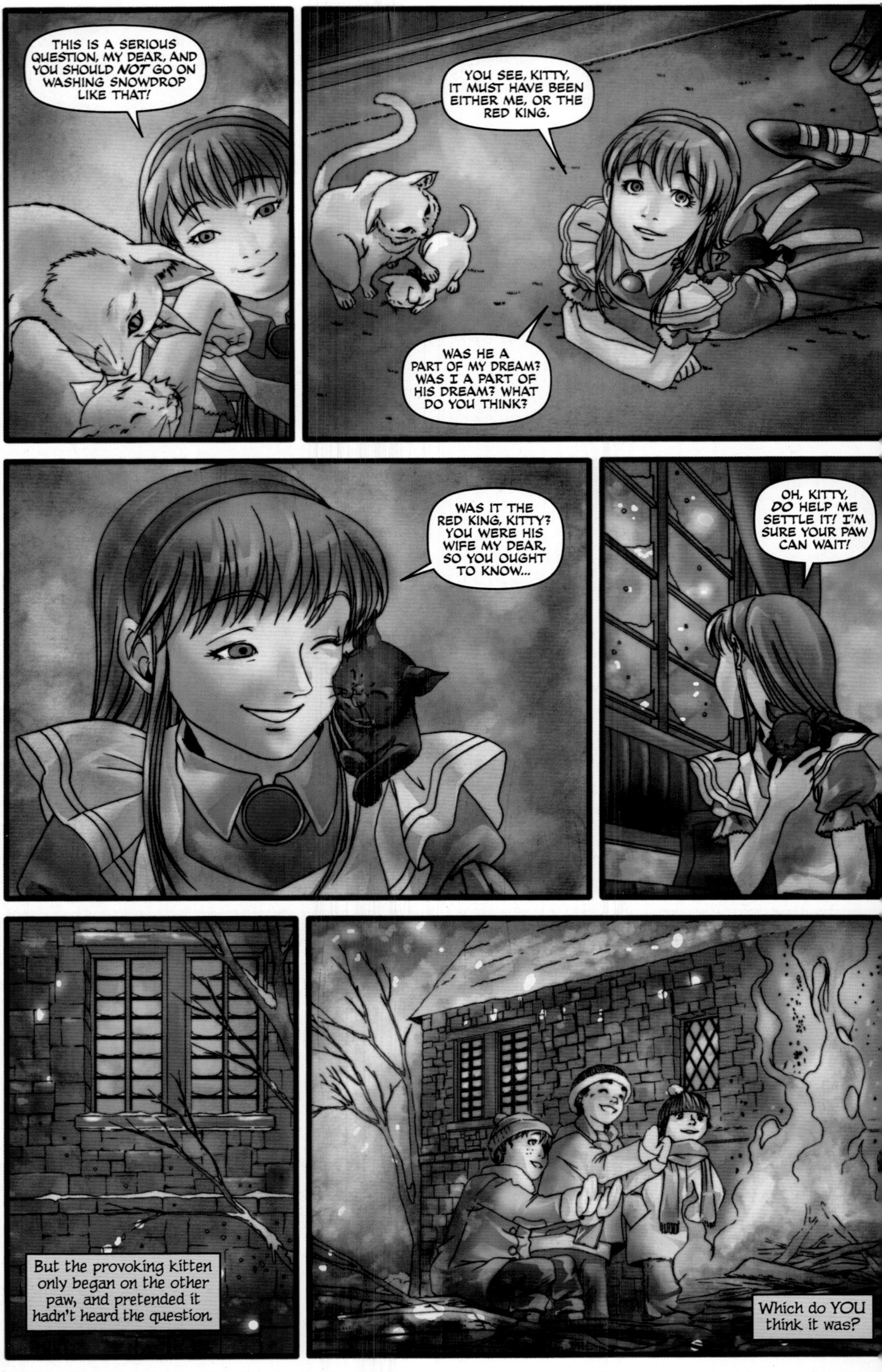
THIS IS A SERIOUS QUESTION, MY DEAR, AND YOU SHOULD *NOT* GO ON WASHING SNOWDROP LIKE THAT!
YOU SEE, KITTY, IT MUST HAVE BEEN EITHER ME, OR THE RED KING.
WAS HE A PART OF MY DREAM? WAS I A PART OF HIS DREAM? WHAT DO YOU THINK?
WAS IT THE RED KING, KITTY? YOU WERE HIS WIFE MY DEAR, SO YOU OUGHT TO KNOW...
OH, KITTY, *DO* HELP ME SETTLE IT! I'M SURE YOUR PAW CAN WAIT!
But the provoking kitten only began on the other paw, and pretended it hadn't heard the question.
Which do YOU think it was?

Bonus Materials

The Poetry of Wonderland

"All in the Golden Afternoon"

All in the golden afternoon
Full leisurely we glide;
For both our oars, with little skill,
By little hands are plied
While little hands make vain pretence
Our wanderings to guide

Ah, cruel Three! In such an hour
Beneath such dreamy weather,
To beg a tale of breath too weak
To stir the tiniest feather!
Yet what can one poor voice avail
Against three tongues together?

Imperious Prima flashes forth
Her edict to 'begin it'-
In gentler tone Secunda hopes
'There will be nonsense in it!' -
While Tertia interrupts the tale
Not more than once a minute.

Anon, to sudden silence won,
In fancy they pursue
The dream-child moving through a land
Of wonders wild and new,
In friendly chat with bird or beast -
And half believe it true.

And ever, as the story drained
The wells of fancy dry,
And faintly strove that weary one
To put the subject by,
'The rest next time' - 'It is next time!'
The happy voices cry.

Thus grew the tale of Wonderland
Thus slowly, one by one,
Its quaint events were hammered out -
and now the tale is done,
And home we steer, a merry crew,
Beneath the setting sun.

Alice! a childish story take,
And with a gentle hand
Lay it where Childhood's dreams are twined
In Memory's mystic band,
Like pilgrim's wither'd wreath of flowers
Plucked in far-off land

"She's All My Fancy Painted Him"

She's all my fancy painted him
(I make no idle boast);
If he or you had lost a limb,
Which would have suffered most?

He said that you had been to her,
And seen me here before;
But, in another character,
She was the same of yore.

There was not one that spoke to us,
Of all that thronged the street:
So he sadly got into a 'bus,
And pattered with his feet.

They sent him word I had not gone
(We know it to be true);
If she should push the matter on,
What would become of you?

They gave her one, the gave me two,
They gave us three or more;
They all returned from him to you,
Though they were mine before.

If I or she should chance to be
Involved in this affair,
He trusts to you to set them free,
Exactly as we were.

It seemed to me that you had been
(Before she had this fit)
An obstacle, that came between
Him, and ourselves, and it.

Don't let him know she liked them best,
For this must ever be
A secret, kept from all the rest,
Between yourself and me.

"Child of the Pure Unclouded Brow"

Child of the pure, unclouded brow
And dreaming eyes of wonder!
Though time be fleet, and I and thou
Are half a life asunder,
Thy loving smile will surely hail
The love-gift of a fairy-tale.

I have not seen thy sunny face,
Nor heard thy silver laughter;
No thought of me shall find a place
In thy young life's hereafter -
Enough that now thou wilt not fail
To listen to my fairy-tale.

A tale begun in other days,
When summer suns were glowing -
A simple chime, that served to time
The rhythm of our rowing -
Whose echoes live in memory yet,
Though envious years would say 'forget.'

Come, hearken then, ere voice of dread,
With bitter tidings laden,
Shall summon to unwelcome bed
A melancholy maiden!
We are but older children, dear,
Who fret to find our bedtime near.

Without, the frost, the blinding snow,
The storm-wind's moody madness -
Within, the firelight's ruddy glow,
And childhood's nest of gladness.
The magic words shall hold thee fast:
Thou shalt not heed the raving blast.

And though the shadow of a sigh
May tremble through the story,
For 'happy summer days' gone by,
And vanish'd summer glory -
It shall not touch with breath of bale
The pleasance of our fairy-tale.

"A Boat Beneath A Sunny Sky"

A boat beneath a sunny sky,
Lingering onward dreamily
In an evening of July –

Children three that nestle near,
Eager eye and willing ear,
Pleased a simple tale to hear –

Long had paled that sunny sky:
Echoes fade and memories die.
Autumn frosts have slain July.

Still she haunts me, phantomwise,
Alice moving under skies
Never seen by waking eyes.

Children yet, the tale to hear,
Eager eye and willing ear,
Lovingly shall nestle near.

In a Wonderland they lie,
Dreaming as the days go by,
Dreaming as the summers die:

Ever drifting down the stream –
Lingering in the golden gleam –
Life, what is it but a dream?

Whither and Why this Wig Wearing Wasp?

When we set out to adapt "Through the Looking Glass" we knew it was going to be really different to "Alice's Adventures in Wonderland" because the first book contains many of the more well known characters and stories. "Through the Looking Glass" is a little bit darker and stranger, and has some quite lengthy poems in it which make it more of a challenge to adapt.

What we weren't at first aware of was that there is an even less well known chapter, a missing piece of Carroll's text which had been lost for over a hundred years. The chapter was called "A Wasp in a Wig" and was only discovered again in 1974, when some galley proofs came up in a manuscript sale at Sotheby's auction house, London. The author of "The Annotated Alice", Martin Gardner, wrote to the anonymous owner of the proofs, and the owner very generously sent him a copy.

The missing chapter is certainly not one of the most spectacular scenes in terms of action, but it does have that darkness and oddness we find in the rest of Looking-Glass. Alice meets an old wasp under a tree, who wears a yellow wig, and they chat. That's about it really. So why was it excised from the book? There is a straightforward answer, which is that the illustrator of Carroll's Alice stories, Sir John Tenniel, suggested it be cut. Tenniel is the man responsible for creating the look of all the wonderful characters, a look which has changed very little over the years, despite the numerous different adaptations. Even Tim Burton's recent movie interpretation acknowledges Tenniel's illustrations in its design. So why did Tenniel object to the chapter? Martin Gardner's "The Annotated Alice" has the note from Tenniel to Carroll:

"My Dear Dodgson:
Don't think me brutal, but I am bound to say that the 'wasp' chapter does not interest me in the least, and I can't see my way to a picture. If you want to shorten the book, I can't help thinking – with all submission – that *this* is your opportunity.
 In an agony of haste,
     Yours sincerely,
         J. Tenniel"

It seems so strange that a whole chapter be cut from this classic work of fiction simply because the illustrator cannot think of a way to draw it. It seems especially odd to us as comic writers, who frequently ask artists to draw the impossible. Where would the industry be if artists just suggested difficult scenes be cut out completely? (Hopefully this won't give any of them that idea!)

There is a theory that Tenniel took offence at the part where the wasp says "one eye would do as well as two" because Tenniel himself only had one eye. There is also another theory that Tenniel was pushed for time, having a pressing deadline for some Punch illustrations (Which also rings true to a comic writer!).Whichever it was, Carroll obviously respected his opinion enough to cut the chapter, and until now, it has remained cut.

We have re-introduced "The Wasp in a Wig" into the story, just after the chapter with "It's My Own Invention," the White Knight's chapter. We did this partly because it is always nice to see things how the author originally intended them, so it's kind of 'directors cut', and partly because we want Érica Awano to get one up on Mr Tenniel, and show everyone how drawing a wasp in a wig is done! Joking aside, Érica has risen to the challenge and the scene is at once funny and surreal and unsettling, which is all we could ask for.

We could not have adapted the missing chapter (or indeed either book) without the invaluable resources at http://www.alice-in-wonderland.net/ or "The Annotated Alice" by Martin Gardner. Both are highly recommended to all fans of Carroll's Alice stories.

Moore & Reppion, 2010

The Wasp in the Wig

Lewis Carroll's "Lost Chapter" from "Through the Looking Glass"

...and she was just going to spring over, when she heard a deep sigh, which seemed to come from the wood behind her.

"There's somebody very unhappy there," she thought, looking anxiously back to see what was the matter. Something like a very old man (only that his face was more like a wasp) was sitting on the ground, leaning against a tree, all huddled up together, and shivering as if he were very cold.

"I don't think I can be of any use to him," was Alice's first thought, as she turned to spring over the brook: - "but I'll just ask him what's the matter," she added, checking herself on the very edge. "If I once jump over, everything will change, and then I can't help him."

So she went back to the Wasp - rather unwillingly, for she was very anxious to be a queen.

"Oh, my old bones, my old bones!" he was grumbling as Alice came up to him.

"It's rheumatism, I should think," Alice said to herself, and she stooped over him, and said very kindly, "I hope you're not in much pain?"

The Wasp only shook his shoulders, and turned his head away. "Ah deary me!" he said to himself.

"Can I do anything for you?" Alice went on. "Aren't you rather cold here?"

"How you go on!" the Wasp said in a peevish tone. "Worrity, Worrity! There never was such a child!"

Alice felt rather offended at this answer, and was very nearly walking on and leaving him, but she thought to herself "Perhaps it's only pain that makes him so cross." So she tried once more.

"Won't you let me help you round to the other side? You'll be out of the cold wind there."

The Wasp took her arm, and let her help him round the tree, but when he got settled down again he only said, as before, "Worrity, worrity! Can't you leave a body alone?"

"Would you like me to read you a bit of this?" Alice went on, as she picked up a newspaper which had been lying at his feet.

"You may read it if you've a mind to," the Wasp said, rather sulkily. "Nobody's hindering you, that I know of."

So Alice sat down by him, and spread out the paper on her knees, and began. "Latest News. The Exploring Party have made another tour in the Pantry, and have found five new lumps of white sugar, large and in fine condition. In coming back - "

"Any brown sugar?" the Wasp interrupted.

Alice hastily ran her eyes down the paper and said "No. It says nothing about brown."

"No brown sugar!" grumbled the Wasp. "A nice exploring party!"

"In coming back," Alice went on reading, "they found a lake of treacle. The banks of the lake were blue and white, and looked like china. While tasting the treacle, they had a sad accident: two of their party were engulped - "

"Where what?" the Wasp asked in a very cross voice.

"En-gulph-ed," Alice repeated, dividing the word in syllables.

"There's no such word in the language!" said the Wasp.

"It's in the newspaper, though," Alice said a little timidly.

"Let's stop it here!" said the Wasp, fretfully turning away his head.

Alice put down the newspaper. "I'm afraid you're not well," she said in a soothing tone. "Can't I do anything for you?"

"It's all along of the wig," the Wasp said in a much gentler voice.

"Along of the wig?" Alice repeated, quite pleased to find that he was recovering his temper.

"You'd be cross too, if you'd a wig like mine," the Wasp went on. "They jokes, at one. And they worrits one. And then I gets cross. And I gets cold. And I gets under a tree. And I gets a yellow handkerchief. And I ties up my face - as at the present."

Alice looked pityingly at him. "Tying up the face is very good for the toothache," she said.

"And it's very good for the conceit," added the Wasp.

Alice didn't catch the word exactly. "Is that a kind of toothache?" she asked.

The Wasp considered a little. "Well, no," he said: "it's when you hold up your head - so - without bending your neck."

"Oh, you mean stiff-neck," said Alice.

The Wasp said "That's a new-fangled name. They called it conceit in my time."

"Conceit isn't a disease at all," Alice remarked.

"It is, though," said the Wasp: "wait till you have it, and then you'll know. And when you catches it, just try tying a yellow handkerchief round your face. It'll cure you in no time!"

He untied the handkerchief as he spoke, and Alice looked at his wig in great surprise. It was bright yellow like the handkerchief, and all tangled and tumbled about like a heap of sea-weed. "You could make your wig much neater," she said, "if only you had a comb."

"What, you're a Bee, are you?" the Wasp said, looking at her with more interest. "And you've got a comb. Much honey?"

"It isn't that kind," Alice hastily explained. "It's to comb hair with - your wig's so very rough, you know."

"I'll tell you how I came to wear it," the Wasp said. "When I was young, you know, my ringlets used to wave - "

A curious idea came into Alice's head. Almost every one she had met had repeated poetry to her, and she thought she would try if the Wasp couldn't do it too. "Would you mind saying it in rhyme?" she asked very politely.

"It aint what I'm used to," said the Wasp: "however I'll try; wait a bit." He was silent for a few moments, and then began again -

> "When I was young, my ringlets waved
> And curled and crinkled on my head:
> And then they said 'You should be shaved,
> And wear a yellow wig instead.'
>
> But when I followed their advice,
> And they had noticed the effect,
> They said I did not look so nice
> As they had ventured to expect.
>
> They said it did not fit, and so
> It made me look extremely plain:
> But what was I to do, you know?
> My ringlets would not grow again.

So now that I am old and grey,
And all my hair is nearly gone,
They take my wig from me and say
'How can you put such rubbish on?'

And still, whenever I appear,
They hoot at me and call me 'Pig!'
And that is why they do it, dear,
Because I wear a yellow wig."

"I'm very sorry for you," Alice said heartily: "and I think if your wig fitted a little better, they wouldn't tease you quite so much."

"Your wig fits very well," the Wasp murmured, looking at her with an expression of admiration: "it's the shape of your head as does it. Your jaws aint well shaped, though - I should think you couldn't bite well?"

Alice began with a little scream of laughing, which she turned into a cough as well as she could. At last she managed to say gravely, "I can bite anything I want,"

"Not with a mouth as small as that," the Wasp persisted. "If you was a-fighting, now - could you get hold of the other one by the back of the neck?"

"I'm afraid not," said Alice.

"Well, that's because your jaws are too short," the Wasp went on: "but the top of your head is nice and round." He took off his own wig as he spoke, and stretched out one claw towards Alice, as if he wished to do the same for her, but she kept out of reach, and would not take the hint. So he went on with his criticisms.

"Then, your eyes - they're too much in front, no doubt. One would have done as well as two, if you must have them so close - "

Alice did not like having so many personal remarks made on her, and as the Wasp had quite recovered his spirits, and was getting very talkative, she thought she might safely leave him. "I think I must be going on now," she said. "Good-bye."

"Good-bye, and thank-ye," said the Wasp, and Alice tripped down the hill again, quite pleased that she had gone back and given a few minutes to making the poor old creature comfortable.

Creating Wonderland

THE COMPLETE ALICE IN WONDERLAND • Issue One, Page Two.
Script by Leah Moore and John Reppion

This is a three panel page with one wide letterbox type panel across the top of the page and then two tall panels under it. We have tried to open the layouts up as much as we can where we have the room, just so the backgrounds become a real feature of the story. We love how you handled the interior of the house on the tryout pages so we want to give you plenty of room to show off!

Panel One.

This is a wide panel with Alice crawling along the rabbit hole towards us. We can see the round bright shape of the rabbit hole entrance in the left background, and the rabbits backside going out of shot to the right in the right foreground. Between the rabbit hole entrance and the rabbit, the centre midground we have Alice crawling along on her hands and knees as she follows the rabbit. Roots hang down and brush against her face, and little bugs and beetles hurry out of her way as she passes by. She doesn't lo keen remotely scared. One caption from the narrator.

Cap: The rabbit hole went along like a tunnel, and then dipped suddenly down, so Alice had not a moment to think about stopping herself.

Panel Two.

This is a tall shot with Alice falling into shot at the top of the panel. She keeps falling for the next four panels, and we imagine that instead of her skirt inflating like the Disney film, that she should slowly tumble head over heels over the course of the four panels. We thought this would look like she was actually falling rather than floating, and it would enable her to reach out for objects at different angles making the panels more interesting to draw and read. In this shot she is just falling into shot, so maybe we can only se two thirds of her, with her feet still being up out of sight off panel top. She is reaching out to take a jar labelled "Marmalade" off a shelf she is falling past. The rest of the panel is a dark vertical tunnel, which has items of furniture randomly placed here and there on the walls. We had the idea that the items on these panels could prefigure the rest of the story, and kind of resemble things Alice might have herself at home (I think we stole this from the David Bowie film Labyrinth by the way). The walls are dotted with roll top desks, and little glass fronted cupboards and bookcases, it has tall grandfather clocks and rocking chairs. The shelves and cupboards have all kinds of things on them (apart from the marmalade Alice grabs) including a teapot, a cup and saucer, a top hat, a little toy rabbit with buttons for eyes, some playing cards, chess pieces, a nursery rhyme book, open at Humpty Dumpty, to name just a few. You don't have to fit them all in, but it would be cool if there were things to spot in each panel, and if those items were ones that cropped up again in the rest of the book. Some (like humpty dumpty) don't happen until issue 3 or 4 but that will be a nice thing to realise when you re-read it for the second time. One little thing we also thought of was that in each of the four falling panels there should be a framed picture somewhere of the Cheshire cat. They don't have to be in the same frame, or in the same place in the panel even. In the picture in Page Two Panel Two, it's the whole cat, in Page Two Panel Three, it is vanishing away, so we can see through part of it, in Page Three Panel One it's just the head that's left, and on Page Three panel Two it's just the smile. There are two captions from the narrator and one balloon from Alice.

Cap: She found herself falling down what seemed to be a deep well.

Cap: Either the well was very deep or she fell very slowly, for she had plenty of time as she went down to look about her.

Panel Three.

This is another tall panel, but Alice is further down the panel now. All the objects and pieces of furniture are different now, so we have an overstuffed armchair, a cuckoo clock, a candelabra, and other items dotted here and there. Maybe there's a framed print of a Gryphon or a copy of The Jabberwocky on a bookshelf. Alice is opening the jar of marmalade as she falls, peering into it to see if there is any actual marmalade inside. Her feet stick out towards the left now, her body turning as she falls. There are two balloons from Alice.

Alice: Well! After such a fall as this I shall think nothing of tumbling downstairs! How brave they'll all think me at home!

Alice: Why, I shouldn't say anything about it, even if I fell off the top of the house!

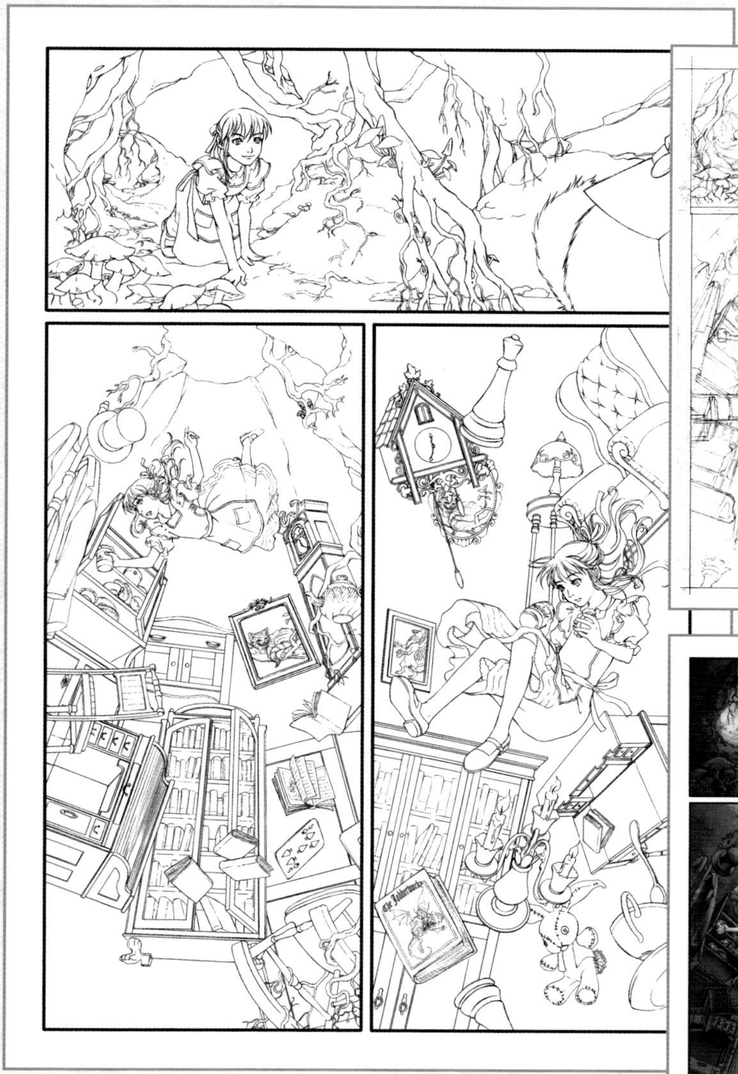

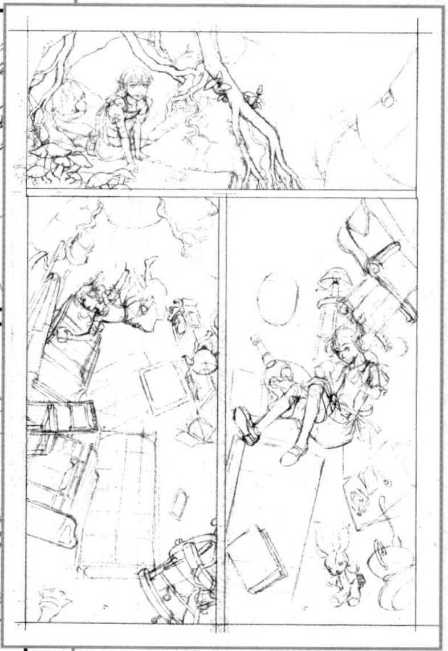

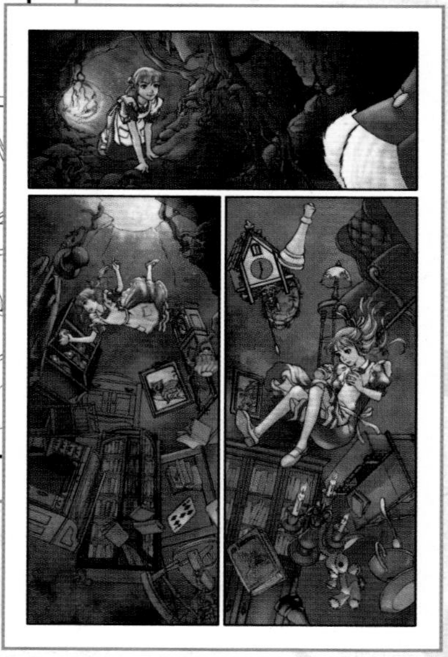

Left: Érica Awano's finished line art for page 2 of this issue
Top right: Érica Awano's rough layout for page 2 of this issue
Bottom right: PC Siqueira's final colors for page 2 of this issue

Notes for the art and colors by Leah and John

Firstly I'd like to say Hello Érica! We are really glad to have you working with us on this project, the samples you did look fantastic, and it will really help us with the scripting knowing the art is in a safe pair of hands! If you need any further reference or inspiration then the original illustrations by John Tenniel are fantastic. The character faces are so weird and unsettling, and the whole vibe is that little bit darker than the Disney Alice we all know and love. The other person I had floating about in my head was Arthur Rackham although his style is obviously more scratchy and busy, where yours is really clean. I just liked the darkness of his drawings, especially the nursery rhymes, and fairy stories, there's a sense of menace there. Obviously quite a lot of Alice's adventures are not at all menacing, but there are parts where things become a bit strange, so maybe bear Rackham in mind for those bits?

For the colorist (these notes were made before PC Siqueira was selected for the project): We would love it if the colouring on this book was very old fashioned looking. The watercolour illustrations you can find in some editions of the book have really nice washed out pastel palettes to them, or maybe like the hand tinted Victorian photographs? I think because we have no time of day (Alice jumps about in space and time so much there's no sunset or night time really, so the light source is usually just a bright sunny day) and because Erica's style is so lovely and clean, we could get away with doing quite simple colouring and shading. I think watercolour is the best way to describe it.

THE COMPLETE ALICE IN WONDERLAND • Issue Two, Page One.
Script by Leah Moore and John Reppion

This is a two panel page with one big two thirds splash panel at the top and one wide letterbox panel underneath that.

Panel One.

This is the reveal of the Mad Hatter's tea-party. It's a lovely shot, and I think there is only one small caption, so we can let your artwork do all the talking. The tea-party is round the back of the house in our version so we didn't have to reveal it at the end of last issue, and could save it for this one. The back of the house is also a beautiful and surreal garden, with big apple trees overhanging, and lots of strange containers full of masses of flowers. The back of the house still has the weird furry thatched roof on it which makes the house resemble the march hare himself. The windows of the cottage are set into the thatch slightly so they are like eyes peering out from under the fur. The house is the backdrop, and on the left we have a great big tree overhanging the scene, and sending dappled sunlight and shade across the tea-party. The midground is taken up by a really long table, which actually continues off out of shot to the right. The tea table is surrounded by chairs of all kinds, including a big leather armchair at end of the table on the left of the shot. Three of the chairs are occupied, facing us at the left end of the table. Next to the big armchair we can see the March Hare drinking from a tiny delicate tea cup, and presumably speaking to his dinner companions. The March hare is always shown as a kind of scruffy figure, with straw sticking out of his hair, and a shabby old coat on. He's much taller and skinnier than the White Rabbit, and has that frightening weirdness that so many of the characters possess. Next to the March Hare is the Dormouse who is asleep, his nose almost resting on the table in front of him. The Dormouse usually has some kind of little coat on, and I almost pictured him wearing a little fez for some reason, like a sleepy old professor. Next to the Dormouse is the Mad Hatter, who for some reason is like Iggy Pop or Bob Dylan in my mind. A gaunt old dude with twinkling eyes and long fingers. He of course has his famous hat on, with the little card that reads "In this style 10/6" tucked into the hat band. He is wearing an outrageous outfit which I will leave to you to design, as it's bound to be fun. The rest of the chairs are empty, although there is a place set for each chair at the table. There is a cup and saucer at each place, and I would love it if these were all different styles and colours of cups and saucers. There are tea plates at each place, and of course teapots full of tea here and there long the centre of the table. There are plates of bread and butter and pots of jam, and little stands of cupcakes. In the left foreground we can see Alice as she walks into shot and towards the strange party. I think she could be full figure, but see how the composition looks to you. One caption from the narrator.

Cap:	There was a table set out in the garden, and the March Hare and the Hatter were having tea at it.

Panel Two.

This is a shot from behind the three characters at the table, looking over to where Alice is approaching the table in the right midground. From this angle the Hatter is on the left, and the Hare is on the right, with the Dormouse still in the middle asleep. From this angle we can see the table and all the cups and saucers as the characters pour themselves tea, spill the milk, help themselves to bread, and generally cause chaos. Alice looks a bit annoyed as she approaches. The Mad hatter and the Hare share one balloon and Alice has one balloon.

Mad Hatter and March Hare:	No room! No room!
Alice:	There's plenty of room!

Notes to Érica from Leah and John

Hi Erica, hope the first issue hasn't been too hard, and that you are all settled in to the book now. It always takes us a while to get into our stride on a book, and I imagine that's even truer for artists, so let's have some fun with the second one, now we're all relaxed. We LOVE the layouts and pencils we've seen so far!

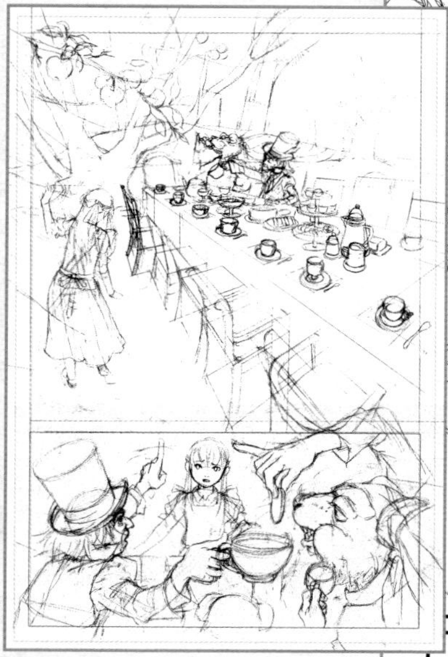

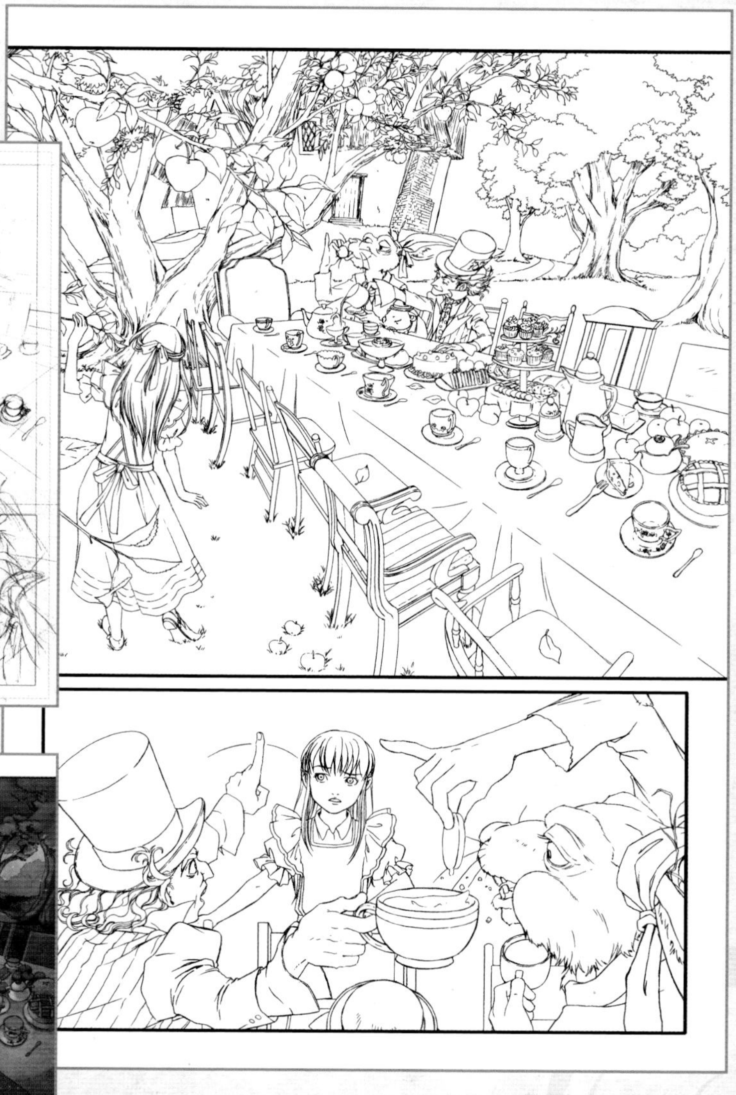

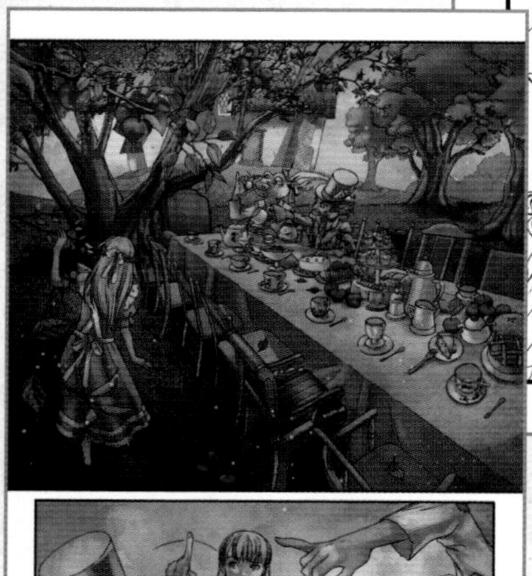

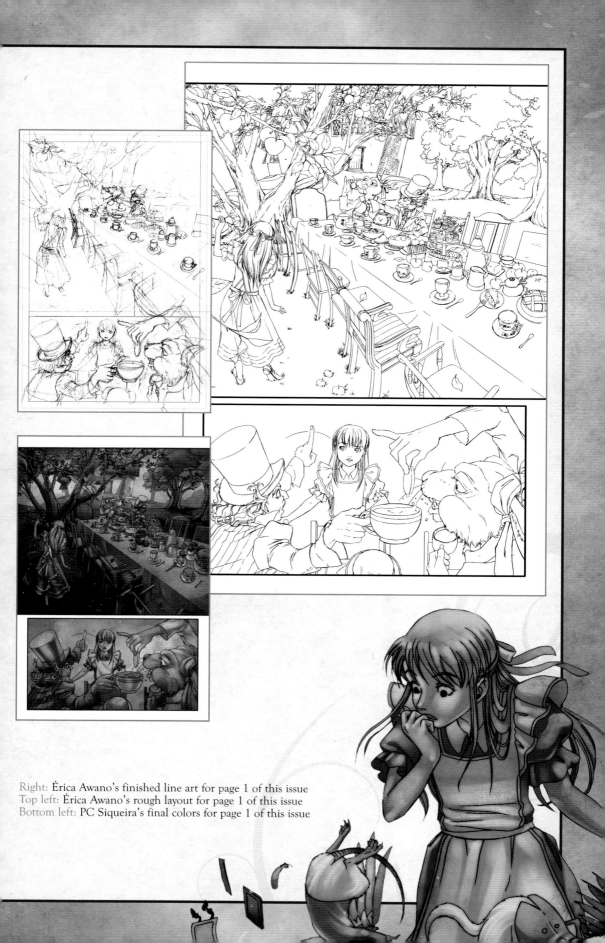

Right: Érica Awano's finished line art for page 1 of this issue
Top left: Érica Awano's rough layout for page 1 of this issue
Bottom left: PC Siqueira's final colors for page 1 of this issue

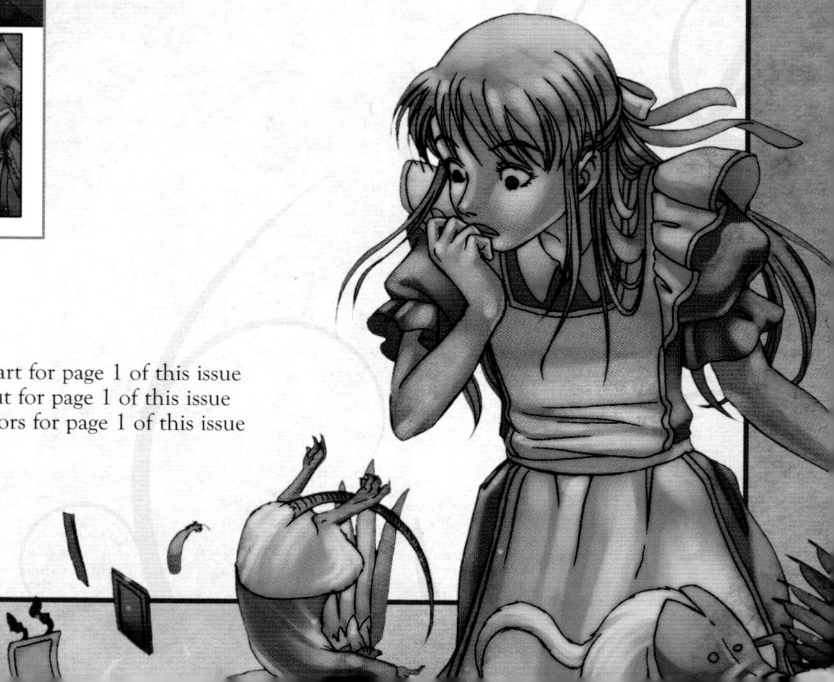

This is a five panel page with one wide panel across the top, and two panels on the middle and bottom tiers.

Panel One.

      This is a wide shot, so there is plenty of room for any crazy details you want to put in, objects you want to sneak into the panel, or whatever. We are inside a little dark shop, the really old fashioned kind with dark wooden shelves lining the walls, and a glass fronted cabinet for the counter, so you can see more shelves under it. The shop is stuffed to the gills with things, and like the rabbit-hole pages at the start of the first issue I thought this might be a great place to put in reminders...of the other issues and the other characters. I thought there might be a tea set, a top hat, a chess set playing cards, comfits, thimbles, wool and knitting needles, a croquet set, pepper pocket watches, and everything else you can think of. I would love it if this shop almost seemed like the shop the other characters had come to, to get everything they needed to make the rest of the story. Obviously this is a lot of work and these two pages are set entirely in the shop and then there's even more later on, so I don't expect everything to go into every panel. It's a dark shop, so hopefully you can make the corners really shadowy and then you can get away with only drawing the things closer to us, that aren't in shadow! The shop has a window over in the left background, with shelves across it with jars of sweets displayed. The floor space is stacked with boxes and larger items for sale. The whole place is very claustrophobic feeling. Behind the counter there is an old sheep who is wrapped in a shawl (the same shawl as the White Queen had?) and has half moon glasses on. She is busy knitting something with several knitting needles at once. I think it would be great if over the course of these pages the thing she knits gets progressively longer and/or weirder...so if she starts off with what looks like a sleeve we see it grow into a sweater with four sleeves, or some kind of weird scarf with extra pieces on or something, just because all the sheep does is knit and I want it to progress a bit just to keep it interesting. Alice is stood looking round her in great surprise. The sheep is looking up at Alice over her half moon spectacles and doesn't look very impressed! The sheep has two balloons.

Sheep: Be-e-ehh!

Sheep: Yes? What is it you want to buy?

Panel Two.

      This is a small shot of Alice two thirds figure as she goggles in amazement around herself at the weird and wonderful shop. She has one balloon.

Alice: I don't *quite* know yet, I should like to look all around me first, if I might.

Panel Three.

      This is a wider shot from behind the counter so the sheep is in the left foreground with what looks like dozens of knitting needles poking out of her knitting. She is glaring across her counter at Alice who is stood looking around her in amazement. The Sheep has two balloons.

Sheep: You may look in front of you and on both sides if you like, but you can't look *all*
                                    around you...

Sheep: ...unless you've got eyes in the back of your head.

Panel Four.

      This is a wide panel again, and we have closed in on Alice. She is closer to the shelves now, and has her hand out to touch one of the items on the shelf. We can see the shelves are stuffed with items and all kinds of exciting things in jars and boxes. Alice is reaching out to the right of the panel with her left hand, and is looking back over her shoulder at the sheep presumably. We can see her face as she speaks to it. She has one balloon.

Alice: Well it would be very queer if I did! I should get quite ill looking forwards and
                                    backwards wherever I went!

Panel Five.

      This small panel is almost a repeat of the last panel but cropped so we can see Alice in the left of the panel, still with her arm up to touch something, but now she is looking at the shelf again, and it appears to be suddenly empty! All the objects have slid out of her sight almost literally bunching up onto the shelves beside and behind Alice so they don't get seen by her. She is very puzzled as to why there isn't anything there now, and she can see the other shelves are full in her peripheral vision so its even more confusing. She has one balloon.

Alice: oh! It's gone! But I'm sure it was there a moment ago?

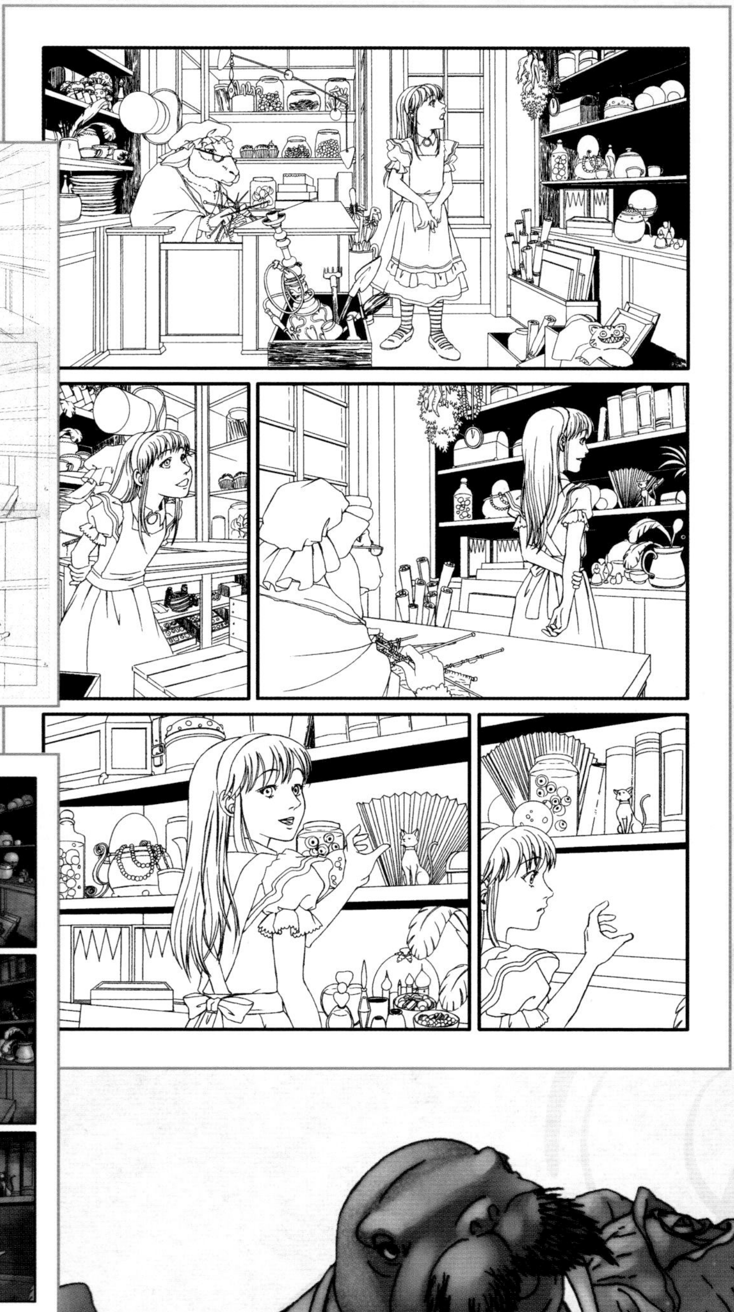

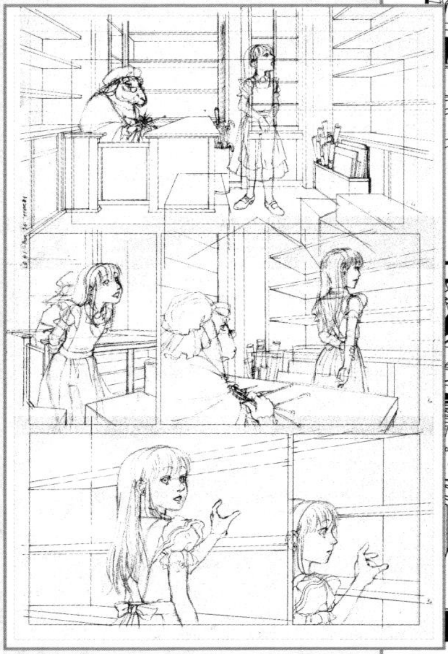

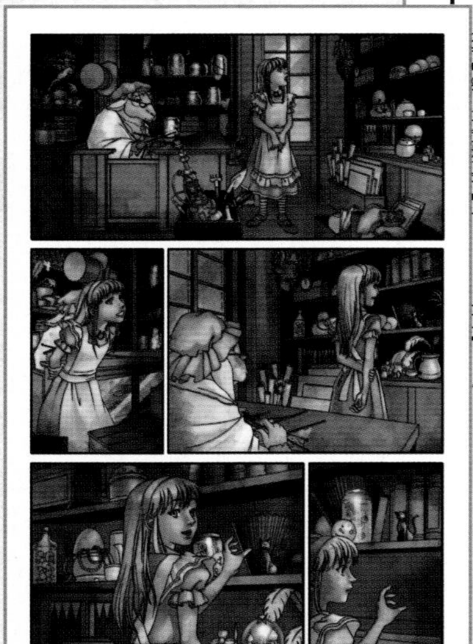

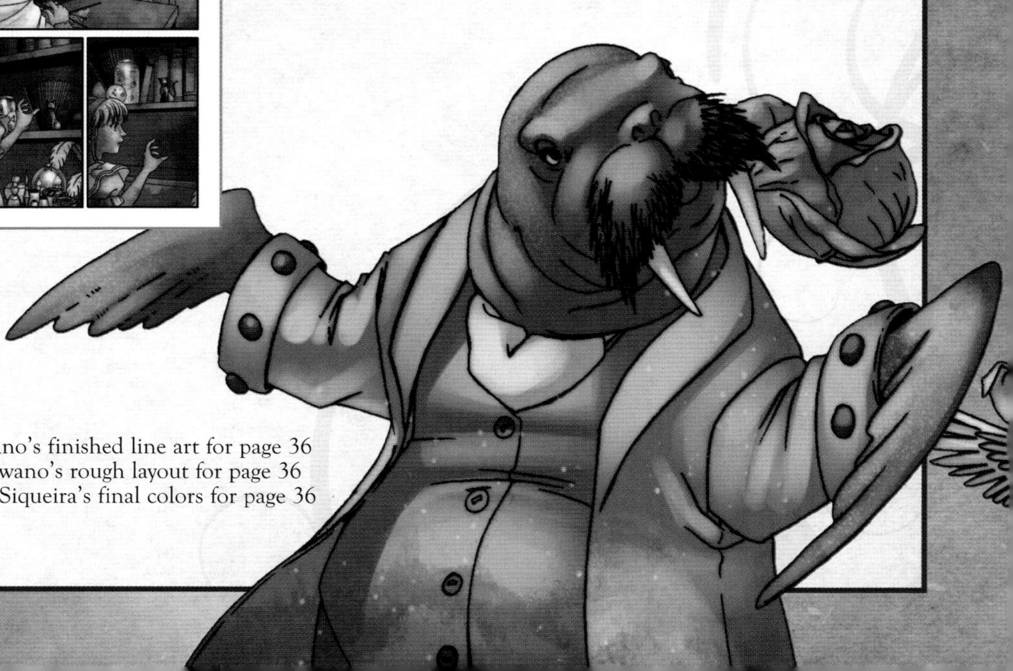

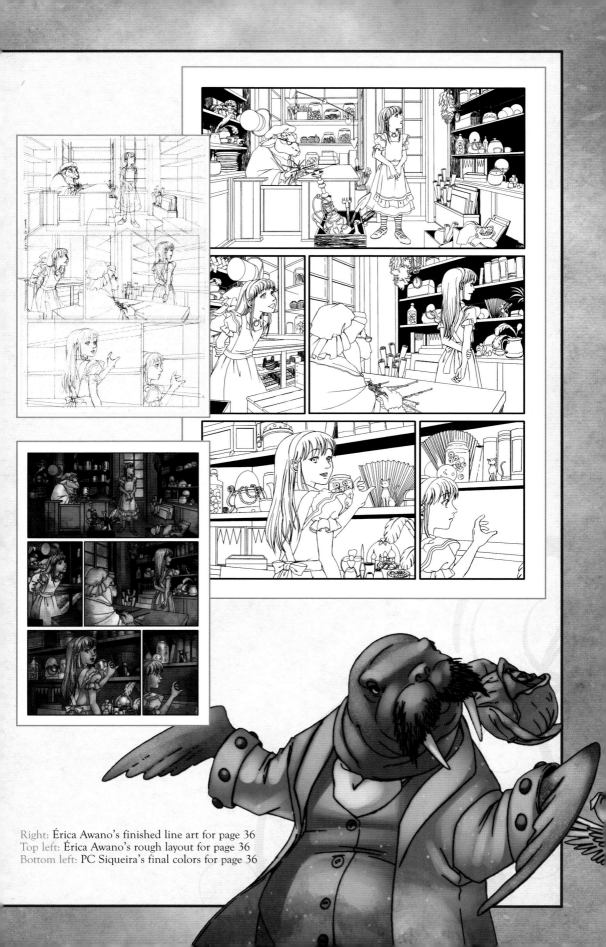

Right: Érica Awano's finished line art for page 36
Top left: Érica Awano's rough layout for page 36
Bottom left: PC Siqueira's final colors for page 36

This is a three panel page, with a big two thirds splash panel at the top, and two underneath it.

Panel One.

In this panel we have Alice approaching us up a grassy slope: at the bottom of the slope in the background we can see the brook which separates this square from the eighth square. The other side of the brook is kind of indistinct really: it's hard to know what's over there. The grassy slope has big gnarled trees every so often, and there is one in the left foreground. The tree is really old and gnarly, and so is the creature sitting underneath it! There is an old man with the head and hands of a wasp dressed in a dark jacket and trousers with a yellow and black striped waistcoat on. He has a yellow handkerchief tied around his face, which almost covers his hair, and ties under his chin like a head scarf. What hair we can see sticking out from under the scarf at the back, is really untidy, tangled and importantly also yellow! He has antennae sticking out from under the front of the headscarf, and his hands are little wasp pincers (I looked on Wikipedia and there are some amazing wasp reference pictures!) He has large compound eyes, and weird hairy little mandibles to either side of his mouth. I have no idea how you make a wasp look old, but he is old, so maybe his mandible hair is grey? Lord knows! He reminds me of Vincent Price in the original version of The Fly before it was remade with Jeff Goldblum in it! He is sitting with his back to the tree in the left foreground and Alice is approaching him as she walks up the slope. He is certainly the most unpleasant creature we have seen her meet so far, even worse than the gnat! It is a windy day so leaves are being caught up and carried a little way. The grass and flowers are being blown into swirls by the gusts, and the trees sway overhead. There are two balloons from Alice and one from the wasp which has failed to even notice her yet.

Alice:	He sounds *very* unhappy! I don't *think* I can be of any use to him, but I'll just ask him what's the matter.
Alice:	If I once jump over, everything will change, and then I can't help him.
Wasp:	Oh, my old bones, my old bones!

Panel Two.

This is a small shot of Alice as she approaches the wasp. She is bending over slightly to speak to him in the strange patronising way people do when talking to old people. She looks concerned. She has two balloons.

| Alice: | It's rheumatism, I should think. I should hope you're not in much pain? |
| Alice: | Aren't you rather cold here? |

Panel Three.

This is a wider shot with the wasp looking round at Alice suddenly. She looks quite startled by the sight of his strange features and shiny compound eyes. The wasp has two balloons.

| Wasp: | How you go on! Worrity, worrity! |
| Wasp: | There never was such a child! |

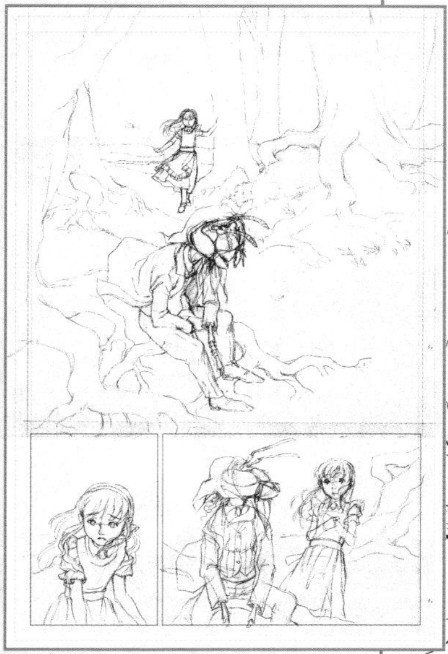

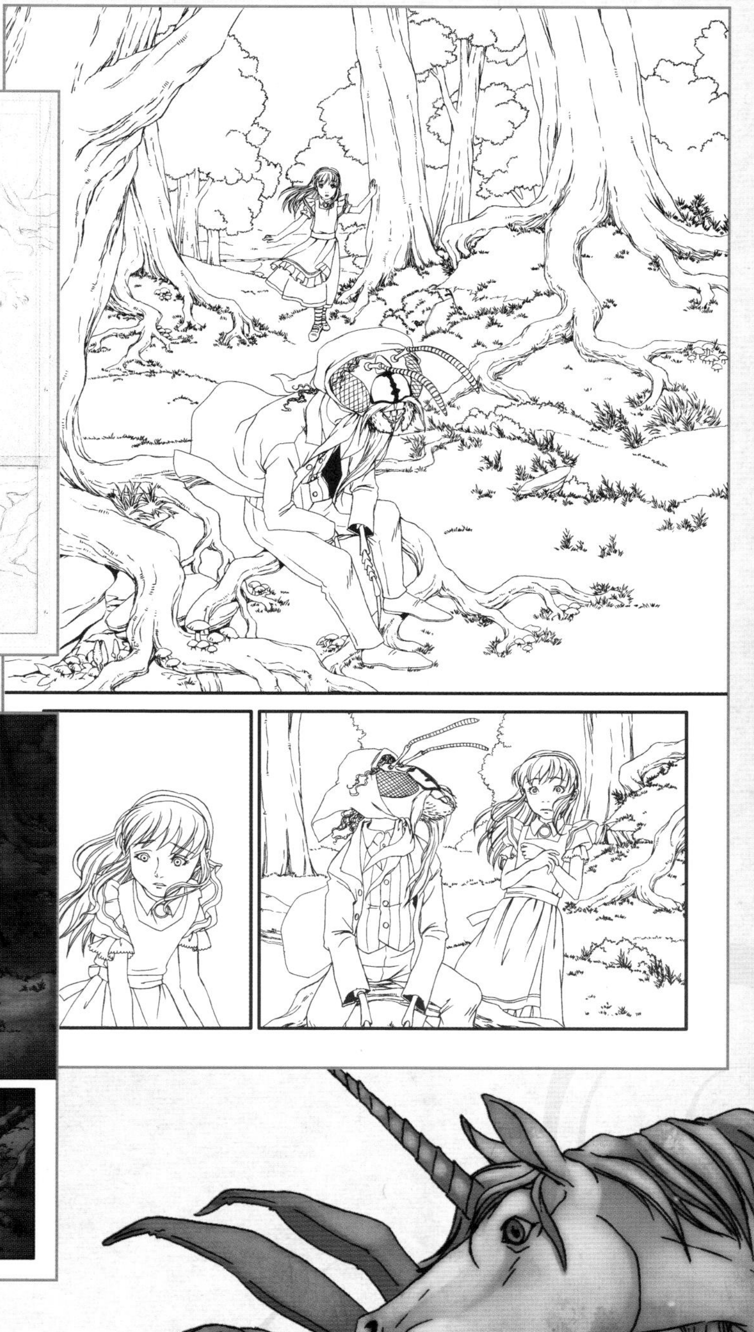

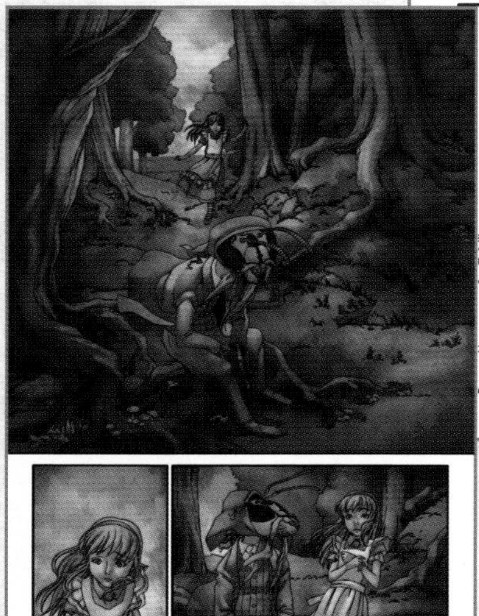

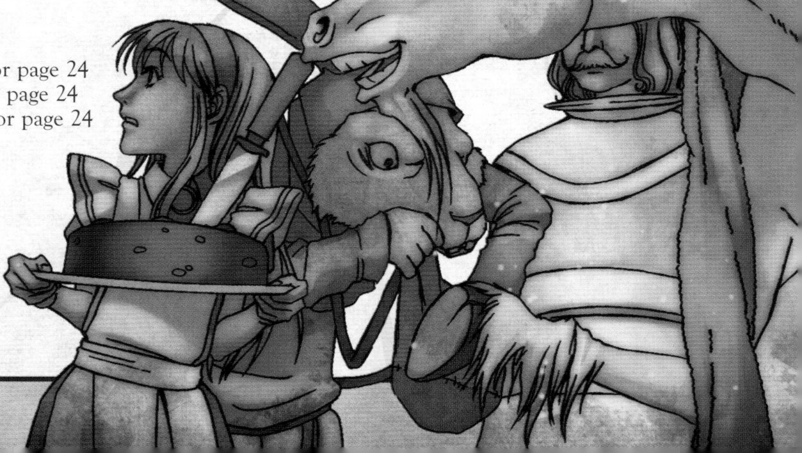

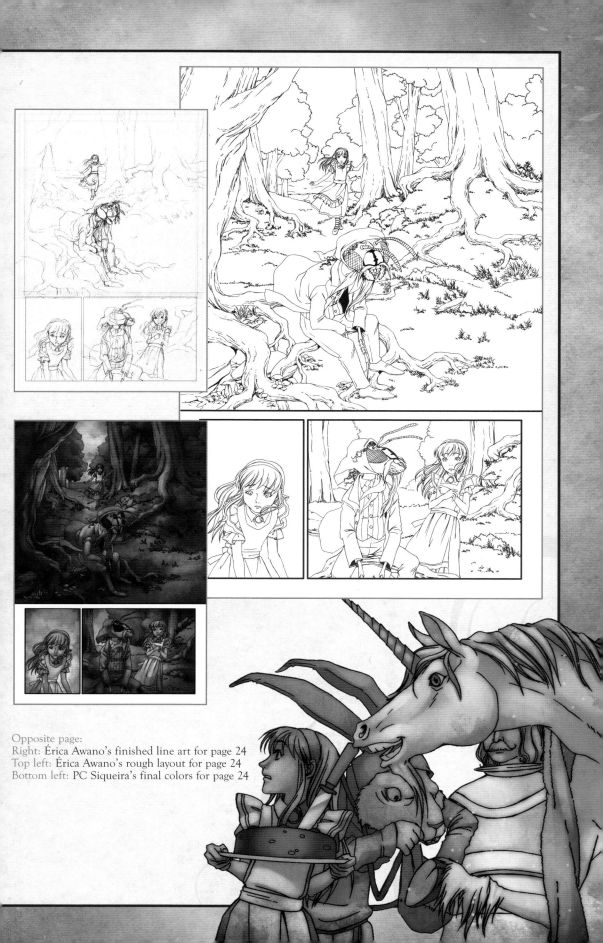

Opposite page:
Right: Érica Awano's finished line art for page 24
Top left: Érica Awano's rough layout for page 24
Bottom left: PC Siqueira's final colors for page 24

The Workings of Wonderland

An interview with writers Leah Moore and John Reppion by Brian Hofacker of Dynamic Forces

Following up on the success of *The Complete Dracula* and *Sherlock Holmes*, Dynamite presents *The Complete Alice In Wonderland*. For the first time ever, Lewis Carroll's classics *Alice's Adventures in Wonderland* and *Through the Looking-Glass* with "The Wasp in a Wig," the "lost chapter" (from *the Looking-Glass*), are adapted into one complete tale. In this All Ages adaptation, writers John Reppion and Leah Moore are joined by Érica Awano for a 4 issue adventure down the rabbit hole! John and Leah gave DF's Brian Hofacker the answers to what went into their trip to Wonderland!

Brian: One of the most powerful and influential aspects the greatest works of literature share is the ability to expand their genre. For instance, with *Hamlet* Shakespeare annihilates the structure of the revenge tragedy by adding, among other things, psychological complexities to his revenger. Likewise, Lewis Carroll's *Alice's Adventures in Wonderland* presents quite a few contradictions of expectations to what one would find in a typical fairy tale. Having worked on the tale, what do you consider to be the ways that Lewis Carroll's tale expands the fairy tale genre?

John Reppion: Whilst Alice is an outsider in Wonderland, she is much more in control than the characters in other, more traditional, fairy tales ever are. Whilst things might worry or upset her, Alice is never in any real danger. In that sense, perhaps Wonderland sanitises the genre a bit, removing the (metaphorical) dangers of wolves and witches and lonely woods and replacing them with problems of etiquette and conversation. At the time of Carroll's writing the story, the children he was writing it for were living a very comfortable life, and I suppose the lack of real danger in Wonderland represents, to some extent, the lack of real danger in their lives. In that sense, perhaps Wonderland is a middle (or upper) class fairy tale?

BH: Characters such as Gatsby, Hamlet, Hester Prynne and Captain Ahab can easily be looked at as not very likable and are often described as careless, indecisive, seductive and obsessive. Alice, as well, can be considered a less than pleasant girl who at most times is stubborn, curious and opinionated. How do you feel about Alice, is she a likeable character? And what opinion do you hope readers develop from your adaptation of her?

Leah Moore: I have to say that Alice is, for the most part, quite rude and quite pleased with herself. The bit that struck me was where she is trying to work out if she has been swapped with another child and reels off their distinguishing qualities to compare with herself. The fact that she points out that they don't have any toys, that they don't know anything, or that they live in "a poky little house" really shocked me. I have kind of expected a Dickens-style sentimental view of the poor, and to hear Alice being so snooty was strange. In reality though, children do make their judgements based on these things, and if we are honest I think adults do too. Possibly even judging Alice by our own modern day sensitivities is unhelpful, as her behaviour might not have seemed so uncharitable at the time. In our adaptation we have retained as much of the original dialogue as we possibly could, so I think a lot of her character will remain the same. We haven't taken out the parts where she seems a bit stubborn or aloof, because it's all part of the character of Alice. Her way of conversing with the other characters drives the plot along, and the other characters are not exactly innocent of exactly the same type of behaviour as Alice. The Hatter is certainly as rude, the Caterpillar is very blunt and annoying, and there aren't actually any characters who you feel are genuinely easy going, carefree people. I think the most sympathetic character in Wonderland is Bill the poor lizard who gets fired out of the chimney, wedged upside down in the jury box and generally mistreated the whole way through. My other favourites are the guinea pigs who have to be suppressed; they seem to have the right idea!

BH: Along with the characteristics of the fairy tale genre, the lack of logic and unpredictable nature of *Alice's Adventures in Wonderland* places the tale in the genre known as *literary nonsense*. These sorts of stories often create an endlessly fun discussion of the lessons, or lack of, to be learned from *Alice*. Do you think there is a lesson to be learned from *Alice*, or do you think that the joy is in its having no lesson at all?

JR: The moral of the story is certainly not the driving force: we are not being propelled towards a resolution which will put everything into context and give the story a meaning. I don't think there is any real moral to Wonderland, it's very much a story for story's sake - "getting there" and the route we (and Alice) take is the real reason for its telling. Carroll even plays with the concept in a conversation between the Duchess and Alice where the former keeps trying to find the moral in everything. I tend to think of Wonderland as a cleverly constructed maze - there is a far shorter and easier route from A to B but getting lost on the way is the true source of the fun.

BH: Lewis Carroll (and artist John Tenniel) filled *Alice* with caricatures of personal, political and professional acquaintances. Along with many others, the author even represents Charles Dodgson (who wrote under the pseudonym Lewis Carroll) as the dodo in Chapter 3 "A Caucus-Race and a Long Tale." Are all of these references included in *The Complete Alice*? And should readers be on the look out for any new additions?

LM: We haven't specified to Erica that she should alter her artwork to include specific people's likenesses, so unless she draws the characters very like how Tenniel draws them, the reference will only be present in the dialogue, which we have tried to give you as completely as we can. Some of the characters have a really distinct way of speaking (the Gryphon for example), and we have always tried to keep in any characterisation there. Also if Carroll has a character acting in a certain way, we have tried to get that into the scripts to pass on their demeanour, their way of standing or moving, so the comic doesn't lose anything of the original. The best example of this is the really horrible part where the Duchess turns up at the croquet ground and walks along with Alice, with her pointed chin digging into Alice's shoulder. This is such a weird thing for someone to do, and the Duchess is such a frightening character, we really wanted to make sure the reader of our adaptation felt as uncomfortable reading it as we did reading the book.

BH: Although the hero journey of typical fairy tale "heroines" such as Cinderella and Snow White contain important lessons, it can be said that their journey contains an incomplete or unsatisfactory reward due to their marrying the prince, which prevents them from becoming the master of their worlds or returning to the journey. Alice, of course, is a less typical heroine, and her ending is also quite different. How would you define Alice's ultimate reward? Would you say it is more or less satisfactory than the typical marrying of a prince?

JR: Alice's ultimate reward is being herself in a stable, normal world. If Wonderland does have a moral, it could be argued that it is "be thankful for what you have", although that seems rather too humble in face of all Alice's snootiness. In that sense it is a far more satisfactory reward than the re-defining of a person's character via marriage or the acquisition of riches or similar because Alice is still just Alice and she is thankful for that. She will grow up naturally (without the aid of cakes or mushrooms or bottles labelled "drink me") and become the person she is supposed to become. The natural order of things is restored.

BH: That said, how would you explain the sunset ending of *Alice's Adventures in Wonderland*?

LM: I think it's more Carroll letting the reader relax again. Alice's adventures are fraught with disturbing changes in location, in size, they have characters who are for the most part either threatening (the Cook, the Queen, the Duchess) or who change their behaviour depending on who they are with. The Hatter is argumentative unless he is near the Queen. He seems really at the mercy of Society. The White Rabbit is really horrible to his servants, and then really scared of Alice when she grows and then really scared of the Queen, but then bolder with the king and is very much more diplomatic, or more of a social climber perhaps? Certainly he's no Machiavelli or Iago, but he does have a public face and a private one. When Alice escapes the courtroom and wakes up under the tree, she escapes a world that seems very much fuller of adult cares and concerns rather than children's ones. Wonderland is full of 'High Society' and the etiquette of that world, social strata are indicated mainly by playing card suit, a kind of weird caste system really, and the other characters seem to be distinguished from each other by how much education they have received, their relative intelligence. In the real world, she knows the boundaries she operates within, she can remember her lessons and play games and not have to worry about being trapped in complex arguments with strange people. The framing of the whole story with Alice's big sister who tries to imagine the world Alice describes is really interesting, as that is presumably Carroll's role in the narrative. He tries to imagine the wonderful things that would amaze and amuse this small girl, and yet at the end he knows she will grow up one day too. The final part of the first book is a wish that the adventures Alice (and presumably her readers) has in childhood are passed on to the next generation of little girls and the next. I imagine he would be pleased to see that this is exactly what has happened, in many media and internationally too.

BH: And finally, if Alice were to ever return to Wonderland, how do you think she would get there and what would she find?

JR: After she passes through the looking glass you mean? Well it all depends on how old she was and what sort of life she had really – Wonderland is a dreamscape and reflects what is going on in Alice's mind at that time. There's been a tendency to re-imagine Wonderland as this dark, ruined place after it has been "neglected" by Alice – a nightmare version of the dream – which, I suppose, is perfectly possible. If we're talking about Alice Liddell though, although her life had its ups and downs, she seems to have been quite happy and well off for the most part. You could argue that, without the confusion and excitement of childhood, Wonderland might be rather a boring and mundane place to visit. That said, our dreams are different every night aren't they?

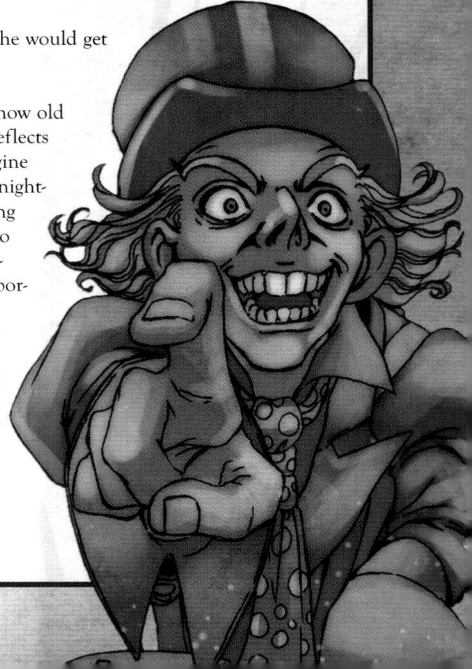

When not out saving the world from space monkeys or rescuing damsels in distress, Brian Hofacker works for Dynamic Forces and Dynamite Entertainment, conducting interviews and producing reviews of comic books. Brian also writes a weekly column, "What's in Brian's Bin" for DynamicForces.com.

Dynamite Entertainment presents:

The Complete Alice in Wonderland™

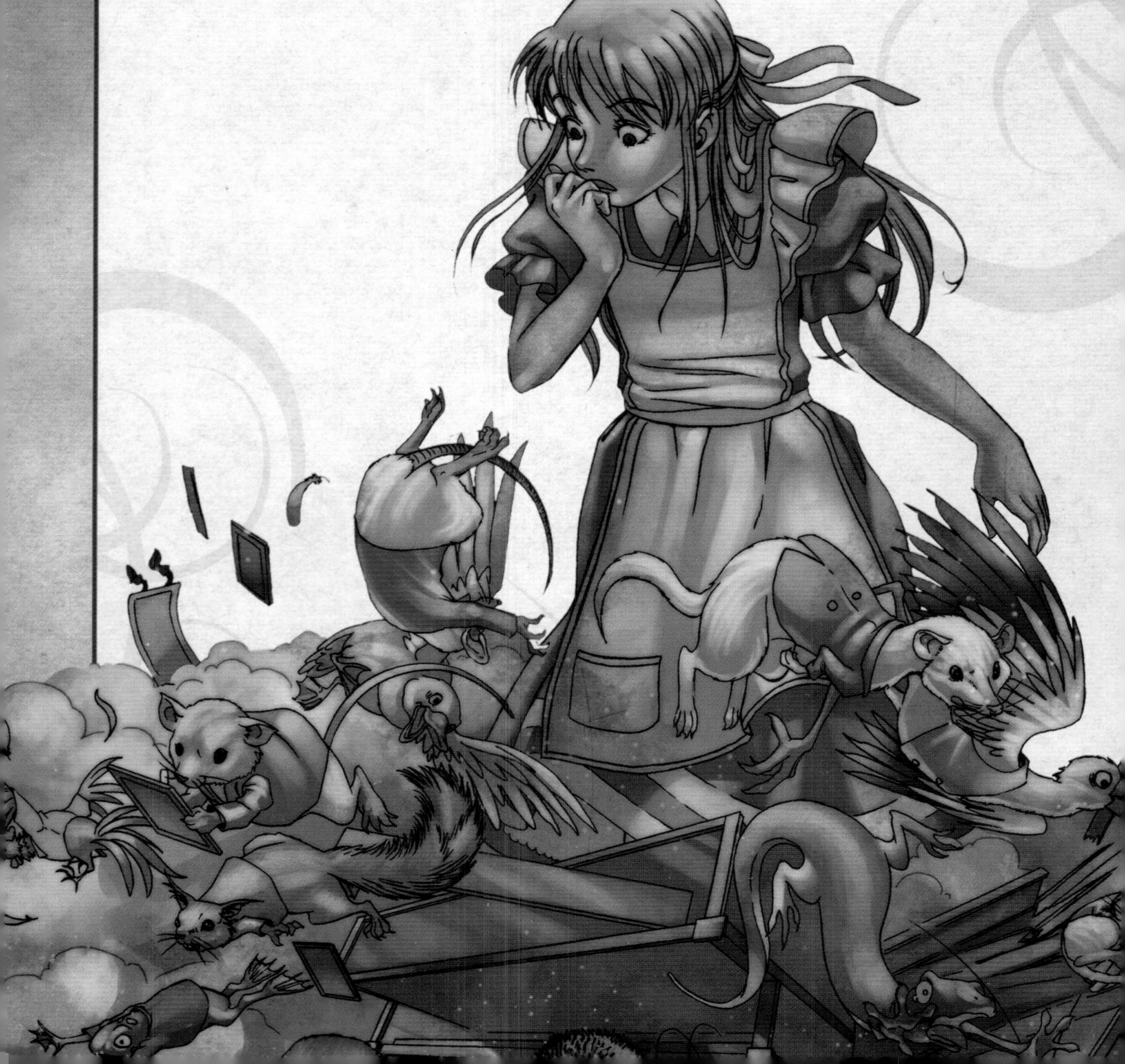